D0849214

Presidential Emergency

Walter Stovall

Presidential Emergency

E.P. DUTTON | NEW YORK

Library of Congress Cataloging in Publication Data
Stovall, Walter.
Presidential emergency.
I. Title.
PZ4.S89Pr [PS3569.T673]   813'.5'4   77-7037
ISBN: 0-525-18325-6

Published simultaneously in Canada by Clarke, Irwin & Company Limited,
Toronto and Vancouver

10 9 8 7 6 5 4 3 2 1

First Edition

TO MY DAUGHTER SUSAN

Presidential Emergency

DAY ONE

1 The Warning

Forbes maneuvered his way awkwardly into the teeming lobby. Messengers, maintenance men, and preoccupied people scurrying to work jostled and dodged each other with a minimum of apology. At the newsstand he set down his suit bag, underseater, and attaché case and purchased a pack of cigarettes.

"Getting out of town for a few days, Mr. Forbes?" asked the newsdealer. He was a rotund man who doubled as a low-volume bookmaker. Forbes was one of his spot players.

"I need a few days off, Benny," Forbes replied amiably, "before I go on the disabled list." He glanced at the headlines on the rack of newspapers as he accepted his cigarettes and change. He had read them all several hours earlier.

"Don't stay too long," said the newsdealer. "I'm feeling a breeze."

"I think I'll stay with the chalk, Benny. The hotiolas are getting expensive." The banter was harmless. Forbes was a moderate, irregular bettor who enjoyed the action but prudently stuck to favorites; he had a subjective dislike for long shots; he merely noted that his bookie was on a winning streak that would cost him money.

He collected his luggage and stuffed himself into an elevator. He was too distracted to notice the tall man leaning against the wall next to the newsstand with a copy of the *Daily News* held in front of him. Had he looked back, Forbes would have seen the man glaring at him over his newspaper. He also would have seen that the man was missing a finger. As the elevator door slid shut the man snapped his newspaper under his arm, had a few words with the newsdealer, and walked hastily from the building.

Moments later, Forbes nudged his office door open with his shoulder. He stacked his bags neatly just inside. He managed his own inclinations. He laid the attaché case on his desk.

Thack Forbes was compactly built with dark hair and opulent sideburns. He had the merry mouth and bright, dark brown eyes of his father. He was of medium height but appeared taller. He had an appealing if not commanding presence; in his world he unquestionably looked as if he belonged. Despite the fact that he was approaching fifty, he had no liver spots on his hands and was frequently addressed by strangers not as old as he as "young man."

Just a few more hours, he thought with an obscure twinge of irritation, as if he had forgotten something important and would discover what it was only after it was too late to go back and get it. He checked his inside jacket pocket. His passport and airline ticket were there.

The July sun streamed through the slats of the venetian blinds. The window was raised two inches in defiance of the city's energy-saving regulations on air conditioners. The humid Manhattan breeze ruffled the stacks of newspapers, pamphlets, and brochures that cluttered the tops of the credenzas and filing cabinets. A potted rubber tree plant gathered dust.

He picked up the telephone.

"Good morning, beautiful. . . . Of course I am. Every time I get out of bed I'm ready to strike a blow for democracy. It's the most charming form of government. . . . I hope this doesn't shatter my image, but the answer is no. It may surprise you to learn that I don't sleep with every woman I have dinner with. It was business. Besides, she isn't my type. . . . Hell, yes, you're my type, but it's too early to go into it. . . . Sure. Any other time, but this is Monday morning. Bring in the memo when you're ready. And some coffee."

Forbes took a sheaf of papers from the attaché case and hung the jacket of his gray double-vent suit lopsidedly on a chair. It clashed inoffensively with the yellow walls and the ponderous dust-and-walnut curtains.

He sat down and shifted in his swivel chair to block the glare of the sun. He liked sunlight and fresh air but hated heat. A pair of half-moon glasses was perched on the end of his nose. He loosened his tie. He jotted notes with a green felt-tipped pen.

His concentration was off. Every moment or so he glanced at the suit bag and underseater and at the clock. The clock was a platter-sized campaign button emblazoned with the monogram "TMF Associates." It was the only thing in the room, apart from the luggage and his clothes, that belonged to him.

The clock reminded Forbes that the office was improvised and temporary. It also made him uneasy at the prospect of a busy day, which he ordinarily relished.

Forbes was a Monday person. Saturday had been spent "expediting" his candidate from kaffeeklatsch to shopping center rally to the head table at a well-attended banquet. On Sunday he had watched the candidates on television, conducted a political strategy session, and fed half-truths to the press on an off-the-record basis. He must have taken a hundred calls from reporters at his East Side apartment. On any other Monday the experiences of the weekend would have effervesced in his restless brain. They would have galvanized his interest, rubbed his intuition, given him a dozen ideas for tricks and tactics. But this Monday was different. It had a wispy dread about it; it was out of proportion, outside his experience.

It was a dread born of misgiving and contradictory conclusions. The reasons were plenty and plausible. He was flying to Georgia later today to join his former employer, the president of the United States. In three days he would be on Air Force One en route to the People's Republic of China. Almost no one thought the visit was a good idea, except the president—and, presumably, the Chinese. Certainly it looked like dumb politics, being in China on the very day of the national nominating convention. It was a damned good thing, Forbes supposed, that the president wasn't running for a second term; few men who had held the nation's highest office had managed to become so unpopular in just three years. This China trip was no help, either, to the vice-president. He had broken with the president and launched an insurgent candidacy; he would have to rely on adroit management and arm-twisting at the convention to win the nomination and head the ticket in November.

Forbes lit a cigarette. The gold butane lighter was a gift from the president. He studied the miniature presidential seal as he tried to shed his discontent. What was it Disraeli said? "What we anticipate seldom happens; what we least expected generally occurs."

T. Morgan Forbes had been known as Thack (for Thackeray) since his prep school days. He was the owner, president, and sole stockholder of a political consulting firm. The business paid well enough. Forbes had the right track record and knew the right people. He took pride in his work; a Forbes candidate knew what to emphasize, and where, without fear of being accused later of talking out of both sides of his mouth. "Fence-straddling will make your ass tired, but it offends fewer voters than you think" was a maxim he liked to quote at doubters. Forbes didn't need a large staff. He made all the decisions. A young assistant asked all the questions. A secretary did all the work. Forbes knew what counted in politics: a feverish imagination and the ability to sound as if you knew what you were talking about.

He practiced his profession as a juggling act of temporary gains and temporary losses. He preferred, naturally, to be ahead, but he did not grow anxious or resentful if he dropped behind, as long as the situation remained fluid. He gravitated automatically to fluid situations. If he had a flaw as a politician, it was a good memory; he could not distinguish between what to remember and what to forget. This shortcoming was offset, however, by his conviction that morality and politics ought to be dealt with separately. Being a man who relied on an accommodating disposition in the absence of substantial physical courage, he found it easy to think one way in private and act another in public. In his world this was an asset. Political reverses are transient, and triumphs are more the product of luck and timing than personal heroism.

He inhaled deeply on his cigarette and adjusted his half-moon glasses. His secretary came in without knocking. She was a slender brunette with high cheekbones. She placed a stainless-steel carafe of coffee at his elbow and handed him a typewritten sheet of paper. It contained a list of times, addresses, and names; there was a notation next to each to check something or call somebody.

"Hello, Thack. Here's the menu." Alison said "hello" in a breathy way that implied she was dying to hear a startling political secret. Her acute, magnificent eyes and parted lips asked more urgent, basic questions. At first Forbes thought it was a case of hero worship. Alison had majored in government at Radcliffe. She was an observant, willing learner. She had given him the impression when he hired her that she looked on him as one of the country's most skillful political technicians and that she wanted to learn the business at the master's knee. Within weeks, however, she had made it clear that she wanted to go to bed with him, as if her education would be incomplete unless she gained firsthand knowledge of his private abilities as well as his public expertise.

At the moment she really did want to hear a political secret. You know as many as I do, Alison, he thought, you just don't have the experience to realize it.

"Let me see." He looked at the paper and screwed up his face in mock seriousness. He did a parody of a man gazing up and down at the bill of fare in a restaurant. "I'll start with more highway development funds and then an anti-abortion amendment. Do you happen to have, by the way, a private poll showing our guy ahead by sixty points?"

"Too early for that, sir. But we have a very nice civil service union endorsement. Very nice." They laughed. Forbes scanned the schedule; the first appointment was in eleven minutes.

"Retype the afternoon schedule for Steve. Remind him he has to sit in on the *Newsweek* interview. And remind him, for Christ's sake, to be on time. Nothing for me after eleven-thirty, right? No calls or anything. I'm on a three o'clock flight to Jaw-ja, gateway to mysterious China."

Alison stood in front of the desk, hand on hip. Forbes poured a half cup of coffee. He tore open a packet of sugar substitute.

"Why are you so devoted to that man, Thack?" Her tone made it clear she would pounce on a sympathetic answer.

"What man, Alison?" He was cheerful but noncommittal. He stubbed his cigarette.

6

"What do you mean, 'What man'? You know 'what man.' Our world leader. Our president."

"Where did you get the idea I'm devoted to him?"

"If you aren't devoted to him, why are you going on this trip? It's the biggest laugh of the year. You want to know what I think? I think he's practically a basket case. I think he's gone bananas."

"Alison, you ought to write a newspaper column." He was still smiling; he was amused at her outburst.

"Just why can't you tell me, then, why you're going on this cockamamie trip with President Ha-Ha Hamilton? Or don't you know?" It was the secret she was dying for.

"If I told you that, Alison, my love, you'd know as much as I do. You're too young for that."

"Bullshit."

She shook her head and smiled at him. She walked partway to the door and then stopped and slowly turned around.

"Thack, do you think I'm attractive?"

"Extremely."

"And bright?"

"Very. That's why I hired you."

Again hand on hip. "Then why don't you ever pay any attention to me? The times we've been out for drinks, you've done all the things that the men I know do when they're trying to put the make on me. But you don't even make a pass. What is it? Do you really think I'm too young?"

"No." Forbes was being truthful. Where sex was concerned, he didn't think any woman over the age of twenty-one was too young.

There was a pause and then Alison said, "Have you slept with a lot of women?"

"I wouldn't say a lot."

"That's the reputation you have."

He chuckled kindly. "Alison, a lot of men—not all, but a hell of a lot more than you suspect—take women one at a time. I don't think numbers count. Every woman I've known has been different, whether I went to bed with her or not. In bed every woman I've known has had different needs. I guess you could say that about the men you've slept with."

A suspicious look clouded her face. "Not the ones I've slept with. No such luck." She clasped her hands in front of her and twisted her fingers. "Usually everything is going great and then it turns to shit. Either they charge in like a stallion before I'm even ready or they want to get into a long discussion or something. A couple of them couldn't even get it up. One bastard thought he'd show me how with it he was and go down on me. Do you know what he did? He *bit* me!"

"Well, one way to improve things is to tell them what you want."

"Does Mrs. Leatherbee tell you what she wants?"

Forbes leaned back in his swivel chair. He gave her a look that indicated she had said too much for the time being. Alison understood immediately and looked down at the carpet.

"I'm sorry, Thack."

"Forget it. Look. My idea of sex is pleasure, not something you do to prove a point. It takes a while to learn how to get the most out of it. Hell, I'm nearly twice as old as you and I'm still learning."

She smiled at him again, a fraction ruefully this time. She closed the door without slamming it.

Forbes watched her go. He understood her exasperation. She was sophisticated but suffered from immense ignorance in spite of a great deal of experience. He expected he eventually would sleep with Alison. Probably at the end of the campaign, if the past was a signal. It made no difference to him that she was younger than his oldest daughter. If there was

8

such a thing as an Agamemnon complex, he definitely didn't suffer from one.

He adjusted his tie and drained his coffee cup. He slipped on his jacket and selected a manila folder. He left by his private entrance. The corridor was softly lit. He wondered at Alison's question. Why *was* he going on the China trip? He was working for Caswell; Caswell was paying him well, very well. There was only one answer. He was going because the president had asked him to go.

He let himself in at the last door on the right. The conference room was in a cluster of offices leased by Liberty Aircraft, which was owned by Caswell's family. They were sublet to Eric Caswell for his congressional campaign. The campaign headquarters itself was in the suburban district Caswell wanted to represent. Forbes had insisted on a separate office in Manhattan. He had pointed out that by being in the city he could stimulate more "free media," the jargon in his trade for news coverage of a politician. He had not pointed out that it meant rent-free office space for TMF Associates.

Caswell and his campaign entourage had not arrived. Tied up in traffic, probably. Driving in from Long Island was murder on a Monday morning in July. Forbes sat down at the rectangular table. Before each chair was a legal pad, placed there by Alison. He opened the manila folder and skimmed the morning's agenda. There was still the question of scatter-site low-income housing. Let's lay back on that one for the time being, he thought, stay vague as long as we can. Better lay back on offshore oil drilling, too. He guessed that everything big could be put on hold until he got back from China. Besides, the convention in Pittsburgh to pick the party's new presidential nominee would have everybody's attention for the rest of the week.

Forbes thought of campaign issues the way a football coach thinks about his game plan. What the hell good was it, putting in an intricate pass play, if you didn't have the people to bring it off? In politics what was the point of drafting a position paper on tax reform when it was easier and more effective to attack government spending in a ninety-second television spot?

He knew that someone like Alison would view this attitude as cynicism. He thought of it as simplicity. For Thack Forbes at the age of forty-eight simplicity was his professional byword. Every proposal and stratagem he put forward during a campaign could be framed on a three-by-five index card. It was the same with every political problem he dealt with. But today the problem, whatever it was, would not reduce; it would not clarify itself in twenty-five words or less.

T. Morgan Forbes was not a profound man, but he was intelligent and shrewd. Some years ago, when his father died, he had realized, without effort, that nothing any longer surprised him. It was a useful, liberating revelation. It sharpened his sense of humor, lowered his blood pressure, and gave him a feeling which in pious men passes for virtue. It did not lessen his capacity for excitement. His glands pumped efficiently; his tastebuds were keen; he was not burdened by a reputation for being patient, although he knew to bide his time and enjoy himself while he was doing it. Women found Forbes sexy; it was his eyes and his assertive charm. On his forty-first birthday he had left his wife. He had thought it over for a week. He had been married for eighteen years and saw no hope that he and Claire could rekindle the bodily impetuosity he thrived on. He provided adequate alimony and generous support for his two daughters, whom he was fond of but not devoted to. He moved first into a hotel and then into an apartment. He became happily promiscuous.

When Hamilton decided to run for president, he asked Forbes to be his campaign director. Forbes accepted and moved to Washington. After the election Forbes went to the

White House as a special assistant to the president. He was in charge of political affairs and spent a lot of time lobbying on Capitol Hill for Hamilton's programs. He reviewed requests for federal judgeships. He accepted the protective lethargy of the federal bureaucracy and stayed on friendly terms with the civil servants. Rarely was he frustrated by the obstructive power of an unhappy or hostile bureaucrat.

Forbes left Washington under circumstances that still baffled him. The administration of Joseph Hamilton had started life as a fuzzy hash of colorless policies. His cabinet members and executive appointees were amiable, cautious men. Someone described them as pleasant hicks. They seemed to fit the nation's mood and needs: not bold and imaginative, but not grasping or ambitious, either; just the types to shape the Era of the Even Keel. Then it began. One by one these lackluster nobodies became corrupt monsters. The secretary of the interior was indicted for land fraud he allegedly committed when he was governor of Colorado. The secretaries of labor and agriculture departed amid accusations of receiving kickbacks. The chairman of the Federal Communications Commission resigned after he was charged with conflict of interest in a cable television ruling. In each case the evidence was circumstantial, but the public indignation was strong and effective.

Hamilton's esteem dipped further when he personally negotiated the treaty that dismantled the U.S. naval base at Guantánamo Bay in Cuba. Hamilton had begun his career as a foreign service officer. Foreign policy infatuated him. He supposed that domestic policy would take care of itself. He mistakenly thought that the rules of diplomacy and elective politics were the same. An anti-Hamilton furor still raged over his attempts to negotiate a mutual nonaggression treaty with Peking. The Soviet Union, Japan, and India had expressed sharp concern.

One drizzly night after the president's ruinous loss in the

11

Florida primary—which finished Hamilton's hopes of renomination—a reporter telephoned Forbes. He wanted Forbes's reaction to a report that he, Forbes, had once owned stock in an Illinois harness racing track dominated by underworld figures. Forbes thought the reporter must have the wrong man. He asked for details. Ah, come on, Mr. Forbes, you know what I'm talking about: Colony Investment Corporation. Forbes once *had* owned stock in Colony Investment Corporation. He had bought it from a retired New York detective named Frank Parisi. But it was genuine, registered stock, not some fly-by-night scam, and he had no idea his capital had gone into a racetrack. Furthermore, he had sold it. End of interview.

Forbes made a few calls; Parisi knew nothing, nor did anyone at Colony Investment. He issued a denial; it was a silly thing to do; a denial in Washington, even an authentic one, is regarded as a quasi admission. He sensed he had been set up and told the president of his sentiments. A search for leaks was undertaken; phones were tapped. "Mafia Link to the White House Hinted," screamed the headlines. The House Ethics Committee staff investigated. Forbes was cleared but discredited. He resigned.

The door to the conference room swung open. Eric Caswell strode in at the head of his retinue. With them was an elderly, white-haired man with a quizzical expression that came from poor eyesight.

"Thack, say hello to Mr. Justice Roundtree." Caswell was a reedy young man with lank, blond hair. He was grinning with self-satisfaction, like a kid on Christmas morning who had gotten the most expensive bicycle on the block.

"Good morning, your honor," said Forbes, extending his hand. Roundtree had retired five years ago from the Supreme

Court; he had been a difficult justice to pin a label on: he had voted to suspend constitutional liberties in the Houston riots and had written the opinion guaranteeing prison inmates the right to vote. Caswell's father had persuaded Roundtree to depart from his long-standing nonpartisanship and endorse the young politician. It was understood he would do no campaigning; he was too busy completing his memoirs. His ruddy face was sagging and tinged with gray. Forbes knew he had been ill lately.

They seated themselves. Caswell seated Roundtree himself.

"Let me add my thanks, your honor," Forbes began. He was hoping, but not fervently, that Roundtree might reconsider and make a few pro-Caswell speeches. "I'm sure I'm only echoing what Eric has told you personally when I say that having you in his corner"—he nodded toward Caswell—"has blessed and enhanced our effort. As a political tactician I must say, too, that having people like you involved in a campaign makes it a hell of a lot easier for people like me to do my job."

Everyone, even Roundtree, smiled.

"Now," Forbes continued, taking a typewritten sheet from his manila folder, "here's the endorsement statement we've prepared. We're painfully aware that it lacks your style and eloquence, so we expect you to make extensive revisions."

The old jurist laughed. He donned a pair of wire-rimmed glasses and quickly skimmed the paper. "I find this totally acceptable," he said, pushing it back across the table. "I don't believe my style and eloquence, as you call it, Mr. Forbes, would add to it."

More smiles.

"Thank you, your honor. You've already done Eric the courtesy, I believe, of posing for a photograph with him. You know, of course, that if you change your mind and want to take a more active part in the, ah, political process, all you have to do is give us the word."

"Mr. Forbes, if I thought there was more that an old man like me could do, you would have heard long before now. My book and my rose bushes are more than enough work for me."

Forbes gave Roundtree a brief account of the campaign's progress.

"I would guess," Roundtree said at length—his presence had grown patriarchal; the others at the table, except Forbes, looked at him with expressions of reverence, as if he were a village elder dispensing wisdom to the cottage apprentices—"that over the years I have come around to the opinion that political campaigns are necessary but not particularly enlightening."

A look of consternation crept across Caswell's face. Was there a defect in his Christmas bicycle?

Forbes spotted the potential for trouble. He moved quickly to ease the tension. "I don't think you'll get an argument from us on that count, your honor," he put in, "but I'm sure you'll agree that a politician has to take advantage of modern techniques if he's serious about getting elected."

"Of course, of course," Roundtree replied. The anxiety abated. A warm sense that Forbes had put the imperatives of latter-day political life in proper focus settled over the group. Forbes glanced to make sure that Caswell's fears had been quenched. They had. A smile had dislodged his dubious frown.

"My point is," Roundtree went on; his tone was conciliatory but firm, "there is a tendency to mold these campaigns into emotional orgies that draw attention away from the issues involved. I remember that in my first campaign—it was for the state assembly and I was a young man—I lacked the money to

14

do many of the things that were considered modern for that time. That time, I should add, was before most of you were born. There were no airplanes, no television, and the radio was largely a toy. The poster was the principal advertising vehicle. My opponent had virtually covered the district with his posters. Since I couldn't afford them, I simply drove around making speeches to the effect that my opponent had resorted to the base tactic of ripping my posters down. It aroused much resentment, and I believe my charges were taken to heart by the voters. In any case, I was elected."

Everyone laughed.

"I think it's fair to say"—Forbes grinned—"that we would follow your example, your honor, if we had to."

Roundtree himself beamed at the success of his anecdote. "I don't want to leave the impression that I'm humorless about the political process. Or indifferent. Otherwise I would not have agreed to endorse Eric. But you can see that modern techniques actually paralyze what small powers of discriminating accuracy a man can normally muster in the polling booth."

"That's what we're aiming for," shouted Caswell, eager to display his worldliness. "We want every man, woman, and child to be thinking 'Caswell for Congress' and nothing else when they pull that lever."

Forbes and Roundtree exchanged a few reminiscences on social life in Washington. They were couched in terms that made them sound like inside advice to Caswell.

Presently Roundtree said he must be going. Everyone stood. He made his way to the door. Caswell shook his hand vigorously and thanked him a couple of times more than was necessary. Forbes decided that a final formality was in order.

"Your honor, I'm joining President Hamilton today in Georgia. I'm flying with him to China. May I convey your best wishes to him, sir?"

15

Roundtree stopped as though he had received a blow. His face was ashen. The room fell silent. Forbes was afraid he was about to have a seizure. Finally, Roundtree said, "Yes . . . that would be kind, Mr. Forbes . . . yes, please do. . . . That would be all right, I suppose. Yes, please convey my . . . best wishes."

Roundtree walked out. His shoulders drooped. He looked decrepit.

"Jesus, Thack, did you see that old bastard?" That was Caswell. He had returned from walking Roundtree to the elevator. "That was the worst reaction I've seen yet to this China business. I thought he was going to cave in right on the spot. How do you think that would've looked, getting endorsed by a corpse?" There were a few bad puns. Everyone laughed.

Forbes steered the conversation to the remainder of his brief agenda. His mind was on Roundtree. What was it that nearly knocked the guy over when I mentioned Hamilton and China? he wondered as he absently ticked off the list of things to be accomplished while he was gone. After each item Caswell nodded assertively, as if they had occurred to him much earlier.

The talk around the table was filled with phrases such as "allocation of resources," "attitudinal climate," and "leadership issues." Forbes noticed Alison at his shoulder. She placed a "while you were out" memo in front of him; it said, *VEEP of USA PERSONALLY on fone your office. Says must speak to you NOW!*

Forbes toyed with the idea of telling the vice-president he would get back to him later. He decided against it and nodded to Alison.

He closed his office door behind him. He hesitated before lifting the receiver. This is damned odd, he thought, the vice-president calling direct. Most vice-presidents, especially Melville, would tell an assistant to do it. He tried to anticipate the conversation but came up with nothing.

16

"Good morning, Mr. Vice-President. What can I do for you?"

"How are *you*, Thack? Good to hear your voice." Vice-President Melville was a principal beneficiary of Hamilton's depleted political stock. Lawrence Melville was the former governor of Pennsylvania and one of the richest men in the world. With each disclosure of wrongdoing at the highest level of government, Hamilton's popularity slipped and Melville's soared. A Gallup poll showed that 70 percent of the American people would rather have Melville as commander in chief; only 27 percent stuck with Hamilton; 3 percent had no preference. Melville had disavowed all loyalty to the Hamilton administration and challenged the president's renomination; he obliterated Hamilton in the early primaries. Hamilton saw he was beaten and declared he would devote the balance of his tenure to a tireless search for world peace. "You know, it's been a *long* time.

"Say, Thack, they tell me you're doing one *hell* of a job with young Caswell's campaign." Melville's voice was characterized by a lazy affability; Forbes could imagine him winking at whoever was with him, listening in. "I just want you to know how much I *personally* appreciate what you've done. Eric's father appreciates it, too. There aren't many real pros like *you* around these days, Thack."

"Thank you, sir. It pleases me to hear that from you." Forbes wondered what the hell he was driving at.

They talked a few minutes about Melville's main opponent for the party's presidential nomination, a congressman from New Mexico named Darrow. Melville asked for an assessment of how the voting would go at the convention. Forbes said he thought Melville would be nominated on the third or fourth ballot. It was a widely held opinion.

"Say, Thack, you're on your way to *Georgia* today, aren't you? I wonder if you could stop by Washington? There are a couple of things we really need to discuss. Some things I need to talk about with a *pro* like you. I've got a big night coming up in Pittsburgh, you know."

"Well . . ." You have to hand it to this guy, thought Forbes. Here I am, an old, close ally of the man he jobbed for the presidency, and he wants me to "stop by Washington" for a chat.

"One of our planes is coming down this afternoon. It can fly on *your* schedule, Thack." By one of "our" planes the vice-president meant one of the Melville family jets or one of the fleet leased to Trans-Columbia Oil Corporation, the keystone of the Melville family fortune.

Forbes quickly weighed the offer. Hamilton would be outraged, he was certain of that; Hamilton hated Melville, hated Melville's private jets. On the other hand, Hamilton would soon be out of a job. Come January, Melville might be numero uno. Forbes would need the patronage of numero uno. What the hell, Melville had come to him; no harm in playing hard to get.

"That's very gracious of you, sir. There are some loose ends I have to take care of before I leave. It's difficult to tell how long they'll take. I'll take the shuttle. But thanks just the same."

"Suit yourself." The affability had vanished. When Melville offered someone something, he expected it to be accepted. He wasn't used to being turned down. "My secretary is coming on the line. Tell her approximately when you'll arrive. A car will meet you."

Forbes gave the secretary the information on his travel plans. He replaced the receiver.

"Alison, get me a seat on something out of Washington for Georgia. Late afternoon or early evening. I'm stopping off in the nation's capital for high tea."

"You have another call," Alison said coolly. "Mrs. Leatherbee on three. From Georgia."

Forbes stepped back into his office. He lit a cigarette and picked up the phone.

"Nell, the damnedest thing just happened. Larry Melville called. He wants to meet with me today. Can you beat that?"

"Oh?" Nell Leatherbee sounded surprised but not floored. Assistant Treasury Secretary Leatherbee was the woman who could be said to claim the greatest amount of Forbes's attention; her husband, not a clever man and not at all close to his wife, preferred the family ranch in Texas to life in crafty Washington. She had been sorry to see Forbes leave Washington, but she also knew she hadn't seen the last of him. They talked on the phone every day and saw each other at least once a month, in New York or Washington. "What do you think? Are you going to do it?"

"Yes. I don't know what he has in mind, but I sure as hell want to find out."

"Thack, I only have a minute." Her voice had a quality of forced nervousness. "Things are falling apart down here. Joe and Osborne are tearing each other's hair out over the China agenda."

"Oh, Christ, Nell, they've been tearing each other's hair out ever since Osborne became secretary of state. They'll never see things the same way, but they'll get the job done."

"It's more complicated than that. I can't go into it now, but I just want you to know what to expect. Another thing. Joe isn't looking too good."

"I'll bet *you* are. I can't wait to see you."

"I can't wait to see you, either. God, it's been almost three weeks. Am I ever glad you'll be down here tonight."

Forbes looked at his watch and put out his cigarette. "I've got to run. Keep the grits and fried chicken hot for me," he added in an atrocious attempt at a southern accent. "Oh. Do me a favor. Don't mention this Melville thing. I want to tell Joe myself."

"Sure." She pecked a kiss into the phone. "I've got to run, too," she said and hung up.

Damn, thought Forbes as he walked back to the conference room, it will be at least midnight before I get to the piney woods of south Georgia. Why did Hamilton, an Indiana boy who had never had a kind word for Roosevelt, pick that place for a vacation retreat? He did not share Nell's concern that the president and the secretary of state were locked in battle over foreign policy. It was nothing new.

Forbes took his seat. He wanted to wind up the meeting. The data indicated that Caswell was leading his opponent, a liberal professor, by forty points. Nothing short of indictment or death could keep him from being elected in November. Whatever might go wrong could be repaired when Forbes got back from China.

Caswell was holding forth on Italians. He had often expressed the opinion that they were the most gullible voters. Forbes looked at his watch. He said it was time he got moving to the airport. He told Caswell he would be in touch when he got to Georgia and hurriedly mentioned a few other campaign matters. Caswell and his aides signaled that they understood and filed out. They wished Forbes bon voyage and cracked age-old jokes about oriental women.

Forbes emerged from the elevator. The newsdealer waved to him as he walked across the lobby and sidled clumsily through the revolving door with his luggage. He looked for a cab. The Third Avenue traffic was thick. The early afternoon sun was harsh.

"Oh, Mr. Forbes." The voice came from a black Mercedes limousine standing a short distance away. It was Mr. Justice Roundtree; he was leaning out of the rear window, wearing a dark Homburg.

Forbes walked over to the car. He supposed he could spare a few minutes.

"Delighted to see you again so soon, your honor. Changed your mind about making a speech?"

"I see you are about to begin your journey. It is important that I speak with you. May I drop you somewhere?" He spoke with friendly urgency.

"I'm on my way to the airport."

"Then let me give you a lift. It's on my way, more or less. O'Brien will put your bags in the trunk."

The Mercedes made its way haltingly through the heavy traffic. A glass separated the chauffeur and the back seat. Forbes sat on Roundtree's right.

Roundtree shifted and faced Forbes. He was wearing his wire-rimmed glasses.

"Mr. Forbes, you've known President Hamilton for some time. Do you think his judgment is all that it should be? All that a president's should be, that is?"

Forbes paused before answering.

"That depends on how you look at it, your honor. Obviously the voters in New Hampshire and Florida didn't think something about him was all it should be. Maybe it was his judgment."

"Perhaps judgment wasn't what I meant." Roundtree leaned closer to Forbes. "Perhaps I should have said the president's power to reason. Do you think his mental balance is sound?"

Forbes had heard that before. The president's colossal ego couldn't take defeat. The strain of office was too much. Hamilton was cracking up.

"He gets depressed, I'm sure, although I haven't seen him in a while. A president takes office expecting to serve his full two terms. It takes the wind out of him when he gets to serve only one of them. He looks at what he wanted to accomplish and finds there isn't enough time. You and I might not agree with his goals, and we might despise his methods, but from his point of view, that's our problem. His problem is he's frustrated. That's a long way from being an irrational neurotic. He's in a hurry. He's been hurt. But he's not insane."

Roundtree blinked behind his glasses. The dull light of the Queens Midtown Tunnel surrounded the car.

"May I ask you a simple question, Mr. Forbes? Is it possible for you to avoid this trip? Gracefully, that is?"

"You mean cancel out? Now?" Forbes knitted his brows as he looked at the old man. "Everything's arranged. The president's expecting me. I used to work for him. We go back a long way together, you know."

"This has nothing to do with friendship, Mr. Forbes." Roundtree's voice was almost a whisper. "Certain . . . events . . . have taken place. Events that are now part of a process. To stop the events one would have to stop, to disrupt, the process. Neither you nor I have the means to stop it, Mr. Forbes."

"I'm afraid I don't know what you mean. Anyway I think it's too late in the day to be saying no to the president."

"What I'm trying to impress on you, Mr. Forbes, is that going on this trip is not in your best interest."

Forbes looked away. The car zipped out of the tunnel. There was a billboard advertising a suburban nightclub; Forbes did not recognize the names of the headliners. What is he trying to say, he wondered. Slowly he turned back to Roundtree.

"I believe, your honor, you must have had a conversation with the vice-president." Forbes smiled as if to say: it's not hard to put two and two together.

Roundtree was breathing laboriously. His face was pale, as it had been in the conference room when Forbes mentioned Hamilton and China.

"I haven't spoken to the vice-president. I don't expect I

will," he said softly. He was silent a moment and then said abruptly, "Stay with me for the next few days, Mr. Forbes. There's plenty of room. Or take off on your own. Europe maybe. *But don't go with the president.*"

Forbes was irritated but took pains not to let it show. He understood beating around the bush, but this seemed unaccountably enigmatic. He lit a cigarette. He did not want to sound caustic.

"You've lost me, your honor," he said evenly, exhaling the smoke with a curbed sigh. "If you know something you think I should know, I would appreciate your telling me. I was alarmed, frankly, at your reaction when I said I was going to China with the president. I was afraid it had made you ill. I hope you won't mind my saying I was surprised at your suggestion that the president may be mentally unstable. What really astonished me, though, was your reaction to my mention of the vice-president. That, and your advice that I hide out for a few days. I don't understand. I don't understand at all."

Roundtree inclined his head and straightened his glasses. "Mr. Forbes, you have an imaginative grasp of modern techniques," he said: his voice was a trifle stronger, "but I don't believe you are fully aware of the unforeseen developments these techniques can lead to. They go beyond simple politics, which are by and large a contest of competing interests— business versus labor, church versus state, freedom of speech versus national security, and so on. Modern techniques let men step out beyond the limitations of their own character. This is dangerous. It could be disastrous. Is that clear to you?"

Forbes nodded and attempted an understanding smile. In fact very little of what the old man had said was clear to him, but he was determined to be polite.

Roundtree looked straight ahead. His face seemed to have

shrunk under his Homburg. A black-on-white sign above the highway said: "La Guardia Airport 1 Mile." Finally he spoke again. His voice was weary.

"There is about to be a sudden change. It will be personal and it will be public. At the same time. Imagine a hotel fire. Would you like to be reminded of it by a pair of your singed trousers or by reading about it in the newspapers? I prefer the newspapers."

The limousine stopped in front of the La Guardia shuttle terminal. The chauffeur brought Forbes's luggage and opened the rear door.

A cab pulled up behind them. A tall, angular man with short-cropped gray hair and cruel eyes got out. His face was tanned and lined. He walked up to the open door of the limousine and looked inside. He stared fiercely at Roundtree and then turned and walked into the shuttle terminal.

Roundtree gazed straight ahead again. His eyes were wide with fright. Forbes knew he had recognized the man who stared at him. Forbes held out his hand to say good-bye. Roundtree sat immobile.

"Is he all right?" Forbes asked the chauffeur.

The chauffeur shrugged. Old men act strange sometimes.

Forbes picked up his luggage. It was hotter at the airport than it was in the city. The sky was cloudless. He felt his shirt sticking to his back. He walked into the terminal.

Several miles away, at Kennedy International Airport, Frank Parisi trudged across the parking lot in front of the International Arrivals Building. He carried a small valise. He wanted to change clothes. He had had on the same suit since Saturday. Jesus, what day is this? Monday? His underwear wrenched his crotch in the bright heat. His stomach pulsed with blunt pain. It must be that goddamn sandwich. Vest had been waiting for him when he cleared customs. He didn't like

24

Vest. Vest scared the shit out of him. Vest had kept those dark, hot eyes of his fixed on him while he fumbled in his pocket for the cylinder of capsules. He had nearly jumped when Vest told him to go for a sandwich. He hadn't wanted a sandwich, but he went anyway. He was afraid not to. He knew Vest didn't want to be seen leaving the airport with him.

Parisi felt for his keys. He opened the door of the metallic-green Cadillac. A gush of furnace-like air engulfed him. He stood back to let the car cool off. It had been standing locked for three days under the July sun. Three days. The longest three days I ever spent, thought Parisi, and I spent some long ones in the twenty years I was a cop. To Ecuador and back, for God's sake. What a whacko that doctor had been. Dr. Guillermo Lick. A kraut, no doubt about that.

"Vest said you have something for me," he had said to the wrinkled, bald man who answered his knock. The stucco bungalow was in the sierra above Guayaquil. A recent earthquake had cracked one wall. It was cold and misty. The drive had taken two hours.

"Come in. The compound is in preparation. Will you have coffee?"

"Vest said it would be ready."

"Vest, Vest." Lick flung up a gnarled, spotted hand. "Señor Vest believes he merely has to wish a thing done, and, poof, it is done. This is not a matter of wishing. It is a matter of precision."

The doctor led him to a rear room that served as a laboratory. Work counters were strewn with filthy beakers of all shapes. Burlap sacks filled with everything from Sealyham terrier hair to Congo River silt sat on the floor. A clothesline ran the length of the room. Clipped to it were pages of yellowing paper; they were covered with chemical formulae and notes scrawled in German; a photograph was attached to each page. Parisi noticed that one photograph was of the secretary-general of the United Nations. Another was of the pope.

Lick set to work filling amber gelatin capsule shells with a fine white powder. He made a few notes in German on a yellowed sheet. Parisi could not see the attached photograph.

"Here is your *arzeneimittel*, señor." Lick held out a palmful of the capsules.

"What is it?"

"Ordinary gypsum plaster and oolong tea. And an inert bleaching agent."

"What's it good for?"

"Good for? It isn't good for anything." He cackled and popped two of the capsules into his mouth. He smiled grotesquely at Parisi as he gulped them down.

"What does it do, then?"

"For a single person on this planet, this capsule does instantly what nature itself would do in the course of time. But only for that single person. I, by the way, am not that person. You see, señor, the old wives' tales are not total myths. For each of us there are ingredients somewhere in the world which, if combined in the correct proportions, will kill us. They prey in a matter of seconds on the inherent weaknesses of our poor bodies. I have devoted my life to the search for the ingredients and the precise combinations. For a limited number of people."

"Who is this for?"

"Ah, señor, it would not be useful for you to know that."

Parisi felt the upholstery of the car seat. It had cooled off. He got in and started the engine. He took a key from his pocket and unlocked the glove compartment. A thick envelope lay inside. Vest had told him it held ten thousand dollars. Not bad for three days' work. Vest may scare you when he looks at you, but he pays well. He wondered how Vest had lost his finger.

The car in front of him had a "Caswell for Congress" bumper sticker. To Parisi all politicians were bums. He should know. He had dug enough dirt on them for Vest, and even planted some when Vest wanted it. Senators, cabinet members, even guys in the White House. It took him thirty-five minutes to reach his home in Freeport, Long Island. His wife was out. He opened some ice and poured himself a scotch.

The envelope was on an end table in the living room. He sat on the sofa and tried to open it. This son of a bitch is sealed with cement, he thought. He twisted it until a tiny rip appeared. He inserted his pinkie finger in the tear and pulled. The envelope flew apart. He saw what he thought was a black metal disc spring before his eyes. Then came a searing flash and a crushing roar. The concussion ripped Parisi's jawbone from his face, slashing his jugular vein as it was hurled across the room. His skull was shattered above his forehead. The sofa was pitted with small burns.

2 The Letter

The boarding line was long. The shuttle flight to Washington was always crowded. Forbes exchanged greetings with several people. A couple of congressmen, a Senate staff committee member, a trade association lobbyist. The Big Hello is instinctive among politicians. Show them a familiar face, and they see a conceivable supporter, campaign contributor, or favor-doer.

On another day he would have been happy to see them; they were his tribesmen; they spoke the same language.

Forbes took a seat next to a man he didn't know. He was relieved. He didn't want conversation. He wanted to think.

A final passenger appeared inside the front door of the plane. Forbes recognized him. It was the tall, short-haired man who had looked so savagely into the limousine. He had no carry-on luggage or attaché case. His deep eyes were aflame. He sat a few seats ahead of Forbes. Forbes noticed the man's right hand. The ring finger was missing.

The plane climbed over Flushing Bay and turned southeast. Manhattan looked like a city planner's table model. The stewardess announced the routine for using the oxygen masks and life preservers.

Forbes was distracted. He tried to concentrate on Vice-President Melville. He tried to sort out the possibilities. Would Melville offer him a job, a spot in his campaign? If he did, how to respond? Should he insist on a major role? Ask for time to think about it? How would Hamilton react? The questions refused to yield to deduction. Roundtree and his intimations of danger kept intruding.

The tall man seated ahead of him was on his mind, too. He looked wild, Forbes thought, but he could not imagine how he had been able to terrorize Roundtree. Was the guy some kind of nut? Maybe he was a psycho waiter whom Roundtree had undertipped. Maybe he had lost a case before the Supreme Court.

The stewardess pushed the ticket cart up the aisle. Forbes handed her a credit card. He looked out and saw a harness racing track below in New Jersey.

Forbes worried that he might have offended Roundtree. Perhaps he should have been more indulgent of the old man. He had been annoyed. He had a right to be, he supposed. Roundtree had been vague and dismaying. He was not used to that kind of talk from an intelligent man. He would drop Roundtree a note. Emphasize his thanks for endorsing Caswell.

But the words had come from Roundtree, Mr. Justice Roundtree, retired associate justice of the United States Supreme Court, one of the most distinguished names in jurisprudence. That was no raving lunatic who had said, *"There is about to be a sudden change. Don't go to China with the president."*

The pilot came on the public address system. He said they were over Philadelphia and would begin their descent shortly. Forbes felt for a cigarette. The pack was empty. He thought of troubling the man next to him for one. No, he decided, that might lead to conversation. He didn't want to talk.

Forbes thumbed through an airline magazine. There was an article on fish and water birds. It reminded him of boating with the president. One of the major drawbacks to visiting the Southern White House, to Forbes's mind, was that you usually had to go fishing with Hamilton. Forbes hated to fish. He hoped the president would be too occupied with details of the China trip to take time out for fishing.

A hand appeared over Forbes's magazine. It held a pack of cigarettes. Forbes's brand. The hand lacked a finger. Forbes was startled. He looked up. It was the man from a few seats up the aisle. The man with the ferocious stare. His scorching eyes were fixed on Forbes. Forbes took a cigarette and put it between his lips. The man's other hand shot out. It held a lighter. Forbes bent forward over the flame. He was about to say thanks when the man spun and returned to his seat.

Forbes knew he had glimpsed what had shaken Roundtree. Those eyes that had gazed at him projected raw menace. How had he known Forbes was out of cigarettes? How had he known the right brand? Forbes knew that the man, by some method, had been watching him. But why?

The plane entered the landing pattern. With each turn a landmark came into view. The Capitol, the Washington Monument, the Pentagon. The Potomac River came closer and then slipped past underneath them.

A driver in black uniform and hat called to Forbes as he walked through the passenger exit area. Forbes had never seen the man before in his life. Melville is really laying it on, he thought. The driver said not to worry about his luggage, someone would pick it up and bring it along. Forbes said that was unnecessary, he was returning to the airport in a few hours to catch another plane. The driver said nothing.

There was a line of limousines outside the main entrance. The atmosphere was moist heat, Washington at its worst. The driver opened the door for Forbes. The car looked cool and inviting.

At the same time the door of the car directly ahead was opened by a driver. Forbes saw the man who had given him the cigarette get in and disappear as the car pulled away.

Forbes stood a moment and watched the car drive off. He remembered he hadn't bought any cigarettes. He got in the car that had been sent for him. The chauffeur closed the door gently.

The drive was smooth. It would be at least an hour before official Washington began heading for home in the Virginia and Maryland suburbs and choking the roads. They crossed the Arlington Memorial Bridge onto the Potomac Parkway. The Lincoln Memorial was thronged with camera-laden tourists.

Forbes looked in the direction of the White House. The State Department, among other things, blocked his view. They zipped past the Kennedy Center for the Performing Arts. The Watergate complex came and went. Heat mirages danced on the highway.

The car turned off Reservoir Road. It stopped at the entrance to a gravel drive. Red brick pillars stood on either side. A brass plate with the name "Box Hill" was bolted to one of them. A guard jotted down their arrival and waved them through. The gravel crunched under the tires.

The drive wound through an expanse of colorful, geometrically sculpted gardens. It was shaded by a double row of box elders.

The house stood on a rise, facing a broad lawn. A squad of sweaty gardeners weeded and snipped. A lawn mower groaned. Sprinklers whipped out jets of water.

Lawrence Melville had never moved into the vice-president's official residence, Admiral's House on the Naval Observatory Grounds off Massachusetts Avenue. He did not like the status it conferred. He was a public figure in his own right. He saw his name as more important than the office of vice-president. He lived at Box Hill.

Box Hill had been built by Melville's father. It was surrounded by thirty-two acres of landscaped splendor. It was where the Melvilles stayed when they were in Washington and where they gave lavish lawn parties. It was one of several mansions the Melvilles owned around the world. All were staffed year round.

The car stopped under a porte cochere at the rear. Other limousines stood in a nearby parking area.

A man with thinning hair and a veined nose was at the top of the steps. Chandler Hibbitt had been a newspaper editor in Pittsburgh. He was Melville's chief political adviser and door-opener.

"Great to see you, Thack," he said. "Thanks a lot for coming. We know you've got a close schedule. The boss is really pleased you could make it."

Hibbitt had a relaxed, confident smile. He had worn an ulcerous frown the last time Forbes saw him. That was in the early, dubious months of Melville's challenge to unseat President Hamilton. Forbes didn't particularly enjoy Hibbitt's company, and he didn't trust him. Hibbitt felt the same way about Forbes.

"My pleasure," said Forbes as they walked to the second floor. "Before I forget," he added; he forced himself to sound lighthearted: "congratulations on your campaign. It looks like you're going to pull it off." It was a canon of their profession to grant a fellow practitioner recognition for his efforts, successful or not, regardless of personal feelings. "How do you feel about it?"

"To tell you the truth, Thack, I couldn't feel better. The

only problems we see right now are Ohio and New Jersey. I think we'll have those out of the way before we get to Pittsburgh. How do you see it?"

Forbes knew nothing of Melville's difficulties with the Ohio and New Jersey convention delegates. He thought, however, he detected a note of reservation in Hibbitt's optimism. It didn't matter. The conversation was tentative, in any case.

"You've got a pretty solid organization in Ohio," he said, trying to sound interested and up to date. "The uncommitted people won't wait long. New Jersey? They're always a problem. Stubborn. They like to play games. You know more about that than I do."

Hibbitt ushered them into a small library. The bookshelves reached the ceiling. A vase of fresh flowers stood on a pier table. There was a Hepplewhite sofa and a slab-front secretary. A console telephone sat on a candle stand.

"The boss is with one of the boys from Pittsburgh," said Hibbitt; he motioned toward the door at the end of the room. "It probably won't be more than a few minutes."

The telephone emitted a soft buzz. One of the buttons blinked. Hibbitt picked up the receiver. "Coming," he said.

"This shouldn't take long. Excuse me," said Hibbitt.

He disappeared through the door. Before he closed it, Forbes could see Melville talking to someone. It was the man with the missing finger.

Forbes was amazed, as if he had seen an actor in an Yves Saint Laurent suit in a movie about the Battle of Gettysburg. He spotted a bowl of cigarettes on the secretary. He lit one and sat down on the sofa. The cigarette tasted stale. It seemed to have been in the bowl a long time.

Hibbitt stuck his head through the door and nodded. Forbes butted his cigarette. He felt slightly disconcerted.

Melville walked from behind a large desk. He grinned almost shyly, arms outstretched, palms up, and his head tilted to the side. It was as if he were greeting a beautiful woman. Melville's famous idle charm. He took Forbes's hand in both of his.

"Say, Thack Forbes, it's *good* to see you. *Good* to see you. Man, have *we* got some things to talk about." Melville winked as he said "we." He was a rangy man with incongruously small, thick hands. He was in his middle sixties. Weekly injections of a hormone-amphetamine solution gave him the looks and vigor of a man of thirty-five.

"I was more than happy to be able to come, Mr. Vice-President." Forbes glanced at the man with the amputated digit. He was leaning against a bookcase. His arms were folded. His air of menace had vanished.

"By the way, Thack, this is—" Melville nodded to Hibbitt. He grinned and winked. Hibbitt took the cue. This was an introduction. Melville did not introduce people. He might not have known how. Hibbitt introduced the people Melville wanted introduced.

"Thack, this is Max Vest," said Hibbitt. "Max, Thack Forbes."

Vest walked over. He and Forbes shook hands. Vest's grip was firm. Forbes felt the stump of his ring finger as it pressed the margin of his hand.

"Mr. Forbes and I met on the plane," said Vest. He was smiling benevolently at Forbes. He conveyed the impression that he was sorry he and Forbes hadn't got acquainted on the shuttle.

Forbes was more perplexed than ever. He hoped it didn't show. What had become of Vest's piercing stare? Why did he pretend they had met casually on the shuttle? What was he doing in the company of the vice-president of the United States? Forbes decided to resort to guile.

"Good to see you again, Mr. Vest. Could I trouble you for another cigarette? I forgot to buy any."

Vest lifted his eyebrows as if it were an extraordinary

request. A look of mild surprise came over his face. He was still smiling.

"Certainly, certainly. Here you are."

Forbes took the cigarette and lit it. He wondered if he had imagined the business about Vest on the plane and in the limousine with Roundtree. No, he hadn't imagined it. What the hell *was* this charade about?

Vest said nothing else. Nothing else was said about him.

"Max, thanks for coming down. Chandler will be in touch with you." Melville put an arm around Vest's shoulder. Vest stiffened just noticeably. Melville grinned and winked at Hibbitt. Hibbitt opened the door. Vest left.

Melville turned to Forbes. His face was grave. He looked his age.

"Thack, how much impact do you think this China trip of Hamilton's is going to have on the convention?" He sat on the edge of his large desk. He motioned Forbes to sit on a French Provincial sofa. Hibbitt stood.

Forbes inhaled and looked for an ashtray. Hibbitt placed one next to him.

"None to speak of, I would guess," Forbes said after a few moments. "I've told the president that. I don't know whether he thinks it will or not."

"How many congressional seats do you think it will cost us?"

"The ones that are going down the tubes never had a chance anyway. The close races will turn on local issues in all but two or three cases. The best guess is that we'll lose seven or eight seats. Ten at most. I don't think the China trip will be a major factor in any of them."

Melville strode over to a large window. It looked across a lawn onto a stand of bay trees. The sunlight was brilliant. He gazed out for a few moments. His stubby hands were clasped behind his back. Abruptly he turned around.

"I don't think it will, either," said Melville. "But let's face it. I'm not blind to the fact that Hamilton would love to be renominated. He would love for the convention to become deadlocked between me and Darrow. Have the party summon him from his search for world peace to lead us to victory in November. Or something like that. That's one of his scenarios, isn't it, Forbes?" Melville gripped the back of a chair. His knuckles were white. The muscles of his face were constricted in anger.

Forbes felt Melville's bitterness, Melville's disgust at Hamilton. It made his flesh crawl. He knew the presidency was the one thing in the world Melville wanted and had been made to wait for. He had never seen the depth of Melville's fear that he might be denied it.

"If the president has a convention scenario, I'm unaware of it," said Forbes evenly; he was merely giving a political analysis. "Why should he have? He has less than fifty delegates; they're diehards for the most part; neither you nor Darrow will get them; they'll stick with Hamilton to the bloody end. The guys you have to work on are the uncommitteds. The number of uncommitted delegates going to Pittsburgh is the lowest in party history. Since you and Darrow are going in more or less even, the uncommitteds will be the swing people. If your organization does the job it's capable of doing, I think you'll get them and take the nomination on the second or third ballot. The fourth at the latest."

Hibbitt looked at Melville. Melville nodded to him.

"Look at it this way, Thack," said Hibbitt. "This China trip will be part of the Hamilton administration's record, such as it is. We're looking beyond the convention. The Hamilton record will be an issue in November. The vice-president wants to run on his own program. He doesn't want to run against the Hamilton record."

Forbes became impatient. He had no use for Hibbitt's view of Hamilton's record.

"You're saddled with the record of the Hamilton administration, whether you like it or not," Forbes said. He ignored Hibbitt and spoke directly to Melville. "You're a part of the Hamilton administration, whether you like *that* or not," he continued. "It's always been a factor to contend with when you run a rebel campaign against an incumbent president. Especially when the rebel is the vice-president. The risks are built in. Christ, that's basic."

"Let's be frank with each other, Forbes," said Melville. He walked to an Ipswich chest. Swans and compotes of cheap molded glass were arranged on top. The defunct factory that made them had been a Melville enterprise. The pieces were known as Melville glass. They were collectors' items. There was a National Melville Glass Society. Melville subsidized it. "I'm worried about this trip. What worries me has nothing to do with the convention or what comes after it. What do you know about the details of the trip?"

"Well, the itinerary calls for—"

"Forget the travel arrangements for a moment. Let's talk about the visit itself." Melville studied the glass collection.

"The time frame is eight days. I think the agendas are firm but the schedules are flexible. Chairman Tien and Mr. Huang are not always—"

"What I'm trying to get at"—Melville interrupted again; he walked back and sat on the desk—"is whether the treaty has been revised. Has there been a change in talking points, in the terms in which they'll discuss it?"

Forbes resented the question but did not show it. Hamilton was still president and still in charge of foreign policy. If Melville got to be president, he would be in charge of it. But not before. Forbes was also relieved. Diplomatic maneuvers were outside his sphere of concern. He was happy to be ignorant of whatever Melville was fishing for.

"I stick strictly to the political side, Mr. Vice-President. Of course, I would give the president my opinion on the political implications of any treaty talks if he asked me. But he hasn't. I don't have any reason to think he will. He knows the treaty is political dynamite. He remembers it blew up twice in his face—in New Hampshire and Florida." He permitted himself a sardonic smile.

"I didn't mean to sound presumptuous, Thack." Melville still sounded pompous, but the hard edge had left his voice. "It's just that I need to know as much as I can about this trip before I share something with you that's . . . well, it's something you and I must try and understand together."

Melville took a tray of cigarettes from his desk and offered one to Forbes. Forbes took it and held it between his fingers. Hibbitt moved to light it. Melville held out his hand. Hibbitt handed him the lighter. Melville lit Forbes's cigarette.

"It appears that we are faced with an unexampled situation." Melville sat down on the sofa next to Forbes. He spoke slowly. "Are you aware of the significance of the treaty?"

Forbes stubbed his cigarette irritably. "Mr. Vice-President, let's make sure we understand each other. There is no treaty. There has been a lot of *talk* about a treaty. Certainly the president thinks the treaty is a good idea. He and the Chinese will talk and talk about it. He knows at the same time that he couldn't get one ratification vote for it in the Senate. It's dead and he knows it. He's still a realist."

Melville smiled patronizingly. "Thack, do you think the president is being as realistic as he ought to be?"

"He's the president. He takes his own chances."

"Of course. I mean, do you think his outlook is as broad as it should be? He hasn't had an easy time. His perspective on many things, like the treaty, may be out of focus. Is he reluctant to listen to good advice?"

"He wouldn't listen when Senator Hall tried to talk him out of the trip, if that's what you're getting at. He knew Hall had been sent by you."

Melville studied Forbes closely. "You have a lot of respect for Hamilton, don't you, Thack?"

"Yes."

"To maintain that respect you have to stay loyal, don't you?"

Forbes didn't want to discuss his feelings about Hamilton with Melville. He also didn't want to offend Melville by declaring rudely that they were none of his business. This might be Melville's way of offering him a campaign job. He resorted to a familiar explanation.

"Hamilton has a plaque on his wall that says, 'Fortune may have yet a better success in reserve for you, and they who lose today may win tomorrow.' That appeals immensely to me."

Melville nodded to Hibbitt. Hibbitt opened a desk drawer and took out a small moroccan leather document case. He handed it to Melville, who unzipped it.

"Thack, what I'm about to show you, you will see one time in your life. You'll never forget it. After you've read it, it will be destroyed. You'll understand why." Melville took a sheet of notepaper from the case. It was tan, made of expensive pulp. It had a presidential seal at the top; the seal was a little larger than the one on Forbes's cigarette lighter. Melville handed the sheet of paper to Forbes.

Forbes put on his half-moon glasses. He looked at the handwriting. It was Hamilton's pinched, awkward script.

July 10

Dear Judge Roundtree:

Prayer comes hard for me, so I am turning to you and to our long, deep friendship for confidence and understanding. This is a time of challenge and opportunity, for me as president, for the country, and for the world. Not many men are afforded the chance to see the possibilities for mankind from my vantage point. And I don't hesitate to say that not many men in my position have been as misunderstood in their efforts to bring to the world the stability necessary for productive human advancement. I am convinced that the vast majority of Americans are oblivious to the nights and days I have spent working to alleviate their fears and improve their lives. I have been increasingly frustrated by the people whom the political process has compelled me to work with. I think I can say that, without exception, not a single one grasps my vision, let alone understands it, and not a single one has the fortitude to back me up rather than pursue his own narrow self-interest. This is why I am calling upon your steadfastness and discretion in this critical hour.

What I propose to do when I sit down with Chairman Tien is initial a protocol on my authority as president that will have the weight but not the approbation of a nonaggression treaty. I believe it was Talleyrand who said, "The art of statesmanship is to foresee the inevitable and to expedite its occurrence." By any reasonable standard the time is right for such a move. Nonaggression treaties are misunderstood. The Germans gave them a bad name. Since we have no territorial claims in the Far East, we have no choice but to forge this final link in our relations with the People's Republic of China.

I know the Senate would refuse to ratify a formal treaty at this stage of history. I feel this will serve as a beacon for them and the man who succeeds me. I also know full well that the State Dept. takes the same view as the military in opposing me on this. I have lost all respect for the State Dept. That was the main reason I gave up my career as a foreign service officer. With the amount of vision I was born with I couldn't permit a clique of snobbish, self-important men to have an exclusive voice on our China policy. They had the notion that because they had a flair for speaking Chinese or writing cables, they were entitled to make policy. They thought they could use their little flairs to cover up the fact that most of them were disloyal. That is why I spoke out against them. History has proved me right.

I am prepared to sacrifice everything to ensure that my

vision is achieved. I have received an invitation from Chairman Tien to stay as long as I'd like. "To enjoy the endless hospitality of the Chinese peoples" was the way he put it. I can't think of anybody in this country better equipped to explain America to the Chinese. As I was reared in China, I understand the Chinese. Being an American, I understand Americans. If I take this unprecedented step in behalf of our country, I would in effect be "going home." I haven't replied to Chairman Tien. I will give him my decision before we leave on our historic mission.

I am convinced that this letter will one day be thought of as one of our country's most important documents. It will give not only this generation but generations to come an insight into how history is made. For that reason I'm entrusting it to you.

Jos. Hamilton

It took Forbes several minutes to read the letter. Many of the words were nearly illegible, so cramped was the handwriting. He was amazed that so much could be crowded onto a single page.

Forbes stared at it. He noticed that it hadn't been folded. He was appalled at the self-pity, the grandiose delusions, the bizarre conceptions of history. He felt hurt, as if he had read a letter to another man from a woman he was secretly in love with.

He read the letter again quickly. A fist behind his navel squeezed shut.

For the first time in many years Forbes was surprised.

"What should we do, Thack?" Melville's voice was subdued. He looked earnestly at Forbes.

Forbes walked to the desk and took another cigarette. He lit it with his gold presidential lighter. He realized he was smoking more than usual.

"The obvious thing is to get to Roundtree," said Forbes.

"Have a talk with him. It's clear Hamilton respects him. I didn't know they were so close, but it seems they are." He described his earlier conversation with Roundtree, adding the details of his unusual introduction to Vest. Melville and Hibbitt listened tolerantly; their expressions conveyed that they found the story interesting but not really consequential. Hibbitt cut him short by saying that Vest had a reputation for eccentric behavior.

"Roundtree has tried to talk to him," Melville put in quickly. "I was told this by a good source, a very good source. My source said Roundtree didn't think it did any good." He was on his feet; he picked up a glass swan and examined it; the swans were his favorites. "According to my source, Roundtree said Hamilton thinks only of the treaty and doesn't seem to comprehend the gravity of . . . the other contingency."

"Maybe there's nothing to it," said Forbes. "Maybe he was just rambling on. Maybe it's just carelessness. He's capable of talking very carelessly, believe me."

"Good God, man!" Melville exploded. "Can't you see what we're faced with? We're talking about the possibility of the president of the United States defecting to Red China!"

The words hung in the air. Forbes looked at his cigarette. The ash was precariously long. He was afraid it would fall on the carpet. The ashtray was across the room. He caught the ash in his palm. It felt warm.

Melville nodded to Hibbitt. He moved his shoulders slightly. Hibbitt stepped behind him. He held Melville's jacket and Melville slipped out of it.

Hibbitt put the letter back in the leather case and returned it to the drawer.

"Let's go for a walk, Thack," said Melville. "Leave your jacket here. You'll be more comfortable."

Melville strode across the room in his shirtsleeves. Hibbitt was by the door. He opened it. Melville ushered Forbes into the hall. He may have thought the door opened automatically.

They strolled along the path of a carefully tended garden. Hibbitt walked a few steps behind them. The heat had become hostile. The sunlight seemed to throb. Forbes felt berries of sweat roll down his neck and seep into his collar. He loosened his tie.

"Our main concern—our *only* concern—is to stop him," said Melville. "And it's vital that we do it in such a way that the country never finds out about it. There's the chance, as you say, that he was simply careless. There's also the chance"—Melville looked over his shoulder at Hibbitt, as if to get beforehand affirmation in case there was an argument— "the chance that he's become impaired mentally in some way. Either way, the *possibility* of disastrous consequences can't be ignored. Remember this. Hamilton is the man who has the key to our survival at his fingertips."

Forbes thought of the army major who was never more than a few feet away from the president. The major carried the black attaché case with the codes that could spring a nuclear attack.

Melville stopped and picked a yellow polyantha rose. It was named for a Melville uncle who had subsidized the research that developed it. He held it beneath the bud and twirled it between his short, thick fingers.

"The implications of this are clear—and I'm not talking about this goddamn treaty," Melville continued. "I'm talking about a defected president. The country would be totally demoralized. We would be vulnerable to everything. The Chinese would have us by the balls. For all intents and purposes they would have the president of the United States as a hostage. They would threaten Japan and march into India. The Soviet Union would feel no inhibitions about any adventure it decided on—including an overt move against us. NATO would collapse in days. We would be paralyzed, if not destroyed completely. I doubt we could hold elections in November.

"It isn't hard to picture the reaction if the country found out about this. No elected politician's scalp would be safe. Economic panic. Riots. Attempted coups by the military. Political witch hunts. We'd be helpless to stop it. We can withstand the psychological shock of getting rid of a president who steps out of line in a way we understand—such as lying to us or abridging our constitutional rights. We can kick him out, if we have the goods on him, and feel we've done the right thing. But we have no experience with a president who goes over to the other side."

Melville handed the rose to Hibbitt. His shirt was gray with sweat.

"That's why we can't take this to the House Judiciary Committee and say, 'The president is committing treason. Please vote a bill of impeachment.' That would open the door to a catastrophe which neither the country nor the world could endure. Our responsibility is to stop Hamilton and make goddamn sure the country doesn't get the slightest hint that it ever crossed his mind."

Forbes was painfully uncomfortable. His eyelids were swollen by the heat. He envisioned the chaos Melville predicted. He thought of the letter. He thought of Vest. He thought of Hamilton. He tried to construct a pattern. The matrix was warped. He multiplied the elements and kept getting zero. He wondered why the hell Melville had suggested a walk. It must be a hundred and ten out here.

"What do you propose?" Forbes asked.

"You can imagine my predicament, Thack. I'm in a cul-de-sac. I can't make an obvious move. I'm the vice-president.

My duties—and limitations—are not ambiguous. Officially, I can do nothing. Nor do I want to. On the other hand, I'm aware of the situation. I'm morally obligated to act. Sometimes you can't wait for the firemen, you have to fight the fire yourself. Do you know what I mean?"

Forbes was put off by Melville's attempt at folksiness; it made his pompousness more distasteful, especially in this heat. But he realized that he, too, had to act. He and Melville had to act together.

"If Hamilton means business," Forbes said to Melville, "you'd better be prepared to blow the whistle. Either that, or see the president of the United States appointed water commissioner of Shanghai. Defection is a definite possibility, I'll grant that. It's also possible Hamilton wrote that letter in a desperate moment that vanished like that. If that's the case, he damned sure won't like to see it again. Or know that you've seen it. Why not confront him with it? Jam it down his goddamn throat. Tell him you'll ruin him with it if he doesn't cancel this China trip on the spot. I'll do it if you want."

Melville stared into the distance. His expression had abruptly hardened into the vulgar sharpness that characterizes the David portraits of Napoleon; the expression held for several moments. Forbes wondered if Melville had been listening. Then Melville smiled. His eyes crinkled. He looked at Forbes as if he were a father humoring an eager but clumsy child. He nodded to Hibbitt.

"If we confront him," said Hibbitt, "we'll be in the mess the boss just described. It will come out and the country will go to hell overnight. Besides, hitting him over the head wouldn't do any good if he's been thinking this way all along. I think what the boss has in mind is another approach."

"Which means?" Forbes rubbed the back of his neck.

"Which means," Melville broke in, "taking the political

45

approach. Talking to him in a way he understands, in a way Roundtree obviously *didn't* understand. . . . Let's go inside. We could use something to drink."

Hibbitt mixed the drinks at a small bar in Melville's office. Melville had vermouth on the rocks; he never touched anything stronger. Forbes had a gin and tonic. He was still recovering from the walk in the heat.

"I admire your instincts, Thack, but I'm sure you see why the direct approach won't work." Melville sipped his vermouth; his youthful look had returned. "Let me sketch a line of reasoning. Don't mention the letter. Appeal to his responsibility to the party. Say that whoever gets the nomination—me or Darrow—will have an impossible time in November with this China trip as an issue. It could cost us the White House. Point out how many seats we'll lose. Then—use this as your clincher—tell him I intend to appoint him secretary of state. Tell him that he and I have no basic foreign policy differences. Tell him he can achieve his international objectives and I guarantee he'll get all the credit. You can also say I want to give him access to all the resources that my family is privileged to have. I think he deserves that."

"What if it doesn't work? What if he skips anyway?"

Melville shrugged and smiled wearily. "We'll just have to ride it out. There's only so much you can do. After you've done that, you just have to ride it out, don't you?"

He motioned to Hibbitt. Hibbitt took the morocco leather case from the desk and removed the letter. He lifted the lid of a small cabinet. The cabinet housed a paper shredder. Hibbitt inserted the letter and pressed a button. The machine whirred. Hibbitt released the button and lowered the lid.

They finished their drinks. A steward brought Forbes's jacket. It seemed to have been pressed. Hibbitt made a conspicuous gesture of looking at his watch.

"Is it time already, Chandler? My God, we covered a *lot* of

ground, didn't we?" Melville winked at Forbes. He had re-
treated to his affected nonchalance. Hibbitt helped him with
his coat and put some papers in a briefcase. They moved
toward the door.

"What I want you to do," Melville said, "is to keep in touch
with Chandler. Let him know what progress you're making.
You know how to reach him. If it works, there'll be a spot for
you in the campaign, a *good* spot, one that won't interfere
with your New York thing. If it doesn't, well . . . "

They walked down the rear staircase. Melville paused to
confer with an aide.

"Chandler, what's the story on that guy Vest?" said Forbes
as they stepped outside.

"Max? Works for Trans-Columbia."

"Does he know about the letter?"

Hibbitt smiled stiffly.

Chandler, you always were an asshole, Forbes said to himself.

Melville's limousine pulled up. The vice-president turned
to Forbes. "Say, Thack, I can't tell you how much I *appreciate* you stopping by," he said and got in; as he did, that look
of imperial sulkiness flickered briefly across his face. Hibbitt
got in behind him and closed the door. The car moved off
down the gravel drive.

Forbes watched them leave. A driver appeared. It was the
man who had driven him from the airport. He said the car was
ready. Forbes got in. He was thankful for the air conditioning. The car turned onto Reservoir Road. The guard noted
their departure.

Vest eased his rented car off the Capital Beltway into a
shopping center parking lot. He rolled down the windows.
Air conditioning annoyed him. It offended his sense of fitness.
This heat is nothing, he thought, compared to Kuwait or

47

Oman. Or Ecuador. A flat buff envelope lay on the seat next to him. He reached in his jacket pocket. He felt the plastic cylinder.

Another car, several years older, pulled into the adjoining space. The paint job was faded. A side vent was cracked. The fenders were chipped and dented.

A man with pale skin and blue jowls got out. He was as tall as Vest but thicker and flabbier. It was midafternoon and he already needed a shave. His eyes were heavy-lidded. His mouth was neutral. His suit and tie had been in vogue a few years before. His shirt collar was frayed. His shoes were scuffed.

The man slid in next to Vest.

"Turn on the air conditioner, for Christ's sake," the man said.

Vest glared at him. His face grew taut. His knuckles whitened on the steering wheel. His shortened finger quivered. There was a time when that look had frightened the man. That was years ago.

Vest relaxed. His eyes softened. He turned the ignition and rolled up the window. He turned on the air conditioner.

"How are tricks at the Basement?" Vest asked.

"So-so. What's on your mind? You said this was urgent." The man looked straight ahead. His hooded eyes betrayed no interest.

Vest took a sheet of tan paper from the buff envelope. He handed it to the man.

The man held the paper before him. His hands were broad and hairy. His fingernails were chewed and dirty. He glanced at the presidential seal at the top of the page. The cramped handwriting was difficult to read.

After several minutes the man said, "Where did you get this?" His voice was gruff, accusatory.

"From Roundtree."

The man rubbed his forehead. He looked at the letter and back at Vest. His shoulders sagged. He sighed deeply.

"What do you make of it?"

"I don't think Hamilton is playing with a full deck," Vest replied.

"Who else has seen it?"

Vest said nothing. His stare began to intensify.

The man shifted suddenly and faced Vest.

"Turn off that goddamn double whammy and start talking," he snarled. "Who else has seen this fucking thing?"

The tension in Vest's eyes faded. "Melville," he said, "and a man from New York. Forbes."

"Who is Forbes?"

"Political type. He was Hamilton's campaign manager. He was in the White House for a while. Resigned after he got caught with his money in a racetrack run by the wise guys."

The man looked at the letter again. He saw that it hadn't been folded. He looked back at Vest. He touched his chin. It felt like sandpaper. He bit at a fingernail. "What about confirmation?" he asked. The rasp was gone from his voice.

Vest looked at him quizzically, as if he had been asked a stupid question.

"There is none," he said. "None that I'm aware of. The thing came to Roundtree. An ordinary letter with a stamp on it. I got it from him."

"When?"

"Today."

"This thing is two weeks old." The man tapped the letter lightly with the back of his hand. "How long has Melville known about it?"

"He told me last night."

"But he could have known about it earlier, couldn't he?"

"What difference does it make?"

The man bit harder at his fingernail. "In two weeks any

number of people might have heard about it. What have we got, three days? How the hell are we going to identify other interested parties and track their operations? In three days, for Christ's sake." He shook his head as he considered the exponential possibilities.

"Which raises another question. If other people *do* know, why haven't we gotten any pre-figures? It's goddamn odd that this has been on for two weeks and we haven't had a single intercept."

He realized this speculation was not secure. It conceivably could compromise a countermove. It came from carelessness and uncertainty. Technically, Vest was his agent. Vest had a "special relationship" with the Basement. Strictly speaking, he had no agents. He was one of the "across-the-street boys." The Basement was not authorized to handle cases.

"You see the scope of this, don't you? The ramifications?" The man's voice was plaintive. He said it more to establish an outline in his own mind than to inform Vest. He needed to talk. He didn't look at Vest. "Naturally the propaganda score for the Chinese would be tremendous. Our getting Svetlana Stalin and Castro's sister would be nothing compared to it. But strategically it would be the biggest blow we ever had. I don't know how we could absorb it. . . ."

He listened to the hum of the air conditioner. He watched the heat shimmer on the hood of the car. Shoppers, mostly women in lightweight dresses trailed by carry-out boys with bags of groceries, walked past.

"The problem is," he continued hurriedly, "the president has detailed knowledge of damned near every aspect of our military and diplomatic planning. He knows our intelligence modes, location of agents, disposition techniques, the works. A thorough interrogator could have him spilling his guts in no time. The Chinese are masters at thorough interrogation. In one afternoon over tea and fortune cookies they could find out the capability of every weapons system we have, every trade agreement we're negotiating, not to mention every Chinese agent we've recruited. And Hamilton would think he was discussing the *I Ching* or matching opposites or something."

The man sighed. He looked at Vest. His eyes pleaded.

"Don't you see how this dead-ends? Operationally, I mean? This is a factor that isn't in our equations. A president who's certifiably bughouse. We could deal with this treaty thing. That's what we're in business for. To counteract the fuck-ups of politicians and businessmen, but this . . . This means a short-term action operation against our own president. With three days to put it together. What about this reply? Any idea whether he has replied or how he'll do it?"

"Not definitely," said Vest. "My bet is Novic. I think he's the intermediary."

"Who?"

"Jacques Novic. California oil guy. Has a lot of trade concessions with the Chinese. In and out of China all the time. He's flying to Peking tomorrow night from L.A."

"Oh, yeah. He delivered Tien's invitation to Hamilton, didn't he? I seem to remember he wouldn't cooperate with us. Is he a Commie?"

"Not that I've heard. I think he believes it's bad for business to get too cozy with you guys."

The man grunted. He remembered an overdue payment on his house mortgage.

"You talked to Novic?" the man asked.

"No. I'm closer to this thing than I intended to get. I don't want to get any closer."

"Who's close to Hamilton? Somebody we could use?"

"Forbes."

"Forbes?"

"The political type. He's going on the trip. Melville has asked him to try and talk Hamilton out of it."

"Any chance it will work?"

"Virtually none."

"How do I find this Forbes?"

"He should be at National Airport in a couple of hours. He's on a flight to Georgia early tonight."

The man looked at his watch. A jolt of panic numbed him for a moment. He folded the letter and put it in his pocket. He opened the car door. The sultry air covered him.

Vest reached in his jacket pocket. He withdrew the plastic cylinder and handed it to the man.

"Do you want these?" Vest asked. "They might come in handy."

"What are they?" The man took the cylinder. He glanced at it.

"Pathogenic accelerators."

The man looked at Vest with sullen indignation. An agent, even an irregular one like Vest, wasn't supposed to introduce techniques, much less produce the means for their execution. He briefly considered flinging the cylinder back at Vest.

"Who are they for?" the man asked; his tone was biting. "Forbes?"

Vest said nothing.

"*Hamilton?*" The man frowned intensely.

Vest switched off the air conditioner and rolled down the window. The man got out and slammed the door. Vest drove away.

The man returned to his battered car. He didn't wait for it to cool off. He turned into the afternoon traffic. It was inflexible. He cursed and blew his horn.

He parked near the Forrestal Building. He decided a walk down Independence Avenue would relax him. He didn't notice the heat.

He pushed through the revolving door at the Twelfth Street entrance of the Department of Agriculture building. He descended a flight of stairs. He walked hurriedly down the corridor past the elevators. His breathing was wheezy. He came to a door with the legend "Outlook and Situation Board Export Analysis" stenciled in gold letters. He opened it with a cylindrical key.

"Unbelievable weather, isn't it, Mr. Coombes?" said the receptionist. She was plump and had thin gray hair; she was a few years older than he. "We don't have any business outside in weather like this, do we?"

"Awful, Ruby, just awful." Coombes signed the register. He was about to tell her about the faulty air conditioner at his home and the amount of the repair cost when he realized he didn't have time.

"Give me Donald Duck procedures. I think it's the green one."

The woman turned and looked back and forth at a row of hard-cover, loose-leaf binders on a shelf behind her. She selected the green one and handed it to him. "If you'll just sign this," she said and pushed a form in front of him.

He signed it and walked through the warren of cubicles. In each one a man sat behind a desk absorbed in reading or with a headset on, boning up on a language from a tape recorder. They were all at least twenty-five years younger than Coombes. The place was quiet. No one was kibbitzing.

The Basement was a stopping-off assignment. For the younger men it was necessary duty. It looked good on their records. The training and travel were invaluable experience. All the highly regarded chiefs of station had spent time there. The usual tour of duty was two years. Coombes had been there eighteen.

The mission of the Basement was close stand-by support. If an operation was mounted to topple a head of state, and it looked as if he wasn't toppling on schedule, the "boys across the street" moved in. Coombes had been "across the street" all over the world. Saigon several times, all over Africa, Ecuador, Chile, you name it.

Coombes reached his cubicle. A nameplate on the frosted glass said, "L. Coombes. Deputy." The furniture was imitation mahogany and shiny metal. He took off his jacket and sat down at his desk. His cuffs were soiled. He opened the loose-leaf binder.

A lanky, curly-haired man in his early thirties appeared. It was McElroy, the section chief. "Was that a developmental contact you left the building to see?" His tone was reproving in the manner of a military school upperclassman.

"Oh, hi, Rick. No, I don't think he has much potential. He's a Venezuelan on a bad visa and looking for work. Gave me some petroleum stuff. Looks pretty weak."

"Let's let the people with more experience in evaluation decide that. This shop isn't in the recruiting business." McElroy always spoke with contempt to Coombes. He didn't regard him as a genuine second-in-command. To him Coombes was an administrative accident. He looked on Coombes as a relic, another old O.S.S. hand who hadn't heard that times have changed. On the other hand, he was wary of Coombes, afraid he had friends higher up. He had once seen Coombes playing golf with the chief of the Foreign Intelligence staff.

McElroy noticed the loose-leaf binder. "What do you think you're doing with Donald Duck?" he asked coldly.

"I thought it was time I had a look at it." Coombes tried to sound ingratiating. "I have to keep up with you young guys on these computers."

McElroy shook his head. His disgust was unmistakable. "Don't take the rest of your life getting that contact report on my desk," he said and walked away.

Coombes thumbed nervously through the loose-leaf binder. He knew only the rudiments of computer operation. He wondered if he could grasp enough of the elliptical instructions to execute a Donald Duck retrieval.

The Donald Duck procedures enabled the Basement to tap the government's ten thousand or so supposedly theft-proof computer data stores. It was a tacitly condoned security violation. Everybody did it.

He signed in at the communications bay and sat down at a video display terminal. The room was chilly, almost refrigerated. The Execumat X computer required a low temperature to function. He held the loose-leaf binder in his lap and studied the terminal. It resembled a television screen with an elaborate typewriter keyboard and telephone dial attached. He inserted his plastic authorization card. A technician walked over.

"Need some help?"

"Just practicing," said Coombes. "How do I find the access sequences?"

The technician, a naval petty officer, smiled condescendingly. "Not too familiar with the gear, are you, sir?" He bent over Coombes's shoulder and typed gracefully on the keyboard. The screen lit up in pale blue. A series of letters, digits, and punctuation marks appeared.

"Now hit the MOVE button."

Coombes looked stupidly at the keyboard.

"Top row right," said the technician.

Coombes spotted the button with the word MOVE on it in red letters. He punched it. The screen flashed. The words ACCESS DIRECTORY appeared. Below was a column of seven-digit numbers.

"Those are the access sequences," said the technician. "Ordinary C&P telephone numbers. Dial the one you want. Then hit the MOVE button. That'll give you your entry characters. Dial again, type the entry characters, the number three—don't forget the number three—and hit the MOVE button. That'll give you the file index."

Coombes dialed a number and then pressed the MOVE button. A series of capital letters appeared at the top of the screen. He dialed again and copied them, laboriously punching the keys with his thumblike forefingers. He punched the number three at the end of the line. He punched the MOVE button. The screen flashed. The letters USDHEWPAYSOC-SEC/RY-A2/GG! appeared over a list of smaller letters and digits. He had reached the Department of Health, Education, and Welfare's payroll computer.

"Want to know what the code means?" asked the technician.

"No. I want an access directory and a locator."

"Same as before," said the technician. ACDIR and then semicolon ABC. And hit the MOVE button. By the way, to take a look at a file you dial the access sequence, hit the entry code and the file characters, with CDD smack up behind it. Don't leave a space, or it won't work. And hit the MOVE button. That puts it in Donald Duck."

"What does Donald Duck stand for?"

"The DD system. Diverted Data. Donald Duck takes a file and copies it and sends it back. That way, you can look at a file without tying it up. You can't tie up a file if you don't have primary authority. It would be my ass if they found files tied up in my bay."

"What about making copies? Anything wrong with that?"

"Well, I guess nobody likes having his files Donald Ducked, but there's not a hell of a lot they can do about it. They gave us Donald Duck. They must want us to use it."

Coombes looked at his watch. A wave of anxiety shook him. The chill of the windowless communications bay made him shiver. He wished he had remembered his jacket. He bit his fingernail.

He went through the routine. It produced the list of access sequences and computer locations. He tried more than a dozen numbers and entry characters. The index he wanted finally appeared. He dialed and typed a file code and pressed the MOVE button. He repeated the maneuver two more times with other numbers and letters.

"How do I get print-outs, chief?" he called to the technician.

"The printer's over there. Hit IMP and hit the MOVE button."

He punched the appropriate buttons. The words FILE EN ROUTE PROVIDE AUTHORITY appeared. He summoned the technician.

"Oh, *shit*," said the technician. He gaped at the screen. "You must have left out the semicolon," he said; his voice was panicky. "The file goes straight into our data store if you leave out the semicolon. The CDD won't work without the semicolon. Did you open the file?"

"No." He omitted to say he didn't know how.

The technician sighed. He typed rapidly over Coombes's shoulder. "There. She's back where she belongs. No real harm done. If you had opened the file, the outgo monitor at the home store would have printed FILE OUT FILE OPEN and who was doing it and the time. That would tie up a file. They would have landed on us with both feet. As it was, it just recorded the origin of request and the time. No sweat. Be sure to hit the semicolon. That puts it in Donald Duck."

Coombes typed the routines again. The printer emitted two short scraping sounds and then a longer one. Twenty feet of thin white paper unrolled through a slot. He ripped it into three sections and rolled them up. He returned to his cubicle.

He took the letter Vest had given him from his jacket pocket. He unfolded it. Somehow it did not look the same as it did when he had first seen it. It seemed altered. He scrutinized it. The constricted handwriting had not been tampered with. But the letter itself had changed, he was sure of that.

He shook his head. He put the letter in a safe behind his desk.

He stroked his cheek. His heavy beard was rough. He wanted help. There wasn't time to go through channels. He would have to fast-break it. He would have to mount a one-man "pilot fish" operation. He would have to act on his own. He would have to ferret out the raw intelligence for the planners to use as a reference point for a policy decision and a countermove.

He studied a roll of the computer print-out. He unrolled it as he read. The end of the roll fell off the desk and between his feet. It was from the National Security Agency. It was a condensation of Chairman Tien's invitation to President Hamilton. There was no mention of an offer to Hamilton to make an "extended visit" to the P.R.C.

He turned to another roll. It was headed "CICUSA Hamilton, Joseph Tyler." It was a habit-medical profile. Coombes was amused by the source "REDWING/SPR/GRU-2A." It had come from the Soviets. He noted that Hamilton was partial to in-and-out martinis and susceptible to a cerebral accident. There was no hint that he was inclined to defect.

The last roll was headed USIRS SS734-29-6485 Forbes, Thackeray Morgan.

3 The Threat

Forbes retrieved his luggage. He checked in at a ticket counter and confirmed his reservation. It was nearly two hours until his flight to Atlanta.

Hamilton's letter to Roundtree flooded his thoughts. What in the hell had possessed the president to write it? he wondered. Would Hamilton be amenable to indirect, predictable arguments against this China trip? Forbes thought it extremely doubtful.

He bought a pack of cigarettes and asked for five dollars in change.

"We only give change on purchases," said the woman at the cash register. She was perched on a stool with a magazine open on her lap.

"What do you call this?" asked Forbes. He held up the cigarettes; he was on the verge of losing his temper. A compulsion enveloped him to reach over and shake her by the neck of her ruffled blouse. He restrained himself by gritting his teeth and swallowing hard.

"You paid with a single," said the woman. "I gave you change for a single."

Forbes selected a pack of gum. He fished a ten from his wallet.

"Could I have my change in quarters?"

The woman raised an eyebrow maliciously. She gave him the change very slowly.

He went to the waiting area. He needed to sit down. He could hear his breath. He lit a cigarette. A lady with a small, fidgety boy in the next seat elaborately fanned away the smoke. Forbes moved. He felt the weight of the coins in his pants pocket.

He went to a phone booth and dialed long-distance information. The number he wanted was unlisted. He dialed his office. No answer. He looked at his watch. Alison had gone home early. He looked in his address book and found her number.

"Thack, what a nice surprise. How is our fabulous Larry Melville?" Forbes rarely called Alison at her apartment. He could hear music in the background. Mendelssohn's *Scotch* Symphony.

"In great form, Alison. Look. I need Roundtree's home number. Justice Roundtree. He's not in the book." He knew Alison kept her own list of all the phone numbers from the office Rolodex. He didn't know why.

"Sure. Anything go wrong?"

"No. There are a couple of things I need to go over with him."

"Hold on a minute." She laid down the receiver. He could hear the symphony's third movement. It was a passage he liked. Alison returned and read him the number.

"Can you tell me what Melville said?"

"He wants me to—" Forbes felt his hand tighten on the receiver. He closed his eyes. He wished he could be alone in a dark room listening to Mendelssohn. "I'll tell you when I get back."

"Is everything okay, Thack?"

"Fine, Alison. Thanks. Sorry to call you at home. I'll check with you in the morning."

"I know you're in a hurry, but I need to tell you this. I want to apologize for this morning. Bitching about my sex life and being snide. But, Thack, you're the only man besides my shrink I trust enough to talk about it. I mean, I'm twenty-three years old and I've never had an orgasm."

"It's a matter of keeping the right company. I wish I could talk longer, but I've got these other calls. Talk to you tomorrow."

He dialed Roundtree's number. Roundtree could clear up the mystery of the letter. A woman answered. Her voice was weak. She spoke with difficulty. Forbes could tell she was old.

"I'm so sorry," she said. "Justice Roundtree has been taken to the hospital. Something to do with his circulation. He has an apparatus, you know, for his heart. This is his sister. May I help you?"

"I had no idea. I hope he'll be on the mend soon." Forbes thought of the scene in the limousine when Roundtree had been frightened speechless by Vest. "Please give him my best wishes for a speedy recovery, Mrs.—"

"Miss Roundtree."

"Excuse me."

"Is there any other message?"

Forbes was silent a moment. "No," he said. "Just my best wishes. Thank you."

Forbes hung up. He considered calling Caswell; Caswell ought to visit Roundtree at the hospital. He decided against it. He didn't want to hear Caswell's voice. Caswell would have to think for himself this time.

He thought of Nell Leatherbee. Assistant Treasury Secretary Leatherbee could help him make some sense out of this. He would see Nell tonight. She would pull him close and touch him softly, dissolve his anxiety with her body. No, he thought, he didn't want to talk to Nell on the phone. It would be too difficult to explain on the phone.

He went to the newsstand. He looked over the magazine rack. He was unable to choose anything to read. He noticed someone at his shoulder. It was a scruffy man with heavy eyelids who needed a shave.

"Can I buy you a drink, Mr. Forbes? We need to talk," the man said.

Forbes looked closely at the man. He did not recognize him.

"You speaking to me?"

"I am."

"I'm afraid I missed your name, Mr. . . ."

"Walker," the man said. He did not offer to shake hands.

"Well, thank you very much, Mr. Walker, but right now I'm—"

"Let's go, Mr. Forbes," the man said. He was several inches taller than Forbes.

"I want to buy a magazine," Forbes said defensively.

"Forget it," the man said.

Forbes shrugged. He sensed that there might be a scene or worse if he refused to join the man for a drink. The man's air of clumsy menace was compelling. Forbes had always been cautious of anonymous bullies.

The cocktail lounge was dark and empty. A public address system announced arriving and departing flights. Bubbles of colored light circled a revolving clock above the bar. They found a table at the rear. A waitress appeared. Forbes ordered a gin and tonic. The man ordered beer. They did not speak until the drinks arrived.

"You've seen the letter," said the man in a tone of urgency and without additional preface. "I need your help. In fact, I've got to have it. I wish for your sake—and mine—that I didn't. There's no time to find anyone else."

Forbes eyed the man over his drink. He caught a glimpse of a man and woman coming in the door. He hoped they would take a seat at a nearby table; possibly that would foreclose this improbable situation; instead, the couple sat at the bar. "How do you know who I am?" he asked.

"That doesn't matter," said the man. "We're on the same side. It won't—"

Forbes thought this was his way out, a chance to put the man off with a show of bravura. "That's not good enough," he said, making to leave. "Thanks for the drink, Mr. Walker."

The man put his thick hand roughly on Forbes's arm.

"Sit down," he said in a low growl. Forbes paused a beat and then slid back into his seat; he tried to make it look voluntary, as if he had committed a momentary lapse of manners; his instincts told him that accommodating this man was the only way to placate him. "Listen carefully," the man went on in the same ominous voice. "I said I need your help. Something drastic may be needed to stop Hamilton. You're close to him." He bit at a fingernail. "If you don't go along, I'll forward a lot of information to the state's attorney in Chicago concerning your connections with Colony Investment Corporation. Stuff the congressional people never dreamed of."

"What the hell are you talking about?" Forbes asked sharply. "There's nothing left to that. That crap's old. Old and worn out."

"Not the stuff I'm talking about, Forbes. It's brand new. Even you haven't heard of it." The man took a large sip of beer. "An unlicensed South American weapons deal, for starters. A ten-thousand-dollar retainer, for unspecified services, in *your* name, on deposit in a Panamanian bank. All with the correct dates and signatures."

"That's not true," said Forbes. "None of it." He was beginning to feel cornered.

"Of course it isn't. Only you and I know that." The man

63

leaned back. "It would seem true, though, if it was necessary. I would make sure of it. And you would be in prison for a long time. I'm telling you this to guarantee your cooperation." He paused and sipped more beer and then added, "You'll be perfectly placed if Hamilton has to be terminated."

Forbes hurriedly lit a cigarette. "Terminated?" he said. He looked as if he had been told he was to be locked in a vault with a demented heavyweight boxer. "That means murder, doesn't it?"

"It's a way of stopping a man who has gone haywire."

Forbes continued to stare at him wide-eyed. "You don't know that he's gone haywire."

"No," the man said—he sounded almost casual—"but I can't bank on the possibility that he hasn't. Neither can you. Not after reading that letter."

Forbes was determined to avoid the sunken rocks he felt himself being drawn to. "You've got the wrong guy," he said after a few moments; he stubbed his cigarette. "I don't know anything about terminating, or whatever you want to call it."

The man abruptly thrust himself forward. "Goddamn it, Forbes," he said heatedly, as if he were warning someone who had ignored a don't-feed-the-animals sign, "I don't want to fuck up your life, send you to Joliet for twenty-five years. But I will, so help me Christ, if I have to."

Forbes had heard threats before; they were usually uttered irrationally and laden with ominous allusion. This man was not irrational. He had implied nothing. He had spelled it out. Still, Forbes thought he detected in the man's words a lack of genuine intention to inflict evil or injury.

Suddenly the man was on his feet. "Stay where you are," he commanded, "and keep your eyes on me."

The man strode across the room and stood for a moment behind the couple at the bar. They appeared to be a husband and wife. The bartender and waitress were not about. The man addressed the couple quietly and a second later the husband jerked his head around. As he did the man smashed him squarely in the face with a short right jab; the husband sprawled against his wife and they both tumbled to the floor.

At his table Forbes watched in strange, speechless horror.

"Now get out of here and stay out!" the man bellowed and spun to make sure that Forbes hadn't given in to the temptation to bolt for the door.

The couple struggled to their feet. The husband held a handkerchief to his mouth as his wife helped him from the bar. Almost immediately the bartender and waitress reappeared; they betrayed no hint that they were aware of what had just taken place. The man returned to the table, massaging his knuckles.

"It's not a good idea, using the fists," the man said as he sat down. "You take a chance of breaking something."

"Who do you work for?" Forbes asked, trying to mask the painful bewilderment the man had struck in his soul.

"It's an irrelevant detail," the man said. "In the long run you'll be happier if you don't know. If we can avoid an international nervous breakdown, it won't seem important." He reached into his jacket pocket. He drew out a plastic pharmaceutical cylinder and set it on the table. It contained three amber capsules.

"What I want you to do is simple," the man continued. "Take one of these"—he held up the plastic cylinder—"and get the contents into Hamilton. Don't try to substitute it for his medication—tranquilizers or therapeutic drugs or anything like that. People are damned negligent when it comes to pills. The heaviest speed freak often misses his dose for no apparent reason. Put it in a drink. Or better yet, the sugar bowl. Don't worry about the amount. But don't forget there are only three of them. That's more than enough. A pinch will do it."

The words froze in Forbes's mind. The image was vivid; it

was revolting; it was preposterous. He thought of the stories of medieval Italy and servants lacing the prince's wine with poison. Because his innocence had vanished years ago, the thought frightened him.

"What is this stuff?" he asked. "Arsenic? Cyanide?"

"I don't know what it is," the man replied. "It isn't toxic in the ordinary sense. It wouldn't give you or me a headache. It will work, though—for this target. It's hair or dust or something."

Forbes looked into his glass. He felt a short-lived sensation of being in a land of unknown boundaries and an undecipherable language, possibly in another century. Finally he said, "I don't think I can do it."

The man shifted slightly, violently. He gripped the edge of the table with both hands for leverage.

Forbes felt an explosive blow below his right knee. His breath caught in his throat. He grabbed his leg. He was too stunned to scream.

"Why the—" he moaned softly.

"Shut up," the man said; he looked directly at Forbes; his eyes held no emotion. "I'm through talking. We're in the last ditch. You're in, Forbes. You have no choice. All that's left to decide is whether you go to Georgia in one piece or several. Either way, the question comes down to this: you agree to kill Hamilton, if it's necessary, or I'll kill you."

Forbes massaged his leg. As he did, he got to the undeniable root of his character: he could not endure deliberately inflicted pain. All his artfulness and understanding of the world could not mitigate this single fact of his existence.

"Do we understand each other?" the man said.

Forbes nodded.

"You're supposed to talk to Hamilton, right, see if he'll change his mind about this trip? What are the percentages?"

"I don't know." Forbes continued to rub his leg, suffering a kinship with the Mohammedans who swore devotion to Christ rather than face the rack, the prisoners of war who collaborated with their captors, the suspects who signed manufactured confessions. "I haven't decided how to broach the subject."

"You'll have as much time as possible. Probably until you reach Alaska. Once you take off on the last leg to Peking, it will be too risky to put any hope in persuasion.

"It also may be necessary to terminate before that. You'll be told when to move. Other angles have to be calculated." The man drained his glass. "You may not have to move at all. What's your favorite track?"

"My favorite track?" Forbes was amazed by the question.

"Name one. A racetrack. You like to play the horses, I'm told."

"Saratoga," he replied, wondering what this was leading to.

"The trotters. I see." The man handed him a small slip of paper. "Call this number before six P.M. tomorrow night and the night after. Get a bet down each night for the third race at Saratoga. Call the number again after ten. If the race is clean, you can relax for the time being. But—if your horse breaks coming out of the gate, get ready with the—" He held up the cylinder of amber capsules and handed it to Forbes.

Forbes studied the cylinder. He set it down on the table.

The man smiled faintly. "Keep in mind what I said about Joliet. But don't forget this—" the thin smile vanished— "human beings aren't all that hard to kill."

Forbes looked at the table. "Apparently not," he said sourly.

The man stood up. He gestured to Forbes to remain seated. "Look," he said. "These capsules leave no fingerprints. None. An autopsy won't turn up anything but natural causes. When all is said and done, a danger will be out of the way. Who knows, a war may have been averted. Good luck. You may win some money on the ponies. I hope so."

The man walked out. He left no tip.

When all is said and done, Forbes thought bitterly, the president of the United States might be dead, and it will be on my hands.

Forbes put the cylinder of capsules in his pocket. He put a dollar on the table and after a few minutes got up and walked to the bar. His leg was stiff. He took a seat on a stool. He flexed his knee; nothing seemed to be broken. He lit a cigarette and ordered a Bourbon on the rocks.

"Did you see what happened?" he asked the bartender. "That fight?"

"I'm just temporary help," the bartender replied, as if to say that only a full-time employee could see a customer get his face bashed.

Forbes looked at himself in the mirror behind the bottles. His features looked distorted. He tossed back a slug of Bourbon. It had a medicinal taste. It produced no warmth.

He stared at the label on a whiskey bottle without really seeing it. Nothing seemed real. He could not imagine that the world was hurtling toward the abyss. Hamilton was going to China, he told himself, and it was rotten politics. That's all there was to it. Period. He took another drink and thought of the letter and the capsules. He tried but could not conceive of himself as the last hope of the world, the boy with his finger in the dike.

At the same time it was clear to him that he had strayed—or, more accurately, been stampeded—into alien territory. Until now his life had been governed by a routine of activity, not action; he kept busy, hectically at times, but his instincts and talents were for manipulating events, not forcing their outcome. Suddenly he had been irresistibly induced to refashion his style and methods, even his notions of his own abilities. Yesterday he would have laughed at the suggestion that Hamilton might defect to Red China. If pressed to argue the point, he might have said let him go, the world would survive it. That was yesterday. Today he had been shown the graphic possibility of a world calamity; he had been brutally confronted with the choice of preventing it.

Goddamn it, he said to himself and felt disgusted, why am I being pushed into making this choice? I'm not a man of action. I deal in temporary gains and temporary losses. I don't take chances. I get paid good money to figure out ways for *other* people to take chances.

He paid for his drink. He walked slowly to his plane. He was aware of his leg.

The flight to Atlanta was uneventful. He wished it had been otherwise. The lack of distractions—smooth weather, languid stewardesses—had given him the unwelcomed opportunity to reflect. He was, after all, a murderer. Not a psychopath who had had to be put away for the protection of society or a professional executioner who did his work efficiently. Just a passive amateur. A man who once had consented to the death of another man. The victim had been his father.

"We can keep him alive indefinitely," the doctor had said as he emerged from the operating room, "but, frankly, he'll never be able to function normally again." The doctor went on to explain the anguish in store for the survivors and the enormous expense involved in keeping a human body alive by artificial means.

"Let me think about it," Forbes had said; he was in his early thirties at the time; his mother had died several years before; he was an only child. "I need to talk it over with my wife." He went to an empty waiting room where there was a pay telephone. He knew he would not call his wife, who was at home with their two daughters awaiting word. What he

69

wanted was some time alone to try and understand why his father had done it—had put a low-caliber pistol to his head in his Manhattan law office and bungled the job (no one knew he even owned a pistol); he had left no note, and there was no hint of scandal in his public or private life; in fact, his father had regularly scorned the idea of taking one's own life for any reason; a man who had lived through a war could live through anything, he often said; perhaps his father did have something to confess and had resorted to suicide as the only way of getting it out. Forbes felt a rush of anger and betrayal that suddenly turned to confusion. Why the hell had his old man done it? They had played their weekly game of squash the night before at his father's club; they had made a date for dinner the following evening. His father was having drinks first with some old army buddies, men he had served with in Burma; it was to be a reunion of sorts.

Forbes had been at the restaurant when the call came. It was from one of his father's partners. The partner, whom Forbes had known since he was a child and regarded as a virtual uncle, gave him the details in his soothing, professional voice. Forbes hurriedly called his wife and rushed to the hospital. As he sat in the secluded waiting room, he was taunted by the idea of hating his father, hating him for contradicting a standard of survival he had set for his son. This was followed by a predictable, extraordinary pang of guilt, a tangible feeling that the son had somehow failed the father. But the guilt was groundless because the contradiction did not seem plausible. In fact, the more he thought about it, it did not seem like a contradiction at all. His father was a deliberate man who controlled his own purposes. But the question—relieved, after an hour or so, of hate—still nagged. What could have been his father's purpose in attempting a final act? In Forbes's mind, the fact that his father lay near death could as easily be attributed to a random accident—a gas-main explosion or a

70

fall from a ladder—as to suicide. It was an enigma, hidden and ambiguous.

Now the decision. His father had chosen to die; he had not made good the attempt; now the choice was in the hands of others. Since Forbes did not know his father's purpose, he chose to put the decision in the hands of others. He would murder his father—as his father had chosen to murder himself—but he would not take responsibility for it.

"What's your advice?" he asked the doctor moments later.

"Cease the medication immediately," the doctor replied softly but without hesitation. "It will be gentle, painless. He's in a deep coma. He'll never be aware of it. I think you've made the right decision."

The right decision. The decision Forbes had not meant to make at all. It was several days before he realized he had made it. He was lunching with the partner in his father's firm who had called him at the restaurant.

"Of course, it was the right decision," said the partner over coffee; they had confined their conversation thus far to matters related to the late Mr. Forbes's estate. "Thack, you know perfectly well your father wouldn't have wanted to entangle his family with a problem that would only cause them pain."

"Pain?" said Forbes, looking down at the table; there was a note of dejection in his voice. "My father had what I consider a damned good grip on life. You probably know that better than I do. You were one of his best friends. I don't think pain was something he gave much thought to, other than helping people he cared about get rid of it. But inflicting it on himself? It doesn't make much sense, does it?"

The partner was silent a moment and then said quietly, "No. It makes no sense at all. The only further light I can shed on the episode is that when he came into the office—it was rather late in the day and I'm certain no one was expecting him back—he looked terrified. I don't mean terrified in

71

the sense that he had had a close call or anything like that. I mean terrified in the sense that he was somehow out of control. Out of control of his faculties. I was working on something at the time, dictating I believe, and meant to look in on him. Then there was this shot. . . . Well, you know the rest."

As Forbes left the lunch, he doubted he would ever know what had driven his father momentarily, fatally "out of control." But he would never cleanse himself of the feeling that he had been the instrument of his father's death. On the other hand, he never punished himself with delusions that he had consented to his father's death to become his father *himself*. However, as the years passed, he carefully established a firm distance between responsibility and action and his methods of dealing with them; he acquired the habits of a gambler—except the risks he took were always for others and never for himself. He did not intend for his dead father to end up killing him.

The plane landed on schedule and Forbes confirmed his connecting reservation on a puddle-jumper airline. He called the Southern White House, which was several hundred miles away, to alert them to his arrival. An eager enlisted man was on the switchboard.

Forbes disliked small regional airlines. He retained the bias that the planes were unsafe and the pilots physically unqualified. They reminded him of campaigning in chartered planes, delays at critical times, improvised repairs. This was in the back of his mind until the small jet landed, five stops later, at Valdosta, in southern Georgia.

A marine captain greeted him at the steps of the rollaway ramp. The moonless sky was cloudless. The stars were magnificent. The atmosphere was hot and damp. The sulfurous odor of decomposing pulpwood, a local industry, bit at his nostrils.

"Welcome to south Georgia, sir," said the marine. He shook Forbes's hand. "Sorry we can't offer you better weather. We're in the middle of a heat wave. Record high. Been like this since Saturday."

Forbes said it seemed to be hot all over. A military sedan was waiting on the apron near the small, dimly lit terminal. A lance corporal brought Forbes's bags. He put them in the trunk and got in behind the wheel.

They drove across the small southern city. Stark mercury lights illuminated the streets and attracted swarms of moths. Lush greenery was blackened by shadows. There was little traffic. As they passed beyond the city limits, pine forests formed walls on either side of the road.

The sedan halted at the gate of Moody Air Force Base. An air force guard waved them through. They came to a restricted area. It was bathed by floodlights. A half-dozen Sikorsky helicopters stood on a pad, their rotors drooping. Beyond them, seven huge jetliners of Air Transport Command stood at the edge of a runway. They were the personal fleet of the president of the United States. One of them was Air Force One. Marine sentries patrolled with loaded weapons.

One of the helicopters came to life. Forbes walked across to the landing pad. The blast from the rotor whipped his jacket and tousled his hair. He climbed in. He remembered he hadn't thanked the marine captain; it wasn't like him to forget a thing like that. The lance corporal threw his luggage aboard. Forbes fastened his seat harness. The helicopter lifted off.

Forbes looked out a window. The landscape was dark, devoid of features. Twenty-two minutes later the Southern White House came into view. The scene was floodlit: the large main house and a cluster of smaller bungalows; a small

73

lake and a putting green; rolls of accordion wire around the fringe; guard towers manned by marines with .30 caliber machine guns. The helicopter alit on a pad near the putting green.

A young presidential aide in a short-sleeved shirt was waiting with a car. He looked anxious.

"The old man wants you at Wabash House as soon as possible," said the aide. They hurried to the car. The mosquitoes were thick. They drove toward the compound.

"Tonight?" Forbes looked at the luminous dial of his wristwatch; it was after midnight. He was dead tired; he wanted a shower; he wanted to fall into the arms of Nell Leatherbee.

"I don't suppose you've heard, have you?" said the aide.

"Heard what?"

"Justice Roundtree. He died tonight. The old man is going over a list. He's trying to come up with someone to represent him at the funeral."

Forbes sank back in his seat. "I saw him earlier today," he said. "He gave me a lift to the airport." He said it as if he were alone in the car. "He agreed to help a campaign I'm handling."

The car stopped in front of a bungalow. Fort Wayne House. Hamilton had named all the tan brick dwellings in his retreat after places in Indiana. It fascinated the media. On one side of Fort Wayne House was Elkhart House. On the other was French Lick House. It was known to frequent visitors as French Tickler House. Or just French Tickler. It usually made Forbes laugh. Not tonight.

"Don't keep the old man waiting, okay?" said the aide as Forbes got out. "He's already pissed off that you took so long getting here."

Forbes walked up the steps. An enlisted man brought his luggage. A white-jacketed steward opened the door.

"Welcome back, Mr. Forbes. The second floor is ready for you. Have you had dinner, sir?"

"Thanks, Juan. Place looks nice. I'll get something at Wabash. A sandwich or something. The president wants to see me."

"Shall I send up a drink?"

"I'd love one, but I don't have time. Any messages for me?"

The steward gave him the messages. He went upstairs.

The second floor consisted of a sitting room, a study, two bedrooms, and two baths. There were at least two telephones in each room. The furniture was nondescript but comfortable. A console could be operated to pipe in music. Prints depicting Indiana scenes hung on the walls.

The enlisted man finished unpacking Forbes's things and left.

Forbes sat down on the bed and looked at the messages. Two from Caswell. One written by Nell herself saying she would be at Wabash when he got there.

The telephone chimed.

"For Christ's sake, Thack, what the hell is holding you up?" It was Gil Snyder, Hamilton's chief of staff.

"I just got in, Gil." Forbes was impatient; he didn't understand why he was being pressed. "What's the goddamn hurry? I heard about Roundtree. I'll be ready with some input on the representation list. I need to make a few calls."

"Don't you know what goddamn time it is? You know how it is when he's been up this long. Christ, get the lead out. Let's get this over with."

Forbes tried to imagine what Snyder meant. Hamilton often worked eighteen-hour days. Subordinates were expected to do the same. Snyder himself had declared more than once that nobody ever said working for the president was a piece of cake: if you don't like the conditions, get an honest job. Snyder's voice had a frustrated ring, one Forbes was unaccustomed to.

He hung up. He decided to put off calling Caswell until the morning. He splashed water on his face and slipped into a short-sleeved shirt. It was the uniform at the Southern White House. Hamilton was an overbearing stickler on the point. The president gave men he saw dressed otherwise the look a maître d' gives a diner who arrives without jacket and tie.

Forbes took the plastic cylinder from his jacket pocket. He felt like a foreign body, a fatal virus in an already sickly organism. He was unable to choose how to dissemble his role as . . . as what? Savior of his country? Presidential assassin? Luckless fool outstripped by events? His doubts were academic, however, unless he found out whether he was able to step into the presence of his projected victim with a concealed weapon. He slipped one of the amber capsules into his pants pocket.

He walked across the compound. His leg was uncomfortable but no longer in acute pain. It was not quite 1 A.M. and the temperature was still in the high eighties. The sound of crickets was pervasive. Mosquitoes hummed and stung.

He let himself in at the side entrance of Wabash House. Wabash House was the president's quarters. It was the largest structure in the compound. It was built on the site of an old plantation. It was the gift of a tool-and-die manufacturer who raised campaign funds for Hamilton; it was to be sold after Inauguration Day, with the proceeds going to the outgoing president. Forbes gave his name to an aide. The aide disappeared. Forbes noticed the army major with the black attaché case of nuclear codes seated down the hall.

Gil Snyder appeared. "Jesus, you took your sweet time." His face was taut. "Where the hell have you been? You were supposed to be here this afternoon."

"I stopped by Washington."

"That's nice." His sarcasm came from fatigue. Insinuation was not one of Snyder's habits. "What were you doing in Washington?"

"I went to see Melville."

"You *what?*"

"He asked me to stop by. I didn't know it would take this long."

"What do you and Larry Melville have to talk about?" Snyder looked at him suspiciously.

"I'd rather tell Joe myself. I don't mean to cut you out, Gil, but I'd prefer to do this one-on-one."

"Tonight?"

"When's the best time?"

"There's never a good time to discuss Melville with him. You ought to know that."

"Look, Gil, tell me what's going on down here."

"What do you mean, what's going on? We've been putting in goddamn long days. The working papers for the trip have been undiluted hell. He just finished ten hours with the secretary of state. He raised hell every inch of the way. He's got General Wells in now, and he's reaming the guy a new asshole."

"Is he losing his grip?"

"Christ, I don't know. It wouldn't surprise me. Everyone else around here seems to be." Snyder leaned against the wall. He rubbed his temple. "It's the short-timer syndrome, I guess. Low sand in the hourglass and all that." He looked at his watch. "Let's go in."

They pushed their way through a pair of double doors into a large room filled with overstuffed leather furniture. A tall, lean, stooped man was standing at a broad window made of bulletproof glass that looked onto the lake. His back was to the room. Abruptly he spun around. The hollows at his temples gave his face a somewhat caved-in look. He was holding a glass. He looked unsteady. It was Hamilton.

"Goddamn it, General, you military people have got to stop thinking in terms of containment and start thinking in terms of my concept of strategic alternatives!" Hamilton's booming midwestern twang was unnerving.

Hamilton did not acknowledge Snyder and Forbes. He walked to a bar at the end of the room. He gestured with a brushing motion and watched closely as the steward poured gin into a shaker. He indicated to the steward to add a little more.

General Wells was standing by a couch. His aide, a full colonel, was seated with an attaché case open on his lap. They were in short sleeves.

Forbes looked for Nell. She was not in the room. He guessed she had excused herself; she probably didn't want to add to General Wells's embarrassment by being present while he was getting dressed down. Forbes looked for food but saw none.

Seated in a corner, fully awake and silent, was Tung Yen Fun, Hamilton's old retainer. He was in his seventies. Tung had been employed in the household of Hamilton's missionary parents. He personally had arranged their funerals, first the mother's and a short time later the father's. When Chungking fell to the Communists, Tung fled via Shanghai to the United States and rejoined Hamilton. He was inactive now as a servant and functioned as Hamilton's companion.

"This containment crap is so far out of date it makes me puke." Hamilton shambled back to his spot by the bulletproof window. "We spent years trying to get the Chinese out in the open where we could see how they operate. You military people can't seem to get it through your thick skulls that containment will drive them right back in their holes."

78

"The joint chiefs don't propose a return to classic containment, Mr. President. What we want to see—" General Wells's humiliation was visible. The colonel did not look up from his attaché case.

"The hell you don't," Hamilton broke in; his speech was slurred. "The goddamn hell you don't. That so-called working paper on fallback and second line estimates"—he pointed to a thick document on a table—"is nothing but nearsighted, second-rate horseshit. Second-rate, General. Plain, ordinary second-rate. Now you and the colonel get out of here and get the joint chiefs on the goddamn ball. By tomorrow I want something that reflects *strategic alternatives*. It had better reflect them so clearly that Tung can see it without his glasses."

Hamilton turned and looked out the window. The military men hurried from the room. The president did not bid them good-night.

Forbes studied the man at the window. He was outlined in partial silhouette against the hot, moonless night. Forbes was engrossed by the man's personality. He had forgotten the capsule in his pocket.

"How does a high-powered political consultant from New York get a drink around this place?" he called out. Snyder was startled. He looked aghast at the ceiling as if he expected it to fall.

Hamilton turned around slowly, as if he heard a note of enchanting music. A crooked grin came over his narrow face. "Forbes, where the hell have you been? Let me get you a drink, son. It's been rough here today, let me tell you." He walked slowly to the bar. Forbes joined him.

"I'm flattered, Mr. President," said Forbes with a grin. "From the minute I got here everyone's told me you're dying to see me. Is it true? The last time I was with the president, everyone was dying to see me leave."

"Hell, yes, it's true. Why do you think I call you on the

phone damned near every day? Just because I had to fire you doesn't mean I don't think you've got more political sense than just about anybody in the business." Hamilton smiled at him wolfishly. "I'm in a gambling mood, Thack," he said. "I'm thinking of trying to draw an inside straight flush. I need to bounce it off you. The idea, I mean. Not now. After we've had a drink."

He waved the steward aside. "That's okay, Sergeant. Run on out to the kitchen. We'll call you if we need you." The steward left.

Hamilton stepped behind the bar and surveyed the bottles. He picked one up. "Know what this is?" He held the bottle out in front of him. "This is mao-tai. This is what they toast with in China. Right, Tung?"

The old Chinese nodded from his corner.

"I know you boys would prefer one of my in-and-out martinis," Hamilton continued; he poured a quantity of vermouth into a shaker and piled in some ice. "This is something new. Get us used to mao-tai. We'll be drinking a hell of a lot of it in a few days."

He made a series of circular motions with the shaker and then drained out the vermouth. He poured in the clear mao-tai. He swished it several times and then poured it into stemmed glasses.

Snyder walked to the bar. His face was drawn with consternation. Hamilton handed him and Forbes each a glass.

"Come over here, Tung, for God's sake!" Hamilton shouted. "*Kan-pei! Kan-pei!*"

Tung eased himself from his chair. He trudged to the bar and accepted his glass.

"Tell Forbes what *kan-pei* means, Tung."

Tung looked into his glass. He looked out of place in his short-sleeved shirt, even though he had lived in the West for nearly forty years. He seemed cooperative but not submissive.

80

"At a Chinese banquet, when they toast each other, they drink the contents of a bowl at one hoist. They say *kan-pei* loudly after each toast. It means 'dry cup.' "

He took a half step back.

"You heard what the man said." Hamilton downed his glass.

Forbes sampled his. It was strong and raw. "I don't think I can *kan-pei* this, Mr. President. I'll nurse it."

Snyder tasted his and grimaced. He looked peevishly at Forbes and silently framed the word "Roundtree" with his mouth.

Forbes took the cue. "I was sorry to hear about Justice Roundtree, Mr. President," he said. "Just this morning he agreed to help a candidate of mine. Do you have someone in mind to represent you at the funeral?"

Hamilton drained the shaker into his glass. Snyder looked alarmed.

"Chief Justice Quinn can't very well represent the president when he's representing the Supreme Court," Hamilton said. He leaned on the bar; his thin frame looked weak. "It wouldn't look right. And Melville—"

He uncoiled suddenly. He padded to a leather couch and sat down heavily. He crossed his legs and folded his arms. He held his drink below his chin. His eyes seemed to recede in their sockets.

Snyder looked at Forbes and shook his head slightly. Tung Yen Fun trudged back to his seat in the corner.

Nell Leatherbee walked in through the double doors. She looked tentatively about her, as if she had walked in on a domestic argument. She touched Forbes's hand lightly; they kept up a modicum of pretense in front of other people.

"Bring me that bottle, Nelly!" shouted Hamilton, who had not appeared to notice her entrance.

Nell glanced at Forbes and then at Snyder. Snyder nodded at the mao-tai. She picked up the bottle slowly.

"All of you come over here," Hamilton mumbled and

shifted in his seat. "The president of the United States doesn't like to drink alone." They seated themselves near him. Hamilton took the bottle from Nell Leatherbee.

"I know what they say. I *know* what they say." Hamilton's eyes were out of focus. He poured some mao-tai into his glass; some of it slopped onto his short-sleeved shirt. "I know they say, 'You might not agree with Larry Melville's politics, but, by God, you can't accuse him of taking money.' That's the shit Congress and the bar association threw at me when they made me establish that blue-ribbon panel to screen my new appointees. *My* appointees."

Forbes knew the depth of Hamilton's bitterness at Melville. But he was stunned that Hamilton was so devastated by alcohol. He knew the president drank heavily at times, but heretofore he had controlled it, grown expansive with it. Now he seemed to be using it to feed a deep melancholy.

Forbes glanced at Nell. She looked grim.

"Blue-ribbon panel, my ass." Hamilton struggled to sit up. "Have you looked at these new *appointees?*" He was having trouble with pronunciation. "Nearly every goddamn one of them has spent his life kissing Melville's ass. They own stock in Melville corporations, get grants from the Melville Foundation, get campaign contributions from the Melville family. They serve on Melville commissions and they work for law firms that represent the Melvilles. God almighty, the government sounds like it's being brought to you as a public service by Trans-Columbia Oil."

With great effort Hamilton got to his feet. Forbes and Snyder leaned forward—they were afraid he might fall.

"That Osborne, that self-important turd of a secretary of state, he's Melville's boy." Hamilton was swaying; his eyes were nearly closed. "Gil, tell Thack what that son of a bitch tried to do to me today. Nelly, you were here. You tell Thack what that son of a bitch Osborne tried to sneak past me today."

82

Snyder and Nell Leatherbee looked at each other; their eyes were full of apprehension. Snyder nodded to her.

"Well," she began, "I suppose in effect what he wanted to do was to open up the agendas to more staff participation and save the critical negotiations for—"

"I'll tell you what the son of a bitch tried to do," Hamilton interrupted; he was holding his glass in front of him. "He tried to fix it so I'd be sightseeing while he and his academic types did the hard bargaining. He wanted me to take the fucking guided tour of Peking.

"But he made a mistake, didn't he, Gil? Huh? Didn't he? Tell Thack he forgot who he was dealing with. Asshole Osborne forgot I was brought up in China. I know the Chinese. Look at this." He held out his left hand; it wavered. "This is my Purdue ring."

A tear rolled down Hamilton's cheek. He swallowed with difficulty.

"You don't know what it's like to have missionaries for parents," he said pitifully. "You feel like a freak. You're poor to start with. When you're back home on leave, kids— American kids like you—treat you like you have two heads. You get shown off by relatives at Sunday school. My parents made sure I didn't learn Chinese. They said they had to learn it for their missionary work, but that I shouldn't learn it because I wouldn't be staying in China. I was an American, they said, and English was good enough for any American. God, I *wanted* to learn it.

"I went to Purdue and waited tables to pay my way. I was forever getting invitations to speak to some group or other about China. I always felt out of place. I didn't feel like a bona fide American and I didn't feel like I belonged in China since I couldn't speak the language. When I entered the foreign service and went back to China—"

He drained his glass. He thrust out his chin.

"The foreign service was full of bastards like Osborne. You

know what they're like. Slick idealists. Sold the Chinese out to Moose Dung and then turned around and said they did it because Chiang was too weak to unify the country. Of course he was. They made sure he was. They undercut him at every turn. That's exactly what I told the loyalty review board. I named names. I didn't hesitate. I *named names*. I got elected to Congress for the stand I took before the loyalty board, remember. . . . That was a long time ago. Moose Dung is gone. Tien isn't so rigid. We understand each other. . . . "

He collapsed on the couch. He lost consciousness. The glass fell from his hand. It shattered with little noise.

Forbes, Nell, and Snyder stood up. They looked around them. They were dismayed, ashamed. Tung Yen Fun came over. "Would you be so kind as to summon the steward, Mr. Snyder?" he said. Snyder picked up the phone and spoke into it. Two stewards arrived. They draped Hamilton's spindly arms over their shoulders and took him from the room. Tung accompanied them.

"He gets like this when he stays up too late," said Snyder; he sounded apologetic. "He'll be all right in the morning. Dr. Brabham will take care of him."

Snyder collected some documents. "We'll put the funeral list together in the morning, Thack. At breakfast. Eight sharp, right? The heavy stuff starts at eight forty-five. Osborne and General Wells. I'll have to unruffle their feathers. Don't lose any sleep over the list. He'll probably go with the chief justice when he's slept this off."

"Can you get it to the media that I was consulted?" asked Forbes. "It would help me back home." He was puzzled that Hamilton had shown virtually no personal interest in the death of Roundtree; Roundtree, his state-secret confidant, his postman to history. It only reinforced his confusion at the day's montage of disparate events.

Snyder said he would take care of it and left through the kitchen. Forbes and Nell left by the side entrance. The army major with the black attaché case had gone upstairs to sit outside the president's bedroom.

"Are you staying at Fort Wayne?" Nell asked as she and Forbes walked across the compound. It was still hot and sticky. She took his hand. "I want to come to you tonight."

Forbes looked at her. "What about Austin? What if he calls? He calls at the damnedest times."

"I'll say I was up all night working with Hamilton." She shook her head. Then she kissed his cheek and released his hand. "I'll be over in a few minutes."

Forbes told the steward to send up a bottle of Bourbon. "How's the corned beef, Juan? Good as it used to be?"

"Excellent, Mr. Forbes. I had some sent down when I was told you were coming."

Forbes sat down on a sofa in the study. The steward brought the whiskey and sandwiches. He rang the switchboard and asked for a 7 A.M. wake-up call. He thought of the capsule in his pocket and his sinking feeling returned. He went into the bedroom and put it back in the cylinder, which he concealed in a drawer. He returned to the study and poured himself a drink. He looked at the sandwiches; he had no appetite after all.

Nell walked in. Her eyes were angry, her full lips drawn tight. Her arms were folded. She paced the room. She refused a drink.

"You saw that spectacle," she said acidly. "That was mild, very mild, an exercise in sobriety, compared to the way he's been the last few days. Gil thinks it's because he's overworked, too tense over the China trip. I don't. I think he's unraveling. He was absolutely unmanageable with Osborne."

"I got a look at it when General Wells was in," he said. He was distracted. He had been appalled by Hamilton's belligerence, but he didn't want to discuss it. He wanted Nell to enfold him, transport him in soft moisture.

"Don't play the detached professional, Thack. Please. Not

85

with me. The thought of the man sickens me. He made a pass at me last night. It was disgusting. Trying to play lord of the manor, snapping his fingers and calling me Nelly. So drunk he could barely move. He went through that business of his unhappy childhood, too. No wonder his wife left him."

Forbes gestured to her to sit down. He wanted her warmth. He wanted to confide.

She shook her head and continued to pace.

"Goddamn it, sit down," he said angrily.

She stopped in the middle of the room and put her hands on her hips. She looked at him defiantly.

"Not you, too." She laughed; it was hollow. "Simplemindedness seems to be the order of the day here."

Forbes stood up and held out his arms. He tried to smile. His distress was apparent. "Please come close to me," he said. "I need to feel you near me. I'm sorry I shouted."

She smiled. She walked up to him and put her hands on his neck.

He held her waist. He looked into her wide, green eyes. He felt a wave of desire surge and wane. He lowered his head.

She lifted his chin with her finger. "Let's let all this go," she said. "I need you, too."

"Please sit down, Nell," Forbes said gently. "I have to tell you something. I don't want to, God knows, but I have to tell someone. I'll snap if I don't."

They sat down on the sofa. She took his hand. Forbes recounted what happened. Roundtree and the ride to the airport. Vest. Melville and the letter. The presence of Vest at Melville's estate. The seedy, violent man and the capsules. The threats. The kick under the table. It took nearly an hour. Nell did not take her eyes off him the entire time.

"I know it sounds incredible," he said finally, almost ruefully. He lit a cigarette; it seemed to require a great effort. "I wouldn't believe it, either, if I didn't have those capsules and a sore leg."

Nell squeezed his hand and stood up. She walked across to the table where the liquor was. She poured herself a drink and took Forbes's glass and refilled it.

She returned slowly and handed him the Bourbon. Forbes accepted it without looking up at her. She remained standing in front of him. She sensed that he was absorbed in his dilemma. To sit down next to him, to offer the warmth of her body at the moment, would not console him. She also saw that he needed rational reassurance that his despair was not insurmountable.

"What it comes down to, I suppose," she said quietly, "is whether all this adds up to . . ."

Forbes looked up at her dubiously. "Whether I seriously think he intends to defect?"

"Yes."

Forbes sipped his drink. His eyes were far away. "At the moment I don't seem to have any other choice," he said wearily. "I can't just turn my head and pretend the possibility doesn't exist. As illogical as it sounds, the possibility is *there*. The question is: how to eliminate the possibility. One way is talk, persuasion. What I need is time alone with him. Time to try and talk him out of it. The other way . . ." He closed his eyes and sighed. "If talking hasn't worked by the time we reach Anchorage, then . . ." His voice trailed off.

Nell resumed pacing. Suddenly she turned and said from across the room, "I'll help you. I'll help you talk to him, and if that doesn't work, then I'll help you—"

Forbes snapped to life. He shook his head violently. "No," he said; his voice was charged with anger and finality. "Can't you see I'm already trapped? Somehow I have to act. If anything goes wrong I don't want it to touch you. I don't want you involved, understand?"

She nodded. She also understood that, for the time being, Forbes had said all he wanted or cared to say. She walked over and took his hand. She tugged and he stood up. "I'm trapped, too, in a way," she said softly. "I love you."

They held each other firmly and kissed. The quality of hunger they most often experienced was tempered tonight by Forbes's desperation But it did not distract them from their pleasure. It only inflamed their urgency. Nell's abdomen rippled. She grew warm and the first rumbles of passion gave rhythm to her hips.

Forbes held her tightly, almost roughly. The tensions and fears of the day receded to a temporary resting place in his memory; he knew they would return, but in this moment out of time they did not exist. He stroked her buttocks under her light dress. She wasn't wearing panties. He slowly rose and hardened. He moved his hand in front beneath her dress and massaged her. She pressed against him until she shook.

Still embraced, they backed into the bedroom. Nell freed one arm and switched on the light—they always made love with the light on. Stepping apart, they rapidly shed their clothes. Nell paused at the edge of the bed as Forbes flung his trousers onto a chair. She frowned as she looked at his leg. It was yellow and purple below the knee.

"Does it hurt?" she asked.

"I don't know. Let's find out."

"Let's not. Lie down."

Some time later, perhaps an hour, Forbes stirred. He awoke without quite being aware of it. He tried not to gain full consciousness. He sensed movement in the room. He rolled over. He was alone in the bed. He raised his head.

"Nell?"

"Yes?" The low voice came from the closet.

"What are you looking for?"

"Cigarettes."

"They're in the study."

He sleepily watched her emerge from the closet. She picked up her dress. She fiddled with it briefly in the dark, as if she were adjusting a zipper or a fastener.

"Going?" he asked. He was propped on an elbow.

"Just straightening my dress. I don't want to draw too many looks in the morning."

She returned in a few moments from the study with a lit cigarette. Forbes fell back asleep. She lay next to him, their feet touching under the sheet, and smoked.

4 The Question

Coombes walked across the rear yard. The night was stuffy with moisture. It was dotted with the soft flicker of fireflies. The light from the back porch glistened on the dewy grass. The grass needed mowing. Coombes didn't notice it.

He lived in an unimaginative section of a Virginia suburb. His neighbors were career military people, sergeants mostly, with young children. The rear yards on either side of his were equipped with barbecue pits and sliding boards.

He had difficulty with the garage door. It was warped. He couldn't remember the last time it had been opened. It scraped and creaked. He managed to shove it ajar just enough to let himself in. He swore as he felt a splinter pierce his hand.

The letter Vest had given him loomed in his mind. There was *something* about it, something about the shape of it, as if the parallel lines had been arranged. He wished he had brought the letter with him. He wanted to look at it again. He didn't question its authenticity; he had taken that for granted. The only question left to answer was whether Hamilton would defect.

The idea of relying solely on this Forbes as his circuit breaker unsettled him. There hadn't been time for adequate development and conditioning of him as an agent, he told himself. Forbes was available and he had grabbed him.

He took a small flashlight from his shirt pocket. He beamed it on a stack of dusty cartons and some pieces of rusty lawn furniture. He spied the small trunk. It was behind a bicycle whose tires were flat. A faded lampshade sat on top of it.

Coombes rubbed the back of his neck. He felt his jaw. He noted with satisfaction that his beard was thickening. He shined the flashlight on his watch. His face muscles constricted. It was later than he had realized.

He hurriedly pulled the trunk free and undid the padlock. He lifted the lid. He withdrew a canvas weekend bag and unzipped it. It contained a palm-sized camera, some film, a wallet, and an oilcloth bundle. He loaded the camera and slipped it into his pocket. He thumbed through the contents of the wallet. There was a social security card, a driver's license, and several credit cards. They all bore the name Donald Perry and the address of a Baltimore hotel. He had gotten the name from an infant's headstone in a Delaware cemetery several years ago; the child had been born within months of Coombes's own birth and had died at the age of two; Coombes had sent away for a photostat of the dead child's birth certificate; the rest had been easy. It was one of a number of separate identities he maintained. The others were in his office safe.

He rummaged the trunk and found a leather shoulder holster. He tried it on. It was too tight. It had been years since he had worn it. He had brought it home from Burma. He adjusted the backstrap. It felt moldy. The buckle was rough with rust.

He untied the oilcloth bundle and carefully picked up the .38 caliber Colt Cobra revolver. It had a square stock and a snubbed barrel. It had belonged to a young direct-hire officer; he had been stitched across the chest by a P.V.O. machine gun near Wan Pangsung; Coombes had carried him on his back for miles; he had been dead when they reached the collection point.

More digging and he uncovered a dark metal tube. It was a silencer.

He stuffed the wallet in his pocket and put the pistol and holster, along with the silencer and a box of cartridges, in the weekend bag. He relocked the trunk and pushed it toward the corner with his foot. It upset the bicycle.

This is going to run into a hell of a lot of money, thought Coombes. He imagined the flap over an unauthorized expense account. He tried to calculate the air fare, what the car rentals would come to. He remembered he had forgotten to go to the bank. He would have to get some money from Vivian. Oh, Christ, that would mean a scene. He chewed at a fingernail.

The garage was stifling. His shirt was soaked. Perspiration trickled into his ears. He hurried out. He didn't bother to try and close the warped door.

He threw the weekend bag on a chair. He began fumbling through the bedroom's only closet. His wife watched him out of the corner of her eye.

She had been watching television. She was lying on the bed. Her thin legs were outstretched and crossed. She wore a peignoir over a cotton nightgown. Her hair was in rollers. She was smoking. A glass of Bourbon was on her night stand.

"That suitcase, that small one, is it in here?" His hulky frame was half in the closet. He was on tiptoe, pawing at a shelf. A shoe box became dislodged. It fell to the floor. Something in it broke.

His wife swung slowly off the bed and put on her slippers. She walked to the closet and knelt down. She picked up the shoe box and carried it back to the bed. She did not look at Coombes.

"It's in the living-room closet," she said finally. He left the room and returned presently with a valise. It was scarred and papered with fragments of customs labels. He set it on the floor and opened it.

Coombes felt his wife's eyes on him. They were full of questions. She would want to know where he was going, how long he would be gone. He heard her replace the glass of Bourbon on the night stand.

He went into the bathroom. He lathered his face and fashioned a goatee and mustache. It wasn't difficult with his heavy beard. It altered his appearance.

His wife was standing by one of the air-conditioning vents when he returned with his toothbrush and shaving things. The air in the room was stagnant.

"The man from the repair place was here," she said. Her arms were folded. She tugged at the throat of her peignoir. "He said something about rewinding the motor or something."

Coombes took some things from a drawer and put them in the valise. "They said that might be the problem. That's what they told me when I stopped by the place." He didn't mention the estimate they had given him.

He unzipped the weekend bag. He took out the revolver, silencer, holster, and cartridges and put them in the valise under some shirts.

Coombes stood up. "I need some money, Vivian." He hated saying it.

His wife crossed over to the bed. She sat down and lit a cigarette. She took a sip of whiskey. She stared at the ceiling.

"I'll be out of town for a few days, at least two. I should be back by Friday or Saturday." He wished she would simply open her purse and give it to him. He knew that was unlikely.

"I didn't have a chance to get to the bank," he added pathetically.

"This is—" He cut himself short. He knew he couldn't tell her. "I'm on a case, Vivian." He spoke rapidly; his tone was desperate. "It's breaking fast. There hasn't been any planning. I have to stay out in front of it until Special Ops or somebody works something out. How much cash do you have?"

His wife turned her head slowly and looked at him. "A case? How can you be on a case?"

He looked at her intensely. His throat tightened. A look of pain shot across his face. "It's an unconventional situation, a million-to-one kind of thing. The timing's bad; there's no time for a supportive analysis." He looked away. He bit at a fingernail. "I need as much money as I can get. I'll be taking the car, too. You'll have to get someone to drive you to work."

She walked to the dresser and opened her purse. She took out some bills and handed them to him. "This is all I have," she said.

He counted the money. He shook his head. He put it in his pocket. He slipped on his jacket and looked at himself in the mirror. He thought the goatee and mustache were adequate.

His wife looked at his reflection. "Are you on the run?" she asked; her voice was edged with apprehension.

He didn't answer. He was afraid to say anything else. He had already said more than he meant to. He fastened the valise and picked it up.

"*Are you on the run?*" his wife asked again. Her nostrils flared in anger. "I'm entitled to know, goddamn it." She folded her arms tightly across her bosom. "You leave here in the middle of the night with a gun and disguised like some sideshow magician and all I know is that it's an 'unconventional situation.' What kind of trouble are you in?"

He looked at her from the door. "I'll be in touch in a couple of days," he said and left.

The late-night traffic was meager. It became almost nonexistent as Coombes neared Dulles International Airport. He was distracted by the engine of his dilapidated car; it had developed a new rattle. He stopped at the entrance of the long-term parking lot and took a ticket from the machine. He parked some distance from the terminal.

The terminal lobby was nearly deserted. Men in work-clothes were busy with mops and buckets on casters. He checked his valise and got his ticket. It was under the name Donald Perry. He paid for it with one of the credit cards he had taken from the trunk. He looked around to see if he had been followed. He was sure he hadn't been.

He walked to the boarding gate. The woman at the security station looked sleepy. He noticed his bearded face in a window. He took a seat on the mobile boarding module. The ride from the terminal was brief. He showed his ticket to the stewardess. He took his seat in the second-class section. He looked out the window and stared at the wing light; it pulsed in the humid darkness.

It was the dead of night when the plane touched down at San Francisco International Airport. He had managed to sleep a little. The plane taxied to the terminal. A sensation of haste rushed through his heavy body. His mind began to anticipate, to think several moves ahead. He glanced at the few other passengers; none of them appeared unusual.

Coombes wheeled the rented car onto the Bayshore Freeway and headed north. The valise lay on the seat next to him. The car smelled new, clean. It responded without hesitation as he stepped on the gas pedal. The feeling enlivened him; it imbued him with confidence. He decided he hated his own car.

After several miles he pulled over at an emergency parking area. Candlestick Park stood in the distance. It was veiled in fog and glowed dully in the moonlight. He peered into the rearview mirror.

He opened the valise. He slipped on the shoulder holster

and squirmed back into his jacket. He loaded the Colt Cobra and shoved it into the holster. He patted it and frowned at the obvious bulge under his left arm. He dropped the silencer into his jacket pocket.

He leaned back in the seat. He bit at a fingernail. In a few hours, he reflected, he would have to bring his operation to the surface. He would have to make a call on an insecure public phone and dump his intelligence on Special Ops. He would catch hell, he was sure, for taking the "cowboy" approach.

The "cowboy" approach was the only one Coombes had a talent for. He had never been able to manage the contrivances and conventional precautions of intelligence work. He was too old for it now, anyway. Direct, simple, offensive operations were his forte. If you wanted a document, you hired someone to steal it or stole it yourself. If you wanted information, you paid for it on the spot in negotiable currency and let the seller beware. If you needed an agent to kill a president of the United States who was on the verge of defecting to the Communists, you recruited him and gave him his goddamn orders. He knew the risks. He knew his outlook and methods were officially discredited.

He put the car in gear and pulled back onto the freeway. His wife and his pension did not cross his mind.

The hills of San Francisco loomed on his left. In the bay the beacon atop the abandoned prison on Alcatraz Island beamed through banks of fog. Coombes turned off the freeway and parked on a side street a few blocks above Grant Avenue. He was in Chinatown.

The doorways and shop windows were obscured by a jumble of vertical signs done in Chinese ideographs. The streets looked deserted. Coombes guessed he had not attracted notice.

The night breeze was uncomfortably cool. Coombes had

not remembered that July was different in San Francisco. His rumpled summer suit was useless against the chill. He walked faster. He did it to induce warmth and to listen for footsteps behind him. He heard none.

The New Paradise Travel Agency was wedged between a community center and a shop that dealt in bronze dragon paperweights. Coombes gazed into the darkened showcase. He could make out posters advertising vacations in Hong Kong, Kuala Lumpur, Seoul, and Singapore. A decal in a corner of the window listed a number for nights and week-ends. Coombes made a note of it. He walked to a telephone booth of oriental motif; he exchanged a few words with a sleepy voice and hung up.

He crossed California Street and sat down on a bench in St. Mary's Park. The fog had floated up from the bay. It swathed the stainless-steel statue of Sun Yat-sen. It made the streetlights fuzzy. Coombes tugged his jacket collar about his neck.

The park was filled with flowers. The dark and fog muted their brightness. Coombes had heard that Chinatown was once a coarse red-light district. He found it hard to conceive that child prostitution, opium dens, and the other common evils of the Orient had thrived in this peaceful place where he sat shivering.

The common evils of the Orient. For nine unremitting years Coombes had survived in the Orient. He had known only one common evil. Death. After training as a marine paratrooper he had been shipped to Burma. He was an officer in an O.S.S. detachment of Burmese guerrillas; the Shan tribesmen wore turbans; many were heavily tattooed. They spent their time pursuing and being pursued by the Japanese. The preferred tactic was the close-range ambush. The favorite weapon was the heavy-bladed dah. *Attack only when the Jap is close enough to touch.* Months on end of running, crawling, hiding in dripping teak forests and the squishy Burma mud. He somehow avoided fever, but his teeth rotted. His enormous frame shrunk. His limbs took on the proportions of a coat hanger. He acquired the habit of biting his nails. The Burmese thought he was trying to eat his own flesh.

Coombes looked across the plaza. A bus was struggling up California Street. There was no other traffic. It was past the hour for the cable cars to be running. It occurred to him that he had never ridden a cable car.

When the war ended, Coombes was sent across the frontier into China. He was an adviser to one of Chiang Kai-shek's Nationalist divisions in Yunan province. The dry mountains of Yunan seemed an unbreachable fortress.

The Nationalist commanders and their troops appeared unworried that Mao Tse-tung's Communist peasants were overrunning the rest of the country. They spent most of the time extorting food and other comforts from the local population. They seemed to regard military training as an imposition.

Coombes tried to organize a counter-guerrilla section to combat partisan raids in the district. The local secret police opposed him strenuously. They threw Coombes in jail. The charge was vague. "Failure to observe the supremacy of the Nanking Military Directorate."

He was made to witness the torture of a local merchant. The merchant had refused to allow a Nationalist quartermaster to confiscate his inventory. The torture was supervised by Major Shen Keng Min. Major Shen was the district secret police commandant.

The instrument had been the *teo chen yi*—the iron shirt. A net of steel mesh wire fashioned like a shirt was pulled tightly about the helpless merchant's bare torso. Where his skin protruded through the spaces in the mesh, a corporal scraped a jagged shard of a rice bowl. The man's flesh peeled back in tiny flaps. His nipples were mutilated. The bones of his shoulders were exposed. Blood trickled down his body in dozens of rivulets. He screamed until he fainted.

Coombes thought he would faint himself. He forced himself to take deep breaths to keep from vomiting.

"You see, Captain Coombes, brief but efficient cruelty has its uses," said Major Shen. "This man henceforward will be a cooperative supporter of our fight against communism. He may not be enthusiastic, but he will be cooperative." Major Shen was a small, slender man with a perpetually downcast expression. He spoke faultless English. He wore thick glasses and blinked incessantly. He had been in the service of a neighboring warlord before joining the secret police. He kept fighting crickets as a hobby.

He offered Coombes a cigarette. Coombes declined and bit at a fingernail. Major Shen was amazed. He had heard all Americans smoked cigarettes. He lit one himself. He did not inhale; he sucked on it in short, inconclusive puffs.

"Your purpose in China is to support our fight, too, Captain Coombes, not to concoct unorthodox schemes that contradict the lessons of modern warfare." Major Shen blinked and puffed his cigarette.

"What's the proverb, Major?" Coombes was seated on a low stool. The morning sun slanted through the single high window of his cell. " 'It doesn't matter what color the cat is, as long as it catches mice.' That's it, isn't it? That's how the Reds are playing it. In Burma—"

"Your cooperation is inadequate," snapped Major Shen. "Perhaps a session in the iron shirt will improve it. I will interview you again in a few days. Then I will decide."

The interview never took place. The next day a delegation of Communist representatives appeared at the mountain garrison. They arrived in an old touring car under a flag of truce. They barely attracted attention. They said they had come to arrange the surrender of three regiments of their troops who were dispirited and starving at the foot of the pass. They asked that the commanding general and Major Shen accompany them to their bivouac to inspect their weary men and negotiate the surrender details. The division was hastily assembled on the small, dusty parade field. The general gave a short but stirring—and wildly imaginative—speech on Nationalist military superiority. Then he and Major Shen climbed into the touring car and drove off down the mountain road with the Communists.

The garrison went wild with celebration. The dry mountain air was filled with shouts of praise for Chiang Kai-shek. Drunken soldiers and officers embraced; they swore loudly that Communist capitulation had been inevitable. Bonfires were lit. Weapons were fired into the air. Firecrackers popped.

Coombes and the other prisoners were released. The merchant who had suffered in the iron shirt was too weak to move; relatives were summoned to carry him away. The young lieutenant who unlocked the cells was beaming with confidence. "To win a battle without firing a shot is the perfection of the soldier's art," he said as he undid Coombes's leg irons. Coombes was unmoved by the aphorism. The "victory" celebration repelled him. He walked stiffly to a tavern operated by a dog butcher. He ordered a pot of raucous kaoliang. He drank alone.

Sometime before midnight there was an explosion. It was assumed that someone had been careless with a firecracker near a fuel drum. A series of explosions followed. The Communists had launched a mortar barrage. The headquarters building burst into flame and collapsed. Barracks were splintered. Bodies were ripped apart. Screeches of agony pierced the night. The shelling lasted an hour.

Coombes dashed from the tavern. He had no chance to pay the dog butcher for the kaoliang. He was gasping violently when he reached the garrison gate. The sentry box was deserted. He zigzagged his way to the officers' compound. His two-room bungalow had taken a direct hit. He clawed through the debris. He dug out his M3 machine gun and threw a half-dozen clips of .45 caliber ammunition into a musette bag.

He found the division's second-in-command in a temporary headquarters at the rear of the hospital. Several staff officers studied a map spread on a wooden table. A lantern hung from a rafter cast spastic shadows. The second-in-command, whose bloody right arm was in a sling, announced that the best intelligence available in the chaos was that two Communist divisions, led by tanks, were attacking up the pass. Lacking other orders, he said, he was preparing a "tactical withdrawal" down the other side of the mountain. Coombes wondered if the second-in-command had considered that the line of retreat might be blocked. It seemed pointless to raise the question.

There was no line of retreat. Time, space, and will were the property of the Communists. They were deployed behind the rocks and cliffs that lined the narrow, serpentine road down the back of the mountain. With mortars and heavy machine guns they annihilated the ragged Nationalist exodus. The mortars bracketed the convoy. Truckload upon truckload of Nationalist troops were roasted alive. The smell of burning flesh along the road was overpowering.

Coombes managed to pull himself from the wreckage of the command car. Everyone else inside, including the second-in-command, was dead. The din of the attack was deafening. Coombes was momentarily stunned by the flashing spectacle of the intense machine-gun fire and the mortar bombardment. Then his impulse to live galvanized him. He sprinted to a ravine. He flipped the safety of his M3 on the run. He expected to find an emplacement of Communist gunners; the ravine seemed an ideal spot to conceal a mortar. Instead he found a knot of panic-stricken Nationalist soldiers huddled in the lee of an outcropping of boulders. He motioned for them to follow him. One of them leveled a pistol at him and shouted something. Coombes fired his M3 from his hip. Three rounds struck the man with the pistol in the chest and throat. The others got abjectly to their feet. They followed as Coombes led them from the ravine through a maze of gullies and away from the war.

More stragglers appeared as the days passed. Most of them were other fleeing Nationalist soldiers. A few were civilian refugees. Those who were lucky sheltered in caves. Mostly they lived in the open. They survived on what they could scrounge, which was usually not much more than the smell of a greasy rag. They eventually numbered more than ten thousand. Communist patrols often spotted them but seldom attacked.

It took them six weeks to reach the Burma frontier. Most were sick. Many were dying. All were starving. As they trudged beneath a dusty scarp in the Shan hills early one afternoon in 1949, Coombes, his heavy beard thick with grime, was astonished. Rounding a bend in the road ahead was a column of tanks and trucks with United States markings. Chinese officers and noncoms in Nationalist uniforms leapt from the vehicles. They fanned out through the stragglers' ranks. They barked orders. They assembled the bedraggled soldiers into units. They supervised the construction of kitchens and field hospitals.

A dozen or so Americans hung about the fringes. They did not wear insignias or badges of rank. Coombes recognized most of them. They were old O.S.S. operatives. They did not greet him; they merely acknowledged him. They did not speak much to each other.

Coombes was too weary to wonder why. His clothes were tattered. His stomach was cramped by hunger. He couldn't remember the last time he'd had a bath. He reported to the man who seemed to be in charge of the Americans. The man introduced himself only as "Headlight." Coombes remembered he had been a battalion commander.

". . . Then I suppose you've about had it out here," said Headlight; he spoke with a cultured drawl. He had just listened to Coombes give an abbreviated account of his escape from China. They were seated in a Jeep.

"No," said Coombes without emotion. He had chewed his fingernails to raw, filthy nubs. "I don't know what the mission is, but it isn't hard to guess. I need my teeth fixed. It's hard to chew dog meat with rotten teeth."

"There's a dentist in Calcutta," said Headlight. He was a tall man with an air of authority that transcended military rank; he commanded loyalty rather than obedience. "Take a couple of weeks off. Think it over. This is going to be a long haul. We think the Reds are going to make a move soon. India, Korea, maybe Formosa. We want to keep them busy in the south." He took a deep breath and looked closely at Coombes. "I don't need to tell you that all this"—he gestured to the scene of military activity around them—"is top secret. I mean *tip-top* secret. Not even the ambassador in Rangoon is in on it. In fact, he's denied the Nationalists are here. Of course, he doesn't know we're here, either."

Coombes spent a week in Calcutta. The dentist was British. He talked ceaselessly on the ineptitude of the wogs and what a catastrophe independence for India was proving to be. He did an admirable job on Coombes's teeth, considering the years of neglect. Coombes tried to unwind. He spent an unsatisfactory night in bed with the wife of a French consular official. He got drunk and kicked a beggar to death in Chitpore Road. No one seemed concerned. Coombes did not regret it.

The fog had entirely enveloped St. Mary's Park. It had grown heavy and cold. Clouds screened the moon. Coombes was sharply aware of the Colt Cobra under his left arm. He wondered impatiently how much longer he would have to wait.

When he returned to the Shan hills, he found a Nationalist division refitted with American equipment. The command structure was irregular. There was a Nationalist general, but orders and supplies came from an American trading company in Thailand. The trading company planned all the division's operations. Headlight seemed to be consulted on everything.

Late-night patrols were sent out to probe Communist positions across the frontier. The Americans led them. Coombes commanded a long-range penetration and sabotage unit. He welcomed the assignment; it meant killing at arm's length again. When he formed the unit, he had interviewed the volunteers individually in pidgin Cantonese.

One of them had answered in faultless English. He was a small man with thick glasses who blinked incessantly. Coombes paused. He dismissed the others and invited the man who spoke English so well into his hut. As they cleared the screen door, Coombes slammed him between the shoulder blades with his heavy forearm. The man was hurled across the room. The few sticks of furniture were scattered. Before the man could recover, Coombes crashed his knee at an angle into the man's face, shattering his nose and cracking the bones around one eye. His thick glasses were crushed. He ended up sitting with his back against a wall. He was still conscious.

"I was mistaken to think you might have forgotten me, Captain Coombes," said Shen Keng Min. "I did not realize my memory was so unpleasant for you." He spat blood on the floor.

Coombes clenched his teeth. His hooded eyes were lustrous. He pressed one huge fist against his other palm. He was only a few feet away from Shen. He gave the impression he was about to attack again. Shen Keng Min drew his arms about himself and doubled his knees; he pressed his chin into his chest. Finally Coombes snarled, "Okay, you sawed-off, slant-eyed bastard, what are you doing here?"

Shen Keng Min lifted his head tentatively. "There seems to be a misunderstanding. My practices as a security officer were distasteful, I know, to many Westerners." He wiped more blood from his face and gingerly touched his nose. "It was my duty to—"

He was cut short as Coombes flung a camp chair in his direction. He again drew himself into a ball. The chair splintered harmlessly against the wall of the hut.

"Goddamn it!" Coombes roared. His shoulders were arched; his heavy arms swung at his sides; he looked like a bull straining at a tether. "Who are you working for, Shen? How the hell did you stay alive after you got down off that mountain? We both know a Nationalist secret police officer would be an automatic dead man if the Reds got their hands on him. They got their hands on you. How is it that you're alive? And here?"

Shen felt his battered face again. "Did you know that I am a Taoist at heart? Of course you didn't. How could you have?" He said it simply. He was blinking less because of the condition of his eye. "For years I thought the Nationalists were the forces of good. It was actually a matter of politics and circumstance. However, I did not regard the Communists as evil. In principle, that is." He spat more blood on the floor. "When the general and I arrived at the foot of the mountain, we immediately saw our predicament. We were prisoners. We both resorted to tradition. The general offered to diagram the garrison's defenses. . . . He now commands a Communist division, somewhere in the north, I believe. I offered to divulge all the information I had gathered as a security officer. My sincerity was accepted, but my capacity to tell everything I knew was doubted deeply. My own methods were applied to me, and some I had never thought of. They were quite effective. May I show you my back?" He shifted and began to unbutton his tunic.

"Save it," Coombes said savagely.

"My interrogation had reached the stage where the officer in charge, a Comrade Mee—who, by the way, shares my passion for fighting crickets—had ordered the removal of my testicles," Shen went on. "I had told them everything I knew. Then it dawned on me. What they wanted were my services. But it was up to me to realize it. It was a timely realization." He smiled faintly. "I recalled at the same moment a proverb that goes something like this: 'He who knows that enough is enough will always have enough.' It did not fit the Taoist context, but it fit my situation."

"Have you had enough?" asked Coombes, who knew nothing of Taoism. He showed a clenched fist.

"Quite," replied Shen Keng Min.

"Do you want to live?"

"Yes, very much."

"Let's have a talk with Headlight."

Thus Shen Keng Min joined the blurred, unanchored world of the double agent. He accepted two masters but served only himself. Both sides viewed him as "our spy who comes to spy on us" and used him accordingly. As the Nationalist division prepared for its invasion of China, Shen supplied the intelligence on Communist fortifications—and passed the word north that the invasion was coming. The invasion failed, and Shen vanished.

The beaten Nationalists gave up being an army. They marauded the Burmese countryside and smuggled opium into Thailand. The Rangoon government launched a campaign to dislodge them, fearful that the presence of so many Nationalists in the Shan hills might provoke a Chinese invasion. More

Americans arrived. They tried to pull the division back together. They found that the principal enemy now was the Burmese army. There were occasional skirmishes with some local Communists called the People's Volunteer Organization.

Coombes stayed on for a while. He did not get along with the new Americans. Most of them were on short-term contracts, and they were young. They liked to shoot a lot, which Coombes looked on as a waste of time in Burma. He moved on to Laos for a few months and took command of a force of Meo tribesmen. He was unable to inspire or threaten them to take the field against the Pathet Lao, and, after what seemed a century, he was sent home.

He was woebegone in Washington. He had no feel for civilian clothes. He had forgotten how to eat at a table or drink from a glass. He was assigned to a department in the old building on E Street. There seemed to be no actual tasks to perform, just paper games invented by compulsive men. The ceremonial intricacies of bureaucratic warfare eluded him. He was put on the team that led the revolt against Mossadegh in Iran. It was a violent operation, but it wasn't Coombes's style of violence; he couldn't organize a riot. He tried to circumvent the team leader and precipitate a direct action by the Iranian army. The team leader ordered him back to Washington. He was slated for dismissal when Headlight intervened. Headlight had adapted to the new way of doing things—he was a section chief—but he protected his old Burma associates. Coombes spent three years on one of the nonoperational staffs. He married a childless widow who frequented the same coffee shop. It became clear he hadn't the temperament to be a case officer or the self-conceit to indulge in "hypothetical intelligence." He was transferred to the Basement.

The fog in the park had turned to a fine mist. A small, stork-like figure in a raincoat minced its way across the plaza. As he drew nearer, Coombes discerned a diminutive Chinese blinking behind thick, horn-rimmed glasses. His nose was crooked. One of his eyes was disfigured. Coombes didn't bother to get up or to extend his hand.

"Can this actually be you?" said Shen Keng Min. His English was as flawless as ever. He wore the same downcast look.

"Sit down. I don't have much time," said Coombes. He could see his breath. He bit at a fingernail.

Shen sat at the other end of the bench. He had taken the precaution of wearing a turtleneck sweater. His hands were thrust in his raincoat pockets.

When he disappeared from Burma, Shen Keng Min had fled to Bangkok, where he moved in with a cousin in Nana Road. He turned up later in Singapore and Hong Kong. He finally emigrated to America and settled in San Francisco. He opened a travel agency. In the interest of providing the best accommodations for his clients he traveled widely in the Far East. His business as a travel agent gave him an excellent cover for his work as a spy.

Strictly speaking, Shen was no longer a double agent. Both sides, years back, had abandoned the practice of letting men with no loyalties know their secrets. The Chinese had cut back on what they told him when they found that the Americans had pinpointed the locations of their missile sites in Sinkiang Province; for years the multitude of dummy sites in the Lop Nor basin had befuddled American reconnaissance satellites. The Americans had acutely limited their trust in him when the Chinese suddenly rounded up all but two of the U.S. agents who were keeping tabs on the Sino-Soviet border war. For some time he had functioned mainly as a courier. The pay wasn't what it used to be, but Shen didn't mind. His New Paradise Travel Agency had made him affluent. It had enabled him to move out of Chinatown and into a restored Victorian mansion north of Golden Gate Park. He was still devoted to cricket fighting. He imported his insects illegally from Hong Kong. They won most of the fall tournaments. He fed them a special chestnut meal.

Shen continued to blink as he scrutinized the man who had shattered his features. "Perhaps we should find a more hospitable spot. You do not seem to be suitably dressed for sitting outdoors at this hour," he said; his tone was amiable. He had not aged nearly as much as Coombes since Burma. "Nor does your outfit hide the fact that you are carrying what can only be a pistol. I can recommend a tailor—"

Coombes started from the bench. Shen's fawning cuteness enraged him. He stopped short when Shen Keng Min swiftly withdrew one hand from his raincoat pocket. He was holding a Walther PPK 9 mm automatic. It was aimed at Coombes's chest.

Shen had decided before he stepped out into the damp night that Coombes probably had not changed.

Coombes slumped back to his seat on the bench.

"Please explain what you want, Coombes," said Shen evenly. His voice was assertive. The mist made the barrel of his pistol glisten. "I'm not accustomed to leaving a warm bed to sit on a park bench in the middle of the night. Are you?" He folded a flap of his raincoat over the automatic but kept it pointed at Coombes. "Your facial hair. It becomes you. It looks new. Is it?"

Coombes self-consciously touched his budding goatee and mustache; the hair was wet. He drew a deep breath. He was no longer bothered by the night chill. Finally he said, "I need to fill in a blank."

"A blank? There are many blanks. Please be more specific."

"There's a hole in some information."

"A hole? Is it a large hole?"

"Large enough. All I want you to do is to get a reaction for me. I think that if you put the word out to the other side that

I came to you and said I want a reaction, a yes-or-no answer, I'll get what I need."

"I need a question, Coombes."

"I can't give you one."

"I would say, Coombes, that you will have a hard time getting even a yes-or-no answer from the other side without first posing a question."

Coombes sat silent. He studied his shriveled cuticles and fingernails.

Shen Keng Min adjusted his glasses with his free hand. He flicked drops of mist from the corners of the lenses with his little finger. "This is most unlike you," he said. "I miss your directness. Having a gun aimed at you is inhibiting, I know. It must be, however. For my peace of mind. Do you understand?"

Coombes grunted. He realized he was actually beginning to sweat.

"You know, of course," Shen continued, "my whisper is not as loud as it used to be. I no longer command immediate attention. A soft word from me pricks few ears nowadays. I must shout to be heard. And what I shout must be worth listening to. I am an actor, so to speak. While we are together, you must be a playwright. You must give me the lines that will please and interest our audience. Do you have a good play?"

This was too clever for Coombes. He sunk his teeth fiercely into the shredded skin of his thumb.

"Like this," Shen Keng Min prompted. "Two old ginseng-root dealers meet on a mountainside after many years. One comes from far away. He says, 'I have a riddle I cannot solve. . . .' Something like that. Go ahead."

Coombes exhaled a long breath. He knew he would have to give it a try. He had no other choice. "It's about this guy," he began slowly. He hoped—but had little faith—that he would

110

get the hang of it; he had never been good at this kind of talk. "This guy who was . . . who was—who *might* be thinking of getting another job. That's it. The guy owned a noodle factory, and a guy who worked for him bought him out in a proxy fight, and the guy who lost the noodle factory *might* be thinking of going to work for another noodle factory."

He sat erect and folded his arms. He looked like a schoolboy who had completed a difficult recitation.

Shen Keng Min unobtrusively slipped his pistol back into his raincoat pocket. He rubbed his chin. His blink speeded up. "That *is* an interesting play, Coombes. *Very* interesting. You are correct in saying it has a hole in it."

Coombes blurted abruptly, "Do you understand what the hell I'm trying to say? I need to know whether—"

Shen raised his hand and interrupted. His voice was edged with authority. "Let us pay attention to the drama. It's the only way, Coombes. I believe you mentioned another noodle factory. Is this a serious competitor?"

Coombes paused a moment and then continued, almost casually, "You know how it is." He was slipping into it. "The competition used to be cutthroat. Nobody could figure out what the price should be. It's not so bad now. Big demand for noodles, plenty of room for everybody. But"—he began to hurry his delivery—"if this guy was to go to work for the other noodle factory, Christ, I don't know. . . ." He looked at the ground and shook his head.

Shen Keng Min leaned forward. His expression remained downcast, but he clearly enjoyed the discomfort the word game was causing Coombes. The mist had become very cold. "Why would our audience believe that a man would join a competitor simply because he had lost his own noodle factory? Strange things happen in the noodle business, but this stretches credibility."

"For God's sake," Coombes snapped, "he's gotten an offer."

111

"An *offer?* Do you mean to say he's received an *offer?* How do you know this?"

Coombes felt helpless. Once again he had said more than he should have. He was confused. He tried to regain his composure. He thought of the letter Vest had given him; he remembered how it seemed to have changed shape. "There's a pretty solid indicator that the other noodle factory, the competitor, has said something to him. It sure as hell sounds like an offer."

"This indicator. How did you learn of it?" Shen persisted.

"Indirectly. First- and secondhand," said Coombes.

"Then it is not known at this point in the drama whether the other noodle factory has in fact made a serious proposal to . . . our main character?"

"That's what I need from you," Coombes said desperately. "More important, if there is an offer, I need to know if it's been accepted."

Shen Keng Min gathered his raincoat collar about his neck. "I take it that you would like to know this before our main character visits the other noodle factory?"

Coombes nodded.

"That may not be possible. As I said, the noodle business is strange." Shen paused and stared across the park. The old Kong Chow temple was illuminated momentarily by a flash of lightning. Lightning was virtually unheard of in San Francisco at this time of year. It would probably rain soon. As the thunderclap died he continued, "You know, Coombes, in many ways I am a better judge of crickets than I am of men. The chirp of a champion cricket is unmistakable; it is clear and metallic. I favor small ones with long necks and wings with fruit-blossom patterns on them. They are fearless. Men have lost much money to me because of their confidence in large crickets such as purple-necks. That's taking nothing away from purple-necks. They are superb fighters. But when they are pitted against the blossom-wings, they seem to forget about cracking the smaller cricket's neck. Perhaps they look upon it as a mismatch and refuse to snap their mandibles with full viciousness. No amount of prodding with the mouse bristle can spark their anger. Blossom-wings, on the other hand, need no prodding. A blossom-wing harries and bites furiously until the larger cricket is disabled. Eyes pulpy, antennae broken, thorax shattered. Then the blossom-wing attacks head on. It amounts to little more than a *coup de grâce*, usually. Still, men are eager to back the purple-necks, and I am eager to set my blossom-wings on the sandboard with them."

The thunder and lightning grew more frequent. Coombes was biting his fingernails rapidly. "Why not let two blossom-wings go at it?" he asked. He did not sound as though he was interested in an answer.

Shen turned slowly and faced Coombes. He looked at him without blinking for a few moments and then said, "I have only seen your main character on television and in the newspapers. He does not have what I consider a pleasant face, but it tells much about the man who wears it."

"What the hell are you talking about?" Coombes said impatiently. It occurred to him that he had never seen President Hamilton in person, either.

"I have some ability as a physiognomist," Shen Keng Min continued imperviously. "The art of reading faces. A man's face is the reflection of his soul. Eyes, chin, ears, nose, complexion, they are a public record of a man's character. The face of your main character, it is like a cadaver, strong but without direction. I tell you, Coombes, I do not think it is the face of a man who would take a job at another noodle factory. Not even if he got an offer. That face has no imagination."

"Knock off this goddamn hocus-pocus," Coombes put in sharply. "Time's running out, for Christ's sake. I need facts, not some crap from a Chinese guessing game."

Shen Keng Min shrugged. "As I said, I am a better judge of crickets than men."

"This is priority interest, Shen," Coombes went on hurriedly. "I need an *answer*. I'll call you at noon today, understand? I want a simple yes or no. Is he or isn't he?"

"*Noon?*" His tone left no doubt that Coombes was demanding something that bordered on magic.

The mist had turned to a light rain. Lightning fired the sky.

"Jesus, man, we have less than three days," said Coombes. He stood up.

Shen Keng Min stiffened. It was obvious he was holding his pistol on Coombes through his raincoat pocket. He remained seated as Coombes left the park.

Coombes crossed Stockton Street and walked past Victory Hall. A strong wind whipped the light rain. It stung Coombes's face. He shivered from the chill. He quickened his pace. His suit was a mess already. It will really look like hell, he thought, if it gets soaked.

He turned in the rented car at the airport. The girl at the counter wore a nameplate identifying her as Cee Cee. Her hair was short and frizzed. She was casual and friendly as she handed him his receipt. "Thank you very much, Mr. Perry," she said, smiling. Coombes mumbled a reply. He checked his bag for the next flight to Los Angeles. He had taken the time on the freeway to return the Colt Cobra and silencer to the valise.

The telephone booth was designed for handicapped persons; it was spacious enough to accommodate a wheel chair. Coombes dug several scraps of paper from his pocket. On one was a telephone credit card number he had overheard once in Washington. He dialed and gave the credit card number to the operator. After several rings a drowsy male voice came on the line.

"This is a friend of Gustave's," said Coombes.

"Who?" replied the voice; there were sounds of yawning and smacking.

"A friend of Gustave's."

Silence.

"Hello? This is a friend of Gustave's."

"Hold on. . . . I'm taking this in the kitchen, hon. Hang the phone up for me."

More silence. Then "Yeah?" and a click.

"This is a friend of Gustave's."

"I got that. What's up?"

"I'm landing at Van Nuys Airport at six-thirty. Is the drop still operative?"

"Yes."

"I need a comprehensive personal-security floor plan and up-to-the-minute surveillance. Jacques Novic, Pacific Palisades. And a one-hour surveillance stand-down. Can you make the diversion? This is priority interest. Premium rate."

"Premium rate?" The voice sounded dubious. There had always been several weeks' notice for "premium rate" jobs. This was only a couple of hours.

"You heard me. And a car. Can you swing it?"

"Okay. Van Nuys Airport. Six-thirty." Click.

Coombes replaced the receiver. He had some time until his flight. He bought a cup of coffee in a cafeteria and took a seat at a table. The place was empty of customers except Coombes. He poured huge amounts of sugar and non-dairy creamer into his coffee. A few drops spattered on the table.

Shen Keng Min's face kept popping into his mind. The image jumped from Burma to St. Mary's Park. Burma was more frequent. He remembered with a shudder that he had neglected to tell Shen to camouflage the message to Peking. He didn't know who else owned a piece of Shen, who watched him; the last thing he wanted was a third party in on this. Then he remembered the noodle-factory business. He

115

relaxed a fraction. He decided Shen would be appropriately vague.

"Not much longer till your flight, Mr. Perry." A woman's voice startled him. "Mind if I have a seat?" It was Cee Cee, the girl from the car-rental counter. She had a container of coffee. "Mind if I have a seat?"

Coombes was tense. It was partly because he was unaccustomed to the alias and had forgotten the cover story that went with it. It was also due to the fact that it had been years since a strange woman had spoken to him. He looked at her noncommittally. She sat down opposite him.

"Get caught in the rain?" asked Cee Cee. She was smiling. She stirred her coffee carefully.

Coombes nodded. He tried to remember whether he had seen her before tonight.

"The radio said it's going to rain all day," she went on. "It's something, isn't it, rain this time of year? Bet you're glad to be going to L.A., aren't you. Get back here very often?"

Coombes was unsure how to respond. The girl had remembered his credit card and gossiped at the airline ticket counter. That was easy. But why? He could not conceive that someone would acquire personal information just to make conversation.

"What do you want?" His eyes were hooded. There was a note of menace in his voice.

"I just thought . . . I'm sorry." The girl made a move to leave.

"Who are you?"

"You looked like you might want some company. I mean, it's so late and there's nobody else. . . ." She looked as if she might cry.

Coombes got abruptly to his feet. He walked from the cafeteria. It did not cross his mind that the girl might have found

116

him attractive or merely wanted to talk to someone. He did not look back at her.

Most of the passengers in the boarding lounge were well groomed. They still looked sleepy. Business types flying to Los Angeles for the day. Coombes gazed out a window into the drizzly predawn darkness. The wind had subsided. He was filled with self-disgust. He had drawn attention to himself. There was no way in hell that girl would forget him now. He focused on his reflection in the window. Thank God he had thought of the goatee and mustache.

A small light shone at the rear of the New Paradise Travel Agency; it came from a gooseneck lamp on the desk next to the telephone; the rest of the room was dark. Shen Keng Min sat in a chair against the wall, away from the dull glow. He blinked at the telephone. It would be early evening in Macao. He hoped Po Lung was having a streak of bad luck. Otherwise, it would be difficult to coax him away from the *da-show* mat for an overseas call.

The telephone rang. Shen picked it up swiftly. The operator said his call to Macao was ready.

Shen Keng Min and Po Lung exchanged inquiries about the other's health, family, and fortune. Shen said his luck had been exceptional lately and asked how fate had been treating Po Lung.

"Badly," said Po Lung. "I've been barred from the Central Hotel casino again. They say it is final this time." Po Lung had been detained several times for switching dice at *da-show*.

"Ah, well," said Shen Keng Min, "the Central Hotel attracts unadventurous tourists who gamble only for curiosity's sake."

"Exactly," said Po Lung, "and they are not unduly troubled by their losses—which have been small but steady." He

117

paused and then, almost as an afterthought, asked, "Can I be of service?"

"It's about crickets."

"Crickets. Yes. I anticipate a rewarding season."

"It should be most profitable," said Shen Keng Min, "particularly if there is anything to the rumor that an unusual cricket, an American species, in fact, will compete."

"An American cricket? I don't believe an American crick—"

"I know. It is a new rumor. I don't know what to make of it myself. I hear it will make its debut outside America."

"In Macao?" asked Po Lung eagerly.

"No. Beyond the Portas do Cêrco. And soon. Within a day or two, perhaps."

"That's impossible. There can be no crickets to fight until the autumn."

"It seems doubtful, I know. However, much interest has been shown in the rumor. Ask our colleague in the north. He will have more details."

The words "our colleague in the north" settled Po Lung's mind. This was another of Shen Keng Min's secret messages. Po Lung recalled that he had been poorly paid for the last one.

"I see," he said. "There will be expenses."

"A draft for five hundred dollars American will be waiting for you at precisely seven A.M. at the perfume counter in the Miramar Hotel. You will enjoy the ferry trip to Hong Kong, I am sure. If you have been able to tell me whether the match will take place, the money will be handed over to you."

"Is this some kind of secret agricultural experiment?" asked Po Lung.

"No," replied Shen Keng Min. "Just a rumor about a new kind of cricket."

DAY TWO

5 The Implication

The heat was blistering in south Georgia, although it was less than three hours since sunrise. It held the presidential vacation compound in near photographic stillness. The scene was broken here and there by the movement of Secret Service agents · murmuring into their walkie-talkies. Staff members moved torpidly from one bungalow to another. A handful of reporters and television cameramen had arrived. Everyone was in short sleeves.

Forbes walked across the compound toward Wabash House. He had lain in bed for several minutes after the wake-up call. Nell hadn't been there. He wished she hadn't left before he awoke. He had wanted to talk to her, to be reassured before he faced the day. He had recalled vaguely that she had been up during the night.

His leg throbbed with a cloggy ache below the knee, but the pain was not enough to make him hobble. The image of the disheveled man who had kicked him flashed in his mind. It was replaced shutter-like by the thought of the amber capsules. His intuition told him that his days of solving his problems on three-by-five index cards might very well be coming to an end. The threads of history were enmeshing him. He would have to act, and soon, but he wanted to be as damned certain as possible that *he* would survive the consequences. He wondered if he should ask a doctor to look at his leg. He decided he would have a clearer view of the choices he had to make once he was out of the hot glare of the morning.

"Hey, Thack, got a second?" It was a wire-service reporter. He shouted as Forbes was nearing the side entrance of Wabash.

"What's new, Ron? It's been a long time." Forbes was habitually cordial to people in the media. "I suppose you wish you were in Pittsburgh?"

"That's what I need to talk to you about," said the reporter. Forbes guessed he was looking for something to freshen up a story that had been on the wires for several hours.

"I'd love to, Ron," he said—he looked conspicuously at his watch—"but I'm due inside right now."

"This will only take a minute," the reporter persevered.

"Okay, shoot, but make it quick."

"Has the president discussed the possibility with you that this trip to China might profoundly affect Vice-President Melville's chances of getting the nomination?"

Forbes tried to assume his blandest no-comment smile. It was a much-asked question, but this morning it unsettled him. "No, he hasn't, Ron. I can only tell you what the president himself has said many times before—that the contest for the nomination is the concern of the men seeking it. His only concern is the affairs of the presidency."

"But won't the effect of—"

"Sorry, Ron, I'm late. Wish I could be more helpful. You're signed on for the trip, aren't you?"

"Sure, but—"

"Let's have a drink before we leave. Good to see you

again," he said. A marine sergeant opened the door. He walked into Wabash House.

He was greeted by a short-sleeved young aide with a clipboard. The aide scanned his list. He said a place for breakfast was set for him in the North Dining Room. In the Southern White House the North Dining Room was reserved for Hamilton's inner circle.

"Gil Snyder will be a few minutes late," said the aide.

"He had a long night," said Forbes.

A credenza stood inside the dining-room door. Stacks of morning papers were arranged across the top. Forbes selected a *New York Times*, a *Washington Post*, and a *Wall Street Journal*. He ignored the daily news summary mimeographed for the president by the White House communications office. He knew from experience that it was tailored to gratify Hamilton; it lacked disagreeable but relevant particulars.

The table was covered with a beige cloth and set for two. It was next to a window that looked onto an expanse of pine forest. The presidential seal ornamented the china and silverware. Forbes gave a white-jacketed steward his breakfast order. The steward, an army corporal, reappeared with military brusqueness and poured coffee from a Pyrex carafe. Forbes ripped an envelope of sugar substitute and shook it into the cup. He stirred the coffee as he slowly turned the pages.

He started with the *Times*. The obituary of Justice Roundtree was on page 1. He noted with professional satisfaction that Roundtree's endorsement of Eric Caswell was mentioned. He supposed Alison had called the fact to the attention of the *Times*'s obit desk. He would congratulate her when he called. There was no mention of who would represent Hamilton at the funeral.

Moments later, Snyder sat down and motioned to the steward for coffee; the presidential chief of staff said he was skipping breakfast. His manner was lively; he was brimming with self-control. He was the same age as Forbes but larger and fleshier; his hair and eyebrows were ginger. He carried a loose-leaf leather folder, and he got straight to business.

"I've just seen him on the Roundtree thing," he said; he was seated across from Forbes; "and he's all but decided on Chief Justice Quinn. I'm pretty sure that's who he'll go for. Thank God *that* was no hassle. The problem now is Larry Melville. The Man will jump through his asshole if that bastard goes to the funeral. I don't see how he can manage it in light of the convention, but you never know. What do you think? Will he?"

"I have no idea," said Forbes. He folded his newspapers and set them on the floor next to his chair. He lit a cigarette. He had smoked a half dozen since he got up.

"You must have spent quite a while with him yesterday," Snyder said warily.

"Roundtree was still alive at the time." Forbes studied the ash on his cigarette. "By the way, I need some time with him, preferably this morning. When can you factor me in?"

Snyder drew a long breath. "Look, Thack. This thing with Melville. It's bound to raise a lot of dust. I can't block any time for you with the Man until you give me an outline—"

"Why the hell not?" Forbes broke in sharply.

"Anything remotely to do with Melville turns out to be a pain in the ass," Snyder replied; his ginger eyebrows were furrowed. "*My* ass, sooner or later. I've got too many identifiable problems without letting myself in for a surprise. A loaded, unknown surprise."

Forbes leaned forward. He stubbed his cigarette. His eyes pleaded. "You've got to get me some time with him. An hour—forty-five minutes, at least. Please, Gil. I'd background you if I could, but it's out of the question. Please trust me. A half hour. I'll take a half hour, for Christ's sake."

"Not a chance," said Snyder; there was a note of finality in his voice. "You know what this is, don't you?" He tapped the leather folder. "This is today's 'must inventory.' The Second Coming would need a month's notice to buy time on it. You're asking me to break discipline, to jeopardize a 'must inventory' to give you time to discuss God knows what with him. You, of all people, should know that isn't how it works."

The steward set a plate of poached eggs and bacon in front of Forbes. He wasn't especially hungry, but he hadn't eaten in nearly twenty-four hours. "He told me last night he has an idea he wants to kick around with me," he said casually between bites. "Why not this morning?"

Snyder looked at him coldly. "Don't pull that crap on me." He studied a spoon engraved with the presidential seal. A trace of smugness distorted his stern expression. "Besides, he said nothing to me about it."

"Goddamn it, Gil," said Forbes; his face was taut. The pine trees beyond the window shimmered in the heat. "I wouldn't ask for this if I didn't think it mattered. You know that. It's bad performance management, I know, to bypass the chief of staff, but this is a special case."

"Bad performance management!" Snyder heard his voice rise; he immediately lowered it. "It's rotten, incompetent performance management. You come to me with some off-the-wall story about a special case and expect me to open the door, no questions asked. A special case involving Melville, for God's sake. You saw what happened last night when Melville's name came up. Today's inventory will take at least sixteen hours. I can't afford for him to get sidetracked."

"He was drunk last night," Forbes shot back desperately. He was sorry the moment the words left his lips.

Snyder glared at him. Forbes felt his own despair and Snyder's stony accusation of disloyalty. Whether the president had been drunk was beside the point; to say he had been was to speak the language of disloyalty. Snyder tolerated many things; disloyalty was not one of them.

"That was a lapse, Gil. I'm sorry," said Forbes quietly. He put down his fork and lit a cigarette. A steward cleared the table. "This is big, that's what I'm trying to get across."

Snyder's glare softened. He was not the kind of man to overlook Forbes's past labors in Hamilton's behalf. He saw that Forbes was disconcerted, not disloyal. "Check the prelim strike list after eleven," he said. "There may be some open time. I'm not *guaranteeing* anything. Depends on the prep with Osborne and General Wells. They see him at noon. I'll be with them until then. I have a lot of stroking to do. He sandpapered them yesterday. Osborne and Wells both."

Secretary of State Osborne and General Wells, surrounded by their subordinates, were in the corridor at the foot of the stairs when Forbes and Snyder emerged from the dining room. Osborne looked self-assured, even belligerent. The general wore an expression of suspicious apprehension. Neither appeared to have slept much. Snyder greeted them and gestured for them to follow him. They were halted by a commotion on the staircase. They inclined their heads upward, as if on cue. The president and his entourage were coming down. A Secret Service agent led the way.

Hamilton wore a large, floppy hat; fishing lures were attached to the band. The desolation was gone from his narrow face; his eyes seemed to glow in their deep sockets; his rawboned body moved with an angular jauntiness; the rejuvenation from the bout with the mao-tai was the work of Dr. Brabham, his personal physician, who was at his side. The aged Tung Yen Fun struggled a step behind, leaning on the banister for support. An army major carried the black attaché

124

case of nuclear codes. He and another Secret Service agent brought up the rear.

The president surveyed his audience from halfway up the staircase. He smiled slyly. He pronounced a series of brief orders. Each functionary assented as he heard his name. "Gil, first of all, it's Quinn for the Roundtree thing. I've already called him. Tell Al to put out the statement. 'The president is profoundly saddened' . . . and so on . . . 'but he is engaged in intensive preparations for his visit to China.' That kind of thing. On the diplomatic and military stuff. I want a good mesh. I want it when we sit down. Around noon, isn't it?"

"Yes, sir," Snyder replied crisply.

"No coordinated staff presentation. We'll do that later. But a goddamn good mesh." Hamilton stroked his cheek; small patches of whiskers sprouted here and there; he insisted on shaving himself and often did a haphazard job.

"Osborne"—his Indiana twang rose an octave—"restructure the internal agenda discussions, understand? I'm not buying that shit you came in with yesterday. How the hell can I bargain with them if all I have to go on is a piece of paper slapped together by you and your college boys? You work it out with Gil, but, by God, I'm to be consulted on every point on that agenda. Got that?"

"Yes, Mr. President." His nostrils were distended and his lips were stretched thin in suppressed outrage.

Hamilton pushed back his floppy hat and slouched on the railing. "General, I don't have to say any more about strategic alternatives, do I?"

"No sir, Mr. President." General Wells was standing at near attention.

"Good. I didn't think I would." He descended another step and stopped. "One other thing. Gil, the tax people are on the home mortgage thing. Nell Leatherbee's handling it. Make sure Congressman What's-his-name, the banking guy, gets a call. I want to see that this afternoon, too."

Snyder unobtrusively passed his "must inventory" to an aide; it would require extensive revisions.

The president and his entourage continued down the stairs. The crowd in the corridor began to disperse. Abruptly Hamilton paused again and called out, "Where's Thack Forbes? I'm going fishing and I want Thack Forbes to go with me."

"Over here, Mr. President," said Forbes, raising his hand. He was leaning against a wall.

Snyder spun around and caught Forbes's glance. He shot him a hard look that said, "Don't cross me, buddy, or I'll put your ass in a sling."

"They're biting today, I can feel it," said Hamilton, fairly bounding from the staircase. He put an arm on Forbes's shoulder.

The presidential fishing party swept unceremoniously out of Wabash House and started for the lake. They resembled a flock of confused geese. The sky was faded blue and cloudless. The sunlight was bludgeoning. The Secret Service detail formed a protective wedge. Photographers and television cameramen scrambled for shots. Reporters elbowed each other and shouted questions. Hamilton waved and smiled and said it looked like a great day for fishing.

The lake was glassily smooth. There was no hint of a breeze. The Secret Service and the press secretary kept the media people at a distance.

Hamilton, Forbes, and Tung Yen Fun made their way onto a narrow pier. They were trailed by the major with the black attaché case and the Secret Service detail. Several flat-bottom boats with low-horse-power outboard engines were moored on either side. A speedboat for emergencies was tied up down the shoreline. The security men lowered themselves into the boats. A helicopter circled overhead.

Tung disappeared into a shack at the end of the pier where the tackle and other aquatic paraphernalia were stored.

Hamilton was not an instinctive outdoorsman, but he believed the president should exhibit an enthusiasm for physical activity. He chose fishing because he had found he was embarrassingly clumsy at golf and tennis. The lake was abundantly stocked with perch, bream, redbreast, bass, and other fish which thrive in southern freshwater. This ensured that the president always brought in an impressive catch. The media portrayed him as an avid, resourceful fisherman.

Tung emerged from the shack. He wore a deep-orange life preserver. He tossed two others onto the pier. He was laden with bamboo poles, a tackle box, nets, a rod and spinning reel, and a screen-wire cage of crickets. He squatted and patiently readied the equipment. Among his duties on the lake was baiting Hamilton's hook.

Hamilton relied on a pole and a line. He had never tried to master the subtler aspects of the sport. The rod and spinning reel saw no action; the lures in the band of his floppy hat were for effect. In fact, Hamilton hated the taste of fish.

"Crickets are the best bait down here, isn't that right, Tung?" said Hamilton as he slipped on a life preserver; the Secret Service demanded he wear one on the lake. Tung did not answer; he was absorbed with the gear. "We tried worms, but we have better luck with crickets." Actually, Hamilton dreaded earthworms.

Forbes donned a life jacket and sighed submissively. He knew this was likely to be his only time alone with Hamilton. The thought of the letter—that goddamn illogical, unbelievable letter—consumed him. He also experienced a passing tremor of grating uncertainty as he anticipated Hamilton's reaction to the news that he had visited Melville. The heat was relentless.

The miniature flotilla putt-putted away from the pier.

Forbes was in the bow of the presidential boat with his back to what lay ahead. Hamilton sat amidships. Tung was at the tiller. Hamilton gestured offhandedly as they reached the center of the lake. Tung cut the motor and proceeded to stretch a number of poles over the sides. Within seconds the cork of a starboard pole bobbed vigorously. Tung landed the fish with the use of his net and rebaited the hook from the cricket cage.

The boatloads of Secret Service agents pitched listlessly before and aft and alongside of them. They spoke out of the sides of their mouths into their walkie-talkies and reconnoitered the horizon with binoculars. The army major was in one of the Secret Service boats.

"What did you get?" Hamilton asked over his shoulder.

"I believe this is a bream, Mr. President," said Tung. He dropped the hook back in the water and continued to haul in fish of various kinds at frequent intervals.

"We must be over a bed," said Hamilton; there was a note of distraction in his voice. "Don't you think so, Thack?"

"A what?" Forbes's ignorance of fishing lore was almost total.

"A bed. You know, a school or something. We must be sitting on top of a bunch of fish that are mating or whatever fish do. Breeding, anyway. They say you can smell it. I never have."

Forbes gazed across the lake. He watched the helicopter settle onto the landing pad next to the putting green. It was a few degrees cooler on the lake. It helped him compose himself. He lit a cigarette. Finally he said, "I stopped by Washington yesterday. I saw Larry Melville." He sucked a deep puff and braced for Hamilton's furious response.

"Oh?" The president sounded as though he had been told there was a minor fluctuation in the stock market. Forbes exhaled a long breath of relief.

Hamilton glanced over his shoulder as another fish plopped into the boat. "Never did much fishing as a boy." Forbes was flabbergasted that the president should launch into a reminiscence after what he had just told him. "My dad wouldn't stand for fishing," Hamilton went on, "looked on it as idleness. Besides, the Chinese don't fish the way we do."

Tung Yen Fun looked up in mild surprise.

"Where my people came from"—Hamilton shoved his floppy hat to the side of his head—"part of Indiana they call Crawford Upland, the fishing was good, but my folks never went for it. Worked limestone and went to church till Dad got the call and became a missionary.

"Lincoln grew up in Spencer County, too, you know. Went to a 'blab' school in Dale. No books back then. Kids just learned what the schoolmaster told them. Indiana's never had much luck in claiming Lincoln as one of their own. There's a memorial, and they built a state park—pretty lake, place to camp, and so on—but not many people know about it. People want to claim a president for their state if they can. Looks like Indiana's stuck with me," he said with a chuckle.

Forbes found he was amused by Hamilton's folksy reflections. He decided to enjoy the president's even temper while it lasted.

"I haven't decided whether I'll go back to Indiana or not," Hamilton went on; he adjusted his floppy hat again. "If I do, it won't be right away. I don't have a place there, not a real place. The house in South Bend belongs to Janet. I have a good notion that she'll file for divorce when my term's up. She was all for me when I was on the way to the top, but she couldn't stand the sight of me on the way down." His brow lowered; he paused for Forbes to agree with his appraisal of his broken marriage; Forbes nodded. "Of course, that would mean living in a hotel in Indianapolis, at least for a while. You, you'd rather live in a hotel any day than a house, but I can't do it." Forbes smiled with mock indignation. Hamilton, however, was in dead earnest. "I'm not sure I approve of it, an ex-president living in a hotel. . . .

"The state party people have asked me what my plans are, but hell, that's mostly courtesy. I don't seriously believe they would ask me to run for governor or senator. Not that I would accept if they did. And they won't. They would have to be in miserable shape to pick a man who couldn't get himself nominated for a second term as president of the United States. An ex-president is pretty much a museum piece. Nothing much left for him but his memoirs and the chance when the incumbent fucks up to say what a tough job it is to be president. And there are plenty of chances to do that. I wonder if Melville knows it. Do you think he's optimistic about the nomination? He damned well should be."

Forbes was unsure whether the president had understood that he had visited with Melville the previous day. He decided to try again. "Melville asked me to tell you—"

Hamilton gestured absently for quiet. He slowly rubbed his forehead. "You know, Thack, about this trip. I know it's unpopular. People think the president is so isolated that he loses touch, forgets how to read the mood of the country. That's bullshit. It's a matter of viewpoint. I have another viewpoint. From where I sit, knowing what I know, I believe in this trip. No matter how unpopular it is. I know some of the media say it's downright stupid. Politically speaking, I'm inclined to agree. It will hurt Melville or Darrow, whichever gets the nomination. I'd bet on Melville if he was working harder for it personally; he's got the money and the organization, and a man would be a fool to take him lightly when he has his heart set on something. At the moment I think Darrow is working harder personally, and that counts; you know it does. But this trip will hurt the nominee in November. I'm aware of that."

He looked around again as Tung Yen Fun landed another fish. Then he turned back to Forbes.

"There's no love lost between me and Larry Melville. I don't think that's a secret," he continued; his tone remained mellow. "No president is going to be on brotherly terms with a vice-president who has uprooted him after one term. Hell, if I'd been in his place I might've done the same thing. You don't get this job without taking the gloves off. I know it. You know it. But if Melville wins, I think he'll made a good president . . ." His voice trailed off.

Forbes seized the opening. "What he asked me to tell you was that if you'll call off this trip, he'll appoint you secretary of state."

"That's a new one," the president said evenly. "Did he say why?"

"He said he could see no major differences in your foreign policy views. He said you could call your own shots."

Hamilton smiled patronizingly. "I wonder if Melville thinks it's that simple," he said. "I *know* it isn't. Foreign policy is my ball game. I would be a *very* independent secretary of state. I'd make Osborne look like a houseboy. Has Melville thought of that? Anyway, there are some things I *can* accomplish when we get to Peking. They haven't been discussed—I haven't even touched on them with Osborne or General Wells; the media would get them and blow them sky high—but there are some novel possibilities. I'm still the president. You know how much the treaty means to me, don't you, son?"

Forbes knew. He lit another cigarette. He also knew Hamilton trusted him as more than just an accomplished political strategist. They had been through many battles together. Forbes was a realist; he knew that Hamilton had never intended to abandon their friendship, only the public part of their political association. Because he knew the president trusted him—and he trusted the president—he found Melville's implications about Hamilton's frayed sanity irreconcilable with what he was hearing from Hamilton himself; Hamilton was as lucid as he was relaxed.

"One possibility," Hamilton continued—he knitted his eyebrows and rested his chin on his hand—"is a protocol. That's not a treaty by any means, but it carries a lot of weight. It would strengthen our overall posture with regard to the Chinese. For one thing it would show them that our policy is consistent. If you remember, we more or less gave the Chinese a free hand to take care of Taiwan. It hurt some feelings, but we faced the fact that the Chinese were going to insist that Taiwan was their problem, whether we liked it or not. So you can see why this protocol would mean so much. It will give us a leg up militarily with the Chinese. Why, it would make us all but allies. Improve our diplomatic and trade relations beyond anything we can imagine. It may upset the Japanese for a while, but it will force the Russians to be more openhanded with us." He leaned back and stretched broadly, flexing his bony fingers. "That's a possibility. A protocol. I can't bring it up now. If I decide to do it, it will have to be on my own when Chairman Tien and I sit down. It's just a possibility."

"Couldn't it wait until after the election?" Forbes said tentatively. "If it means this much, it wouldn't do any harm to wait a few months, would it? Melville wants you as secretary of state. If you drop the trip, he gets a clear shot and gives you the State Department. It's horse trading. He gets the presidency, you get the treaty. What should I tell him?"

Hamilton's face was impassive, as if he had heard that the choice for dinner was sardines or bologna. "Oh, I don't know," he said. "Tell him I need to know more about what he has in mind. I want to keep as many options as I can. Tell him I'll think about it on the trip. Who knows, he may not win it.

. . . By the way"—his expression brightened again—"I haven't mentioned this to anyone, either, but I'm thinking of extending the trip beyond the time frame. I haven't been back there since forty-seven, you know. Moose Dung was running the revolution from a cave at the time. He had shied away from the Japs and saved all his muscle to use against Chiang. Stubborn bastard, from all I heard. Couldn't bargain with him. Even the Russians wouldn't have anything to do with him. I said so in my cables. That was a foreign service innovation in China, believe me. The other junior officers were eating out of Moose Dung's hand. They reported that Moose Dung was the peasants' savior and Chiang was a ham-handed vulture. The facts showed it was the other way around, and I said so in my very first campaign."

Hamilton removed his floppy hat and examined one of the fishing lures on the band. He appeared preoccupied. Forbes had heard that many of his conversations recently dwelt on his China service and how he had used it to enter politics.

Still scrutinizing the lure, he continued: "When Senator McCarran—it was Pat McCarran who suggested I run for Congress; he said to me, 'Joe, that was the best testimony we've heard yet. You came forward with names and dates. Let's get together. I have some ideas on how you can capitalize on it'—when he asked me to repeat my loyalty board statement before his committee, I did it gladly. It was easy. I told them what I had seen and heard—that the foreign service was the reason we lost China to that gangster Moose Dung." He fanned himself a moment with his hat and then put it back on his head. "Tien is a different man altogether. He's tough, tough as Moose Dung ever was, but flexible. He's from Chungking. His father was a member of the Rotary Club. I grew up in Chungking. My parents are buried there. You knew that, didn't you? I think it would be a hell of a good idea, as a matter of fact, for an American president to just let his hair down and take a vacation in China. Especially an American president who was reared there but who has a realistic position on China. It would create God's own amount of trust and mutual good will. How does that sound?"

The word "vacation" crackled in Forbes's brain. He could almost feel the sticky composition of the amber capsules on his fingers. The sunlight was tangible; drops of perspiration rolled down his shins and into his socks. He felt his chest tighten.

"Do you really want to know how it sounds, Joe?" he rasped.

"Naturally," Hamilton said after a moment. His sunken eyes widened with surprise. He had not expected Forbes's severe reply.

"It sounds like shit," Forbes said harshly. "This trip is unpopular enough as it is. Forget Melville. Forget the political damage. This is the kind of thing that brings the nuts out of the woodwork." He flung his cigarette into the water. "What I'm trying to say is that I believe you've put yourself in personal danger."

"In danger of what?" Hamilton sounded amused.

"Of getting yourself killed."

The president threw his head back and laughed, holding his floppy hat in place with one hand. "Do you have any idea how many assassination threats I get—*every day?*" He sighed and gestured to the boatloads of Secret Service agents bobbing on all sides of them; the helicopter was again circling overhead. "With that many bodyguards—and the woods around this place are crawling with them, too—who could possibly get close enough to do me in?"

"I mean it, Joe, you ought to call this thing off." Forbes's tone was still rough.

"Will you come off this crap, Thack, for God's sake?" Ham-

134

ilton sounded exasperated. "Hell, nobody in the world can get near me—except the people I trust and the—"

"We have exhausted our supply of crickets, Mr. President," interrupted Tung Yen Fun.

The bottom of the boat around his feet was covered with fish. Tung jerked the cord that ignited the outboard motor. "It is a curious thing about crickets," he said. "In China they are valued for their fighting ability. Often the smaller ones outdo the larger ones—the purple-necks."

Hamilton snapped his head around. "I never heard that," he said with skeptical astonishment.

A heavy, bluish haze hung over Van Nuys Airport. The San Fernando Valley was overshadowed by the last traces of night. It was an hour past dawn, but the light was still dim.

Coombes made his way back to his seat moments before landing. He had thought at the last minute to lock himself in the toilet and recheck his palm-sized camera. It had been years since he had done any microfilming.

He walked briskly to the men's room nearest the baggage-claim area. The "drop" was behind the paper-towel dispenser. As he swung the door open he was confronted by a burly man with crew-cut blond hair and dressed in dark double-knit slacks and a tan windbreaker. He was as large as Coombes but younger and brawnier.

Coombes dropped to a defensive crouch. He covered his midsection with one arm and lifted his other hand, the knuckle of the middle finger protruding, to the level of his chin. His lip curled. A brute sound rose in his throat.

The burly man promptly lifted his hands shoulder high, palms out, in a nonaggressive pose. Coombes loosened a bit.

"What the hell are you doing here?" Coombes snarled. "This was supposed to be a—"

"I know it's a breach," broke in the burly man frantically, "but there's been a pre-emption."

"A pre-emption? What kind of pre-emption?"

"The stuff you wanted. The Novic stuff. The GSL people got an identical request three hours before you called. I got the stuff you want, but I thought I ought to let you know."

Coombes leaned against the wall. He bit at a fingernail. "Any idea who?"

"Can't say."

"Why not?"

"I don't know. I can't find out. GSL would be on my ass if I asked too many questions."

Someone came in and stepped up to a urinal. Coombes nodded to the burly man and they walked out.

In the parking lot the burly man handed Coombes an envelope. Coombes opened it. It contained a floor plan of the home of Jacques Novic and the location and combination of his wall safe. A handwritten notation in the margin said the house was empty, unguarded, and accessible.

"How about the surveillance?" Coombes asked. The haze did not seem as heavy on the ground as it did from the air.

"Good for an hour. No more," replied the burly man. "I've diverted with a suspected kidnapping. It's only a rich drunk from the neighborhood. He's sleeping it off in Palm Springs. He'll turn up soon, so don't waste any time."

"What about a car?"

The burly man pointed to a five-year-old, tired-looking sedan at the other end of the parking lot. It looked remarkably like Coombes's own rattletrap. "It's stolen but unreported," the burly man said and handed him the keys.

"Can you stand by?"

The burly man looked at his watch. "Forty-five minutes," he said. "Longer than that, I'll be late for duty."

"Christ," muttered Coombes. "How far away?"

"Two miles. Near the highway." He scrawled a telephone number on a scrap of paper.

Coombes turned off Interstate 405 at Brentwood Heights. The haze showed no signs of lifting. The burly man's warning of a "pre-emption" swirled in his head. He tried to separate and distribute the possibilities. *Who* could be anticipating him? His speculative processes refused to function. He was too weary. He would have to rely, as he had always done, on endurance and instinct.

The traffic was unexpectedly light. He paused at a stop signal. He repeated the process of strapping on the shoulder holster and the Colt Cobra. He pocketed the silencer. He drove into Pacific Palisades.

He wheeled slowly onto a palm-lined street. Jacques Novic's house was a Tudor manor with a peaked roof. Coombes craned to detect any sign of activity as he drove past. The house and the narrow surrounding grounds were settled in early-morning lifelessness. The same was true for the neighboring houses.

He parked at the corner. He attached the silencer to the snubbed barrel of the Colt and stuck it in his waistband. He took a last look at the floor plan and stuffed it back in his pocket. He shoved the valise under the glove compartment, and walked as hastily as he could up the block.

A light shone behind one of the upstairs cathedral windows. Coombes guessed it worked off a timing device to discourage burglars. He thought of trying to enter by the massive, elaborately carved front door but decided against it. The room he wanted was in the rear just off the terrace behind the glass-panel doors.

The flagstone terrace was overhung with live oak and bougainvillea. A bird twittered high in one of the live oaks. There was a kidney-shaped pool and cabana at the foot of a gentle grassy slope. The crest of the slope was flattened by a

137

driveway. A late-model car, a Buick or a Mercury, was parked nearby.

Coombes mounted the terrace steps and tried the panel doors. They were unlocked. The view inside was blocked by heavy magenta curtains. He pulled the Colt and cocked it with his thumb. He slid open one of the glass panels. He calmly brushed a space between the curtains and eased himself into the house, leading with the revolver.

He paused to let his eyes adjust to the murky light. He scanned the room; its features stood in fuzzy outline. He methodically made his way to a light switch and flipped it. A chandelier blazed overhead.

The room was large, plush-carpeted, and furnished in what appeared to be a boldly discordant motif. A japanned Queen Anne secretary stood against one wall; a heavy, imitation eighteenth-century bachelor's chest, against another. There was a Regency bamboo chair, and a glass-topped coffee table with Polynesian-style caning between two nondescript sofas. The avocado-green walls were hung with bullfight scenes. There were several closets with doors more ornately carved than the one at the front of the house. A huge television set rested atop a low, hand-decorated table.

Coombes had no appreciation of interior design. If he had, he would have understood why the home of one of the country's more talked-about wealthy men was unguarded. Nothing in it was really worth stealing. He also would have understood why President Hamilton and Jacques Novic appealed to each other; for each, accumulation was everything, taste nothing. In Novic's case, the less said and more paid to the interior decorator, the better.

The wall safe was behind a ceramic plaque. Coombes found it easily. He disengaged the hammer and shoved the revolver back into his waistband. He read the combination from the floor plan and twirled the dial. The tumblers clicked. He turned the handle and opened the door. A bulb lit the interior, like a refrigerator. It was almost bare. He thumbed through a small stack of envelopes. Toward the bottom he came to a buff-colored one with no address on it. He turned it over. The back flap bore the seal of the president of the United States.

He extracted the envelope cautiously. He ran a heavy finger across the back of it. It was unsealed. He opened it gradually. It contained a single sheet of stationery. He unfolded it. He recognized the constricted handwriting. His huge body trembled as he read it.

Most Honorable Chairman Tien:

Mr. Jacques Novic, the gentleman bearing this message, is, of course, no stranger to you. Like myself, he retains a friendship with the People's Republic of China that extends back many years and beyond many difficulties. He enjoys my total confidence. I trust it will please you to have a similar faith in him.

It is with the warmest pleasure that I look forward to my visit to the People's Republic of China. I am fully optimistic that we will be able to reach concrete and mutually agreeable accord on the questions that now hinder complete cooperation and respect between our countries.

It also is with the humblest gratitude that I accept your gracious invitation to enjoy as long as I like the hospitality of the Chinese peoples. I am profoundly honored to acknowledge the wisdom of your invitation. I am certain it will lead to the deepest understanding between the Chinese and American peoples.

> Your colleague in peace,
> Jos. Hamilton

Coombes braced himself as he felt his shoulders sag. He carried the letter to the bachelor's chest. He placed it face up on the top and secured it with a pair of heavy ashtrays. He took the palm-sized camera from his pocket. He hoped to God the glare from the chandelier would be enough light. He opened the lens to f/2 and set the shutter speed as slow as he dared for a hand-held operation. The film magazine had fifty exposures. He began snapping away. He envisioned the way the pinched script would look when it was enlarged and projected on a screen.

There was a noise.

He snapped two more exposures and stopped. The room was suddenly quieter. The deeper silence seemed to echo the noise. He gently placed the camera on the chest. In the same motion he grasped the square stock of the Colt Cobra.

The noise again.

He spun and dived to the carpet. He drew the Colt and cocked it as he went down. The fall nearly knocked the wind out of him. He lay prone with the revolver held straight ahead.

Coombes thought for a fraction of a second that an animal might be in the room. A guard dog with its larynx altered so it couldn't bark. Then he remembered the "pre-emption."

The chandelier went out. The room was plunged into semi-darkness. Coombes rolled and aimed in the direction of the light switch. Abruptly an ornately carved closet door next to it flew open. A tall figure burst forth and darted across the room.

Coombes fired a muted shot and missed. He fired again and the figure staggered. He fired a third time and the figure tumbled behind one of the nondescript sofas. Keeping the revolver trained in the direction of the sofa, he scrambled to the light switch. The chandelier flashed on again.

Layers of smoke like a mackerel sky floated toward the ceiling. The air reeked of cordite. Coombes stalked across the room, the pistol leveled in front of him.

A motionless arm stretched from behind the sofa. The hand was contorted claw-like. The ring finger was missing.

140

Coombes stood over the body. It was Vest. His eyes were open. His ferocious stare was locked on his face.

"Christ," said Coombes under his breath as he removed the silencer and reholstered the Colt. He was gasping. He felt his rib cage; he didn't think he had broken anything when he hit the floor. He was angered that he had neglected to check the room when he came in and confounded at why Vest had taken this ridiculous chance. Vest had wanted the letter, that was obvious. But for whom? Melville? Could Melville be foolish enough to sponsor a burglary? He gave up. His capacity for deduction had been sapped by fatigue.

He rolled the body over. Blood from wounds in Vest's neck and abdomen oozed into the carpet. He removed Vest's wallet and replaced it with his own containing the "Donald Perry" credit cards and driver's license. He stuffed the keys to the stolen car into Vest's trousers. Vest was unarmed; it seemed out of character; Coombes couldn't account for it; to him it was an unforgivable error.

Vest's wallet contained nearly two thousand dollars. Good, thought Coombes, I can use it.

He retrieved the camera and placed the letter back in the safe. He discarded the idea of tidying up the room. Police investigators would be thoroughly baffled by the body of a man with a nonexistent identity and the keys to a stolen car. Fingerprints didn't matter; Coombes had taken care years ago to expurgate his from all government files. Ballistics made no difference, either. The Colt was army issue, but it had never been registered in the Federal Supply Control System. Its last official owner was in an unmarked grave in Burma.

There was a telephone on the japanned secretary. Coombes lifted the receiver and dialed the number the burly man had given him. The phone on the other end came off the hook in the middle of the first ring.

"This is a friend of Gustave's."

"Yeah?" snapped the voice.

"I need an assist. Triple-O," Coombes replied hurriedly.

"Where?"

"Down the street. On the corner. You'll see the car. I'll be in the car," he said and hung up.

He pulled the glass doors shut. It was only a shade brighter outside. More birds twittered in the live oaks. He hoped the film would turn out all right.

"Give me the skinny," said the burly man. He had pulled up to the stolen car in less than three minutes. Coombes climbed in next to him; he held his valise on his lap. "Is this going to cause me problems?"

"That 'pre-emption,' " Coombes said, "he was inside. The dumb son of a bitch panicked."

"And?"

"And I had no choice. Look, I told you this was premium rate, priority interest. I got what I needed."

"*What do you mean, you had no choice?*" The burly man scowled.

"I mean I left an unidentifiable corpse inside."

"Jesus," sighed the burly man, "how the fuck—"

"Don't worry. I repapered him. And I hung that stolen car on him. With the keys."

The frown on the burly man's face slackened. "You guys, I don't know," he said, shaking his head. After a pause he added, "Where to?"

"Find me a cab. . . . I want something to keep me awake. I'll need it before long. A pill or something."

"Take one of these. Take a couple with you." The burly man handed him an aspirin tin as the car screeched away from the corner. Coombes removed three green heart-shaped Dexamyl tablets and dropped them into a pocket of his rumpled jacket.

The burly man dropped him at a hotel cab stand in Hollywood. "Let me know if there are any problems with your voucher," Coombes said.

"Los Angeles Airport," he said as he was about to step into the cab. He said it loud enough for the burly man to hear.

At the airport he went directly to the line of taxis at the arrival level. "Topanga Canyon," he told the driver and gave him the address of a crumbling motel.

Coombes brooded as the cab turned onto the freeway and carried him north again. Puffy clouds hovered over the Pacific Ocean. He was fretful about his noon call to Shen Keng Min; he *had* to know whether "the guy would take the job at the other noodle factory." The microfilm of Hamilton's reply would weigh heavily in Special Ops' analysis, but Special Ops would be damned reluctant, the bastards, to commit themselves to a short-term counteraction without confirmation from at least one hostile source. Never mind that he had produced a gold-plated, double-barreled one on this side in less than twenty-four hours. The bastards. . . .

His dejection was relieved somewhat when he foresaw the chance of a couple of hours' sleep at the motel. He settled back in the seat. The expense of his operation had all but vanished, he reflected. The airline and car-rental costs would be charged to a dead nonentity. The loss of his emergency separate identity did not trouble him. He would simply have to establish another one. He would be back in Washington sooner than he had expected. He was now carrying more, much more, than enough money to pay back his wife. There would be plenty, too, to cover his air-conditioner repair costs.

6 The Cabal

The second-story study at Fort Wayne House was cool to the point of discomfort. That was the way Forbes wanted it. He could take no more thorny sunlight or suffocating heat. He had drawn the blinds and set the thermostat at sixty. A single, small lamp on a desk against the far wall provided the only light. Several unread newspapers lay on a table at the end of the sofa. Next to them was a telephone. He smoked apprehensively and eyed the bottle of Bourbon across the room. His leg had ceased to throb. He was thankful for that.

The day had been indecisive and odd. He had tried and failed a dozen times to see Nell Leatherbee; she had replied to each of his messages that it was impossible for her to get away from the home-mortgage bill sessions. He had tried and failed to get more time with the president; Gil Snyder was rationing Hamilton's time down to the minute. He had agreed to talk politics with several reporters but had pleaded pressing business and canceled the interview; he had felt too exposed.

One of the uncanniest moments had been his call to New York. A voice that Forbes could have sworn belonged to the rumpled man who had threatened to kill him had answered.

Alison came on the line almost immediately and explained that it was a technician from the telephone company. The campaign was going smoothly, she said; Caswell had had the presence of mind to make a public statement of condolence to Justice Roundtree's family; she also gave him the results of a "vital issues" poll—the campaign was conforming 97 percent to voter preference, she told him—and said he didn't sound very relaxed.

"You know how it is, Alison. The president wants everything right now. There's no way to say no to him."

"You always said you liked working that way. For Hamilton, anyway."

"I'm out of shape. My timing's off."

"You said you didn't think there would be anything for you to do down there."

"I was wrong."

They discussed a few other details of national politics and then Alison said, "I've been thinking about your office, Thack."

"My office?"

"Yes. It's so barren. The walls, I mean. The only thing in there is your button clock. I saw some very reasonable Hoogh prints. I think they would appeal to you."

"Hoogh? I don't think I ever—"

"He did some very interesting things with light. He was Dutch. Dark foregrounds with an open door and brightly lit backgrounds. That's his favorite effect. Two or three figures polishing the candelabra or setting the table or doing some kind of housework."

Forbes told her to select the prints she thought would be most pleasing. Then he had said, "Alison, why don't you close up the office for the rest of the week? The only real work we're doing on Caswell's campaign is keeping his foot out of his mouth. With all the noise from the convention, Eric could

145

swallow his shoe and nobody would notice. Hell, take a few days off."

"Well, God, Thack—" Her tone made her message clear: her boss didn't think the Caswell campaign was very demanding and by extension the work she was doing wasn't all that critical—her boss, who was rapidly becoming her unconditional prospect for sexual fulfillment, the man she would take her clothes off for in a phone booth. Forbes had meant merely to say that things were quiet for the moment and that a holiday for his secretary would be appropriate. He realized his blunder instantly.

"No, forget that. Sorry, Alison, no lounging in East Hampton for you. The convention may be a problem. Make sure Steve monitors the platform in detail. Tell him to tailor Eric's statements to our positions, never mind what the platform says. But no flat disavowals. We'll do that later, if we have to. The same for this China trip. Eric's on record against it. Tell Steve to make sure he stays against it."

"Aren't you satisfied with the campaign, Thack?"

"Caswell could beat the guy he's running against if he never made a speech or spent a nickel on media. Not by the margin he's going to get, but he could do it."

"If it's so easy, couldn't you give me a little more to do? I'd love the experience. I'm, well, overqualified to be a secretary. You said we'd talk about it later in the campaign. Well, it's later in the campaign."

"Sure. Of course. Write me a memo on it. We'll do the restructuring the minute I get back. Oh. Good work on the Roundtree obit. That's the kind of touch that makes a first-class campaign. Thanks, Alison."

Forbes attributed his lapse of sensitivity toward Alison to the fact that his conversation with Hamilton on the lake was reverberating in his memory. It had worn his mental faculties and political intuition to a frazzle. He was tempted to doubt

146

what he had heard. Anything was possible in this weather, he thought. The letter to Roundtree that Melville showed him had been one thing: it was consistent with what he knew about Hamilton. Hamilton was often impulsive, sometimes erratic—in private—in conversation and on paper. Forbes also knew the president was an equally devoted believer in second-thinking. At bottom Hamilton was a cautious man. He was often mistaken but not often blind. But today the man seemed—*seemed*—to have exhibited a rashness, a disregard for his own experience and instincts, that Forbes had never seen before.

He lit another cigarette from the glowing butt of his previous one. He glanced at the telephone with creeping despair. In a few moments he would have to pick it up and relay what he knew to Chandler Hibbitt. He felt a pang of hatred for Hibbitt. He inhaled deeply. But as much as he despised Melville's coat-holder, it was nothing compared to the loathing he felt for the other call he had to make—to the bookmaker whose number the rumpled man had given him.

His thoughts shifted bluntly back to the scene on the lake. Despite his apparent recklessness, Hamilton had laid it out; he had been deliberate, thoughtful, he had even been charitable toward Melville. Yet, Forbes thought, what he had said was out of harmony with the odds that he would say it. Somewhere in the equation there seemed to be an imaginary number. Could it be Hamilton's hold on sanity? Did the letter plus Hamilton's disjointed musings in the boat really add up to the defection of the president of the United States? He crushed his cigarette.

He crossed the faintly lit room and poured a stiff, neat Bourbon. He belted it. He poured another two fingers and returned to the sofa with the glass. He sipped it. He lit another cigarette with his presidential lighter. Hell, he thought—he felt a little drunk—maybe Hamilton just wants a

147

vacation in China, like he said. Maybe he's homesick. Maybe
. . . He recalled Melville's prediction of world chaos; the
rumpled man's threats rang in his ears.

Resignation set in as he looked at his watch. He set the
whiskey aside and walked to the bathroom. He splashed
water on his face. He rebounded quickly from the unsubstan-
tial amount of alcohol. As he dried himself on a towel with the
presidential seal on it, he realized that the suite had grown almost frigid as a result of his fiddling with the thermostat. In
fact, he felt a slight chill under his short-sleeved shirt. He
damned well didn't care. Anything but that heat. He took his
jacket from the closet and slipped it on as he walked back to
the study. The small rip in the lining of the jacket's rear hem
escaped his notice.

He placed the call through the Southern White House
switchboard. The number was the Melville-Monongahela
Bank and Trust Company above Liberty Avenue in Pittsburgh. Hibbitt had an office there. The bank was owned by
the Melville family. The president was Melville's brother; he
styled himself as a patron of the arts and spent most of his
time on galleries and museums; a Melville brother-in-law had
charge of the bank's day-to-day operation.

Hibbitt's office was actually a modular computer terminal.
It encoded incoming calls digitally, routed them onto a UHF
radio channel, and signaled them back over another circuit.
At the same time it automatically alerted Hibbitt—at one of
the numerous extensions he or an assistant manned twenty-
four hours a day around the country, including all the Melville private jets—that it had a waiting call. The system was
an adaptation of the Navy's Ophidia Red network, for which a
Melville electronics manufacturer had been the prime con-
tractor.

Hibbitt himself dialed the bank from Washington and was
put through to the computer, which repeated the process.

148

Both Forbes's and Hibbitt's voices were encoded and "demodded" beyond detection by anyone else. Had the Southern White House switchboard tried to reach Forbes during the call, it would have gotten a "dead" line and assumed the Fort Wayne House phone was out of order. Forbes was unaware of it.

"Sorry to keep you waiting, Thack. Have you heard what happened?" Hibbitt sounded as if he were speaking over a ship-to-shore phone. The microsecond message switch from computer tape to radio channel and back to tape needed adjusting. It flattened his tone and clipped syllables off his words.

"We've got a bad connection," said Forbes. "I'll call you right back." He fumbled with the receiver as he lit another cigarette.

"Oh, no, no, no. How's this? Better?"

"Yes."

"Did you hear about the Ohio delegation?"

"No." Actually, he had discussed it at some length with Alison; he thought the lie would discourage Hibbitt from getting chatty.

"They pledged to us as a body. It looks solid, at least for the first ballot. We think it'll hold up all the way. It looks like we might take it on the first ballot. What do you think of that? The *first* ballot."

"Great, Chandler," he answered monotonously.

"Well, I suppose you've had quite a day. . . . Got anything for me? For the boss, I mean? A hash total?"

Forbes felt bleak and bitter. Hibbitt's feigned breeziness angered him. Jesus Christ, he thought, you must have to try and be as coy as Melville to work for the son of a bitch.

"Here's what I have," he said; he said it curtly. "Hamilton said he would think about it. He said he'd let Melville know."

There was a pause. "So?" said Hibbitt.

"So that's it," said Forbes. "He said he'd think about it on the trip."

Another pause. Forbes could not tell whether it was the ship-to-shore effect or whether Hibbitt was putting his hand over the mouthpiece.

Hibbitt came back on the line; he still sounded demure. "I don't quite follow you, Thack. What's he going to think about?"

Forbes clenched his teeth. He snorted a breath of cigarette smoke. "For the love of Christ, Chandler," he burst out, "the secretary of state thing. Melville's offer."

The phone seemed dead again.

Finally: "The trip. He said he'd think about it. Do you think he *meant* he'd think about it on the trip?"

"Maybe," said Forbes. "I don't really know."

"In that connection, Thack, was there any discussion, any talk, of the extended visit?"

"Look. I haven't forgotten the letter, but my impression is that Hamilton's just toying with the idea of taking a vacation."

"A *vacation?*"

"I'm telling you, my impression is that's all there—"

Another void on the phone.

"What *about* a vacation?" It was Hibbitt's voice again. He had assumed a dictatorial tone. Forbes knew from experience that he often sounded that way when he was weak and frightened. It was an accent he used on underlings when he was getting heat from Melville. It was a side of Hibbitt the media never saw. Forbes ignored it.

"That's all Hamilton has in mind, as far as I can tell," Forbes said evenly. "Spend some time in the land of his father. Lay a wreath on his parents' grave. That kind of thing. I believe that letter was nothing more than the confused mishmash it looked like. Something off the top of his head. In fact, Hamilton agrees the trip will have an impact on the election.

150

But what the hell, that's politics. As far as the treaty goes, he said a protocol was a possibility, nothing more. Just a possibility. It's his pet project. But no decision—"

Silence. When Hibbitt spoke again, the ship-to-shore effect was definitely back. Nonetheless, the distress in his voice was unmistakable. "Have you forgotten what we're *dealing* with?"

"We may be overreacting, overreacting in a large way." Forbes noticed he had said "we." It worried him. He had meant to keep a distance between himself and Melville and Hibbitt. "There's another thing, Chandler. This is important." He had begun to sweat despite the low temperature in the suite; he shifted this way and that and removed his jacket; he threw it on the sofa next to him. "I need some help. A man cornered me before I left Washington and—"

"Yes?"

"Well, it doesn't make any sense. I'd never seen the guy in my life and he threatened me—"

Static grated on the line.

"Hibbitt!"

"I think we're about to lose the connection." Hibbitt's sprightliness had returned. "Listen, Thack. Try to get to Hamilton again. Plead with him. Anything short of telling him the boss has seen his letter to Roundtree. Call me here again in the morning."

"Goddamn it, Chandler, I'm trying to tell you this guy at the airport—"

Click.

Forbes hurriedly dialed the Pittsburgh number again. He was put through the bank switchboard. A male voice came on the line. Mr. Hibbitt had just left for the day, the voice said. Forbes said it was urgent. The voice said the message would be relayed. He tried Elkhart House. The steward said Mrs. Leatherbee was expected around seven. He slowly replaced the receiver.

151

One more call to make. Forbes reached for his jacket. He saw the tear in the lining. It seemed to have been made with a blade of some kind. He had not noticed it before. He wondered how it had happened. He dug in a side pocket and withdrew the scrap of paper. It had an unfamiliar area code. He dialed the number with the vague expectation that he would see his hand tremble.

A woman answered with the last four digits of the number. Her voice lacked inflections; her delivery was dry-cleaned, like that of a television personality.

"My name is Forbes. You don't know me. I was—"

"Oh, yes, Mr. Forbes. We've been expecting your call."

"How do you spell your name, please?"

"Pardon me?"

"How do you spell your—"

"Would you like to hang up and place your call again?"

Forbes lit a cigarette. He picked up the glass of Bourbon and took a swallow. He saw it was pointless to try further to find out who was on the other end of the line. He knew this was no way to speak to a horse shop. If this was a horse shop. The late-afternoon sun filtered through a crack in the venetian blinds. "I want something in the third at Saratoga," he said at length. It was still in the high nineties outside.

"Yes?"

"I don't have an account or anything. I mean, I don't know how—"

"An account has been opened for you."

"Who opened it?"

"I couldn't say, sir."

"I haven't seen a sheet."

"Here's the line. Exclusive had a sharp reversal of form last time out. Shock Absorber was out to score by a head. Vegas Junket could not handle this track in two starts. Exclusive, nine to two; Shock Absorber, five to one; Vegas Junket, four to one."

Forbes took a long draw on his cigarette. The ash fell between the sofa cushions. He was amazed at himself. He was about to bet on a race that he had every reason to believe was fixed. He hesitated. Did he have a choice? He decided he did not. The rumpled man's threat was precise: unless he did as he was told, he would go to prison—or, more likely, die. He had a swiftly passing urge to ask which horse was least disposed to break in the gate. He recalled the rumpled man's words: "If the race is clean, relax until Wednesday." He wondered what the woman would say. Instead he asked, "Who's paying for this?"

"I beg your pardon?"

"Who's going to cover my bet—if I decide to place one?"

"The account will be billed. Winnings will be paid to the account."

"I see. In that case I'll take a hundred on Shock Absorber to win."

"Very good. One hundred dollars on Shock Absorber to win in the third race at Saratoga. Will there be anything else?"

"No." Forbes crushed his cigarette. He was sweating again.

"We'll expect to hear from you again after ten tonight. Thank you for calling."

He replaced the receiver carefully, as if only a premeditated movement would ensure the possibility of future self-governed acts on the part of T. Morgan Forbes. He was shot through with doubt. What he needed was to touch base with certainty, to reconnect with some object that stood for substance in his world. He reached for one of the newspapers on the end table.

Forbes read newspapers diagnostically. He paid attention to by-lines; he had learned which reporters to trust and which not to. He concentrated on political stories attributed to un-identified sources; he had been an unidentified source himself often enough, God knows. Somewhere in each story was an implication or a reference to the source's identity. He also searched for random, inverse details: a prominent name buried in a story, an unlikely address. The process relaxed him and absorbed him completely.

He had been reading for three-quarters of an hour when he saw the item: "Frank Parisi, Retired Policeman, Slain by Let-ter Bomb." He drew no conclusions—just as he had been un-able to disentangle the contradictions of his father's suicide sixteen years earlier—but doubt explicitly reasserted itself. A man who had figured at least marginally in his single profes-sional disaster had turned up dead in an ominous fashion. (The news did not particularly sadden him.) He put a ciga-rette in his mouth and then decided against lighting it; he tossed it into the overflowing ashtray. The voice that had an-swered his office phone lingered in his mind. He took a light sip of Bourbon, and contemplated, in shadowless silence, the notion that there was a Grand Design—set in motion by whom? managed by whom?—that interwove the whole un-happy world into a unified web of conspiracy.

Nell Leatherbee drove a trifle faster than the law allowed along the two-lane asphalt highway. The compact car was from the Southern White House motor pool. She steered with one hand. With the other she anxiously smoothed an imagi-nary wrinkle from her Italian cotton sundress. The dress was yellow, her favorite color. It agreed with her shoulder-length brown hair and tanned skin. Capezio sandals emphasized her slender ankles. She wore enormous sunglasses.

Fields of corn and tobacco, backgrounded by pine forests, lined the road. Irrigation sprinklers spurted here and there. The sun was in the west but still high and barbaric. Being a child of Texas, Nell accepted summer heat as a matter of course, likewise the car's air conditioner. Stifling weather in July was as natural to her as her menstrual cycle. Had it been fifteen degrees cooler, she might have become concerned, as if she had missed her period—something she unequivocally did not want at this stage in her life. Two sons, both in college, were exactly what Nell Leatherbee had planned for.

She rounded a familiar curve and slowed for a railroad crossing she knew was ahead. On her right was a cornfield; in a few months it would be dry and tumbled and thick with quail. She took comfort that this part of the flat south Georgia countryside was a well-worn track for her. Her stays here predated the Hamilton presidency by many years. She had first visited as a girl with her wealthy father. He had bred hunting dogs. Each January they had been guests at one of the region's huge plantations during the national field trials for bird dogs. Several of her father's dogs had won prizes. She had relished the trips; she had been the center of attention at the endless parties. She knew it had been in part because she was the daughter of handsome, rich Griffin Scott; she had imagined it had something to do with being a Texan; time and an eastern education had convinced her it was because she was strong-minded, ingenious, and almost beautiful. After her father died, leaving her, his only child, the immense Scott Ranch west of Fort Worth, she had made the visits to Georgia with her husband.

Her husband. She eased the car over the crossing and picked up speed. Austin Leatherbee had been a problem for some time; he was fast becoming a calamity. She was angry at herself for not having foreseen it. It had forced her to yield on a number of formerly solid fronts, to accept expedients shaped entirely by someone else. She did not welcome this role reversal, nor was she amenable to it; to her it meant only one thing: an intolerable compromise of self-determination.

She did not blame Austin, any more than she would have blamed a dog that loved to chase cars and inevitably got run over; she blamed herself, as she would have done had she owned the dog and failed to teach it to stay out of the street. She was not, however, sympathetic to her husband. Not only did he have limits, he implicitly acknowledged them. By her standards that was inexcusable. Circumstances, events, had limits, not people of will and originality.

A line of cars and trucks appeared ahead. She instinctively whipped into the other lane and passed them; she could not stand to be slowed down on the highway. Her thoughts turned to Forbes. She would have been able to find time to see him that morning if she had not been forced to deal with the mess her husband had made. She wondered if she really loved Forbes; she had told him often enough that she did. She still found him as attractive as she had the first time they met, on a late-night campaign flight in the early weeks of Hamilton's race for the nomination. His appeal transcended charm. They had been equals in bed from the start; Forbes had confidently insisted on it; he had said that the only genuine pleasure in bed was shared pleasure. It had taken her a while to adjust to that; her previous experience—she thought it laughable that the only other man she had slept with was her husband—had been that the man dominated or the woman controlled; in any case, until she met Forbes her sex life had been a numb disaster. She believed Forbes had recognized from the outset that her political desires were compelling; he had known so much about her early career—details of her unsuccessful congressional campaign, sums of money connected with her work as a party fund-raiser, anecdotes about her two years as ambassador to Sri Lanka. In natural sequence she cultivated him politically as she was drawn to him personally; ingrained habit permitted her to observe the distinction. Accordingly, Forbes provided her entree to

Hamilton's inner circle. Not once had he treated her as a pro-tégée, but always as a competent politician.

Which brought her husband back to mind. Austin had tried to discourage her from running for Congress. He had presented the unsure, childish argument that a woman had no business in politics. She couldn't believe it. After her primary victory he had stirred dissension among her campaign staff. Later, when she was raising money for state elections, her husband donated a small amount to the opposition; she knew he had done it to embarrass her, and she promptly informed him that only concern for her political future in her conservative district prevented her from divorcing him. When she was named ambassador, Austin had accompanied her and her younger son to Colombo; he had returned home "to run the family ranch" as soon as appearances had been satisfied. The "happily married" pretense was maintained, but barely, when she got the cabinet job. Like Nell, Austin Leatherbee was basically selfish, but he lacked his wife's tricky, pointed ambition and her resolution to survive. Consequently, Nell saw herself as surpassingly bright and her husband as totally foolish instead of just plain weak. Her lawyer had received the same impression during two telephone conversations with her earlier in the day.

The lawyer had confirmed suspicions that she had held for several months. There were no two ways about it: the ranch was in deplorable financial shape. The facts were tenuous, but an accountant and a private detective had sniffed the heart of the crisis—Austin had plunged heavily in a deep-sea mining venture; he had maneuvered land titles and borrowed from Texas and Florida banks; he had put up huge chunks of the ranch as collateral. The investment was lost; the banks were calling in their loans.

"It comes to this, Nell," the lawyer had said. "The ranch may be on the verge of bankruptcy."

She had given him his instructions. The lawyer was to initiate negotiations with the banks and other creditors the minute the extent of the problem was defined; stall, buy time, anything; he was to do what he could to put the blocks to Austin. In the meantime . . .

Nell was unsentimental about the ranch. She valued it because it was *hers*. She felt much the same way about her sons; they mirrored her taste and prominence; the fact that Austin was their father was a biological coincidence of no importance. She looked on the ranch as property; it provided things. She had discovered long ago that the most precious thing it provided was independence. The feudalistic pretensions of her neighbors, whose families had also owned their land for generations, was missing in her. She had thought Austin viewed the ranch as the best source of income he could hope for; he had professed a love for the cattle business; in fact he had shown an aptitude for it. He could have stayed on as long as he liked, as long as the ranch turned a profit. Now that abject moron had undermined the foundation stone of her independence.

A small cement-block-and-glass diner appeared on the right. Nell signaled and turned off the highway. She stopped and got out. She paid no attention to the wilting heat.

The building was whitewashed and topped with a rectangular sign identifying it as "Buddy's Fine Food—Home Cooking." For several miles east and west billboards proclaimed that the motorist was approaching it. It was known locally as Buddy's. Most times of the day it was packed with television and newspaper correspondents. Buddy's was the nearest place to the Southern White House to get a bite to eat. Facing it at a hundred yards on either side were signs affixed to trees that said, "Whoa! You Just Passed Buddy's!" It was deserted now. The media people were attending the late-afternoon news briefing given daily by Hamilton's press secretary. Nell had timed her arrival to coincide with their absence.

A bell tinkled as she opened the door. A lizard purse hung from her shoulder. The dining room was neatly configured with Formica-surface tables and booths upholstered in aquamarine vinyl. It was cooled by a noisy, five-ton air conditioner; a strip of red paper blew from the fan guard. Coiled fluorescent lights glowed starkly overhead. There was a strong suggestion of fish and grease. Buddy's menu offered a variety of overpriced fried fish dinners.

Buddy himself was behind the cash register. A television set was suspended above him. He was alone in the dining room. The single waitress was on her break; she would return in time to work the dinner crowd. He had watched Nell from the moment her car pulled up. The media people and Buddy's other seasonal patrons got the feeling he eyed them individually, with more than passing interest, as they came in; they couldn't explain why. Buddy had been the subject of countless feature stories since the establishment of Hamilton's vacation retreat; his recipes—they were actually the work of his wife, who toiled unseen in the kitchen, and were uniformly unappetizing—enjoyed national circulation.

"Evening, Miss Nell," said Buddy; his voice had a harsh, ringing quality. Only one side of his face worked; the other side was paralyzed; he had been struck by lightning as a child. "Television boys're all fired up about the trip. Asked me what I thought about it. I told them. Told them to be careful what they eat. Them Chinamen eat a lot of dog meat, they tell me. It'll be on the seven o'clock news." Buddy ordinarily greeted his customers with a grunt or a nod. He spoke to Nell because she had been coming to his restaurant since she was a girl at the side of her wealthy father. He had once tried to remind her that he remembered her when she was not more than this high, but she had cut him short.

Nell did not reply. She stood in front of the cash register with one leg thrust forward a fraction and delved in her purse. The cash register sat atop a glass case lined with boxes of cigars and souvenirs for tourists. Postcards depicting the diner hung from a metal rack. She withdrew a dollar bill and asked for change for the telephone. Buddy opened the cash drawer and handed it to her and resumed his gaze out the window.

Five telephone booths were positioned anywhere they would fit along the passage leading to the restrooms. Until the influx of media people, there had not been a public phone in the place. The booths were initially installed outdoors. Buddy moved them inside when the media people complained. Nell chose the one farthest down the passage and closed the door. She inserted a coin, dialed, and told the operator to reverse the charges.

"Ah, let me see . . . yes, of course, we'll accept the call," answered the receptionist, who clearly imparted that she was perplexed at receiving a collect call from Assistant Treasury Secretary Leatherbee.

"Let me speak to Chandler Hibbitt," said Nell.

"One moment, please."

In a matter of seconds Hibbitt came on the line. "This is Chandler Hibbitt, Mrs. Leatherbee. Nice to hear from you. Can I help you?" He sounded like a man whose wife was in his office when his mistress called.

"You haven't heard from me yet, Chandler," Nell replied; there was a trace of exasperation in her voice; she was offended at the idea of having to call Hibbitt. "Check your watch. We agreed on a schedule, remember?"

There was a pause and then Hibbitt said irritably, "Why didn't you call the Pittsburgh number? That was the arrangement. You were supposed to call the Pittsburgh number. It's goddamn risky for us to talk on this—"

"Take it easy, Chandler," Nell broke in. "I'm at a pay phone. No one's around to listen."

"You should have called the Pittsburgh number."

160

"I don't like talking to your computer. When I talk to you, I want to know I'm talking directly into your ear. I want to be able to see you on the edge of your chair in that big old house of Larry Melville's, ready to jump like you've been goosed the second he yells for you. I don't seem to be able to picture you like that when I talk to your computer."

She omitted to say that she had dialed him collect, person-to-person at his Washington number to make certain the receptionist was aware of the call and to make certain there was at least a telephone company record of it. She guessed Hibbitt would eventually figure it out.

"Very funny, Nell," said Hibbitt; there was a small, clear note of resentment in his voice. "Very funny." He tried to regain control of the conversation; he mentioned the encouraging number of uncommitted convention delegates who had declared for Melville in the past twenty-four hours.

"Well, if that's the case," said Nell, thinking her business with Hibbitt would be concluded much sooner than she had anticipated, "I assume the urgency has gone out of our backup plan. I'm happy to hear it. Now tell me the status of our deal to settle my little Texas problem. What did you call it, Chandler? 'Our foreign exchange transaction'?"

"Oh, I wouldn't say the urgency has gone out of it," said Hibbitt with distinct self-satisfaction. "I wouldn't say that at all."

"What the hell are you talking about?" Nell asked hotly; she was close to rage.

Hibbitt's tone turned abruptly grim. "He has indicated he's going to do it," he said.

"Indicated he's going to do what?"

"What we feared he might do."

"You aren't making sense, Chandler. I'm not aware we feared he might do anything. By 'he' I assume you mean Hamilton?"

"Of course I mean Hamilton." Hibbitt's voice sharpened.

"I don't believe it."

"It does sound unreal, doesn't it? I wouldn't believe it myself if I hadn't heard it from Thack Forbes."

"*Thack Forbes!* Thack told you that? Thack told you Joe Hamilton *indicated* he was going to defect?"

"In so many words."

"What were the words, Chandler?"

"They were heavy. Forbes spent a lot of time with Hamilton today, Nell. Apparently Hamilton poured his heart out."

"What were the *words?*"

"The information Forbes gave us is concrete enough. The boss is ready to act. My instructions are to tell you to be prepared to go ahead with the alternate plan. . . . The Syrette was in Thack's jacket lining. You were able to retrieve it, weren't you?"

Nell shifted impatiently in the telephone booth. Taking orders had always been difficult for her; taking them by relay from Chandler Hibbitt was too much. "Put me through to Melville," she said; her face constricted as she spoke; she felt her lips draw thin.

"The boss would love to speak to you if he had a second to spare, but he has his hands full, believe me. My God, you can imagine—"

"*Put me through to Melville.*"

Hibbitt sighed and then said, "Let me see if he can take a call."

"You had better see to it that he can. If you don't, I'm hanging up, and as far as I'm concerned this conversation never took place."

Hibbitt put her on hold. She wondered if she really would hang up. She was unaccustomed to making threats she doubted she could make good. Her thoughts drifted for an instant to her husband; she entertained the thought that it was

162

his fault. She checked herself; that was not her style. She had consciously thrown in her lot with Larry Melville; she had elected her course on her own; she would stand by her own judgment. Hanging up was out of the question. If getting what she needed from Melville meant adjusting her attitude toward Hibbitt, she would adjust, no matter how distasteful she found the accommodation.

"Nell, is this causing you some *problems* we hadn't *counted* on?" The voice turned out to be Melville's. The vice-president of the United States sounded solemn but gracious and confident. Nell was relieved that it was Melville; she was relieved that she would not have to defer to Hibbitt.

"Hell, yes, it is," she snapped; she snapped, because she knew Melville would indulge it—in her case. "I have just been told by your caddy that there's a chance Hamilton might do it. A very real chance. I mean, it's utterly preposterous."

"It's a fact, Nell," said Melville; he spoke easily. "I *suggest* you have a talk with Thack *Forbes*." He had the disconcerting habit of emphasizing what seemed to be random words. "Ask Thack to *tell* you about the *conversation* he had with Hamilton. I know it sounds preposterous, but *there* it is. An *indication*. A *clear* indication. We can't ignore it."

The telephone booth had grown uncomfortably warm. Nell cracked the door an inch. "But Larry," she said; her voice was tinged with anxiety. "This is incredible. What about the letter? What about Thack? He's been threatened, you know, and kicked around in the bargain. Where on God's earth does this leave us?"

"Everything until *now* has been a precaution. *Something* of a training exercise."

"A precaution?" Nell sounded subdued.

"Yes. We knew this was likely to *happen*. More than likely. The hints have been getting *more* conspicuous all the time. Don't ask me, please, where the information *came* from. I'm *sure* you don't want to know. It's lucky, goddamn lucky, we took it seriously. It would have been easy—*and* disastrous—to overlook the evidence, and I *confess* I had to look at it very, *very* hard before I was *convinced*. If you feel you have been used, *I* apologize. But, believe me, Nell, the bit of deception was necessary. Vital, in fact. I think we agree on that, don't we?"

Nell had an image of Melville holding one of his glass swans as he spoke. She failed to understand why he treasured that collection of cheap glass. "Does this mean the planning has changed?" she asked.

"No," said Melville, "not at all. The planning is on schedule. Don't you see? This is what the planning was *built* on. This eventuality. We were *hoping* like hell it wouldn't come to this, but it has. Thank *God* we were able to prepare for it."

"Am I still expected to—"

"Your role hasn't changed, Nell. You're the person on the *scene* who has to evaluate the conditions, the timing. You have to watch Thack, judge him, *determine* whether he's moving within the *time* frame. If he seems hesitant *about* committing himself, you'll have to move in and act *on* your own. You *have* the equipment, I believe. Let me *caution* you. Be *extra* careful with it. Another thing. It will be best if Thack isn't *told* about the early planning. For consistency's sake."

"What's in it, Larry? The Syrette, I mean?"

"It's . . . I'm *told* it contains a *particularly* virulent strain of meningococcal bacteria. Let's see. Yes. If you should even suspect you're infected"—he sounded as if he were paraphrasing from a written form—"you're to call *Chandler* immediately. He has an emergency *procedure.*"

"Spinal meningitis?"

"Do we have anything else to discuss? Oh, yes. I think you'll want to tell your financial people, your lawyer or *whoever,* that the bank we discussed, the one in Europe, is ready for a visit. All your man needs is a signed document from you

164

authorizing transfer of funds. I'm told that he should *open* an independent account, outside Texas if possible. A legal angle. The lawyer will know what to do. . . . Nell, I want you to know I am *happy* to be of help in a case like this. I *want* members of my team to *understand* from the start that they *should* come to me when they have problems in these areas. It's a quality I'm looking for in a *cabinet* member in my administration. I think you're going to make an outstanding treasury secretary, by the way."

"Thanks, Larry."

"You *have* your timetable for calling Chandler. That stays the *same,* too. Call the Pittsburgh number from now on. I think that's a better idea. It will be more convenient. I'm glad we had a chance to resolve *any* questions you had. I appreciate it, Nell. Good-bye."

"Good-bye."

Nell opened the door of the telephone booth. She did not get up at once. She understood plainly how vulnerable she was. She had the momentary illusion that she was a game bird in one of the nearby fields, a quail or a dove, and had just been flushed from the undergrowth. She wondered whether the birds, after so many noisy autumns, had an inkling that during a specified period each year they would in all probability be in the sights of a gun every time they took flight. The illusion passed. She noticed her palms were moist. She decided against freshening her makeup and walked out of the restaurant.

The clang of metal cookware resounded from the kitchen as she left; Buddy's wife was putting the finishing touches on dinner. Buddy was standing on a stool behind the cash register. He was tuning the television set for the evening news.

Hibbitt, similarly conscious of the hour, slid back a panel of the étagère in Melville's office. The space contained three television sets. Melville and Hibbitt watched the three network news shows together every evening. It was a ritual. Hibbitt watched with a consuming but uncritical eye; it was a trait left over from his years in the newspaper business; his role was to note Melville's comments on the day's events and pass them along to the press secretary.

"Tape them," said Melville; he was standing at a window; his back was to the room. The shadows lengthened from the stand of bay trees across the lawn; a drooping mist clung to the trunks. "I'll watch them later. How much time until the plane?"

Hibbitt checked his watch. "Less than an hour," he said. He activated the automatic mechanism on the videotape machine and closed the étagère panel. "Would you like me to get Senator Hall for you before we leave?"

It had been a rough day for Hibbitt. This was his first moment of identifiable tranquillity since midafternoon. Forbes had been easy enough, but Nell Leatherbee had upset him. He did not know how to deal with someone, especially a woman, who had direct access to Melville; he was used to people who *asked* him if they could speak to his boss; it was his fulcrum of power. Melville himself had been demanding and irascible. The worst had been when Hibbitt reported that Ohio's uncommitted delegates were swinging to the vice-president. It was Melville's first significant success in days in the final rush for delegates. It would have filled most men with at least temporary contentment; it made Melville even more ravenous. Matters were aggravated by the fact that Melville had received his weekly hormone-amphetamine injection; the reaction had been predictable: an initial gush of youthful spunk that gave way to mild depression; for the rest of the day his moods had alternated. Hibbitt ran his hand carefully over his thinning hair. He needed a drink. The time had long vanished since he saw himself as more than Melville's provisional servant.

166

"No," said Melville. "Call him from the plane." He picked up a glass of vermouth he had been nursing and held it across his chest between sips. "On second thought, forget Hall. I'll see him at the dinner for the New Jersey delegation. It's at the William Penn, isn't it?"

"Yes. Nine o'clock."

"Hall turns my stomach, that chubby idiot. I can't for the life of me think why I agreed to let him serve as national chairman. There's no way he could be worth that much. He's a homosexual, too, did you know that, Chandler?"

Hibbitt was at the small bar for his second drink. He was pouring what he had intended to be a light scotch. He splashed more whiskey into the glass. He pretended to ignore the question.

"I said, did you know Hall was a fag?" Melville had turned and was facing the room. His eyes were crinkled but he wasn't grinning.

"I've heard it, yes," said Hibbitt tamely. His veined nose was taking on its late-afternoon glow. He avoided Melville's eyes.

"You know, Chandler," said Melville—he was leaning against the windowsill; his legs were crossed—"I've never understood homosexuality." He mispronounced the word with an unaccented *o*. "I don't understand how a man stimulates another man the way a woman does. . . . Have you told your wife? It would seem to me a very difficult thing to keep from her. Have you told her?"

"Yes." Hibbitt looked into his glass.

"*Good.* Of course, it would have been extremely hard not to tell her, wouldn't it? Especially after the time you were arrested in Harrisburg. Have you told your sons?"

"No."

Melville had brought up the subject at every opportunity recently, it seemed to Hibbitt; on each occasion he employed the same commentary and the same questions. As a man capable of broad ignorance and insensitivity, Hibbitt was ill-equipped to spot the same qualities in someone else; but he wondered whether Melville realized that these discussions were painful to him; he was too frightened to ask.

"You should tell them," said Melville, crossing over to his desk. He slumped into his chair and put his stubby fingers together in a peak. "You'll have to one day, you know. They'll find out sooner or later. After all, it's accepted as natural in San Francisco and New York. Coming out of the closet, I think it's called. I look on it as an illness, like a cold, the same way I look at alcoholism. Your last stay in the hospital gave you the confidence to handle liquor, didn't it? I believe you've got the other thing, the homosexuality, more or less under control, too, don't you?"

"I suppose so," Hibbitt said quietly.

"No brushes with the police or anything?"

"No."

"The Harrisburg thing has been taken care of, if I remember correctly. That's something we don't have to contend with. I don't suppose the police make as big a thing as they used to about cracking down on people like you. Still, you have to be careful. The FBI or somebody runs a security check on people in the executive branch. It's pretty thorough, I'm told. As far as I know, homosexuals are still regarded as security risks. Be damned certain you stay out of Schenley Park while we're in Pittsburgh." He leaned forward and studied something on his desk for a moment and then looked up. "What do we have from California? How are things with our friend Vest?"

"No word yet." Hibbitt drained his glass and put it down. He desperately wanted another drink but dared not take it. He knew his emotions could not withstand an inquisition of

168

his drinking habits. Besides, it would be hard enough sober to refrain from cruising when he got to Pittsburgh tonight.

"*Nothing?* What time is it in California?"

Hibbitt looked at his watch again. "Nearly four-thirty," he said. "I can't imagine why he hasn't made contact. I spoke to the security people at Trans-Columbia. I said I needed to speak to him as soon as possible. They're good about tracking people for us. I'm sure they're on it."

"Trans-Columbia?" Melville sounded doubtful. "Surely there was a better way than that."

"I asked them informally," replied Hibbitt; he was regaining his composure. "Of course, they'll put the request at the top of the list. They always do for things coming from this office."

"*This* office?"

"My Pittsburgh office, I mean."

"Did Vest make contact with his intelligence source?"

"I don't know." Hibbitt spoke easily now that he no longer felt threatened. "I went precisely according to the guidelines we decided on and left the operational details up to him. All he got from us were the Hamilton letters and the suggestion of Jacques Novic."

Melville was scrutinizing a piece from his glass collection. "Vest is a good man," he said. "Brutal, but good at what he does." He put the piece down and continued. "Chandler, this thing Forbes told you—Hamilton and his vacation in China— what do you suppose the odds are that I could have guessed that the man would say a thing like that today?"

Hibbitt considered the question a moment and then said, "Astronomical, at least."

Melville walked back to the window and resumed his gaze. "Yes, astronomical," he repeated meditatively; "about the same odds that Charles the Second had of reclaiming the throne of England when Cromwell died. . . . I want another vermouth. More ice this time."

Hibbitt promptly delivered the drink. Melville accepted it with an outstretched hand, not bothering to glance where it came from.

"I'm making a point," Melville went on, "a crucial point."

Hibbitt knew what was coming. He had heard it numerous times in one version or another over the past year. It was now Melville's incessant private refrain. He had returned to it constantly since he had decided to arrange Hamilton's assassination.

"This country has reached a juncture in history where we are actually *behind* the times." Melville gestured as he spoke, as if there were a cheering crowd in the gathering darkness beyond the window. "I don't mean militarily or economically, or necessarily socially. I mean *culturally*."

He turned and faced the room, to make certain he had Hibbitt's full attention.

"We have evolved into a culture"—his nasal voice sharpened to a near-whine—"that allows amateurs to govern us, to set our tastes and standards, and even to deny the existence of the *few* sparks of genius that allow us to survive. I find that intolerably hypocritical, don't you?"

Hibbitt nodded agreement. On the other hand he found Melville's monologue less effective and articulate than usual. Moreover, it lacked cohesion as discourse; it was what the police would call "rambling and confused" if they found it in a suicide note.

Melville was now pacing the length of the room. "This country was, in fact, built on the industry and farsightedness of a few, a *very* few families, of which mine was among the foremost. The time has come for *us* to reclaim our *natural* right as its leader." He paused and sipped his vermouth.

"Every single nation that has *mattered* on this globe has

170

been *dominated* by a single unchallengeable leader. Their *cultures* demanded it. We must have it, too, if we are to regain our position of *natural* strength."

He paused at the window again. "Let's face it. The men who wrote the Constitution were rural men attuned to an agricultural age. How could they possibly have foreseen our technology, our modern techniques? The Constitution is out of date. It just isn't an instrument of progress anymore. On the contrary, it's a positive hindrance to it. It's hardly a source of justice if it can justify laws that force *me,* whose birthright it is to lead, to contend as an equal with Darrow. Or serve as a subordinate to *Hamilton.*" His face drew into a vicious frown as he spoke the president's name.

He returned to his desk. "The time has come for the institutional union of the government and the country's strongest families. I don't mean creating titles or anything silly like that. I mean it is time for us to become the *visible, dominant leaders of this country,* not just the manipulators of power. The idea—*my* idea—is to harness directly and irrevocably the resources of the Melville family and the government of the United States. And I will *not* allow a trivial aberration like this trip of Hamilton's to forestall this idea. I will not allow it!"

Hibbitt remained respectfully silent for an appropriate period and then indicated it was time for them to leave for Pittsburgh. He helped Melville with his coat and held the door.

7 The Suspect

The duty officer knew he had a problem. His face wrinkled into a scowl as he scrutinized the computer print-out. He was a navy commander; silver oak leaves pierced the collar of his summer uniform. He felt a tightness in his stomach. A tightness he pretended, as a good officer, wasn't there.

He lifted his eyes a moment from the print-out and glanced at the mug of coffee at his elbow. A fringe of steam floated above it. He decided he had no taste for coffee. He looked across the desk at the telephones. There was a white one, a red one, a green one, and a black one. He picked up the white one.

"This is the duty officer," he said. "Send the 'city-list' controller down here. On the double."

He had been transferred to the National Security Agency three months ago. He had managed to get an administrative job. A prudent career officer steered clear of operational assignments at NSA. Operational assignments often put a man in a position to mar his record. The promotion-minded remembered the *Pueblo*. The duty officer was prudent and promotion-minded. His superiors regarded him as a practical, efficient officer who was slow to jump off the deep end. Once a month he drew a tour as officer of the watch.

On this Tuesday night his watch was in signal traffic security. The SIGTRAFSEC shop was a brightly lit clutch of windowless offices in the NSA complex at Fort Meade, north of Washington. SIGTRAFSEC's routine had been supercharged since President Hamilton began preparing to embark for China. Every secret technique, code, and piece of equipment used by government agencies had been checked in infinitesimal detail for leaks.

The "city list," on which the duty officer's eyes had frozen, was a digest of the interdepartmental activity of all the government's computers since noon of the previous day. The task of monitoring it had been given to SIGTRAFSEC for the course of Hamilton's trip. SIGTRAFSEC personnel had protested the extra assignment; they weren't busboys, for Christ's sake. Each entry on the print-out showed which information had been requested by another department's computer, how long it had been away from its home data station, and the retrieval and return times. A separate line recorded the subject of the information and an enciphered authorization code. Unauthorized retrievals were marked with triple asterisks.

The duty officer absently touched the pinch clip of his security-clearance badge. It was attached to his shirt pocket flap; it was peach-colored, meaning he was authorized to go anywhere in the three-story Operations Building and the nine-story annex. The white telephone caught his eye. He thought of picking it up again.

There were three acute raps on the door.

"Come in," said the duty officer.

The door opened and a wiry air force sergeant appeared.

"You sent for me, sir?" The sergeant kept one hand on the door handle.

"Are you the city-list controller?" The duty officer was behind his desk.

"Yes, sir."

"Come in and close the door."

The sergeant eased the door shut. He looked resentfully at the duty officer's security badge. His own was robin's egg blue and restricted him to his own area. He knew the duty officer could pull rank on any of NSA's thousands of employees who were at work deciphering the electronic secrets of the country's enemies and allies and devising ways to shield America's own communications from interception. He was offended by the knowledge that the duty officer didn't know how SIGTRAFSEC did its job but could tell SIGTRAFSEC people what to do.

"Have you gone over the intracity intercepts?" asked the duty officer.

"You mean the international schedule, sir?" replied the sergeant. He sensed the duty officer suspected an irregularity; he was stalling to get an answer ready.

"I mean the city list. You're the city-list controller, aren't you?"

"Yes, sir," said the sergeant defensively. The duty officer's security badge again struck his glance. The son of a bitch is going to cause trouble, he thought, and he doesn't understand a thing about SIGTRAFSEC.

"This is timed off at fourteen-thirty," said the duty officer, holding up the print-out. It was a sheet of perforated white paper covered with lines of jerky, chain-printed letters; it resembled an enlarged bank statement. "It's nineteen hundred now, a few minutes after. This shows at least forty unauthorized retrievals. Have you indexed them and checked them out?"

"You mean a selective sequential, sir?"

"If that's how you check out unauthorized retrievals, that's what I mean. Have you checked them out?"

"We don't keep the city list on the front of the stove, sir," said the sergeant, trying to head off a reproach. "It isn't one of our normal routines. We're short-staffed as it is. A lot of people on leave in the summer. Anyway, each department monitors retrievals on a per-file basis. It's something for the departments to keep up with. Operations threw the city list to us on an emergency basis."

"I take it these retrievals haven't been checked?"

"The overnight crew has been handling them. I can have these done now if *you* want me to, sir."

"All right, sergeant. Complete them as soon as you can. But I want this one immediately." He turned the print-out halfway around and pointed to an entry near the bottom. The sergeant studied the heading. Three asterisks were next to it.

"***CICUSA Hamilton, Joseph Tyler REDWING/SPR/GRU-2A."

His eyes dropped to the second line.

"USDAOUTSITEXPAN 170821-7 170821-7 ODEARL KUDOVE 11."

The sergeant lifted his head. He touched his cheek and looked at the duty officer out of the corner of his eye. He was surprised to see the president's name but did not say so; it would have been unprofessional.

"The Agriculture Department is the origin of request," said the sergeant. "The file was gone from its home data station for less than a minute. Whoever retrieved it sent it straight back home." He spoke with the air of a man proud of his mastery of technological mysteries. "If the retrieval had worried the home data station, we would have heard about it by now. You see, sir, *all* retrievals show up on the home station monitors when a file goes through the memory buffer register. Anybody who sees an unauthorized retrieval on his monitor, and doesn't like it, screams like hell. That's s.o.p."

The duty officer was baffled by the jargon. "Where did the file come from?" he asked impatiently. "Where's the home data station? In the Agriculture Department?"

"File headings are nonpublished items. You have to go through a hell of a long list of access sequences and computer locations to find the heading you want."

"You mean to say somebody can actually retrieve something from another computer simply by *looking it up?*"

"More or less. People Donald Duck files all the time."

"They do *what?*"

"Donald Duck. It's a duplicating capability, like an acoustic delay line. The generating loop has been modified. Nearly every machine in town has it. It isn't supposed to be used on classified stuff, but it's such a time-saver, I guess people cut corners with it." The sergeant gained confidence as he went on. He was sure the duty officer would relax as soon as he understood the insignificance of the city list.

"Look, sir," he continued, "there's no way this could involve a security violation. To operate a computer console and retrieve classified data, you have to have a damned high clearance in the first place. Otherwise you wouldn't be allowed near the equipment. This city list shows unauthorized retrievals, *not* security violations. If a data station doesn't want its files Donald Ducked, it's up to that data station to do something about it. SIGTRAFSEC has enough work without doing somebody else's. We'd never get home if we checked out every unauthorized retrieval."

The duty officer was almost convinced. The tightness he would not acknowledge in his stomach had disappeared. He felt vaguely sorry for having wasted the sergeant's time. He persisted nevertheless, partly to gratify his superior rank.

176

"What's the authorization code? Is that Agriculture Department, too?"

Outside, sultry night was falling on the enormous parking lot and the heavy, chain-link barriers topped with electrified wire that encircled the installation. The uniforms of the armed marine guards were spotted with perspiration.

"It's enciphered," replied the sergeant.

"Can you decipher it?"

"I'll do it upstairs. I can have it back to you in five minutes."

"Can you do it by phone?"

"I'm not supposed to, sir. It's against—"

"Use the phone, sergeant. I'm authorizing it."

The sergeant raised one eyebrow a degree; it was the only dignified way left that he could protest. He dialed the white telephone and read the final two cryptonyms and digits from the print-out entry. He paused and looked blankly at the duty officer until he got the information he had asked for.

"It's a Department of Defense authorization code," he said as he hung up. "No prior transmissions on the second cryptonym. You don't see many Department of Defense codes on Agriculture machines. It's probably a TDY shop."

The duty officer's stomach slammed shut—for real this time. His face whitened. "I want the rest of that city list checked out within an hour," he said crisply as he sat down at the desk. "I'll check this one myself. That's all."

The sergeant stood motionless for a moment. He could not understand the duty officer's agitation. Nobody gives a fuck about the city list, he said to himself. For an instant an image of the roof of the Operations Building stuck in his mind; an outpost of antennae siphoned electronic impulses from the atmosphere and funneled them to the cryptanalysts; U.S. listening posts around the world were intercepting Chinese mil-

177

itary and diplomatic messages and beaming them to NSA. What the hell, thought the sergeant, an officer can *always* find an excuse to break balls. Then he backed out of the room and closed the door.

The duty officer picked up the green phone and cradled it on his shoulder. He flipped through a telephone directory, put his finger on a number, and dialed. The other end answered immediately.

"This is SIGTRAFSEC duty officer. I'm reporting an unauthorized data retrieval. A station under your authority is involved."

There was a pause and then the other end said, "Under our authority, okay. How do you know that?"

"I had it checked."

"Okay." The other end sounded cheerful. "Give me the last two digits."

"One-one."

"One-one, no kidding?"

"That's correct."

"One-one copy. Thanks for the call."

"You want a call back?"

"This is fine. Thanks. Have a good night," said the other end, still cheerful, and hung up.

The duty officer replaced the receiver. His stomach unwound. He wondered if he had made a mistake about the authorization call. He decided he hadn't.

A crack ran like a lightning bolt down one wall of the motel room. The owner had never considered repairing it. His guests were not thin-skinned about such things. The air conditioner gurgled ineffectually. Fragments of a sandwich lay on a piece of wax paper on a table by the bed. The bedclothes were in disarray. The wax paper was puckered and greasy.

Coombes stood at the window. He was looking through a space in the threadbare curtains. His eyes were bloodshot; his perception was distorted by lack of sleep. He was stripped to the waist. His huge torso reeked of perspiration odor; he was afraid that a shower would make him drowsy despite the Dexamyl. The hair on his chest and stomach showed numerous signs of gray; it was almost as thick as his day-old mustache and goatee. His belly and the pouches of fat below his ribs rolled over his belt. In one bulky hand he held a can of barely chilled cola.

His view was of the garbage cans and the potholed parking lot at the rear of the motel. The southern California sun was brilliant in midafternoon. A convertible with its top up rounded the corner of the building and stopped. A man and a woman got out; both were well tanned, stylishly dressed, and wore sunglasses. The man carried a suitcase that obviously had nothing in it. They went into the room next door. It was the third time since Coombes got there that morning that a couple had occupied the room.

Coombes abandoned his vigil and sat down on the edge of the bed. He shoved the sandwich aside; crumbs and shreds of meat fell onto the floor. He picked up the telephone and dialed the switchboard number for long distance.

"Palomino Lodge, good afternoon. Your number, please?" It was the woman who had checked him in. She had looked him up and down disdainfully. She had streaked hair and was related to the owner. She believed that anyone who checked into this motel deserved to be looked at with disdain—especially if he arrived by taxi and looked as if he had spent the night in a doorway.

"This is Mr. Vest in seventeen. Put through my calls to San Francisco again," he said gruffly. He was uneasy about using Vest's identity; he was no longer confident that switching aliases would protect him. He had been hesitant and awkward when he signed Vest's name in the motel register; he was unsure whether the woman had noticed.

"Your party is not at either of the numbers. Now, why don't you stop calling the desk every ten minutes? I've got plenty to do besides making calls for you, Mr. Vest." Her voice was hoarse and insolent; Coombes thought she had stressed the "Vest" a little too much. "While I've got you on the line, I'll tell you that the call you made to Detroit, Michigan, was four dollars and thirty-six cents. We collect immediately on calls over five dollars. With these calls to San Francisco you will owe more than five dollars. You'll have to come to the office now and pay for the Detroit, Michigan, call. So we can keep things straight."

Coombes slammed down the receiver. The rest of the sandwich tumbled onto the floor. His instinct was to charge, shirtless, into the motel office and demolish it—and the creaky-voiced woman, too. He sprang to his feet and stood a moment trembling with his hands on his fleshy hips. He took a series of deep breaths to compose himself; it was a trick he had learned in Burma. He calmed down. He put on a clean shirt and brushed his teeth and walked to the office.

The woman was seated with her back to the screen door. Coombes chewed at a fingernail until she got up and came to the desk. He marshaled all the courtesy he had and said he was unaware of the Palomino Lodge's pay-as-you-go telephone policy. Then he took a fifty-dollar bill from Vest's wallet and slapped it on the desk.

"I'll be making more toll calls," he said; his fury was returning but he managed to hold it in check. "This ought to cover them. If it doesn't, tell me when I check out. Not before. I'll be leaving in a couple of hours. I want a cab at six on the dot. Understand?"

The woman looked up; her eyes had been fixed on the fifty-dollar bill. "Yes," she said tentatively, and then added with a whimper, "The telephone rule, it's not my idea. You have to realize you get all kinds up here in Topanga Canyon. You can't be too careful."

Coombes did not hear her. He had turned and walked from the office, slamming the screen door behind him. The sunlight made him blink.

His rage turned out to have been for nothing. His calls to San Francisco were not completed. Shen Keng Min was not at the New Paradise Travel Agency or at his home north of Golden Gate Park. It was nearly five o'clock. Five hours past the time Coombes had *told* Shen he had to have a yes-or-no answer from Peking.

Coombes replaced the receiver. He stared stupidly at the remains of the sandwich. He could hear the couple in the next room; the walls were that flimsy; the man was asking the woman to tell him that he was a better lover than her husband; she said, oh, yes, oh, yes, there was no comparison. The talking ceased and the sounds of lovemaking resumed. This was the third time that Coombes knew of since they checked in.

Then the sounds began to torture him. They were sounds of exertion and tender eagerness; Coombes was personally familiar only with the former; the latter he could only listen to in thirsty loneliness. He realized that he was an old man who had never understood what lovemaking was about; he didn't know how to please both a woman and himself. No woman had ever told him he was a good lover. He rushed to the bathroom and turned on the shower full blast. He leaned against the lavatory, gnawing a cuticle. The din of the falling water obliterated the other sounds; it reminded him of a teak forest during the monsoon.

He tried to set his thoughts in order. Weariness made it difficult, and he was distracted by what was going on next door. He cursed Shen Keng Min. Shen had wrecked his time-table; he had planned to dump the whole operation on Special Ops five hours ago; Shen was his link to Chinese intelligence; Shen had *agreed* to provide the ingredient that was indispensable to the success of his pilot-fish operation—independent verification from a hostile source of Hamilton's intentions. He knew it was poor tradecraft to employ an irregular courier as a kind of cutout; Christ, he told himself, it was his only choice. *Why the hell hadn't Shen been there to take his call?* he wondered as frustration tore at his mind. He pounded the lavatory with the edge of his fist. He imagined the hysterical reaction in Special Ops when they heard, at this late hour, that he had relied on Shen Keng Min for independent verification and didn't get it.

Gradually his concentration returned. Coombes was not a self-pitying man. Nor was he speculative. He dealt in suppositions which his senses could confirm. He was slow to draw an inference, slower to generalize. He had collected intelligence; he did not pretend to evaluate it.

As the water beat on the shower-stall floor he totaled up in his mind the information he had assembled since the previous afternoon; he tapped one forefinger against the other as the items occurred to him. He had a letter written by the president of the United States stating that he, Joseph Hamilton, was thinking of defecting to Red China (or words to that effect); he had microfilm of Hamilton's other letter saying he *would* defect. He had gotten the first letter, which was addressed to Justice Roundtree, from Vest, a hired gun and strong-arm man who operated in the shadowland between government and the international corporate world; he had gotten a copy of the second letter (and killed Vest while he was doing it; of course, he hadn't known it was Vest when he fired the Colt Cobra in the dusky light of Jacques Novic's gaudy mansion); he had recruited Forbes and given him the

182

pathogenic accelerators—which he had gotten from Vest; Forbes was in place to "terminate" Hamilton if it came to that.

What else had he found out? Novic was flying to China. The reply letter was in Novic's wall safe. Melville had seen the original letter; Roundtree had seen it; Vest had seen it, but he no longer mattered; Forbes had seen it. The original letter. It continued to trouble him. He was goddamn certain that something about it had changed between the time Vest had given it to him and when he had tucked it into his safe in the Basement.

Where did knowing all this leave him? With a handful of loose ends and nothing to tie them to, he thought. He had known when he started that he was launching a high-risk operation, but he did not believe it was possible that so much could have gone wrong.

What the hell, then, had gone right? he asked himself. The microfilm and Forbes. Those were his successes. Forbes was following instructions, Coombes had confirmed that. Forbes had telephoned the headquarters of the labor union in Detroit which Coombes had set up as the "betting blind" for the stop-or-go racetrack signal. The union often provided foreign cover for Basement operations.

Coombes looked at his watch. It was almost nine o'clock at night in Georgia. He walked back to the telephone. He left the water running even though the sounds beyond the walls had stopped. He told the woman at the desk to dial the Detroit number. A female voice answered with the last four digits of the number. It was the same flat voice that Forbes had spoken to three hours earlier.

"This is the typewriter representative," said Coombes. "It's impossible for us to decide anything today."

"It can't be done today. I understand."

"We'll try again tomorrow. I'll check with you to see if the other party is still showing interest. Same time. And then I'll let you know if there's a decision."

"Very good. You'll check tomorrow to see if the other party is interested and later on a decision. Thank you for calling. Good-bye."

Had the woman at the front desk eavesdropped, she would have been unable to tell that Coombes was speaking in a prearranged code. The elliptical conversation meant that Coombes was still not ready to give Forbes the green light to use the amber capsules. Forbes would find it out himself later tonight when he was told that his horse had not broken in the gate in the third race at Saratoga.

Coombes hung up and put on his tie and rumpled jacket. He guessed his taxi was waiting. He rubbed a spot in the steam on the bathroom mirror and looked at himself; his goatee and mustache needed trimming; the whiskers were thickening over the rest of his face.

There was only one thing to do, he concluded as he fastened the lid on his valise. Fly back to Washington and state his case in person to Special Ops. The telephone was out. Things had grown too involuted to convey them persuasively over the telephone. Particularly since he had taken the "cowboy" approach. Besides, the telephone was insecure.

He picked up the valise and walked out. He didn't bother to turn off the shower.

The inertia of early night had descended on Washington. A steady light rain had fallen until a short time ago. It left the atmosphere steamy. The streets and sidewalks seemed to be covered with mold.

Ordinarily at this hour Twelfth Street was deserted. The revolving doors at the side entrance of the Department of Agriculture building would have been locked for several hours. Tonight they were unlocked. A man with his hat tipped low on his forehead stood a few feet behind them in the dark. He held a walkie-talkie. He was acting as a scout and could not be seen from outside.

From the corner of Independence Avenue a half-dozen cars were parked at various distances. At least two men sat in each of them. They wore somber, watchful expressions.

Inside the building, down a flight of stairs and behind a door marked "Outlook and Situation Board Export Analysis," the mood was resentment and bewildered anxiety.

"Goddamn it, he's Basement. That means he's my man. I'll take care of him." This was Sprague, the deputy director for Clandestine Services. He was seated in the section chief's chair; his fists were on the desk; his chin was thrust forward.

Across the room, the Basement chief himself, McElroy, leaned uncomfortably against the wall. He looked as if his collar were too tight. He occasionally fingered his curly hair.

"Of course he's your man. No one has questioned that. But he's my problem." This was Rice, the deputy director for Counter Intelligence. He was seated on the edge of a sofa; his hands were on his knees. "This *entire* shop is my problem," he added. He glared at McElroy. McElroy glared back at him for a moment and then looked away.

"I didn't come down here to get a consensus of what ought to be done," Rice continued; his tone was reproachful arrogance. "It's as clear as the way to church what *has* to be done. And, mind you, I'm making every allowance for the vulnerability of our, ah, data storage capability."

The talk had been going on this way for some time. Sprague was on the defensive. The Basement, a section in his department, was under attack; he took it as an attack on his own ability. McElroy, too, had to be defended; he personally had spotted McElroy as a comer and selected him as section chief; a bad word against McElroy was a bad word against his judgment of men. The fact that Counter Intelligence was fidgety about a compromise of national security counted for very little with him at the moment.

Rice, on the other hand, was posing in the role of impartial investigator. That's how Counter Intelligence did its job, he said repeatedly. The truth was, he intended to make sure the chips fell where they would make him look good and anyone else who got hit look less than competent.

Thus these professional conspirators were arrayed against each other.

"I don't think it's fair to single us out," said McElroy; he tried to sound indignant. "It's common practice. I can name off the top of my head—"

"This is an internal matter," broke in Sprague. His bald head had reddened. He regarded McElroy as a good intelligence officer but a tenderfoot at interdepartmental warfare. He lowered his voice once he had the floor. "Don't you think it's good policy for each department to wash its own dirty linen? That's how you did things when you ran the Basement, isn't it?"

Sprague and Rice had both served as Basement chief earlier in their careers. They were each at least twenty-five years older than McElroy.

"Dirty linen isn't the issue. There's no point to insisting that it is," replied Rice. He had leaned back. He was examining his key chain; the pendant was a five-franc piece minted in 1844; "heads" was a Caesarized profile of Louis Philippe. "The issue is the unauthorized retrieval of top-security data by a member of this section who hasn't been heard from since yesterday afternoon."

The door opened. A man stuck his head in the office. He was a member of Rice's "sweep team." "It's the safe," the man said. "The combination's no good. The technician says the tumblers have been monkeyed with. He thinks he can work past them but it will take a while. You want him to blow it?"

"No. Explosives cause too much confusion," said Rice. "Tell him to take his time. An explosion might damage something."

The man withdrew his head and closed the door.

"He's been something of a misfit, I gather," Rice continued.

"You mean—" said McElroy, jerking a thumb toward the door.

"I mean Coombes," Rice said emphatically.

Sprague jumped to his feet. He shoved his hands onto his hips and bent forward a degree or two at the waist. "You're out of line," he said; his teeth were clenched. "Evaluations of officers in this section are none of your concern. And loose talk about one of *my* men being a misfit doesn't go. All right?" He sat down and plunked his fists back on the desk. "Keep this in mind about Coombes. He's been aboard since before the Creation. Like us."

"For the love of God," said Rice. He sighed and made an elaborate gesture of putting his key chain back in his pocket. "He's been an embarrassment for years. He should have been fired the minute he got recalled from Iran. He's never had the finesse for intelligence work. We wouldn't let him go back to Indochina, either, remember?"

"I'm not aware *we* had any say about it," Sprague said sarcastically. "You were in Logistics at the time, if my memory is correct. Or whatever it was called back then. I was in Johannesburg."

"The point is," Rice persisted—he was unimpressed by the suggestion that he was presuming too much influence—"he doesn't have any real usefulness anymore. I don't know why we've let him stay on. We wouldn't have, if it had been up to me. I take it McElroy feels the same way."

"I don't know what you mean," said McElroy. He looked as if he had been addressed in a foreign language.

"Don't you?" said Rice. He raised an eyebrow. "The fitness

reports on Coombes since you took over this section read like the first draft of *The Hunchback of Notre Dame*. You did write them, didn't you? They have your signature. And"—he looked at Sprague—"*your* initials. They're fascinating stuff, by the way. And a prima facie case, at least, for dismissal for cause."

McElroy glanced at Sprague and then at the floor. Sprague tried not to look like a man who was bluffing with a pair of deuces.

"There are some things about Coombes you ought to be interested in," Rice went on; he crossed his legs. "They aren't noted in the fitness reports, so I assume you aren't aware of them. For one thing, all his documentation has been truncated. I mean, there are gaps in our own records, Grand Canyon–sized gaps. Do you know there is no fingerprint available on him? Not a single one in town. That's goddamn strange in this day and age, don't you think? There's no record of his assignment to this section. It's as if he simply materialized here about twenty years ago. In case you're interested, he's still listed as a salesman for that mutual fund Headlight ran as a cover in France. And Coombes never set foot in France. He's broke, too, did you know that? His current bank account shows less than two hundred dollars, and he has loans out all over this part of the country, more than half of them overdue. I don't suppose these details surprise you, do they, McElroy?"

McElroy was about to reply, but Sprague intruded. "This is the most irregular goddamn Counter Intelligence operation I've ever seen. And I've seen some odd ones. As I understand it, this rumpus started when some panicky bastard at NSA went crazy over a misuse of computer technique. You know as well as I do that isn't a security problem. It's administrative. I'd have thought you were too busy to take an interest in administrative procedure. The inspector general may feel the same way. We'll discuss that later if it's necessary. In any event, you're mixing apples and oranges." Sprague took out his handkerchief and patted perspiration from his brow and head. "Mixing them, I might add, by going over the head of the man's division superior. Since when does Counter Intelligence run a check against an officer without first notifying his deputy director? Doesn't fundamental courtesy count with you people anymore? I'm surprised, actually, that untidy clerical habits upset you. Personal record-keeping in this organization is notoriously behind. It has been for years. Good Lord, if you looked in my 201 file you might find I'm on the staff of the National Gallery. I was once, you know. If you went to my bank, you'd wonder how I'm getting by. I wonder myself. As far as this computer thing is concerned, that's your problem, not mine. It's your machine—what do you call it now? BEEHIVE, I believe—and it's up to you to keep it secure. It's not my fault that someone, *anyone* it seems, can . . . what's the word?"

"Donald Duck," said McElroy.

"It isn't my fault that your computer has no protection against this Donald Duck." Sprague was now relaxed; his hands were no longer balled into fists. "If you're looking for security violations, I suggest you have a chat with the electronic wizard who persuaded you that you needed a computer with a greater conversion capability. Take *him* up to the mountains and roast *him* over a slow fire."

"How do you know about conversion capability?" Rice asked sharply. "That's classified on a strict need-to-know basis. No one's supposed to know that about BEEHIVE."

"You didn't think you were the only one who knows how to ask questions, did you?" said Sprague; his nose was upturned, as if he had detected a fetid odor. "I was shocked, frankly, at the strange things that find their way into your precious data store. Which raises this question. Why the hell is a habit-medical profile of the president in BEEHIVE? I didn't know we were tossing our commander in chief in with C.I.'s job lot of terrorists and scandal-mongers, even for filing purposes. Since the thing was pinched from the Russians, it seems to me it ought to have a place of its own. Of course, it doesn't have any real value, does it? Just stuff culled from the newspapers. Perhaps we got it during an expensive operation that flopped; somebody felt Finance breathing down his neck and said, 'Hey, I've got a hot item,' and managed to hide it in BEEHIVE. We all know it's still done. We haven't overcome our weakness for self-justification. That's how it got into BEEHIVE, isn't it?"

Sprague leaned back and clasped his hands behind his head in triumph. McElroy, who had been slumping against the wall, straightened up.

Rice uncrossed his legs and placed his hands on his knees again; he was known to be hard to buffalo. "Computer vulnerability, as I said, is a separate matter. And I don't need *you* to remind me that it's serious. It will be dealt with, I assure you. At the moment what we're dealing with—what we're confounded by—is an intelligence officer of questionable reliability who has got hold of top-secret information, who—"

"*Questionable reliability?*" Sprague put in heatedly. His fists were clenched again.

Rice was unruffled by the interruption. "An officer of questionable reliability," he continued, "who has disappeared with top-secret information at a very sensitive time."

"What's so sensitive about it?"

"My God, man, the president is leaving for Red China the day after tomorrow."

"So?"

Rice blew a long breath. "Look at it this way. A highly classified document is floating around. The man last seen with it is in desperate need of money. The same man has been in-

190

communicado for twenty-four hours. In less than forty-eight hours the president flies off to a country whose intelligence service would dearly love to get the document. Do I have to draw you a picture?"

Sprague slammed his fists on the desk; his cheeks were puffed. "How long has Counter Intelligence been on this diet of wild goose?" He stood up abruptly and rolled his eyes toward the ceiling. Then he fixed his gaze on Rice. "This highly classified document, as you call it, isn't worth a shit and you know it. *Nobody* would pay for it." He inclined his head to the side. "The Chinese may be hard pressed, but it's unthinkable that they would lay out good cash for this rubbish."

At that moment the door opened again. A tall, muscular man walked in. He had iron-gray hair and was dressed for tennis. It was Headlight, the deputy director for Foreign Intelligence.

Sprague and Rice looked at him with astonishment; they were his equals in the hierarchy; they dated their service from the same year; but Headlight had moved over from the "dark" side some years ago. McElroy seemed puzzled; he knew Headlight by reputation only.

Finally Rice asked, "What the hell are you doing here?"

"Kibitzing on an official basis, more or less," replied Headlight; he spoke with a patrician drawl. His white knit shirt, shorts, and Adidas did not seem out of place. He had been the Basement's first chief.

He smiled and extended his hand to McElroy. "I don't think we've met," he said congenially. "I'm Headlight." He might have introduced himself as "Jim" or "Mike"; the air of anonymity he had nurtured in his younger days clung to him; it was mostly because his *nom de guerre* had become habitual among his colleagues.

"Rick McElroy. I'm the section chief."

"Rick, excuse my poor manners"—Headlight continued to smile—"but I have to ask you to leave us learned elders alone for a while. I may have to introduce some things that aren't the business of a section chief."

McElroy looked to Sprague for guidance. Sprague nodded. McElroy left.

Professionally, Sprague resented Headlight's presence; tactically, he welcomed it; Headlight might prove advantageous in his battle against Rice. A man takes help where he finds it when Counter Intelligence is on his tail.

"This is a Counter Intelligence operation," Rice said pointedly. "I can't see any reason for you to be here."

"The director asked me to come down," said Headlight; he took up the position against the wall that McElroy had vacated. "As a consulting partner, so to speak. He thought I could help. Coombes and I go back a long way together. I've known him since Burma."

"Perhaps you know where he is?"

"No. That's not my line of work anymore."

"Your visit here. Does it have memorandum status?" Rice looked at him out of the corner of his eye; he had his Louis Philippe key chain out again.

"I suppose, in a limited way. I'll simply note that I came here to cooperate and include generally the facts you stick on my information."

"It's on the record, then?" Rice asked.

"Yes."

Sprague loosened his tie. "Have you seen the summary?"

"Of course."

Everyone was silent a moment and then Rice spoke, in his official voice. "Based on the events of the past twenty-four hours, I propose to bring Coombes in. If that's still possible. And recommend Class A disciplinary proceedings." Sprague tried to interrupt; Rice raised his hand and continued. "This will be the substance of the charges: he knowingly employed an unauthorized procedure to retrieve a top-secret document from BEEHIVE; and he has been absent without leave from his post. I'm prepared to go further if I have to."

Headlight was no longer leaning against the wall. He was standing with his legs apart. His arms were folded across his chest. "This is inconsistent with your fitness-report digest. Coombes isn't even qualified on computer functions."

"He knew enough to penetrate BEEHIVE."

"Apparently anyone can."

"The point is, Coombes did it."

"Penetrate it? He may have stumbled into it."

Rice tossed his key chain into the air and snatched it with a grasping motion. "We know he did it this time," he snapped. "We don't know whether he's done it before. It doesn't matter what the document is really worth. The instrumental fact is, it was taken by an officer who, by the written testimony of his section chief, is unreliable. It would be helpful," he added bitterly, "if I got some support from Clandestine Services— and Foreign Intelligence, since you're here—in trying to establish a pattern. I'm not trying to hang the man. I'm trying to do a job, and I've got at least two unwarranted obstructions in my way."

"Let Headlight in on your little theory; why don't you?" Sprague said acidly. "What you think Coombes has done with this exceptional document."

Rice changed directions. "You mentioned you had some private wisdom for us. Something unfit for the section chief's immature ears."

Headlight sat down on the edge of the desk. He stroked his jaw. "We've had a priority-interest signal from Peking," he said.

"A *what?*" Rice's eyes narrowed.

"It doesn't have any meaning, on the face of it. It didn't

come from one of our established sources." Headlight knitted his eyebrows. "It arrived through a courier. A low-grade courier, I should say; we haven't used him on high-priority stuff in years. The problem is, the signal appears to be in open code. We think it's a reply. Apparently, only the sender of the original message can understand it."

"This courier," Rice said, "did you query him?"

Headlight leaned back and flattened his palms behind him on the desk. His tanned legs dangled; one thigh was marked with an S-shaped scar; it was an old shrapnel wound. "We've been trying to trace him since the signal arrived. He seems to have gone to ground. Maybe you can make something out of it. It says, *'Special cricket unexpected at noodle factory. Wrong season for crickets.'* "

Sprague shook his head.

"That's all there is to it?" Rice asked.

"That's it. It may be an old code. Something left over from years ago. If it is, we'll track it down sooner or later. The smart money says it's a one-shot open code."

Rice looked at his key chain; he twirled the Louis Philippe coin pendant between his fingers. "I'll tell you what it suggests to me," he said. "I think Coombes is trying to set himself up in the used-rug business."

"You think he's trying to make a sale?" asked Headlight. His eyes shone with disbelief.

"Precisely," said Rice.

Sprague was on his feet. He strode from behind the desk. "I resent the hell out of this," he said; his voice was strained. "I resent your absurd conclusion and I resent the methods you used to reach it." He paced the floor between Rice and Headlight. Suddenly he halted and faced Rice; his nostrils were flared in anger. "This isn't an investigation. It's a goddamn lynching. A cover-up lynching. It's clear what you came down here for. You came down here for one purpose. To hang somebody—somebody outside Counter Intelligence—for your half-assed computer security.

"And you"—he swung around to Headlight, whose assistance he now seriously doubted—"you walk blithely in and drop this tidbit about crickets and noodle factories. 'Oh, we can't tell what it means,' " he mocked. "Hell no, you can't. But you know goddamn well it's like waving a bloody shirt when Counter Intelligence is on a rampage. A blind rampage, at that." Headlight said nothing. Sprague turned back to Rice.

"You figured old Coombes for a soft day's work, didn't you? The people he works for want him thrown to the wolves—you believe that, don't you, from reading the fitness reports? If a man has poor fitness reports, his superiors are happy to get rid of him, no matter how it's done—that's what you thought, isn't it? Then you throw out this wild assumption that he's selling things to the other side. I suppose you expect us to overlook the fact that this blue-ribbon document that you've built your case on is pure junk."

Sprague walked back behind the desk. He slumped into his chair. He glared pugnaciously at Rice.

"It's an assumption I'm obliged to make," Rice said simply. "He needs the money."

Headlight returned to his spot against the wall. His face was taut. "Have you run across many instances of people selling stuff this way?" he asked; he touched the scar on his thigh. "I mean, would a man try to sell something he knew was going to be missed?"

"If he was inexperienced, yes," replied Rice. "And if he had gotten away with it before."

"Coombes is hardly inexperienced, is he? Clumsy, but not inexperienced."

"His record is nothing to win Officer of the Year with."

"If you were in Coombes's place, would you go about it this way?"

"There are any number of ways. This is an obvious way."

"Would you do it this way?"

"No."

"Well?"

"Look," said Rice; the Louis Philippe coin became a blur as he twirled it. "Try to keep my operation in perspective. And context. Everything indicates that Coombes should be suspect. To my mind he is suspect. At the moment that's what counts. I'm doing what I'm paid to do. For the sake of discussion I'll concede that the document, the habit-medical profile on Hamilton, is overrated."

"It's worthless," interjected Sprague. "Why don't you say so?"

"Just because it's overrated doesn't mean it isn't attractive," Rice continued unperturbed, "or worth a great deal. Intrinsically its value may be small. Like the paper a stock certificate is printed on. But if an overrated document is offered for sale by a covert American intelligence officer, then *all* the values are changed."

"Covert?" It was Sprague again. "How can you say the Basement is covert? It isn't even operational."

"Of course it's covert," Rice replied strongly. "No one knows it's here. That's the accepted definition of covert. The Chinese don't know it isn't operational—I say the Chinese presumptively; the Soviets wouldn't be in the market for the thing because it came from them in the first place, unless they wanted to backtrack to see how we got it. The French and the British wouldn't need it; the Israelis wouldn't want it. But the Chinese . . . When a service as restricted as the Chinese makes a buy from an American, you can be goddamn sure they have more in mind than the information; they're looking to compromise the officer. We've done the same thing."

"With damned little success," said Headlight.

"We became selective because we could afford to," Rice

shot back. "We don't jump up and whistle anymore when a foreign officer comes to us with something. We look at his information first; if it's hot, we get friendly; if it's no good, we offer him cab fare home and show him the door. The old method was to pay equal attention to where the stuff came from, with a view to getting something of value eventually.

"If a Russian comes to us and says the chairman of the Communist party is shacking up with the *première danseuse* of the Bolshoi Ballet, we say how interesting. But if the same Russian shows up with a bundle of passionate billets-doux from the party chairman to the ballerina and some signed champagne tabs, we talk terms. Time was, we would automatically suppose this Russian was practically living in the party chairman's armpit and start a recruiting operation. We don't do it much anymore, but the technique is valid. It fits what we know about the progression of the Chinese system."

"You're just guessing," said Sprague vehemently. "You can't name an example of a significant Chinese penetration. They don't go in for it. They spend most of their time reading technical journals and trying to persuade Chinese scientific types to return to the homeland."

"They've reached the point where they need an interior source," Rice said flatly. "For authentication, if nothing else. They've gone as far as they can by scouring nonclassified sources. They realize they aren't moving fast enough. In short, they need an agent. The logical next step is recruitment for a penetration. Their style is passive: seize an apple that falls in their lap and make the most of it. Coombes is a classic apple."

The door opened again. The man from Rice's "sweep" team looked in. "We've got the safe open," he said. "The problem was the slides and pins in the lock. They've been altered. The technician can explain it, if you're interested. He says it looks like a professional job."

Headlight, Sprague, and Rice glanced at each other. They

said nothing. They followed the sweep team man down the passageway to Coombes's cubicle. Several other Counter Intelligence men were inside. The technician was replacing a stethoscope in a small case; it was his principal tool. The safe was behind the desk. It was covered with fingerprint powder. The door gaped open.

They took turns getting on their knees and peering into the safe. They each examined the contents and put them back. There was an envelope containing three passports and an assortment of credit cards and driver's licenses; they were the separate identities that Coombes used on the Basement's "across-the-street" operations. There was an electric razor and an old newspaper. That was all.

Rice got to his feet. He ordered one of his men to clean out the safe and make a list of the things in it. "I'll sign for them. We're taking them with us," he said to Sprague; he looked around. "Where's McElroy?"

"Here." McElroy was at the door.

"Who was the duty officer last night?" Rice asked.

"We don't post a duty officer in the summer," McElroy replied.

"No duty officer?"

"No."

"Why the hell not?"

"We don't post one in the summer."

Rice looked hard at Sprague; he did not try to hide his contempt. Sprague's expression was neutral. Rice nodded; he wished to reconvene the closed meeting of the deputy directors. They walked back up the passageway in silence.

"Need I say more?" Rice asked over his shoulder as he closed the door to McElroy's office.

Sprague tried to object again, but Headlight spoke first. "The safe was tampered with. That's obvious. What's also obvious is that it was done with a skill Coombes doesn't have. At this point it's another piece in a puzzle. I don't necessarily agree that Coombes is the man who can fit the pieces together."

"I'd like to know who else can," said Rice.

Headlight again leaned against the wall. "Let me tell you about Coombes," he said; his drawl was mellower. "He was with me in Burma. He's as tough as they come. There's a widely held view in this organization that he's *too* tough, too slapdash, that we're too sophisticated for a man who's all lion and no fox. But we forget a built-in contradiction—this section itself. The Basement exists solely for ad hoc offensive operations. Frankly, I can't think of anyone I'd rather have backing me up during the terminal phase of a destabilizing operation."

"The man's courage isn't an issue," said Rice.

"Coombes is what the British call a mud-picker," Headlight continued. "A demon in combat and a disgrace to the regiment on parade. It says a lot about the man, but basically it means his imagination dries up when the pressure is off; his mind goes into low gear when he's behind a desk. No one argues that Coombes is a plodder in the office. His fitness reports reflect it. Do you see what I'm getting at?"

"That Coombes is essentially a goon?"

"In a sense, yes. More accurately, I'm saying that Coombes doesn't have the imagination to go into the used-rug business."

"But the indications—"

"The indications are that Coombes has taken something from BEEHIVE and that he's missing. And that his safe was diddled. The implications are more extensive. And more urgent, in view of Hamilton's trip. I agree that Counter Intelligence has to act. The way you've theorized it, I suppose you have to act in a hurry. But keep my 'cricket' signal in mind—we don't know why we got it. If Counter Intelligence assumes it's connected to Coombes, then I—Foreign Intelligence, that is—must assume it isn't. For the sake of balance.

"God forbid that either of us should drive the other up a blind alley. I mean, we don't want to create a situation where we might be denying ourselves a full appreciation of some very ripe opportunities. I wouldn't want to do anything to hamper you. Especially since you suspect a used-rug dealer at work. On the other hand, I don't want a Counter Intelligence operation that is grounded in conjecture to jeopardize a chance for us to do some business in Peking."

"*Grounded in conjecture?*" Rice said shrilly.

"Reasonable conjecture, but that's what it adds up to," said Headlight. Sprague smiled slightly. "As I see it," Headlight went on, "we have to reach a mutual concession. Otherwise, we'll stifle ourselves by fouling the other's lines. Let's try this out. You put together a low-key operation for bringing Coombes in. Nothing elaborate. Just a simple stakeout of his house. No charges in advance. No sweat session after you've got him. That way, you'll have your man, and I'll have room to maneuver on this 'cricket' thing. How does that sound?"

"If I say I don't like it," said Rice, "will you tell the director that I torpedoed a potential China breakthrough?"

"That's about the size of it."

Rice knew he had been had. He did not look at Sprague. Sprague had the good grace to keep his face straight.

"Let's get out of here," said Headlight. "I, for one, expect a busy night." He ushered them from the office. "It's damned odd about that safe," he said as he closed the door.

For the second straight torrid night the Georgia sky was moonless. Forbes turned off the two-lane highway and onto a scrawny dirt road overhung with Spanish moss. He eased the car to a halt and switched off the lights to maintain the air conditioning. The road was popular among local teen-agers as a lovers' lane; several other cars, and one or two pickup trucks, were parked in the distance, all with their windows rolled up and steamy; it was a time-honored practice among the passionate young of the region. It was the only way they could take off their clothes and not be eaten alive by the teeming mosquitoes. Forbes thought it was the perfect spot under the circumstances to plant a story.

He lit a cigarette and settled back to wait. He imagined that the panic his arrival had caused among the occupants of the other vehicles was beginning to wane; he had not turned out to be a deputy sheriff intent on shaming them—or worse—with a big flashlight as they struggled desperately to disengage and slip back into their jeans and tank tops.

The word from the bookie a half hour earlier had exhilarated him: Shock Absorber had not broken in the gate in the third race at Saratoga (she had not finished in the money, either, but that mattered not at all to Forbes). It meant he still had time to act independently, to devise a ploy that would slip the collar of strangling intrigue he had felt tightening around him since he read of Frank Parisi's grisly death—and that would save him from having to murder again; it meant taking a risk for his own sake, but it definitely was not a death wish. He knew he was improvising from experience, not instinct. This time, he was out to preserve life, not forfeit it, even by passive consent.

Presently another car pulled up behind. The headlights went dark. Through the rearview mirror Forbes could make out the form of a tall, overweight man getting out and cautiously making his way forward. The man peered closely through the window, made sure it was Forbes, and opened the door and got in.

"Sorry to have to set up the meeting like this, Mark," said

Forbes once the car was dark again, "but I couldn't afford to be seen talking to you at the compound. You understand, don't you?"

"Sure, sure," replied Mark Beard. Mark Beard was a middle-aged syndicated columnist and one of the most notoriously unreliable members of the Washington press corps; he was also one of the Hamilton administration's most hostile and widely read critics.

Forbes had arranged to meet Mark Beard at this remote spot because he knew it would appeal irresistibly to Beard's bent for inside information. Mark Beard had a reputation as a fast-moving, deep-digging opponent of corruption in government; he kept his career afloat by grabbing the wildest rumor or fuzziest fragment of gossip and embellishing it with a speck or two of truth. Politicians and bureaucrats feared him—and used him. Those of any prominence could tell him anything—invented or true, harmful or beneficial, about anyone or anything—and virtually depend on seeing it in print. One key to planting a story with Mark Beard was to make certain he thought he was getting it exclusively. The other was to make certain the story was tainted with scandal. Mark Beard had written several hysterically inaccurate columns that helped seed the cloud under which Forbes left Washington.

Beard shifted uncomfortably in his seat. Had the light been sufficient, Forbes could have seen the nervousness in his almost colorless gray eyes. Forbes sensed his anxiety and sought to put him at ease.

"Look, Mark," he said amiably, "before we start I want you to know that the things that happened before, the things you wrote about me, I want you to know I never took them personally. I know you were doing your job—and I think you did it well, by the way." This kind of lying came easily to Forbes; his object was to disarm Mark Beard with flattery for the purpose of manipulating him. "Ready?"

"Sure, sure," replied Beard, his ego massaged by compliments and forgiveness. "What's this all about, Thack?"

Forbes heaved a deep sigh, partly genuine and partly for effect. "You know how close I am to Joe, don't you?"

"Sure, sure." There was an acute note of surprise in Beard's answer. He had thought—because he believed his own columns—that Forbes had been run out of Washington for good. It had never occurred to him to question the presence of a disgraced man at the Southern White House. To Mark Beard's way of thinking Forbes was dead politically, because he, Mark Beard, had said so. Hearing that Lazarus was back in business at the old stand disconcerted him.

"He calls me for advice three or four times a week," Forbes went on, "and, as I'm sure you know, I eat dinner with him at the White House every month or so." He paused to let this register on Beard and then continued, "I know you don't like Joe Hamilton and the way he's running the country—" he lowered his voice an octave for suspense—"but that's neither here nor there. What I got you out here to tell you is that Joe Hamilton—President Joe Hamilton—is about to make the biggest mistake you or the world ever dreamed of."

Beard was unable to utter, "Sure, sure." He had never been in a position to hear anything like this before. He was accustomed to complaints from disgruntled government employees about misuse of taxpayers' funds or smutty stories told by one politician on another. He had never heard this kind of talk from a member of a sitting president's inner circle. "May I take some notes?" he asked, almost pathetically; Mark Beard was well known for never taking notes.

"No notes," Forbes said crisply. "That was a ground rule. We do this the way I told you on the phone or it's no dice. I told you I don't want my fingerprints on this story. Okay?"

"Sure, sure." Mark Beard was breathing heavily.

"Now listen closely," Forbes commanded, "and don't interrupt me. You can ask questions later. Like I told you, I may or may not agree to answer them." Again Forbes paused to let the suspense expand in the darkened car; he switched off the engine and the air conditioner went silent; up the road, one of the pickup trucks, its occupants' lust either spent or thwarted, drove away. "Joe has let it be known—only to me, as far as I've been able to check—that he intends to take what he calls a vacation when he gets to China. That means staying beyond the scheduled time frame. He says it will do a lot to improve our relations with the Chinese and blah-blah." He lapsed into silence again for a beat or two and then slowly turned and faced Mark Beard. "What this *really* means—and I have this from as good a source as you'll ever come across—is that this vacation talk is a smokescreen. What Joe Hamilton intends to do when he gets to China is—*defect.*"

Mark Beard gasped. "Where did you—"

"Hold it until I'm finished, Mark," Forbes said evenly. "Remember our ground rules. . . . Now, where was I?"

Mark Beard gulped and said weakly, "About Hamilton defecting."

"Oh, yes. Well. I can't give you the background because the story could be traced to me. But I can tell you this: I've seen a document, a classified document, that substantiates what I've told you. Now, I don't have to paint you a picture of the mess this would make, do I?"

"No," Beard replied in a near whisper.

"Any questions?"

Beard swallowed again and then said hesitantly, "Ah, when did you see this document?"

"In the last couple of weeks."

"Who showed it to you?"

"I can't tell you that."

"How did you get a look at it?"

"I can't tell you that, either."

"Where did you see it?" Beard's voice was regaining some of its customary gruffness.

"Uh-uh, Mark," Forbes snapped. He knew how to plant a story; the success depended on the strip-tease effect. He knew he had the columnist in the position of a customer at a carnival hootchy-kootchy; Mark Beard was dying to see more and could only hope guiltily that his cries of "Take it all off!" would be heeded. Like any accomplished stripper, Forbes knew in advance that removal of G-string and pasties was out of the question.

"But, Thack," Beard pleaded, "I have to know at least where you saw it."

"No way," said Forbes sharply. "Now, listen. I've given you something. I haven't asked for anything in return. Just look at what I've given you. And you've got it alone. You've got the big one, Mark, *all by yourself.* Think about it. I've got no axe to grind. I'm trying to keep the country's throat from getting cut." He switched on the engine, indicating the interview was over, and added, "I hope you're going to try and do the same thing."

"Sure, sure," said Mark Beard as he opened the door and got out.

Forbes waited until Beard had maneuvered his rented car around in the dirt road and driven out of sight. He then pulled away in the same fashion. A few cars of young lovers remained. In less than a half hour he was back at the Southern White House and walking across the presidential compound.

He felt confident, on the edge of audacity. He had contrived his course of action on the expectation that if only half the country believed Mark Beard's story—Forbes took it for granted that no responsible reader would believe it—Hamilton would have no recourse but to cancel the trip. Forbes had worked his craft at the top of his form.

Hamilton will go wild with anger and embarrassment—and the country will go into the frenzy Melville had predicted— over Mark Beard's "exclusive," Forbes thought, but I won't have to use those goddamn capsules. Hamilton's dreams of the treaty will dissolve, he said to himself, but I have fore-stalled having to commit murder. He knew his days as Hamil-ton's friend and confidant were numbered because of this breach of trust; but his own were numbered unless he stopped Hamilton. And he knew he had stopped him. He just knew it.

"Thank God for Mark Beard," he said aloud in the darkness as he fairly bounded up the steps of Elkhart House. The light was shining in Nell Leatherbee's second-floor study.

DAY THREE

8 The Message

Peking. The morning of the following day; still last night in the United States. Typically arid July weather on the North China Plain; the outlines of buildings blurred by opaque haze. Loudspeakers blaring martial music; knots of people exercising at *tai chi* in streets and squares; others on bicycles and packed in buses on their way to work, ideological training, or revolutionary dramas.

Colonel Mee shoved his bicycle into a rack near the entrance of the Great Hall of the People. He adjusted his cloth cap. He was director of the Office of Social Affairs. He coordinated the functions of the Military Section of the New China News Agency and the 8341 Regiment, the chairman's personal military unit. This made him in effect the chief of domestic and foreign intelligence for the People's Republic of China. He did not use the title. He was also a respected but anonymous poet.

He was shown immediately into the deputy premier's private office. Some recently excavated pottery figurines from the Yuan Dynasty were on display near the door. Colonel

Mee briefed the deputy premier every morning; the deputy premier in turn briefed Chairman Tien.

The deputy premier greeted Colonel Mee politely. Both men wore small, rectangular, red-and-white emblems reading "Serve the People" over the right breast pocket of their deep gray tunics. Both had endured the Long March, borne victorious arms against the Nationalists, and suffered during the Great Leap Forward. They had outfoxed the Japanese, fought the Americans in Korea, and weathered the Cultural Revolution. They had served Mao Tse-tung and advanced in the feud for supremacy after his death. For the time being they were devoted to Chairman Tien.

"Tea?" asked the deputy premier.

"Yes," said Colonel Mee. He did not remove his cloth cap. He took a seat in one of a pair of chairs upholstered in white linen. A small table sat between them. A pack of French cigarettes lay on top. He took one and lit it with a disposable lighter from West Germany.

"The struggle sessions have been instituted at the university," Colonel Mee began; he knew what was expected of him. "They will continue for the course of Hamilton's visit. As I expected, the sessions are keeping the more vocal schismatics out of public view. Passenger railway service to and from the city will be suspended twenty-four hours before the Americans arrive."

"What about reeducation?" The deputy premier poured from a porcelain service at a sideboard. He placed the cups on the table between the chairs and sat down next to Colonel Mee.

"Most productive," replied Colonel Mee; he sipped from his cup and puffed his cigarette. "At the moment the maximum sentence for 'reeducation through manual labor' is six months. This has been reserved for hard-case 'helicopters.' "

"Helicopters" was Colonel Mee's pet term for troublemakers.

"I have tried to isolate the potentially dangerous ones," he went on, "those with tendencies to act overtly. This morning, for instance, three men were executed at the garrison barracks for defacing one of the chairman's wall posters. There was another execution, incidentally, a woman. She was accused of prostitution. She was one of the instigators of the strike at the tractor factory."

"Unattributed announcements?" The deputy premier sat with his slender hands on the arms of his chair. "Are those ready?"

"A limited number of posters will be displayed that hint of recent nuclear tests at Lop Nor. The Americans have been more forthright during past negotiations when they have heard of nuclear tests. The posters will be displayed near the Peking Hotel—the visiting correspondents will be lodged there—and near the diplomatic quarter. Posters indicating impending earthquakes in Liaoning Province will be more widely displayed. We want to verify the efficiency of our antipenetration patrols. The Americans succeeded in parachuting some agents near Shenyang during the confusion that attended the earthquakes several years ago."

"Surveillance?"

"The usual," said Colonel Mee casually. "The tour guides will be as alert as ever. No American will see anything or talk to anyone he isn't supposed to. If the tour guides encounter trouble, my 'pumpkin' squads will be out in force to intervene."

The deputy premier picked up the teacups and returned to the sideboard. "The chairman asks whether you have finished the poem he wishes to present to President Hamilton," he said as he poured from the porcelain pot.

"It is scarcely a poem," said Colonel Mee, "but it is appropriate. It scans but it does not rhyme." When he was commander of the 8341 Regiment, Colonel Mee wrote hundreds of poems at Mao Tse-tung's direction; they were published as Mao's own work. "In any case," he added, "it is just a souvenir. Hamilton will accept it and treasure it because it is a gift. That is the importance of the poem."

"Might I see it?" asked the deputy premier; he placed the refilled cups on the table and sat down. "Unless it would be indiscreet. I regret to say I do not know Chairman Tien's estimation of poetry."

"He has none that I am aware of," said Colonel Mee. "He sees it merely as a tool. For example, he has absolutely no qualms about classical language or allusions. Mao worried about them a great deal. He was afraid that someone, particularly a young person, might think he was somehow glorifying classical values."

"And you," said the deputy premier; his voice chilled a fraction. "Do you see any glorification?"

"None," answered Colonel Mee promptly; he had a seasoned ear for this trap; he had laid it himself countless times; to "glorify" anything apart from Mao's Thoughts was criminal. He had served a long period as Mao's speechwriter. He had produced many of the Thoughts. He had never advertised the fact. The experience had paid off when Mao died. Colonel Mee had secretly modified a directive from Mao that he himself had composed. Mao's widow, a leader of a rival faction, was blamed for the modification and purged. "It is a challenge to create the proper mood and phase of the climate. Often the old language works best."

"The poem?"

"I don't have it with me. I can recite it if you like."

"Please."

Colonel Mee made the slightest noise of clearing his throat.

> "The brisk youth sits a bright horse.
> He tosses shafts of credit
> To the daughter of Chin Ping-mei."

The deputy premier gazed reflectively for a moment. Then he said, "It isn't up to your usual fluency, you know."

"My fluency has been limited," said Colonel Mee a bit sadly. "Besides, it would be unbecoming for new poems to match the quality of Mao's. Chairman Tien agrees."

"Have you provided a commentary?"

"Yes. There are in fact two interpretations. Naturally the 'brisk youth' is modern China and the 'bright horse' is the example of the Revolution. This holds for both versions. 'Shafts of credit' can be explained as tokens of esteem and cooperation, presumably directed by China toward the United States; the other meaning is armed missiles supporting China's intentions. The 'daughter of Chin Ping-mei' could be taken as a manifestation of the goddess of love or universal friendship. I meant an allusion to the ancient status of Chin Ping-mei as the whorehouse goddess—Soviet Russia, of course."

A look of concern came over the deputy premier's face. "Don't you think that's unnecessarily provocative? Not to mention confusing?"

"Chairman Tien will endorse a provocation if it is satisfactorily disguised. He wants the poem to be forceful but ambiguous."

"But this seems to be primarily directed at the Russians."

Colonel Mee lit another cigarette in an effort to mask his impatience. "Hamilton has been trying for some time to conclude a nonaggression treaty with us," he said a trifle sharply. "His visit here offers us an excellent opportunity to issue a warning to the Russians. The idea is to give the Russians the impression that we still enjoy America's support in our differences with them."

"That isn't precisely the case," said the deputy premier; his voice, too, rose a bit. "The Russians suspect—with good reason—that our accommodation with the Americans is just a practical arrangement."

"Of course. But they don't know how much more we can

get from the arrangement. They know we've obtained enormous quantities of strategic equipment from the Americans, computers and so forth. Our information from Moscow is that they suspect we'll get a lot more. It is convenient to issue this warning while Hamilton is here."

The deputy premier sipped his tea. Beyond the ceiling-high windows the morning haze was beginning to sparkle. "Hamilton was reared here, don't forget," he said. "Won't it be awkward for us if Hamilton knows Chairman Tien is telling him in so many words that we have missiles aimed at Russia? And for no apparent reason, since he surely knows it already?"

"In so many words. That's the purpose of the poem. Mao felt the same way when Nixon first visited us. He wanted an ambiguous but stubborn poem to give to him. I worked for days to strike just the balance that Mao adored—something that blended simplicity and obscurity, in the fashion of a symmetrical aphorism. He didn't think Nixon understood it.

"Chairman Tien wants Hamilton to understand the poem," Colonel Mee continued, "in both its meanings. We will make certain he does. Copies of the blander commentary will be circulated among the foreign press in Peking. The harsher one will be distributed in Hong Kong. The Americans set great store by information about China that comes from Hong Kong. So do the Russians."

The deputy premier rose from his chair and walked to the window. He could see a group of soldiers from the People's Liberation Army; they were in Peking from the provinces on a sightseeing holiday; their leader was reading to them from Mao's Little Red Book. The deputy premier drummed his fingers on the windowsill. He wished Colonel Mee's poem were more graceful and less apt to start something. In both its meanings.

"Do you have an evaluation of Hamilton?" the deputy premier asked; he was still looking out the window; his back was to Colonel Mee.

"Official or personal?"

"Official, of course," said the deputy premier; he slowly turned around.

"It is in the documents. They were sent to you some time ago."

"Yes, yes. I haven't read them in some time. Please refresh my memory."

Colonel Mee put out his cigarette. "Hamilton believes that the coincidence of his childhood in China gives him a unique understanding of us and our special circumstances. His public statements over the years reveal that he is arrogant enough to think he actually knows what is best for us. His early career as a diplomat is widely taken in America as representing a comprehensive grasp of international affairs. We do not take this view. On the contrary we believe Hamilton is susceptible to flattery and can be manipulated. That's a summary. Do you want particulars?"

"No," said the deputy premier. "Do you have a personal opinion?"

"Yes."

"Could I hear it?"

"Is it necessary?"

"I would appreciate it. For guidance."

"Very well," said Colonel Mee; he put his hands together and touched his chin. "I have a somewhat sympathetic view of Hamilton. It comes partly from my background. Hamilton is the son of déclassé parents. I think it is accurate to say American missionaries are déclassé—in bourgeois terms. He understood early in life that he was an outsider. That drove him to seek recognition. He chose elective politics. Western capitalists have a weakness for it." He paused and considered his words. "As you know, I am an ethnic Aini. My parents took

213

me from Yunnan to Shanghai when I was very small. The foreigners, of course, scorned everyone who wasn't white, but I got a double dose of abuse, being a minority peasant in a sea of urban Han."

The deputy premier raised an eyebrow; otherwise, his face was immobile. He was a Han, like 95 percent of everyone else in China. He wondered if Colonel Mee was hinting that he secretly harbored discriminatory feelings against ethnic minorities. He certainly hoped not. Ethnic discrimination was not in accordance with Mao's Thoughts.

"So you can see," Colonel Mee went on, "that I understand the motives of a pariah. It drove me to excel at composition when I became a Communist, and I think Mao felt he made good use of my achievements. It also forced me to acknowledge theoretical virtue. This is essential to intelligence work. It allows me to see Hamilton as both a defeated politician and an unwitting gull.

"Hamilton's visit to China can be of no conceivable advantage to the United States. His own supporters have renounced him and thus renounced their faith in his capacity to speak for them. He is what is known in American political terms as a lame duck. He comes to us, not as a symbol of American unity and purpose, but as a walking specimen of political defeat. As a revolutionary, however, I do not see this defeated politician as someone to be consoled and honored. I see him as someone to be used. One way to use him is to console and honor him, and I would not hesitate to do it."

"Could you find it possible to respect Hamilton?" asked the deputy premier.

"I could respect him if I had to. I don't think it's necessary. Theoretical virtue collapses under the reality of the Revolution."

The deputy premier sat down again. He sipped some tea; it

had cooled; he preferred it piping hot. "One last thing. Chairman Tien wants to know whether you have learned anything more about the message from the Americans."

"We only suspect it came from the Americans," said Colonel Mee. "I made that clear in my accompanying note." His expression betrayed a trace of agitation. "I trust the chairman was told that we know nothing concrete."

"Of course, of course," said the deputy premier. "He thought that perhaps you had heard again from your source. What was his name?"

"A gambler in Macao. He is just a shuttlecock. I'm sure he relayed it from a man I personally recruited during the Yunnan campaign."

"Who is this man? This agent of yours?"

"Shen Keng Min. He is not an agent of mine. He hasn't been for years. That was what caused the alarm. An urgent request from a man who knows he is not trusted here. After all, he has worked extensively for the Americans, too. I have often regretted," Colonel Mee added, "that I did not kill him when I first met him. It was many years ago. I had put him through an intensive interrogation."

The deputy premier got up again and walked over to a sawhorse table next to the sideboard. A single sheet of paper lay on top. It was a copy of Shen Keng Min's message as forwarded by Po Lung. The deputy premier read it aloud. "It is whispered that an American cricket is to be entered for competition out of season. For obvious reasons my principal must know. Please be so kind as to inform me immediately whether this gossip is based on a grain of fact."

It was signed "servant." Both Colonel Mee and the deputy premier had read it as "eunuch." The ideograph was the same for both words.

"I, too, have been speculating on it," said the deputy pre-

215

mier. "Do you think it is possible that it means exactly what it says? That it simply represents an intense interest in cricket fighting?"

"No."

"No, I suppose not. We have no fighting crickets. Revolutionary thought discourages such absurd games. Where do you think your man got the idea that we might afford an arena for an American cricket?"

"It's an old code. Shen Keng Min used it often in the past in signals to me. He is enthusiastic about cricket fighting. So am I. He found it suitable to cloak critical messages in talk about crickets."

"So you think this Shen Keng Min has sent us a message from the Americans. How long do you think it will take to find out what it means?"

"It is not possible to say. If it is from the Americans, it could very well be an attempt to throw us off balance. The American intelligence service has a history of initiating projects in the hope of producing a result. Any result. Perhaps to see if they can detect a pattern of response. They call it 'floating a trial balloon.' That kind of thing happens in capitalist bureaucracies. It resembles Soviet disinformation."

"And your wall posters," said the deputy premier.

"And my wall posters," said Colonel Mee.

The deputy premier put down the sheet of paper. "Be careful how you respond to the message." He glanced at the message again and added, "Chairman Tien has indicated a special interest in an unofficial portion of Hamilton's visit. He's very vague about it. I believe it has something to do with Hamilton's valet. Did you know he is Chinese?"

"Yes. Tung Yen Fun. I arranged his exit from Shanghai. He has a strong superstitious interest in being buried in China."

"Can he be of use with this message?" asked the deputy premier.

216

"Possibly. There has been no contact with him for years. I am exploring the practicabilities. However," Colonel Mee continued crisply, "you must emphasize to the chairman that a response has already been sent. It was phrased in terms of Shen Keng Min's signal. I said we were not expecting a new cricket. I'm sure Shen Keng Min adapted the reply to fit the situation he was paid to address himself to. If it happens that the message came from the Americans—and if they happen to be seeking something specific, some particular information— we certainly will hear from them again. Until then I intend to do nothing. The Americans have a habit of revealing a lot about themselves to people they believe aren't watching them."

Colonel Mee finished his tea; it had grown cold; he did not mind. He got up to leave.

"I was disturbed to hear that you fancy cricket fighting," said the deputy premier. "Particularly since it is associated with gambling. Mao condemned gambling as a bourgeois evil."

"I know," said Colonel Mee from the door. He glanced at the Yuan figurines; they were cast in comic poses; he preferred the more primitive Shang bronzes. "It is a failing of mine. I look on it the way I look on those dollars you acquire from the American diplomats—the money the railway conductor bets for you at the Happy Valley Racecourse in Hong Kong. As I said, I accept theoretical virtue."

He walked out of the Great Hall of the People. He mounted his bicycle and pedaled toward Tien An Men Square. Across the way an old woman carried her grandson on her back; the child's head was shaved to retain a topknot against evil spirits.

Wednesday broke hot and calm on Washington.

Coombes lumbered across the parking lot at Dulles International Airport. He was consumed by fatigue. He had been on a plane all night: the "red-eye" flight from California. He had slept miserably. It was the Dexamyl. His valise seemed to weigh a ton.

He squinted at the early-morning sun. The heat wave that had roasted the eastern seaboard since the weekend was on hold. There were a few gray clouds, but Coombes knew it wouldn't rain and banish the heat; the clouds were too high. Washington would be a caldron again in a few hours.

The worst was over, he thought. His operation was nearly done—cut-diamond perfect or not, finished or unfinished. Any intelligence officer knows how that feels. He had chosen not to initiate his debriefing with a call from the airport. He would wait until he had gone home and showered and eaten. If he knew anything, Special Ops would want him in person, on the double, and keep him all day. Probably keep him on standby until a counter-operation had been outlined and activated.

He even felt a qualified respect for his colleagues. They were skittish bastards at Special Ops, he said to himself, and they were sure to give him a ration of shit for "pilot-fishing" on something like this. And raise purple hell about no independent confirmation. But he knew they would recognize that he had gotten the better part of the job done. Christ, he was tired.

His aged car sat forlorn where he had left it Monday night. It looked as haggard as he did. He unlocked the door on the driver's side. He tossed the valise across the seat; it required an effort. He struggled to get himself behind the wheel. He put the key in the ignition and turned it.

Nothing.

He took a deep breath; he wanted desperately to keep his temper. He tried it again. From deep in the car came a clear, metallic clink. Another try and another clink. His composure dissolved. Coombes felt he had deceived himself. He shook in a spasm of anger. The universe turned smoky yellow; hate vaporized his brain. He hated Special Ops; he hated himself for having entertained the barest goodwill toward Special Ops. He hated his goddamn car. Then he boiled over.

The steering wheel went first. Coombes gripped it with both hands just above his thighs and heaved it from the steering column. This set off the horn. He rammed his hand underneath the dashboard and wrenched loose a multicolored handful of wires. The wailing stopped. He whacked off the turn-signal indicator. He glanced maniacally for something else on which to vent his loathing. Wielding the steering wheel with his left hand, he backhanded it against the windshield; it snapped the rearview mirror and ricocheted into the back seat; the blow produced a cobweb pattern on the shatterproof glass. He snatched the valise. He was going to get his fucking pistol and blow holes in this car big enough to put your fucking foot in. He grappled with the fastener. It was stuck. Doesn't any goddamn thing work around here? The fastener held. A ragged cuticle on one of his fingers snagged and began to bleed. He flung the valise against the far door. He was panting convulsively.

Presently his breathing grew more regular. The glazed look melted in his eyes. He looked over the damage. His wife would bitch until she turned blue; how did he propose for her to get to work? He decided that and other matters connected with this car could wait. His perspective was returning. Special Ops was a bunch of thumbsuckers; they would give him a ration of shit, all right, but they would be damned sparing in their recognition of his work; they would be the same nitpicking, obsessive, self-important pricks they had always been. He seized the valise and got out. He didn't relock the door; good tradecraft didn't matter with this crate, he said to himself. He walked to the front of the car. He arched the valise over his head and swung it down as hard as he could onto the hood. It left a crater-like depression.

A taxi did not trouble him this morning. He certainly could afford it. The driver looked at him doubtfully. Coombes's appearance was appalling.

The cab turned off the access road and headed south on the Beltway. It was too early for the daily crush of traffic. Coombes's instincts were functioning again. He squirmed to catch a glance in the rearview mirror. The driver didn't notice. Coombes saw nothing suspicious behind them.

He settled into the seat but did not relax. He thought of his wife again. He would tell the cab to wait; she could take it to her office. He calculated the impact of his operation and worked out a scenario for presenting it. He would play his strongest cards first—the two letters from Hamilton and the fact that Forbes was in place with the pathogenic accelerators. He concocted an assortment of lies to justify his unauthorized absence. He felt alert, on top of things, in spite of his weariness.

At Exit 6 they turned east off the Beltway. A mile or two later they turned off again. They were within a mile of Coombes's house. The neighborhood was modest but well kept. Traffic signs warned of children at play.

The streets were just coming to life. Here and there a car backed out of a driveway; most of them bore parking decals for military installations.

A block before they reached his street, Coombes leaned forward and said, "Don't make the turn. Stop and then pull across the intersection. I'll get out at the corner."

The driver complied. He came to a dead halt. Then he eased the car ahead.

Coombes peered down the street. He recoiled. He spied pairs of cars, each with four men in them, parked on both corners at each end of the block. The nearest car was less than twenty feet from the cab.

Across the street from his house, an unfamiliar car was in the driveway aimed at the street. There was even a car in his own driveway.

"I'm not getting out," he said to the driver; his voice squeaked. "Drive on."

"What? This is the street you gave me."

"I'm going into Washington," Coombes said; he cleared his throat. "I'm having some trouble with my wife. I've been away for a while. I thought I'd surprise her, try to make it up. I changed my mind."

"Where to in Washington?" The driver looked annoyed.

"The Mayflower."

"Mayflower Hotel?"

"Right. Let's go."

Coombes leaned back and lowered himself a fraction in the seat. He reluctantly decided against strapping on the Colt Cobra; the driver was sure to see it. He would have felt safer with it under his arm.

The cab turned onto the Shirley Highway and headed for Washington. Coombes was perplexed. Why was his house staked out? It must be McElroy; the young jerk must have panicked at his AWOL and called Counter Intelligence. He was certain it was Counter Intelligence. He could spot that surveillance configuration anywhere; they might as well have put up a billboard; a backwoods police department could do better, in Coombes's opinion. He would have let himself be taken if there had been time. But there wasn't; it would take him at least two days to clear himself; by then his operation would be beside the point. He dismissed the notion that one of his neighbors was the target.

The scene quickened once they crossed the Arlington

Bridge. There was a small traffic jam near Dupont Circle.

He paid the driver and got out. He had spent nearly fifty dollars for cab fare; he didn't realize it had gone up so much; it had been years since he had taken a cab in Washington. He walked into the hotel. The doorman stared at him.

The red-carpeted lobby of the Mayflower fitted Coombes's needs. Plenty of space, convenient, observable exits, and a moderate crowd. Early-rising tourists shifted in line at the checkout desk. Luggage was stacked in one place and another. Coombes made for a bank of pay telephones.

A voice with a drawl answered. Coombes could hear the morning news on a television set in the background.

"This is Mr. Walker," said Coombes. "It's about Major Hunt's lacquer ware. The piece with the Hintha bird on it. We won't be able to drop it off until nine o'clock."

"What's the name again?"

"Walker. It's about Major Hunt's lacquer ware with the Hintha bird. The delivery won't be until nine o'clock."

"I'm afraid you have the wrong number. There's no Major Hunt here."

Coombes hung up. He had established contact.

"Major Hunt" was a cryptonym. "Lacquer ware" was a countersign. "Hintha bird" was a request for an emergency meeting at the usual rendezvous. "Nine o'clock" meant nine-thirty. "Wrong number" meant the request would be granted. Had the meeting been deemed impossible or unwise, the reply would have been "what number are you calling?"; meaning Coombes was to call back in an hour.

He walked back to the lobby. A group of conventioneers had assembled for breakfast. Their lapel badges identified them as bankers. Most were with their wives. They were like all conventioneers first thing in the morning; a few greeted each other robustly, imparting self-confidence; the others seemed distracted and hesitant, as if they had lost their bearings and could not possibly find the coffee shop without assistance. They looked at Coombes with distaste.

He took a city bus and got off after several blocks; his valise had inconvenienced several passengers. He walked along Columbia Road. At Eighteenth Street he went into a fast-food restaurant. The smell was french-fried potatoes. He bought a container of coffee and took a seat by a window. He positioned the valise by his leg and undid the fastener; he wanted to be able to get to his revolver.

Outside, the city had come alive for the day. The temperature was on its way to the sweltering point. The few clouds Coombes had seen at the airport had vanished.

A half hour later a tall man with iron-gray hair and wearing a lightweight three-piece suit crossed the street and walked straight for the restaurant. It was Headlight.

Coombes looked closely for backup men. He didn't see any.

Headlight walked directly to Coombes's table. They met here once a week, usually on another day at another time. Coombes reported unofficially on the projects and personalities at the Basement. He was one of Headlight's many acquaintances down in the ranks. All were old-timers; they had been in Burma together. Headlight had realized early that an important secret to success in a large organization was detailed knowledge of the interworkings of its outlying branches. Coombes and the others admired his advancement without jealousy and looked to him as a patron. Headlight collected Asian lacquer ware; it was a taste he had developed in Burma; he favored betel-nut canisters with intricate Hintha-bird designs. He sat down and put his hands on the table.

"What the hell happened to you?" Headlight asked. "You look like you came to town on the back of a truck." There was astonishment in his cultured drawl; he wore an amused smile. "A beard, for God's sake."

Coombes shot a glance out the window; he was still worried about backup men; Headlight himself might have been followed. He furtively touched the top of the valise. "I wouldn't have used the 'Hintha bird' unless I had to," Coombes said apologetically. "For some reason Counter Intelligence is on my ass. My house is staked out. It looks like a carnival camped on the street."

He paused and sucked the cuticle he had torn in his car. Headlight remained silent. His hands seemed to have been manicured. "The Counter Intelligence thing can wait," Coombes went on. "What I need is entrée to Special Ops. Immediate entrée. If I don't have star-quality help, Counter Intelligence will slow me down. I can't afford it now."

"Special Ops?" Headlight took an English cigarette from a gold case and lit it with an initialed lighter. "I have a chip or two out with them—they were damned hard to get. I'd hate to call one in for something less than priority interest."

"This is priority interest," said Coombes; his eyelids lowered as he spoke.

Headlight continued to smile. "Do you mind letting me in on it? After all, I'm your safe-conduct pass. I want to know what I'm getting into."

"Shouldn't we go straight to Special Ops?" Coombes asked plaintively; he knew Headlight demanded a favor for a favor. "This is damned complicated and there isn't much time."

"Better try it out on me first. It will give me an idea of how to break it to Special Ops."

Coombes sat up straight, as if he were a witness in a courtroom. "Hamilton is going to defect when he gets to China," he said. He looked at Headlight for a reaction.

"I said it was priority interest," he added stupidly.

Headlight studied his hands for a moment. He shook his head and clucked. "That's priority interest if I ever heard it," he said. He eyed Coombes closely and then looked absently from side to side. "Where the hell did you *ever* get this idea?"

"I've got documentation," said Coombes sharply, defensively. "Damned good documentation."

"What?"

"A roll of film"—he patted his jacket pocket—"and a letter in my safe."

Headlight clasped his hands. His expression was a fusion of concern and melancholy seriousness; it was the look he had worn at briefings in Burma. "I want you to tell me everything," he said. "Don't omit a single detail, no matter how insignificant you think it is. Even include what you were thinking, if you can remember. All right?"

Headlight propped his chin on his hands. It was clear he did not intend to interrupt. His eyes remained fixed as Coombes tediously recounted, step by step, the past two days—from the meeting with Vest in the suburban shopping center to the discovery that Counter Intelligence had bracketed his street.

It took the greater part of two hours. Several times Headlight had motioned for Coombes to take a breather while he fetched more coffee.

"Is that everything?" Headlight asked quietly.

"No," Coombes replied; he was rubbing his eyes with a thumb and forefinger.

"What else?"

"I killed Vest. I switched identities with him. I'm traveling on his paper now. And quite a bit of his money."

"How did it happen?"

Coombes told him.

"What did you think about it? At the time, I mean?"

"Nothing much. He surprised me. It was the only thing to do, when you think about it. He was obviously after the letter."

Headlight nodded. "Why do you think Shen Keng Min ducked out?"

Coombes cast his eyes downward. "I'm damned if I know. I

can't figure it out. He knew perfectly well I could use a 'fail-ure-to-reply.' "

A busboy cleared the table; he was wearing a uniform supplied by the franchiser.

"I'd break Shen's neck if I knew where to find him," Coombes added with a scowl. "He held a gun on me."

Headlight lit another cigarette from his gold case. "We've got a problem," he said, "a problem of reducing our case to demonstration."

"What does that mean?"

"The letter to Justice Roundtree. It isn't in your safe."

Coombes turned and glared out the window. He bit furiously at a fingernail. "Counter Intelligence has it," he said sourly. "The bastards must have shaken down my office when they put this surveillance on me. I know they have it."

He turned abruptly and faced Headlight. "How do you know it isn't in my safe?"

"I was at the Basement last night. I saw Counter Intelligence open the safe. The letter wasn't there."

Coombes slumped back. He was seized by a sense of futility and shame; he felt as if he had been tricked into performing. "Why the hell did you let me ramble on like that?" His voice had a hard edge.

Headlight blew a breath of smoke. "It wouldn't have worked any other way," he said; his drawl was less pronounced. "You can't go to Special Ops. At the moment you're compromised. This Counter Intelligence operation is no weekend exercise. They think you've gone into the used-rug business."

"The used-rug business? Me?"

"The habit-medical profile on Hamilton. They think you've gone on the market with it."

"Somebody's been watching too much television," snapped Coombes. "BEEHIVE stuff is available to anybody. There's a book on computer procedure. It's beyond me. A technician showed me how to use it."

"They think you've done it before," said Headlight matter-of-factly. "They're tracing your movements to see where you could have been turned."

Coombes sat up and put his arms on the table. "This is some kind of double game. I don't know who's running it, but that's what it is. Somebody's working both sides of the street. Don't you think it's a bit too coincidental that Counter Intelligence jumps me the minute I show up with the goods on this Hamilton thing? This isn't a shot in the dark. It's a goddamn setup. The timing's too good to be *just* a Counter Intelligence operation. Here I am, ready to slam the door on the biggest thing we've ever seen, and what happens? Some bastard doodles on a pad for a few minutes and says, 'Coombes has been turned.' I can't prove it, but it sure as hell looks like somebody is trying to open the door for Hamilton."

He stared out the window. "What the hell are we supposed to do now?" he muttered.

"Your operation hasn't been a waste, I can assure you," said Headlight; he sounded conciliatory. "There are several directions we can take. The thing is, you have to drop out. You're right about Counter Intelligence; they would stop you cold. I have to take it from here. You've simplified things quite a bit, you know. There's a chance we'll hear from Shen. He'll get in touch direct, if he hears anything from Peking. I know Shen; he loves the premium rate. And you've got an agent in play near Hamilton. What's his name?"

"Forbes. But I didn't have much time with him. I don't know if I motivated him enough. He ought to have support. . . . Look. It doesn't matter what happened to the letter to Roundtree, does it? I saw it. That's good enough, isn't it?"

"Ordinarily, yes," said Headlight; he glanced at his watch. "But you're on C.I.'s list. That colors everything. There's no corroboration. Vest is dead. So is Roundtree. Did you know that? He died Monday night."

"What about Melville? He saw it. He got it from Round-tree."

Headlight chuckled placidly. "That would be an unusual scene, wouldn't it? We walk up to the vice-president and say, 'A man we suspect of doing something nasty asked us to speak to you. He says you've seen a letter saying the president is going to do something nasty.' No. I have to come up with something better than that. You'd better let me have the film."

Coombes handed over the tiny spool. He pulled at his goatee. He grimaced and bared his teeth. "I think Forbes needs help. Lots of it. I don't know if he has what it takes. Pathogenic accelerators are easy, but will he use them? I don't know. There's a damned good chance he'll lose his nerve. Remember the hooker who was supposed to stick the curare to Castro? I told Forbes to act before they got to Alaska, but what if he doesn't? There's only one answer. Send somebody in. Maybe in Georgia. Maybe at Anchorage—to make sure Forbes is in shape to go when they take off on the last leg if he hasn't moved before. I should be the one; it makes sense; I recruited him. But he's got to have help. Especially now, since it looks like there's somebody inside helping Hamilton."

"You should get out of sight," said Headlight. "Stay low while I push this through. I'll settle the Counter Intelligence thing. It will take time, though. The less seen of you while I'm doing it, the better."

"Are you telling me not to do it?"

"I'm telling you to run for it. Go to the Eastern Shore. Use the house on Gwynn Island. It's supposed to be closed; nobody'll look for you there. Do you need more money?"

"I suppose, if I have to spend much time away. Vivian will need some cash, too. Can you see she gets it?"

"Of course." He took a plain envelope from his inside jacket pocket and handed it to him; Coombes noted that Headlight had come prepared; it was one of the things about Headlight that he marveled at.

"If I run up some more expenses," said Coombes, "will you certify a voucher? Put me in a Foreign Intelligence slot or something?"

"I told you to disappear," said Headlight. He looked at his watch again. "I have to be getting back. I've got quite a Chinese puzzle on my hands." He shrugged at the poor joke.

"Those pathogenic accelerators. Do you know how they work?" asked Coombes. He reached for his valise.

"I know the principle. They induce anaphylactic shock."

"They do what?"

"It's a kind of allergic reaction. The stuff in the capsules is a calibrated combination of the right proteins. They give the circulatory system a heavy blast. If the target is subject to circulatory problems—heart attack or stroke—blood clots form all over the body. He won't last more than a few minutes."

"Are they guaranteed?"

"You clog up like a grease trap in a matter of seconds. It's pretty disgusting."

Coombes got to his feet. "Keep your head down," said Headlight, who remained seated. Coombes left the restaurant; he always left their meetings first; it was the drill.

It was cool in Union Station. Coombes bought a one-way Metroliner ticket to Philadelphia. He figured his chances of getting on a plane unnoticed were better in Philadelphia.

9 The Attempt

"How many times do I have to say it?" Dr. Brabham was touchy. He didn't like these meetings; he had been reluctant to attend. "It could come at any time."

"The clinical name for it," said Gil Snyder. The president's chief of staff was eating a late lunch at his desk. It was a tuna fish salad sandwich; he was trying with little success to lose ten pounds; Brabham had recommended it. "What did you call it?"

"Ingravescent cerebral thrombosis," said Hamilton's personal physician; he sounded waspish. He was seated across from Snyder.

Snyder pushed his sandwich aside and drained his cup of sugarless black coffee. He looked at Forbes and Nell Leatherbee; he invariably summoned them when Hamilton's health was being discussed. His expression invited comment.

"I say write off this trip," said Forbes, rushing his answer, "and tell him to get the hell into a hospital." He was leaning against the far wall; his arms were folded; he was holding a cigarette. Forbes was gloomy, not far from being depressed.

The story he had given Mark Beard had failed to appear in the afternoon papers. Beard himself had left his motel early, taking the trouble before he departed to inform his Washington office that he was taking a vacation in parts unknown; the subscriber newspapers had reacted furiously upon learning that "Mark Beard's Washington" would be unavailable for at least a week, Beard's secretary had told Forbes. Forbes moodily surmised that the story had frightened Beard so thoroughly that it had dried up his journalistic saliva glands.

"Nell?" Snyder picked up a letter opener and held it between his fingertips.

"I'm with Thack," she said. She sat with her legs tucked under her. She was on one of the Southern White House's numerous overstuffed leather sofas. "He's obviously in no physical shape to undertake anything as big as this."

Snyder slowly circumvolved the letter opener and studied it from different angles. "You've known this for some time, haven't you, Doc?"

"Yes," said Brabham; his tone was cautious, as if he sensed that his medical qualifications were being questioned. "But the symptoms have become more noticeable."

Despite the prestige, Brabham was professionally uncomfortable as the president's doctor; he was unable to dominate the existence of his patient, and his self-esteem suffered. He had once imagined himself as a man of great power, the single person who could order the president to bed, no matter what crisis was at hand. This had proved illusory. Politicians, not doctors, ran the White House; a medical opinion here was just another political consideration.

"The deterioration of capacities has become marked despite the increased dosage of anticoagulants," he added. "You know blood was found in the last spinal tap. That indicates at least a small hemorrhage. *That* was ignored. And the brain scan showed a—"

231

"Okay, Doc," Snyder broke in. "Skip the work-up on the man's plumbing. You said something about symptoms."

"You only need two eyes to see them," said Brabham sharply. It chafed him to be cross-examined by a layman on a point of his own competence. "For one thing, this radical increase in his alcohol intake. That ought to alarm anyone. There are other signs. Less dramatic but just as serious. Difficulty in getting out of a chair, lessening of appetite, careless dress and table manners, generally making all sorts of mistakes. Take a look at the man's handwriting if you need more evidence."

Snyder put down the letter opener. "Jesus, you could be describing me"—he laughed dryly—"except the bit about the appetite. Look, Doc. The man has been working his ass off. So has everyone else down here. Everybody, including you, could do with a day off. We can't spare it. What else have you seen that makes you think he's so sick?"

"A marked change in his emotional behavior," replied Brabham crisply. "You wouldn't believe the tantrum he threw when he heard Melville attended the Roundtree funeral." This he directed to Nell and Forbes.

Snyder's face distorted under his ginger eyebrows. Nell and Forbes exchanged glances of astonishment.

"Don't give me that shit," Snyder snapped. "I can pick up a magazine any day of the week and read garbage like that." Snyder was not unversed on matters of physical and mental health; when it came to Hamilton, however, only Hamilton's political desires carried weight with him. "I called you in here for a reading on his health, not the state of his goddamn nerves."

Brabham was not intimidated. "They're part of the same thing," he said firmly. "There's a latent coagulum in the right cerebral cortex. There are probably other undetected ones. A change in a person's conduct is a symptom. A damned good one, too, when he's in danger of a cerebral occlusion. This is plain medicine, not psychiatry. When you see a man go into sudden fits of rage, or lose interest in things for no reason, then by God, you'd better get ready to see that man suffer a stroke."

Snyder picked up the letter opener again. "As I see it, he has an even chance if he calls it off and a definite maybe if he goes. I don't need to tell you which way I'm voting."

"With the definite maybes," said Forbes despondently. He looked downcast at Nell, whose mouth was drawn tight.

"This is irresponsible as hell," fumed Brabham. "The man ought to be in the hospital. I'm going upstairs right now and tell him he needs a prolonged rest. I'm ordering a series of tests. I need to observe him for at least ten days. I'm calling Walter Reed. I want the plane ready in an hour."

"Tell him anything you want," retorted Snyder. He jumped to his feet; his face reddened. "Observe him all you want. But get it through your head that anything you have to tell Joe Hamilton or anything about him you want to observe, you do right here and on that plane to Peking. Is that clear, Brabham? Forget this crap about Walter Reed. Forget it, understand? Hamilton wouldn't go into a hospital now if his toes were falling off. He doesn't cancel something like this because he has trouble getting out of a goddamn chair. Now get out of here."

"But, Gil—"

"Get out!"

Brabham got up stiffly. "You'll hear about this," he said from the door.

"Great," grumbled Snyder. "Tell me all about it." The door slammed. "That high-handed son of a bitch," he growled.

The afternoon sun flared through the window behind Snyder's desk. He had intended to move his office to another part of the house if Hamilton had won a second term.

"Is Brabham right?" asked Nell; she had untucked her legs and crossed them in front of her.

"Probably," said Snyder; he was still in a corrosive mood. "What difference does it make?"

"Well, my God, if the man is this close to a stroke, shouldn't he—"

"Goddamn it, can't you see the point?" Snyder exploded. "You see it, don't you, Thack?"

Forbes shrugged. He was still leaning against the wall. He was smoking his third cigarette since the meeting began.

"Christ almighty," Snyder raged on, "have both of you gone blind? This China thing is all he has left." He ran his fingers through his ginger hair. "So what if it looks like a grandstand play? And so what if it's stupid politics? I work for Joe Hamilton. He's the president. To *me* that still counts. I wouldn't give a fuck if he wanted to go roller-skating at midnight in the middle of Denver. I'd tell the Secret Service and get the goddamn roller skates." He sat down and took a deep breath. Broad perspiration stains darkened the underarms of his short-sleeved shirt. "I'm sure Brabham is right, medically speaking," he went on; he was calmer now. "But politically it's just another problem. You can't shut down the presidency just because the president's health isn't up to par, any more than you can call off a battle because the general breaks his leg. Brabham doesn't understand that—among other things."

"You're not being fair, Gil," said Forbes. He sat down next to Nell and stubbed his cigarette. "To Joe or Brabham. A stroke isn't a broken leg."

"Let me put it this way," said Snyder. He toyed with his letter opener again. "The president doesn't care if he's in danger of a stroke or a broken leg or the New Guinea clap. It's just another risk. Sure, he wants to make his mark on history and all that. I personally don't think this China trip will amount to a pound of soft shit. Not to us, anyway. The Chinese probably feel differently. What matters is, Hamilton

234

thinks it will. As long as he does, he's going as far as he can with it, no matter what medical advice he gets."

"But what about the symptoms," said Nell, "impaired judgment, uncontrollable temper? Won't that affect his performance? It would affect anybody else's."

Snyder sighed tiredly. "That's all relative in this job. If Hamilton were going to Pittsburgh to be renominated, everything would look different. Brabham would be concerned, but not hysterical. Hell, you've seen it. A winner is high-strung but acts decisively, a loser has impaired judgment; a winner is a demanding man to work for, a loser has an uncontrollable temper. . . . By the way, did you see the wires? Melville picked up a few more uncommitted delegates. Think he'll sign you on, Thack, if he wins?"

Forbes swallowed hard. It hadn't occurred to him that Hamilton might have told Snyder of their discussion on the lake. He wondered nervously whether Hamilton had told him everything. "Where did you get that idea?"

"I hear things." Snyder wore a forgiving, knowing smile. "I also know how to add. Think he'll make you an offer?"

"It depends—on a lot of things."

"Like calling off this trip?"

"Maybe."

"Well, you can tell Larry baby that's out. You can also tell him to look for another secretary of state. Joe says he doesn't think he and Melville would be compatible. That's not exactly what he said, but it'll do." He looked at the wall clock and then consulted a sheet of paper. "Let's see. Nell, it's you and Hamilton at four on the marketable debt thing. What do you call those things?"

"Book entries."

"Yeah." He shook his head. "I'm glad somebody understands our monetary system." He ran his finger down the page. "Thack, nothing official for you. It's dinner here with Hamilton at eight-thirty sharp. Nell, you, too. Just the four of us. Anything the Man wants to talk about. Okay? If you get a chance, Thack, make some calls on the convention. He'll want to hear some inside stuff. All right, you two clear out. I have a feeling I'll have to handle Brabham again on top of everything else."

"Let's take a walk by the lake," said Nell as she and Forbes left Wabash House.

"Christ, we'll melt," said Forbes. "This weather would give an Arab heat prostration."

They nodded to the ever-present Secret Service agents. Both were thankful there were no media people about. At the moment they both were thinking of the dark of the early morning. They had spent the night in Nell's bed at Elkhart House. They awoke at almost the same instant, tranquil and warm. Nell stroked his stomach and slid her slender leg across him. Forbes gently nestled her against his chest and lowered his mouth to hers. They turned in a single, fluid motion and the agonizing ecstasy began. . . . She had been unable to let go of him, and he lay close against her breasts as they lapsed back into sleep; they were in the same position when the phone rang with the wake-up call.

They walked onto the pier. Forbes let his hand brush against hers. He had a sudden desire to pull her close and kiss her. He knew it was out of the question. Appearances mattered to both of them.

Instead he said, "Nell, you're a devastating lover." He smiled at her tenderly.

"Were you thinking about this morning, too?"

"Yes."

They laughed together.

"I thought I'd never stop coming. God." She stopped and looked at him delicately. "I can't believe we're still so alive to each .other after all this time. Do you think it's because we aren't together every day?"

236

"I think it's because we love each other and know what we're doing. And love to do it."

"Thack, I'm telling you. I can hardly sit still when I'm in the same room with you." She shuddered and smiled with her lips parted.

"Want to go back to the house?" Forbes's male vanity had been fed. It gave him enormous satisfaction to know that the woman he loved was stimulated physically by his mere presence.

"Don't tempt me," said Nell coyly. "There's nothing I'd love more than to be in bed with you when I'm supposed to be in a meeting with Hamilton."

The mood was broken when she spoke the president's name. The realities of the conspiracy that encased them squeezed their enchantment to a dismal pulp. There was a long silence.

Forbes agonized over whether to tell Nell of his attempt to plant the story with Mark Beard. He was distinctly conscious of having failed at what he regarded as one of the strongest points of his craft. He had come away from the rendezvous with Beard filled with self-congratulation; he had taken a calculated risk drawn from his own experience—and failed, miserably he thought.

At length he decided to put the episode behind him undisclosed. He reflected that when you win one time and lose another there is no real reason why you won and why you lost. He refused to accept the fallacy that he had some kind of inner divining rod, a mental indicator that made you win if you followed its directions and lose only if you ignored them. Then he told her about the murder of Parisi.

"You know I think conspiracies are a lot of bullshit," he went on, pausing to light a cigarette; he noticed that the amber nicotine stain on his fingers was deepening. "You have to believe in flying saucers and the roller derby to think they exist. But there have been a hell of a lot of coincidences in the past couple of days, coincidences that are beginning to look like more than coincidences."

Nell looked at him intently. Her eyes shone with apprehension.

"The Parisi thing was what put me in this frame of mind. The article said he had just returned from a business trip to South America. South America, for Christ's sake. What was Frank Parisi doing in South America? He was a small-time wheeler-dealer. After I read the thing I realized that Parisi got blown away at about the same time this guy Vest was scaring the holy shit out of Roundtree. An hour later I was standing in Melville's office with Vest himself, and not long after that Melville shows me this letter from Hamilton to Roundtree. Then this gorilla with the capsules pushes me around at the airport, and a few hours later Roundtree drops dead—Roundtree, the guy who warned me not to go on this trip."

"What are you getting at, Thack?"

"That this thing—" he exhaled a deep breath of smoke—"that this flying saucer or roller derby or whatever it is may be real. If it is, there's a good chance something may happen to you. And an even better chance that something may happen to me."

She turned away and gazed at the lake. "You haven't forgotten the bottom line, have you?"

Forbes was quiet a moment and then said, "I still don't know if I can do it." He thumped his cigarette into the water. "I don't know if I can give that stuff to him." His face, with its hint of rogue around the mouth, constricted in pain. "Joe Hamilton isn't just the president to me. He's a friend of mine. He's more than a friend. He's almost like a . . ."

Nell said nothing. She could not bring herself to say there was nothing to it. She saw herself as a model of objectivity when it came to making her own decisions; she weighed the alternatives and made her choices; and lived with them, no matter how sickening she personally might find the consequences. But she found it impossible to choose for others, even the man she loved. Had she tried to tell Forbes what to do, she would be telling him what she, in all likelihood, intended to do herself. Persuasion was another matter. She had no twinges of conscience about persuading someone, even the man she loved, to do something that she personally found abhorrent. It was a nice point, but she observed it imperatively.

"Can you see any other choice?" she asked.

"Choice?" Forbes laughed flatly. "I don't think there's such a thing anymore. You don't have to be very bright to see that the chances of making a real choice are pretty slim. Any way you look at it, in the end somebody else will be making the choice. I'll just be doing a job that somebody else dreamed up." He looked vacantly across the lake. There wasn't a ripple on it. For once he felt at ease with the heat.

Nell broke tradition and took his hand in daylight. "You know what we're faced with," she said softly. "Dr. Brabham didn't leave any doubts, did he? Hamilton is sick, very sick, and irrational. We're the only ones who can stop him. That's what it comes down to, really. It's a question of a decision. We *do* have a choice. One of us has to make it." She felt driven to tell him of her last conversation with Melville—the one that convinced her of Hamilton's ravaged sanity and that he had to be destroyed for the country's safety. She couldn't do it. She had become involved long before, for her own motives. To tell Forbes now would be a betrayal. She couldn't betray him.

Forbes turned and faced her. "What it comes down to is murder. Lying is one thing; I do it for a living and it doesn't bother me as long as I don't get caught too often—" the Mark Beard fiasco flashed across his mind—"I don't have any genuine feelings about stealing. But murder. . . . You can't say you're sorry or pay it back when it's murder. Even if you do it to save the country and the world from going to hell, murder is final."

They looked at each other intensely. A flock of ducks descended on the lake. "I'll let you know tonight what I've decided," Forbes said. "Whatever it is, I don't want you to be a part of it. . . . Hell, the thing may be off. I'll know after I call that bookie or whoever she is. Why don't you go on back? Look over that banking stuff before your meeting with Joe. I need some time alone. You know the saying: wisdom comes from contemplation."

They squeezed hands. Nell turned and walked back toward the compound.

Forbes sat down cross-legged on the pier. Where did real courage come from? he asked himself. From self-righteousness? Loftiness of purpose? Devotion to justice? No. Real courage came from fear. Fear and running like hell. Running like hell and not thinking twice about it. Not thinking twice about it and not looking over your shoulder.

Or so he had unwittingly told himself in the years since he allowed that doctor—a virtual stranger—to end his father's life. The question before him now was whether he was prepared to take the next step. Would he *decide* whether or not to commit murder. Hell, he thought, Joe Hamilton is going to die soon enough without any outside help. Any sane man knows life is too short. If he knows that, how could he conceivably think someone has lived too long?

None of which helped to extenuate his recently revised opinion that he was probably the only man alive who could deter—terminate?—a president who was about to commit treason.

He heard footsteps on the pier. He turned and saw Tung Yen Fun waddling toward him. He carried a folding lawn chair and an umbrella.

"Good afternoon, Mr. Forbes," said the old Chinese. He

240

unfolded his chair and placed it near the tackle shed. He unfurled the umbrella. "You should move over here, into the shade. The heat is quite unbearable, I believe."

Forbes got slowly to his feet and moved to the shade of the tackle shed. He sat down and lit a cigarette.

"What brings you to the lake on a day like this?" Tung asked as he raised the umbrella over his head. "I had the impression that you were indifferent to fishing."

"I'm not fishing. I came for the quiet. The heat's not so bad if you don't move around too much. What are you doing down here?"

"I, too, like the quiet. The commotion at Wabash House becomes unsettling for a man of my age. I come mainly for the crickets."

"The crickets?"

"Yes." Tung leaned laboriously from his chair and unlatched the shed door. A small wire cage, not the one used to transport the fish bait, hung from the ceiling just inside. "Do you hear it?"

"Hear what?"

"The cricket."

Forbes pulled himself closer to the open door. Listening closely, he heard a cricket chirping vigorously. So what? he thought. A cricket chirping its ass off on a scorching July afternoon.

"Don't you find it soothing, Mr. Forbes?"

"I suppose so. I'd never paid any attention to it before."

"Do you know much about crickets?" Tung asked. He smiled contentedly as he listened to the lively resonance from the wire cage.

"No."

"There is a children's story in China. A boy gives up his soul to a cricket for the emperor's tournament; the cricket wins and the boy's family prospers; the boy himself grows up to become one of the emperor's most influential advisers; and he gets his soul back. An amusing story, don't you think?"

Forbes nodded neutrally. He flipped his cigarette into the lake and drew his knees up under his chin. He had always taken Tung for granted in Hamilton's world. He sometimes regarded him as a kind of oriental Uncle Remus; the man would tell a Chinese folktale with no prompting whatever.

"You have never visited China, have you, Mr. Forbes?" The cricket was vibrating energetically. "Are you looking forward to it?"

"I haven't had much time to think about it. Like you said, there's a lot of commotion at Wabash House."

"I am looking forward to it eagerly. I want to pick a site for my grave."

"Why do you want to do that?"

"I am a Christian, but I believe strongly in geomancy."

"In what?"

"Geomancy. I engaged the geomancer who selected the site in Chungking where the president's father and mother are buried," he said with evident pride.

Suddenly a look of fearful uncertainty came over Tung's old face. "I was promised by the man who—how shall I say it? who facilitated my passage from China—I was promised by this man that I would have the services of a geomancer to pick the appropriate site for me. I have depended upon that promise from the day I left China. With all my heart I have depended upon it. I have saved quite a bit of money to pay the geomancer. I hope it is sufficient." There was a quiet but clear note of anguish in his voice. "The site of your grave fixes the future," he added; he seemed to be pleading for understanding. "An ill-chosen burial place can bring misfortune to those you leave behind."

"Who are you leaving behind, Tung?" Forbes was too preoccupied to comprehend the old man's genuine distress.

Tung Yen Fun hesitated; then he said evenly, "President Hamilton . . . and a number of nieces and nephews."

He closed his eyes and settled the umbrella on his shoulder; he seemed at peace again, enraptured by the sound of the cricket. Presently he opened his eyes. He took out his pocket watch and studied the second hand. "Do you know it is exactly ninety-seven degrees Fahrenheit?"

"I know it's hot as hell," said Forbes, lightly stroking his face; he brushed drops of sweat as they trickled from his thick sideburns.

"Crickets chirp more rapidly on days like this." Tung was still looking at his watch. "If you add thirty-seven to the number of chirps in fifteen seconds, you will get the exact temperature."

"How do you know that?" Forbes was resigned to the prospect of more Chinese folklore.

"It is important in cricket fighting. Cricket fighting is a favorite pastime among many Chinese. The man who promised to engage the geomancer for me is an enthusiast of it. The chirping is produced when the males rub their forewings together. The faster they chirp, the less they are inclined to do battle. They chirp faster in hot weather. That is why the tournaments are held in the autumn."

Forbes lit another cigarette. He coughed as he exhaled the first breath of smoke. He hoped Tung would be quiet for a while. He was laboring to reduce the principle of assassination to its intended victim—and to make peace with his qualified expectation—was it a foregone conclusion?—that it was either a dead Hamilton or a dead or imprisoned Forbes (probably dead). Had he intended to kill his father, the outlines of his dilemma would be sharper; he would be able to accept himself as a man of primal criminal instincts, a bird of prey. But these were not Forbes's functioning traits, and as he sat in the shade of the tackle shed he admitted he did not know what to do. Assassination was for intriguers, lunatics, not political consultants. The only sure thing was that whatever he decided would be dictated by circumstance and presence of mind without regard for the Big Picture.

"The cricket is chirping slower," said Tung. He checked his watch. "I calculate the temperature has fallen two degrees."

Melville was behind the bar in his office. It was very rarely that he condescended to pour a drink for someone. The guest and the circumstances had to be extraordinary. The last time was for the king of Saudi Arabia. He had blundered and offered his highness a whiskey; the king finally accepted a glass of water after it had been tasted by an attendant.

"Do you take soda?" he asked. He fussed with the bar utensils.

"On the rocks will be fine," said Headlight.

Melville brought the drinks over to the sofa. He sat down next to Headlight. Both men were drinking vermouth. They were alone. Hibbitt was elsewhere in the mansion keeping in touch by phone with developments at the convention in Pittsburgh.

The vice-president had returned to Washington an hour earlier from the funeral of Justice Roundtree. He had been interviewed outside the church and asked whether he was attending as President Hamilton's representative. He smiled modestly and said that was a question for the president. He declined to answer questions about the convention. He said it would be inappropriate on such a sad occasion.

"You've caused me quite a few headaches," said Headlight, getting straight to the point. "Why didn't you consult me?" His tone was severe. He sipped his vermouth. "The operation I organized for you is barely afloat. It may abort. I warned you that this was an offensive operation. Offensive operations are tricky under the best conditions. You've turned this one into a minefield. That man Vest, for instance."

Melville was profoundly uneasy, too taken aback to be angry. He was totally unfamiliar with private criticism. No one had ever dared question his actions. No one. Now this dapper spy, who sat here with a drink he personally had poured, was vilifying him.

"There were factors you weren't aware of," said Melville curtly, trying to regain the upper hand, "political factors."

"Such as?"

"Things that have no bearing on your . . . operation."

"Vest was a stupid choice," said Headlight bluntly. "He screwed things up from the start. Your guy Hibbitt. Including him was stupid as hell. His modular computer is insecure; the interception protection is perfect, but somebody's damned sloppy about storing the tapes. Hibbitt's emotionally unstable and a homosexual to boot." In Headlight's profession homosexuals were de facto risks; the issue was not debatable.

"Now, *wait* a minute," Melville snorted. "Vest is a damned *good* operator. He's been with Trans-Columbia for years—" he stressed the "Trans-Columbia" to make clear that his family's company hired only the best people—"and I *personally* have no prejudices against homosexuals. A man's private tastes are his own business as far as I'm concerned. You won't find a man more *reliable*—or emotionally stable—than Chandler Hibbitt."

"Vest was all right dealing with South American police chiefs," Headlight went on; there was a note of disgust in his drawl. "But he was out of his depth on this. First, he went to an intelligence officer who was not on the list I drew up. An officer who is far too single-minded for this operation. Second, he turned over that manufactured letter, the original copy. I told you to duplicate it. First-generation Xeroxes are just as convincing as originals."

"How do you know it was the original?"

"I cracked the safe it was stored in." Headlight smiled laconically. "I was surprised I still knew how to do it."

"Could I have it back?"

"No. I'm trying to salvage this thing. I may need it at some point."

Melville set his drink on an end table and walked over to his glass collection. He picked up one of the swans. "I still say Vest is a good man," he said insolently.

"Vest is dead."

Melville turned around. He looked surprised.

"He was shot in Jacques Novic's place in California. I assume he had just planted the other letter there. It was an original, too. Vest's story was that Novic was flying to China and would deliver the letter to Tien. The catch is, Novic has been in Australia for two weeks. He's flying to China, all right, but he couldn't possibly have the letter with him. That kind of thing attracts attention in this business.

"As if things weren't bad enough," Headlight continued—he lit a cigarette from his gold case—"the man in place to make the hit with the pathogenic accelerators is brittle as hell. My man has real doubts about whether he has the stomach for it."

"But Nell Leatherbee is backing him up," cried Melville.

Headlight glared at the vice-president.

"Nell Leatherbee? The woman at Treasury?" he shouted in angry amazement. "How the hell did she get into this?"

"I thought we needed someone else in case Forbes couldn't do it." Melville was trying desperately to convey that some of his planning had been shrewd.

"Who recruited her? Who developed her?"

"I did," Melville said quickly in self-defense. "She's in financial trouble. I had the impression she jumped at the idea."

"You'd better fill me in."

Melville told him about the Syrette of potent meningococcal bacteria that had been sewn in the lining of Forbes's jacket.

246

Headlight shook his head violently. "Don't you know that stuff is traceable? And treatable? If she injects Hamilton, you're in over your head. Even if it doesn't kill him. Think about it, for God's sake. An isolated case of a virulent strain of spinal meningitis in the presidential compound. And who contracts it? The *president!* Every agency from the Public Health Service to the Bureau of Labor Statistics would be on it. You'd better get in touch with her right now. Tell her to go straight into the Georgia woods and bury it as deep as she can."

Melville walked back to the bar and poured himself another vermouth. "Another drink?" He thought sociability might disarm this man, put him back in his place. An offer by Lawrence Melville to pour a mere government employee a second drink ought to have some effect, oughtn't it?

"No, thanks."

Melville sipped the sweet wine and changed course. "If I've made a mistake, I want to apologize to you," he said; his eyes crinkled into a smile. "Personally and professionally." He had unshakable faith in the Melville charm. "I want you to know I still intend to appoint you director. I think we can work well together. I want a man I can depend on to tell me when I've gone wrong," he lied.

Headlight rose from the sofa. "And I want to be the director. If I didn't, I wouldn't be here now. I liked your idea from the start. I'm attracted to pure ruthlessness. What sold me was when you said you wanted it planned and executed professionally. But you weren't able to let go of it, and, well, we know what's happened. As I see it, that's a habit you'll have to break if I'm to be your director.

"Understand this, Mr. Vice-President. I'm quicker than you are. Most of us are, in this line of work. We have to be. We live by results. You put too much faith in control. You relied on Vest because you knew he would do what he was told. It never occurred to you that Vest was a fool. The same with Hibbitt. He takes his orders and thinks you'll protect him from embarrassment while he gets a taste of power. I don't have a personal bias against homosexuals, either. But Hibbitt has a bias against himself, and that makes him a risk." He leaned over and put out his cigarette. "So for the sake of controlling a situation you had no idea how to handle, you put a fool and a risk in harness and turned them loose. I know you'd like to have a man you can dominate. Like Vest and Hibbitt. But I don't work like that. Do we understand each other?"

"Perfectly," said Melville; he sat down behind his desk; he was trying to recover at least his status as vice-president of the United States. "Vest said something about this man Coombes," he said. "He hasn't exactly been a success, has he? I don't suppose it would look too good for him if this got out. For him or any other intelligence type near him."

Headlight understood the threat and replied in kind. "You're right. Coombes has had his ups and downs. He gets things done, though. For example, he microfilmed the letter that Vest put in Novic's safe. It's good work, but clearly a forgery. I have the film myself. Coombes also has Vest's identification. Did you know that one of Vest's cards is a pass to your suite in the Executive Office Building?"

He placed his drink on an end table and stood up. "Let's see. Where does this leave us? We have a politician of doubtful backbone named Forbes with a handful of lethal capsules at the presidential compound; we have a woman who has probably never given a shot in her life with a needleful of enough bacteria to start an epidemic." He walked across the room and placed a typewritten slip of paper on the desk in front of the vice-president. (Headlight had personally typed the message; he had then disassembled the newly purchased machine, part by part, and scattered the pieces in the Chesapeake Bay over the side of his sailboat.) "That's how we start to straighten out this mess," he said, pointing to the paper, "to neutralize the risks, so to ˙speak."

Melville read it quickly and looked up. "Send him to the Executive Office Building? At six o'clock? But why? I'm expecting him to fly to Pittsburgh with me. We leave around seven, I think."

"Send him. Choose your own excuse. But send him," Headlight ordered and walked to the door.

"One other thing. Forbes. He may be a risk, too. As you know, his father committed suicide a number of years ago. Chris Forbes was a friend of mine, by the way, an older man I always felt comfortable with. Nobody could explain why Chris killed himself. I think you ought to know why it happened." Headlight reached for the door and opened it part-way. "We were first looking into mind-expanding drugs and decided to test one of them—it was something like LSD or peyote—on some people we thought could take the fright it would probably give them." He eased the door shut again. "We arranged a cocktail party in New York for some people who had been with us in Burma. We didn't tell them that all the liquor had been doctored. . . . There were the usual reactions, hallucinations and that sort of thing, but the evaluators said they amounted to less than the nightmares men experience during and after extended combat. I knew Chris never suffered nightmares during the war—he was the battalion commander before I took over—and I learned later that he never had them afterward. I supposed that that drugged whiskey highball gave him the first nightmare he'd ever had—and apparently he couldn't take it. I don't know his son, but it's damned inconvenient, for obvious reasons, for him to be connected with this operation."

"Why are you telling me this?" There was a look of creeping dread on Melville's face.

"To reemphasize my earlier point—to make sure you understand who you're dealing with. By the way, if you tried to tape this conversation, you wasted your time. A portable 'screecher' has been running in my car since I arrived."

Headlight left without waiting for Melville to say thanks so much for coming by.

Melville was outraged. It was the first time in his adult life that he had been humiliated. He knew he had to get a call through to Nell Leatherbee to warn her off. He felt cruel. He wanted to hurt someone. Oh, yes. He would appoint that audacious spy. And then fire him. Strip him naked in public, degrade him, ruin him. That would have to wait. He was possessed. He had to inflict pain now. He picked up the phone.

"Hibbitt, you disgusting queer! Come up here," he spat.

It was true that Nell had never given a shot in her life. She wondered how it was done. She knew she couldn't tell Hamilton to roll up his sleeve and say this won't hurt a bit.

She was fresh from the shower. She sat nude at her dressing table in Elkhart House as she applied her makeup. She put down her eyeliner as she studied herself in the mirror. She admired her body. She credited Forbes with that; he admired it and said so often; her husband never commented on it one way or the other. Her breasts were encouragingly firm. What she could see of her stomach was flat. Her skin was smooth. Her eyes were clear.

The telephone had rung incessantly. Once it rang seventeen times straight. She had not answered it. She had thought of telling the switchboard that she wasn't accepting any calls. Then she realized that the ringing had an oddly reassuring effect. She felt like a soldier who was able to read Euripides in the original Greek during an artillery barrage.

She completed her face and slipped on a light cotton dress. It was less than a half hour until her meeting with the president.

There was a folder on her desk. A pack of Forbes's cigarettes lay nearby; he had left them there last night; the folder was the file on the revised "book-entry" regulations. The banking industry wanted the Treasury bill changes; some banks said the rules caused too much costly bookkeeping; the others said the book entries created too much competition with the Treasury Department itself. Hamilton wanted the changes. She hurriedly skimmed the file.

Next to the folder was her attaché case. She unlatched it and took out the disposable Syrette. She held it up for a closer examination. It was an inch long, a narrow tube with a short hypodermic needle protected by a detachable fiberglass sheath. She recalled Hibbitt's instructions. Plunge it into Hamilton's buttocks. That was the most efficient way. What if he's sitting down? In that case aim for the latissimus dorsi, the muscle at the edge of the back just below the shoulder. But surely he'll know he's been stuck; he'll call for help. What then? "You'll be amazed," Hibbitt had said that morning via his computer in Pittsburgh; it was before Headlight had confronted Melville. "This stuff is quick. We tested it on a two-hundred-and-fifty-pound orangutan in Borneo. It was a healthy, full-grown adult male, nearly five feet tall. We used the same dose that's in the Syrette. The thing was disoriented in less than thirty seconds and stone dead in eight and a half minutes. So don't worry about being discovered. Make sure you dispose of the Syrette the way we discussed. And be careful. If any of it infects you, call immediately. There's a doctor ready if you need him. He's in Georgia with the medication."

She had no ethical misgivings as she contemplated the Syrette. Morality was not a consideration. She had elected to act because she was convinced that Forbes would not. She was doing something she believed Forbes had no reason to be involved in at all. Although she had joined the plot for her own motives, it was now a case of stopping a mad president. The distinction was minor. She loved Forbes; she was simply substituting for him, as if he had suddenly lost his ability to balance his checkbook and she was doing his addition and subtraction. She was going to perpetrate a hideous death for a clear, peremptory reason. To preserve her independence. When this was over, she and Forbes would resume their romance, free of the pressure of intrigue; her ranch would be financially sound again with the loan from Melville; she would be secretary of the treasury when Melville was elected president. She did not acknowledge the quantum leap of self-delusion needed to justify her designs. She was used to getting what she wanted. How she got it had ceased to matter.

The Syrette continued to puzzle her. How *do* you use the damned thing? Just jam it in the skin and pinch the tube? How much pressure was needed? How much time? Wouldn't she have to push harder to penetrate Hamilton's clothing? She decided to make a practice run.

She took a cushion from the sofa and placed it on the floor behind the heavy curtains. That ought to be resistant enough, she thought. She snapped the fiberglass sheath off the needle. A drop of fluid oozed from the tip and dropped to the carpet. She drew back with a start. Her hand was trembling slightly. She got to her knees and pressed the curtain firmly against the cushion. She plunged the needle abruptly into the rough fabric. It was easy.

So that's how you give a shot, she said to herself. She pulled the Syrette to extract the needle. It held fast in the curtain. The threaded joint that connected the needle to the tube clung to a strand of the fabric. She flattened the curtain with one palm and tugged again. The needle slipped free. As it did, it dragged lightly over the loose flesh between the thumb and index finger of the hand with which she had pressed the curtain. It left a tiny scratch.

She stared at the scratch for a moment. Then she replaced the fiberglass sheath on the needle. She dropped it into her purse. When she was a girl, she had once been bitten by a rattlesnake on the ranch. Her father had applied a tourniquet and sucked the venom. It was important not to panic, he had told her on the way to the doctor who administered the anti-toxin serum. She did not think a tourniquet or sucking the scratch would work now, but she did not panic.

The phone was ringing again. She paid no attention to it. She checked to see if she had the keys to the car from the motor pool. She had. She walked briskly from the house and drove away from the presidential compound.

Her head was splitting by the time she reached Buddy's restaurant. Three or four newspaper correspondents were at a table. One of them called to her, shouting a question about government policy. She smiled at them the best she could and went straight to the telephone booths in the rear. She swiftly dialed Hibbitt's number in Pittsburgh. Her fever was increasing. She struggled against delirium.

"Melville-Monongahela Bank and Trust. Good afternoon."

"Chandler Hibbitt," said Nell. She noticed black and blue splotches, like bruises, forming on her smooth arms and legs.

"One moment, please."

Her headache was growing unendurable. Her neck was gripped by a toothache-like pain.

"I'm sorry," said a voice after a few seconds; the modular computer made it echo. "Mr. Hibbitt is unavailable at the moment. May I take a message?"

A reporter appeared outside the phone booth. He pan-tomimed that he wanted to interview her. She waved him away.

"This is Nell Leatherbee. Tell him it's urgent."

There was a moment of silence and then the voice said, "Mr. Hibbitt is away from the office. I'll have him return your call the minute he gets back."

"Put me through to Melville," she said. Her voice was nearly a whisper. The splotches were darkening on her arms and legs, the arms and legs she craved to wrap around

Forbes's ardent body. They had also begun to appear on her face and neck.

"I beg your pardon."

"Melville. The vice-president. I have to speak to him. . . ."

"I'm afraid you'll have to speak to Mr. Hibbitt about that. If you'll leave your number—"

She barely had the strength to replace the receiver. She managed to put on her sunglasses. She was almost staggering when she walked out of the restaurant. The correspondents called to her, but she was unable to acknowledge them.

With a difficulty she had not imagined possible for a human being to experience she started the car and drove away. Her fever was approaching 105 but she still had her wits about her. She would go straight to Dr. Brabham and tell him that she had been infected with meningococcal bacteria. She would even tell him how it happened.

The invincible bacteria rampaged through her bloodstream. The hemorrhagic rash had discolored her entire body. She imagined Forbes would be horrified when he saw it. Her face was disfigured and stained. Her neck was so stiff that she could not touch her chest with her chin. Her joints felt as if they had turned to volcanic stone. Her vision was blurred. The white line down the middle of the two-lane highway rose and fell. The adjoining cornfields were green fuzz.

About three miles from Buddy's on the way to the Southern White House was a notorious curve. It was unbanked and sheered off steeply to a shallow slough that was overgrown with blackberry brambles and scrub oak. Wrecks that occurred here were often undiscovered for days. The county authorities had been implored to erect a guard rail but no money could be found for the job. It was at this curve that Nell's car left the road. Her last thoughts were of Forbes and the cornfields.

254

"I couldn't reach Mrs. Leatherbee," said Hibbitt. He was feeling better. The tranquilizer had taken effect. He had never seen Melville so abusive.

"It doesn't matter," said Melville. He was still morose, but calmer. The savaging he had laid on Hibbitt had restored his sense of dominion. "She hasn't done anything. That's apparent. They don't keep it a secret when the president dies."

"Oh," Hibbitt added. "She tried to call later. I decided against taking the call."

"Good," said Melville. "It isn't a good idea for her to be calling here, even through the computer. We probably won't be calling her too much anymore, either. I shouldn't have brought her in in the first place. She really isn't cabinet material."

He toyed with a glass swan and then said abruptly, "Chandler, I want you to drive up to the E.O.B. Be there at six on the dot. There's something I want picked up personally. Someone will be expecting you. I'll explain after you've got the thing what this is all about."

"But we're supposed to be in Pittsburgh before eight," Hibbitt protested mildly; he hated these moments when Melville reduced him to a mere errand boy. "Won't that be cutting it pretty—"

"Call after you've picked up the package," Melville interrupted crisply. "You can fly up later if it's necessary. Check with one of your people."

Hibbitt was perplexed but resigned to carrying out Melville's unexpected orders. His perplexity grew from the fact that the vice-president seldom visited his office in the Executive Office Building adjoining the White House and never conducted any official business there.

Of course, there was no question that Chandler Hibbitt would do as he was told.

10 The Disappointment

Hamilton dawdled over a dish of butterscotch twirl ice cream and gulped from a straight-up mao-tai martini. Butterscotch twirl was his favorite flavor. Tonight it was his dinner. The martini was his third since they sat down.

"I'm damned put out with Nell," he said. He looked gaunt and sullen but self-possessed. He ladled gobs of ice cream with his spoon. "You make sure you tell her that, Thack. I'll tell her myself, too. You can count on it. . . . Missing a meeting with the president without so much as a how-do-you-do. Who the hell does she think she is? This book-entry business is important."

Forbes and Snyder were having tournedos with béarnaise sauce and sharing a bottle of very good Bordeaux. Forbes had barely touched his. They were in the North Dining Room. They were, of course, in short sleeves. The food and wine at the Southern White House were excellent, although Hamilton was indifferent to it; he had been advised that a first-rate cuisine impressed visiting dignitaries.

"There's no need to crawl Thack about it, Joe," said Snyder. He was trying to downplay Nell's absence from the afternoon meeting and from the informal dinner; Snyder believed that occasional lapses of ceremony were tolerable among the president's inner circle. He wanted to ease Hamilton into a reflective mood on the eve of their departure for China. "Thack doesn't know what's happened to her, either. What the hell, we got the thing worked out. The guy from the banks sounded pleased. We can't stroke the consumer people until we get back, anyway."

"I don't give a goddamn," said Hamilton; his voice rose. "You don't stand up the president. For any reason. She didn't make a call or anything. That kind of thing pisses me off royally. It's the kind of crap I'd expect from Osborne." With the mention of the secretary of state's name, the president signaled the steward for another martini.

Snyder was determined to change the subject. "I can't get over that about Chandler Hibbitt," he said as he sipped his wine. "Where did you say they found him, Thack?"

"In that park in Arlington," said Forbes. He felt vaguely guilty that he was unconcerned over the fate of Hibbitt. He was puzzled, too, about Nell; she didn't go in for disappearing acts. His main preoccupation, though, was the amber capsule in his pocket. He was depressingly conscious that he would learn tonight whether he had to use it. He felt isolated and halfhearted, and had little appetite.

Hamilton's attention was engaged again. The steward set the drink down in front of him. "That park has been a fag hangout for as far back as I can remember," he said. He pushed the dish of ice cream aside. "I didn't know Hibbitt—I don't know any of those people who work for Melville—but I'd have thought anybody as well known as this guy would have the sense to stay away from a place like that. That part on the wire. Was that right?"

"Which part?"

"The part about him being naked and his nuts cut off?"

"It said he had been mutilated. I guess that's what it meant."

"That's what it meant," said Hamilton. He tossed back a generous swallow from his fresh drink. "That's what it meant, all right. That's what it always means when they say the body was mutilated. Did you know the guy was queer?"

Snyder and Forbes shook their heads.

"I wonder how it got out so quick," said Hamilton. He looked mystified. "In the media, I mean. Hell, if I'd been in Melville's place, with the convention in high gear, I'd have made damned sure it didn't get out."

"I don't understand it, either," said Forbes, compelling himself to take part in the conversation. "Melville knows how to keep things out of the media. It doesn't make sense that he might have figured it would draw some sympathy." His observation was mechanical and unoriginal, the facile conclusion a professional politician would arrive at.

"You're damned right it doesn't make sense," said Hamilton. His enthusiasm was picking up. "You might get some sympathy with something like this in an election—an election you're way ahead in—but not at a convention. Convention delegates play too many angles to be affected by sympathy. Larry Melville may win the nomination, but it won't have anything to do with sympathy over a fag killing. You don't believe this so-called stampede of uncommitted delegates to Melville, do you?"

"No."

"Hell, no, you don't. Everybody seems to ignore Darrow's people when they talk about uncommitted delegates. Darrow has been all over Pittsburgh, knocking on hotel doors, attending those goddamn receptions, doing the things you have to do to collar these uncommitted people. Melville flies in there once a day, usually at night, and makes a speech nobody listens to, and goes back to Washington. He thinks those delegates believe he's president already. Well, he'd better watch out. Darrow might not look like much, but he's working like hell, and that's what it takes to get nominated."

Forbes nodded agreement. Had he been asked, he would have assessed the situation about the same way. It was a way of political reasoning that Hamilton had learned from him. He was not surprised that Hamilton did not mention the possibility of a deadlocked convention—a conceivable eventuality that could put him in contention for renomination. Even if he were in China.

Hamilton took a slow sip of his martini. "Brabham told me about your breach of the peace, Gil." Snyder nodded. "I know you couldn't make him understand, but thanks for trying."

He turned to Forbes; his expression was suddenly glum. "What I can't understand is this shit from you, Thack. Wanting me to call off the trip. Brabham said you and Nell both agreed with him. Is that right?"

"Yes."

Hamilton's eyes grew fiery in his narrow face. His nostrils flared and his mouth distorted. Forbes recalled in a flash Brabham's diagnosis of the president's condition. This was followed in split-second succession by an image of the letter Melville had shown him.

"Goddamn it!" Hamilton screamed. "It's got to the point where I don't know who to depend on. Nell Leatherbee treats me like a hired hand. And *you*"—he shoved a bony finger at Forbes—"Larry Melville pats *you* on the fucking back and *you* try to tell me how to do my job!"

"Now, hold it, Joe," Snyder put in; he tried to sound soothing. "Thack was only looking—"

"Shut up, Snyder." Hamilton's words were slurred. "Just shut the hell up. You've been butting in all goddamn night. I may have been kicked in the ass by that son of a bitch Melville, but I don't have to say this or not say that because *you* say so. Nell Leatherbee is a stuck-up cunt and Forbes is a two-faced asshole."

Forbes set down his wineglass and pushed back from the table. He was glad of the insult; it was an excuse to flee, to avoid action, at least for tonight. "Excuse me, Mr. President. I think I should leave now. I have some packing to do for the trip."

"Don't you move," snarled Hamilton. "Either one of you." He looked as if he were tormented by an old, secret sore. "By God, I'll call the Secret Service in here and have them hold a gun on you if you try to leave." He glared at them, as if he intended to spring from his chair and attack them. Then he looked down at the table.

Snyder and Forbes looked at each other apprehensively.

Hamilton slowly lifted his head. His expression was strained. "I'm sorry I said that," he said kindly. "I'm really sorry. The pressure's gotten to me, I admit it. I know that's a pretty weak excuse for behaving like that, but I'm genuinely sorry. Let me get you a drink. Cognac?"

He left the table without waiting for a reply and returned from the liquor cart with two snifters. Forbes and Snyder accepted them with forced, nodding smiles.

"What's got me down," said Hamilton—his voice was a plaintive croak—"is that I'm leaving this job without having done the one thing that I really, at the bottom of my heart, wanted to do."

The other two looked at him attentively, although Forbes was barely listening. He was absorbed by the amber capsule in his pocket.

"And that was to make the State Department work." Hamilton looked contemplatively into his martini. "I tried my damnedest to put the brakes on the professional snobs that run the place, but I got sidetracked," he continued, as if his sulfurous outburst had never occurred. "Oh, I know there are some good people at State. Men who aren't afraid to tell the president the bad and the good news. But most of them are these career types who hide behind cleverness and shut off new blood by hollering that I sell ambassadorships. It's funny with those bastards. They make a big racket about merit, but when I put a man in a post who hasn't spent twenty years in the Foreign Service but who's qualified just the same, they get snotty and call him an amateur. And give him a hell of a rough time.

"Take Osborne." He took a moderate sip of his martini. Forbes and Snyder nursed their brandies and worried that Hamilton was liable to veer violently from the subject. "Osborne hasn't been a bad secretary of state. I might have picked him myself if Melville hadn't campaigned for him in the media and wedged him through that screening panel. But he's Larry Melville's boy. I've never gotten rid of the feeling that he always checks with Melville before he makes a move. . . . That was a pretty good mesh he brought in, by the way, Gil."

"It went pretty smoothly," Snyder replied. "I think he really sees that you intend to lead the negotiations."

"The trouble is," Hamilton went on—he set his drink on the table—"it was like pulling teeth to get him to see that's what I wanted. These negotiations can open the way to all sorts of possibilities. One of them—I discussed this with Thack—is some hard bargaining with Tien on the nonaggression thing. I may even consider a protocol."

Forbes's well-being began to disintegrate. He stole a glance at his watch. It was almost ten o'clock—time to call that bookie or whoever she was. Snyder raised his ginger eyebrows. It was his standard reaction to the last-minute surprises he had come to expect from Hamilton.

"For God's sake, don't mention that," said Hamilton. "It'll

depend on the timing. I may have a couple of other surprises when we get to Peking. I don't want to discuss them now. They'll depend on the timing, too."

Forbes felt nauseous. He wondered feverishly whether Hamilton had told Snyder of his "vacation" idea; he guessed he hadn't. He stood up. "I have to make a few calls," he said; his voice was weak. "I'll be back in a few minutes."

He hurried from the room. Hamilton and Snyder stared at him.

The night air was soggy. The leaves on the broad oak tree outside Wabash House were showing their backs; it was a sign of rain. Forbes leaned against the trunk until the sensation at the top of his throat subsided. The marine sergeant at the door asked if he could help. Forbes said no. He wasn't going to vomit after all.

He went straight to the study in Fort Wayne House and poured a tall, straight Bourbon. It warmed his stomach. He lit a cigarette and coughed.

He plopped on the sofa. Where was Nell? His thoughts were riven with anger. He needed her now. She knew goddamn well he did. And Hibbitt. Why did that wretched son of a bitch choose today to get himself killed?

He reached for the telephone and dialed the number of the bookie. The insipid female voice answered.

"This is Forbes," he snapped.

"Yes, Mr. Forbes. I believe you had Spring Outing in the third race at Saratoga. Is that right?"

"You know damned well I did."

"I'm sorry. Spring Outing broke in the gate. Would you—"

Forbes slammed down the receiver. He leapt to his feet and paced the room. He was seized by a turbulent rush of recklessness and despair. He quickly took stock. In his pocket he had the amber capsule. In his heart he had hate. The kind of hate a man feels when he has forgiven too much. What he needed was dignity. A man who hates must have at least a little dignity. Maybe dignity would see him through.

He tried Elkhart House. Sorry, said the switchboard, Mrs. Leatherbee was still out. He needed to talk to someone. He dialed New York. Alison's line was busy.

He leaned back on the sofa and reflected that he was running very low on alternatives. His anger began to recede; it relieved the mental paralysis that the phone call to the bookie had entangled him in. Still he wavered. He knew he had never lacked the love or attention that breeds the swollen ego and vicious destructive urge of a criminal. He thought briefly of his father and breathed freely as he conceived that the span of years and recollections had actually brought him closer to the man who had slain himself without explanation. . . . The thought faded and the need to hear a sympathetic voice returned.

"Oh, hi, Thack," Alison answered sweetly. There was music playing; Mendelssohn again; Forbes wondered why it was called the *Scotch* Symphony; it reminded him of tender Italian skies. "What's up?"

"I didn't get a chance to call earlier." He tried to sound casually businesslike but knew he wasn't succeeding. "I thought I'd better let you catch me up to date."

Alison put her hand over the receiver. Forbes could hear a terse, muffled conversation with a visitor; he imagined for a fleeting moment it was the voice that had answered the phone in his office the day before—the man Alison had said was from the telephone company. (The seedy man who had kicked him at the airport?) He could hear a door close.

She was back.

"I'm not interrupting anything, am I?" Forbes was more than curious to know who had been with Alison.

"Oh, no," she said. "That was the maintenance man. He unstopped my bathtub. Well, let's see. Topic A is Chandler

Hibbitt. Wasn't that awful? Did you know he was gay?"

"No. I knew he was a jerk but not a gay jerk."

"Thack, I'm surprised at you."

"Sorry, Alison. That was pretty poor. I had a run-in with Hibbitt the other day."

"Did you talk to Melville?"

"No. I probably will, though." He knew he wouldn't.

"What have you heard from the convention?"

"Nothing much. It's all China down here."

"The campaign is in suspended animation. Eric went to the Roundtree funeral. I sent flowers from you. Oh. I got the Hoogh prints. A really good one of *Delft After the Explosion*. It's his first one, you know. And a few others. More representative. They're a lot like Vermeer. He does the same kind of subject. Do you like Vermeer?"

"I know the *Allegory of Faith*. It's at the Metropolitan. I saw the *Allegory of Painting* in Vienna a few years ago."

"You'll love the Hooghs. I've already hung them in your office. They make a world of difference. A personal touch, you know?"

"Thanks, Alison. You can have them after the campaign."

"No. They're yours. You'll have another office. You'll need something besides your button clock. Or you can hang them in your apartment."

They chatted a while longer, local political gossip and a new restaurant that Alison said was horrible but very popular.

Suddenly, impulsively, as Mendelssohn's hints of clans and bagpipes grew more emphatic, Forbes said, "When I get back, Alison, I'm going to take you to a great restaurant, a first-class joint, Lutèce or Côte Basque. I'm going to be the most attentive man you ever went to dinner with. And I'm going to make a pass at you. A dead serious, no-tomorrow pass."

There was a silence and then Alison said, with a note of distress, "Did you say that because you know I miss you?"

"No. I said it because I meant it."

"What about Mrs. Leatherbee?"

"She's my problem. You and I can create a problem of our own."

"I'm counting the days, Thack."

When he hung up, Forbes still wondered who the other voice was in Alison's apartment, but he felt more composed. And dignified. Still no word from Nell. It disturbed him. She invariably left a message.

He took another stiff drink and made his decision.

Hamilton and Snyder had left the table when he returned to Wabash House. They were in the large room at the rear that overlooked the lake. Hamilton was standing slump-shouldered at the bulletproof window. A steward manned the bar. Tung Yen Fun sat silently in a corner.

"What the hell could have become of Nelly, do you think?" Hamilton was obviously drunk but mellow. "Think she'll show up in time for the plane in the morning? She's been to China before, but not with me at the head of the parade."

"I can't imagine," Forbes replied. He took a seat across from Snyder in one of the overstuffed leather chairs.

"Think it's something serious?" Snyder asked quietly; he sounded solicitous. He was aware of their affair but discreet enough never to allude to it.

"I don't know, Gil. I just don't know."

"Hell," said Hamilton from the window. "If it'll put your mind at ease, I'll tell Al or one of the other press people to make a few calls. She may have gone back to Washington. Or Texas. Who the hell knows. Anyway, get Thack a drink. No use worrying about it without a drink."

"I'll get it," said Forbes.

He had chosen his moment. It was time to get on with it. He rose and walked to the bar. He looked at the bottles and at the steward.

"What's your name?" he asked the steward.

"Feliciano, sir."

"Sergeant Feliciano?"

"Lance Corporal Feliciano, sir."

"Like this duty?"

"It's okay, sir. The hours get long sometimes."

"Why don't you take off? I'll handle the bar."

The steward braced and then left the room.

"Why the hell did you fire the bartender, Thack?" Hamilton shouted jovially. "I'm in a thirsty mood."

"The kid looked like he needed a break. Anyway, I feel like mixing a few drinks. What's your pleasure?"

Snyder said his Bourbon and soda was holding up fine. Tung Yen Fun indicated that he did not care for a drink. The president said he was damned ready for another mao-tai martini. "Make it dry—dry as a preacher's tongue."

Hamilton brightened. "Say, Gil, why don't we send a note of sympathy to Hibbitt's wife."

"Okay, if you want."

"Don't you think it's a good idea?"

"Sure, if you want to do it."

"And get it out to the media. I know it'll piss Melville off." The president burst into laughter.

At the bar Forbes picked up the mao-tai bottle. He sloshed the raw, clear liquor into a shaker. Now, he said to himself, it's got to be *now*, the unaccepted but only time. He poured in a dash of vermouth and heaped in a handful of ice. He slipped his free hand into his pocket. He felt the capsule. It was sticky and rough with lint. He would simply crush the powder into the shaker and return the gelatin shell to his pocket. This is the perfect moment, he thought, the moment when blandishments and lies count for everything and innocence itself is misled like the village idiot. The moment when time ceases and things happen. . . .

Nothing happened.

"I can't," Forbes said aloud; there was an ancient pain in his voice. "I can't do it."

His soul seemed to shrink. He had been unable to commit murder and he despised himself. He freed his hand. The amber capsule remained in his pocket. His mind was seething with an extravaganza of imaginary perceptions and vivid memories. He closed his eyes and gripped the bar. In a fraction of an instant he wildly summoned up a panopticon of bizarre illusions: Nell committing fellatio on the president; Alison playing gin rummy with the rumpled man; Melville and Hibbitt drinking beer at a baseball game; Caswell and Snyder furtively going through his luggage. Then his brain began to cool. He remembered his last game of squash with his father; he remembered the attempted consolation of his father's partner—*Of course you made the right decision, Thack;* he remembered his agony over having agreed without agreeing to let a stranger end his father's life. As he gradually made his way back to the real present, he felt like an overtrained boxer; when the crucial moment came, he was too weak to get the job done.

"What's that?" Hamilton shouted thickly from the other end of the room. "Want me to call the boy back?"

Forbes shook his head. "No," he said in a voice of consummate defeat.

He slowly completed the president's drink. He poured himself a full tumbler of Bourbon and carried it along as he delivered Hamilton's martini.

"You look like hell, Thack," said Hamilton. He eyed

Forbes's brimming glass. "Goddamn, son, I've never seen you take on that much straight liquor. Think you can handle it?"

"I'll try," he mumbled with a silly smile and sat down. He bolted back a slug of Bourbon. He fumbled to light a cigarette. He felt undignified. Undignified and mocked by his failure to act. He downed more liquor to buffer the insult of cowardice.

At length they finished their drinks. Forbes was not a heavy drinker, and the huge amount of alcohol he had consumed in a very short time had debilitated him. But it had not eased his spirit.

"I'd better call it a night," said Hamilton. He shuffled across the room. Tung Yen Fun trudged behind him. "I don't want to catch too much crap from Brabham in the morning. Won't have time for it. Peking express is pulling out early."

Tung held the door. Hamilton turned and said, "Did you see that bastard Melville on the news tonight? Said they'd have to ask me if he was representing me at the funeral. What kind of fools does he think people are? I'd already said Justice Quinn was representing me." He lurched a fraction. Tung assisted him from the room.

Snyder helped Forbes to his feet. He was unsteady and his eyes were unfocused and dim.

"I'll walk you over to Fort Wayne," said Snyder.

A light drizzle had begun to fall. There was occasional lightning and thunder. The temperature had dropped. The heat wave had broken.

Forbes crossed the compound under his own power, but he was unable to think coherently.

"I'll run a check on Nell if you want," said Snyder at the front steps.

"No. Probably husband, sons, something." Forbes was obscurely aware that he could not phrase a sentence. "She'll show. Be on the plane. I know." He dropped his head. "Tried, Gil. Couldn't. No guts. No goddamn dignity. Got to sleep alone. No dignity."

A steward appeared at the door. "Take Mr. Forbes upstairs and put him to bed," said Snyder. He wiped moisture from his face. "Make sure he's up at seven sharp."

The deputy premier was profoundly skeptical. He thought the idea was ill conceived and certainly ill timed.

"Surely you do not believe a pledge made nearly forty years ago—a pledge based on a superstition—is still valid," he said pointedly. He was seated next to Colonel Mee in one of the pair of white chairs in the deputy premier's office in the Great Hall of the People. Cups of tea sat on the table between them.

"Oh, most definitely," replied Colonel Mee. He was wearing his cloth cap. He had neglected to pin his "Serve the People" emblem on his tunic that morning. "You have only to look to Hong Kong or Singapore to see how potent the belief is. Wealthy men of education and cosmopolitan outlook lavish large sums on geomancers. The custom exists here in Peking today. On a much reduced scale, of course."

The deputy premier turned his head away irritably. "The man is Hamilton's valet. He is vulnerable to publicity. If word reached the Western press that we indulged him in an officially discredited practice—a practice specifically condemned by Mao—we would be made to look like fools. The negotiations with Hamilton are critical. We *cannot* be made to look like fools."

"That is not even a consideration," said Colonel Mee, somewhat condescendingly. "Tung Yen Fun will not utter a word. I guarantee it. His only interest is having a grave site selected by him. In return he will agree to be interrogated. I guarantee that, too."

The deputy premier was silent a moment. Then he thrust out his chin and snapped, "I must take up the question with Chairman Tien. He will certainly want to review the entire matter."

"The chairman has already been consulted," Colonel Mee said evenly. "He agrees with me that the venture should be undertaken. He also agrees that this is an unparalleled opportunity for us to receive firsthand information on the workings of the American presidency."

The deputy premier glared at Colonel Mee. He was angry and frightened. And surprised. He had no idea that Colonel Mee had immediate access to the chairman. He had thought that Colonel Mee communicated with the chairman only through him. Presently he regained his composure. "The possibility that this Tung Yen Fun retains a devotion to geomancy is no reason, as far as I can see, to set out on a course of action that is contradictory to Mao's Thought."

Colonel Mee sipped his tea. "Geomancy is merely a tool. Like my poem for Hamilton. When I make it clear to Tung Yen Fun that his only hope for selecting a grave site lies in his cooperation with me, he will leap at the chance to volunteer information."

"If he has any," retorted the deputy premier. The morning haze had lifted; the sun was shining brilliantly. He turned and looked closely at Colonel Mee. "Is this Tung Yen Fun an agent of yours?"

Colonel Mee smiled faintly. His look gave the impression that if he were indiscreet he could tell a great deal that was known only to a few. "He agreed when I arranged his emigration from China that he would be at my disposal—if I would assure him that a geomancer would be available to him—in China—late in his life. He was quite unconditional in his agreement. He meant it as a vow, I am certain."

270

"Have you used him since?" the deputy premier asked eagerly. His eyes were wide with driving curiosity.

Colonel Mee maintained his knowing smile. He lit a cigarette from a pack on the tea table. "Tung Yen Fun has several nephews and nieces here. They are being brought to Peking for a reunion with their uncle. They will provide the visible proof that the old man needs a geomancer. If such proof is necessary. I doubt it. The superstition is very strong."

"It contradicts Mao's Thought," the deputy premier said flatly.

Colonel Mee abruptly snuffed out his cigarette. "Let me remind you that half the buildings that were erected after the earthquakes several years ago were placed on sites selected in consultation with *feng-shui* practitioners. *That* contradicted Mao's Thought but there was no disagreement that these men should be consulted."

"I leave it to you to make certain this causes us no embarrassment," said the deputy premier in a voice of mild menace. "Oh, yes," he added. "Chairman Tien asked me to tell you that he is pleased with the poem. He thinks it strikes just the right note." His tone made it clear he did not share the chairman's view.

"Please tell him that I appreciate the compliment." Colonel Mee's tone made it clear that he had already received the compliment from the chairman himself.

"Any further word on the message from the Americans?"

"No. But I have located Shen Keng Min. He is living temporarily in Bangkok. He has a cousin who operates a restaurant in Nana Road. I have him under surveillance."

"Will you eliminate him?"

Colonel Mee welcomed the question. "Yes. In a short time. I first want to see whether he will shed any more light on the American message."

271

DAY FOUR

11 The Flight

Air Force One banked a degree or two to the left. The Boeing 747 was cruising above the snow-streaked crags of southeastern Alaska several hundred miles north of Anchorage. The president had ordered the detour to give the passengers a view of the scenery.

The newspaper and television correspondents in the rear of the giant jetliner—most of the president's personal fleet were now jumbo jets—crowded at the windows. They jostled each other and spilled drinks on the blue upholstered seats. Photographers snapped away, mostly color film for their private portfolios. Despite the unruliness, most of them expressed awe at the spectacle in the distance.

In the foreground were the stark, brown heights of the Cathedral Spires, displayed vividly in the sub-Arctic sun; snow embellished the crests and nestled in the crevices down the sheer face of the massif. Beyond a ring of smaller peaks—and what seemed from that altitude a small desert of snow—stood Mount Foraker.

The horizon was dominated by Mount McKinley, a hulk of jagged white.

"Know what the Indians call it?" asked Hamilton. He craned from his adjustable chair for a view of the tallest mountain in North America. He was seated before a computer-operated console in his personal cabin immediately behind the elevated flight deck. The cabin was a reproduction in miniature of the Pentagon's war room and known officially as the "command authority compartment."

"What?" said Snyder. He looked up abstractedly. His back was to the window. He was thumbing a file on the opposite side of the cabin. He was seated before a shelf that could be unfolded for desk space.

Forbes and Tung Yen Fun were at windows closer to the flight deck.

"Mount McKinley," Hamilton said.

"No, what?"

"Denali," said Hamilton. He had flicked on one of the ten screens arranged across the front vertical surface of the console; it pinpointed the position of a formation of Soviet fighter bombers over the Chukchi Sea thousands of miles to the north. "It means 'Tall Boy' or something like that. I found that out when they were expanding the national parks. All those mountains down there are a national park, you know."

They would be landing in less than an hour at Elmendorf Air Force Base. It would be their last stop before Peking. Hamilton had prepared a short speech on Chinese-American friendship to deliver at planeside.

The door at the rear of the cabin opened. A State Department aide appeared. The smell of cooking food seeped in. The president's private galley was directly behind his cabin. In the space immediately below, the secretary of state and his staff were busy on final details for the negotiations with the Chinese. The president's personal staff worked in an adjoining cabin; it, too, was below and was connected to Hamilton's compartment by a spiral ladderway that opened onto the galley. The aide handed Snyder a thick loose-leaf binder and closed the door behind him.

"Want to have a look at this?" Snyder asked. "It's the frozen-assets proposals." When Mao Tse-tung's Communists had taken charge of China, they confiscated millions of dollars in American currency; the United States in turn seized millions in Chinese government assets in America. The question of exchange had been under discussion for some time. Hamilton wanted to settle it.

"I'll look at it later," said the president. He had switched screens on the console. A report on the weather in south Georgia was on display. "Wouldn't you know it?" he said and shook his head. "The day we leave, it cools off. And the rain has stopped." He looked calm and mildly bored. He had eaten a light lunch and hadn't had a drink.

"Too bad it was raining when we took off. I thought the band did all right, though." Hamilton insisted that a military band turn out when he appeared in public and strike up "Ruffles and Flourishes" and "Hail to the Chief." A band had been on hand when they landed in California to refuel at Edwards Air Force Base.

Forbes was still at the window when the plane completed its turn and headed south. McKinley National Park slipped from view. He was subdued. A Vitamin B_{12} injection from Dr. Brabham had conquered his hangover, but he was stagnated by remorse and fear. Nell gripped his thoughts. One moment he was anxious and confused—and hurt—that she had failed to show up for the trip; it was totally out of character for her to do something like this without offering some kind of explanation. The next he was relieved that she was not aboard this potential coffin.

He wanted to be alone, but it was impossible in the plane. He had tried to be convivial with the correspondents, but he wasn't up to it; they wanted to discuss the convention, but he

274

had grown to detest Melville almost as much as Hamilton did. The amber capsule in his pocket felt like a poisonous insect; he was afraid to touch it. He stared out the window at the dazzling Alaska landscape.

Then things began to happen.

One of the assistant press secretaries came in. He whispered something to Snyder. Snyder slumped at the fold-down desk; his face turned pale. He asked the assistant press secretary to repeat what he had just said. Upon hearing it again, Snyder nodded for him to leave the cabin.

Snyder got up slowly. He bent over Hamilton's shoulder. He spoke softly. An image of an American aircraft carrier in the Mediterranean was on one of the screens; jet fighters were whooshing from the flight deck. Hamilton listened carefully. His sunken eyes gleamed with alarm. His mouth turned down at the corners. He nodded to Snyder.

"Thack, could you come into the galley with me a second?" said Snyder. There was hopelessness in his voice.

Forbes turned from the window. He walked slowly the length of the compartment. Hamilton looked up at him, but his glance held no promise or assurance.

The galley personnel sensed the gloom in the air and stood still and quiet.

"It's Nell," said Snyder; tears brimmed in his eyes. "They found her. Her car was at the bottom of that curve on the road to Buddy's. . . . It's worse than that, I'm afraid. She had spinal meningitis."

At that moment Dr. Brabham's voice roared in Hamilton's cabin. Forbes and Snyder hadn't noticed him scurry up the spiral ladderway and through the galley. "I don't want any goddamn arguments, Mr. President! Every soul on this plane is getting a gamma globulin shot. Starting with you. They're already worried about an epidemic in Georgia. Drop your trousers. *Now!*"

Forbes slumped against a stainless-steel food storage case. He methodically lit a cigarette.

"Dead?"

"Yes."

Forbes looked at Snyder. His eyes were distant, but in his mind things were falling rapidly into place. "Tell Joe I'll bring him a dish of ice cream." His voice was without emotion. "It's butterscotch something, isn't it?"

Snyder nodded. He had the impression that Forbes wanted solitude and the galley was the only place he was likely to find anything resembling it. He patted him on the shoulder and left.

At once Forbes saw with the brightness of an epiphany that he had to act. There was no time to mourn for Nell. The words of the rumpled man rang in his head: *Remember, a man isn't all that hard to kill.* The threat was all the more compelling because he knew it was a knife that cut both ways. Still, uncertainty grated on him. His first murder—of his own father—was by ignorant consent. If he murdered again, it would be a murder of his own deliberate making. Would he murder again? (Was there a skulking, malicious force lying in wait for him here, on this plane, to maim or kill him if he didn't?) Would he murder the president, even though failure to do so would place his own life in peril? In a matter of minutes he would have his answers.

He took a small dish from a cupboard. It had a presidential seal in the center. He lifted the lid of the ice cream box. All the containers but one were butterscotch twirl. He dropped his cigarette on the deck and ground it out with his heel and looked for the ice cream scoop.

Someone else bustled up the ladderway and through the galley. More noise from the president's cabin. The chief press secretary had brought word from the convention in Pittsburgh.

"It's Darrow!" he screamed. "The fourth ballot! The fourth goddamn ballot!"

Then Hamilton. He beamed with amazement.

"So that prick Melville didn't make it after all."

Forbes could see him through the galley door. He was hitching up his trousers. He had received his gamma globulin shot.

"Goddamn it, I want a statement out immediately," Hamilton shouted wildly. "Use the electronic thing and get it out through the White House. Congratulate Darrow. Make it heavy. Say I think he'll make a great candidate and a great president. But not a word about Melville, understand? Not a fucking word!"

More members of the president's personal staff filed up the spiral ladderway and through the galley to Hamilton's compartment. They were grinning and whooping. One by one they bared their buttocks as a team of navy corpsmen administered gamma globulin injections. The press secretary said the correspondents were eager for a visit from the president.

"Tell them I'll be back there in a minute." Hamilton was in top form. He felt vindicated.

The excitement in the president's compartment intensified. One of the screens on the computer console was tuned to a commercial television channel. The commentator in Pittsburgh said the nominee was expected any minute now at the Civic Arena; a shot of the Bedford Avenue drive-in entrance showed a mob of boisterous Darrow supporters.

A steward pointed out the ice cream scoop to Forbes. He paid no attention to the commotion next door. He could not afford to be distracted by it. It was time to act. He dug out a helping of ice cream and set the dish on the counter.

Someone pushed open a cooler next to the ice cream box and extracted a double armload of bottles of champagne.

"Isn't this terrific?" he shouted to Forbes. "Melville getting his ass kicked in his own hometown."

"Great," Forbes replied tersely. He couldn't remember the man's name.

The corpsmen headed for the ladderway to go to work on the correspondents at the rear of the plane. Forbes saw they were about to overlook him. He stopped them by the ice cream box and lowered his trousers for his injection.

The jubilation mounted over Melville's defeat. Corks popped from champagne bottles. Forbes could hear occasional distinct, antithetical expressions of harsh delight and rather frivolous political analysis above the general uproar.

"The son of a bitch should have known better than to mix it up with a pro like Darrow."

Forbes took the capsule from his pocket. That was the first time he had ever heard Congressman Darrow characterized as an adroit politician.

"Darrow knew hard work would beat a heavy checkbook."

The champagne flowed. For a brief moment it reminded Forbes of the night Hamilton was nominated.

"The fourth ballot! Christ, I thought they'd deadlock if it went that far."

Forbes broke the capsule in two. He sprinkled the white powder over the ice cream. The galley workers were distracted by the celebration and did not notice. He tossed the halves of the amber gelatin shell into the waste receptacle.

He was ready to make his move. He was not surprised that the news of Nell's death was drowned in the political excitement.

Hamilton was leaning against the door to the flight deck. He was sipping champagne and smoking a cigar. His eyes did not seem so deep in their sockets. He was expansive and relaxed.

Forbes made his way through the crowd. He smiled at a

few people, trying to give the appearance of enjoying himself as much as everyone else. He guided the dish of ice cream past the swarm of shifting bodies and gesturing arms.

Snyder was holding a plastic glass of champagne. He was by the computer console. He did not appear especially festive. Tung Yen Fun was still looking out the window, a nonparticipant in the confusion.

Forbes finally reached Hamilton.

"A little something special for you, Mr. President," he said. He tried to sound ceremonious.

Hamilton looked at the dish of ice cream. Then he looked into Forbes's eyes.

Suddenly Forbes spun and hurled the dish the length of the cabin. It ricocheted off the ceiling and spattered several celebrators. Cries of "What the hell?" went up. Then the compartment became hushed.

Forbes slowly turned back to face Hamilton. Their eyes met again. They both understood.

The president was about to speak when he froze. His champagne glass fell to the deck. The cigar crushed between his fingers. His jaw dropped. His eyes bulged. He looked like a man screaming behind soundproof glass.

He collapsed.

All heads turned in the silence toward the crumpled body in front of the door to the flight deck.

Forbes was standing immediately over him.

Snyder snapped the spell.

"Get Brabham!" he yelled. "Everybody out of here!" He began shoving violently.

Tung Yen Fun politely nudged Forbes aside and knelt down with great effort over Hamilton. He gently took one of the president's hands and pressed it against his chest.

Instantly Brabham appeared at the rear door. He breasted the crowd of aides and deputies, who were elbowing their way from the cabin as if escaping from a fire. The head of the Secret Service detail was right behind him.

Brabham quickly examined Hamilton's unconscious body. He shot a glance at Snyder. His eyes were aflame with accusing anger.

"Fuck you, Brabham," Snyder growled. "Get to work."

Two corpsmen rushed in.

The Secret Service agent snatched open the flight deck door. The captain and the other crew members reacted as if it were a regular occurrence. He seized the radio phone.

"Elmendorf," he said crisply into the instrument. "This is Big Bird. We want immediate clearance to land. We have a critical problem with Doughnut." "Doughnut" was Hamilton's Secret Service code name. "It's medical. We need ambulance and hospital standby. Do you copy?"

"Emergency ambulance. Copy," crackled the reply. "You have immediate landing clearance."

The corpsmen loaded Hamilton's stricken body onto a stretcher. They carried him to his narrow sleeping quarters next door. Brabham held the mask of a portable oxygen unit on the president's face. Tung Yen Fun, tears coursing down his cheeks, hovered over the stretcher, still clasping one of Hamilton's hands.

The correspondents in the rear of the plane were all clamoring at once to use the air-to-ground communication system to telephone the story of the president's seizure to the world. The press secretary angrily denied permission.

Snyder sat down in Hamilton's chair at the computer console. He picked up a telephone receiver and speedily punched a series of buttons that put him in direct contact with the White House.

"This is Snyder," he said incisively. "No. . . . Shut up and listen, goddamn it. Hamilton's just had some kind of attack. It looks serious; he's unconscious. Get on the horn to Pittsburgh and tell Larry Melville to get his ass back to Washington pronto. The son of a bitch is going to get to be president, at least for a little while.

"Alert State and Defense. You know the form. And don't give it out to the media. We'll handle that. What? How the hell do I know where he is? He's in Pittsburgh, for Christ's sake. Call the national committee. Call his office. But get to Melville and get him back to Washington. The country has to have somebody running it, even if it's him. And when you get to Melville, tell him to get to his office and stay put until I get back to him. . . . Yeah. You, too." He replaced the receiver and exhaled a long breath.

Forbes was at the other end of the cabin. He had picked up the ice cream dish; it was unbroken and he was staring at the presidential seal in the center of it. The cabin was littered with bottles, champagne glasses, and cigarette butts. There were smudges of butterscotch twirl on the ceiling and on the floor around Forbes's feet.

Snyder looked at him wearily from Hamilton's adjustable chair. "Put that down," he said quietly.

Forbes looked at him a moment as if he did not recognize him. Then he reared back and sailed the dish side-armed against the flight deck door. It shattered explosively.

Air Force One crossed the Chugach Mountains and touched down at Elmendorf Air Force Base outside Anchorage in less than fifteen minutes. Three ambulances rolled up as the giant plane came to a halt at a remote part of the runway.

Hamilton was still unconscious. He was on a litter. Attendants lowered it to the tarmac and lifted it quickly into one of the ambulances. Brabham crawled in. Tung Yen Fun waddled as fast as he could to the open back door; someone thrust out a hand and pulled him in. Secret Service agents with automatic weapons at the ready jumped aboard. The ambulance sped away, siren wailing.

Across the field an air force band packed its instruments and climbed back into its bus.

A small body of celebrity-seekers and a few Hamilton admirers with placards drifted away from a restraining fence.

Forbes was at last yielding to the shock that comes from finding the world's course had not failed even though he had gone as far as he could to warp it. Snyder guided him by the arm. He shoved him into one of the other ambulances. At the same time he blocked a dozen or so correspondents who tried to wedge in after him.

"We're on the president's staff," Snyder shouted to the driver. "Take us to the hospital." They didn't speak during the two minutes it took to get there.

"I'll find a place and work the phones," said Snyder as they pulled up to the emergency entrance. "You find the press people and see if they need some help with the media. Biography. That kind of stuff. Tell them to say nothing about his condition, even if they find out. We'll let Brabham handle that."

Snyder dashed into the building. Two Secret Service agents guarded the double doors.

Forbes waited and then went inside. He had no idea where to go. He had no intention of following Snyder's instructions. He wandered down a corridor. No one else seemed to be about. All the activity devoted to saving Hamilton's life was at the other end of the hospital. Forbes hadn't been in a hospital since the night of his father's death. The light in the place was faded yellow, like most hospital corridors. The tile floors were highly buffed, a military habit. He found a bench outside an office and sat down.

He looked up and saw Tung Yen Fun trudging toward him. His old face was twisted in disillusionment. "They ordered me from his room," he said dismally. "They wouldn't even let me stay with him." He continued down the corridor.

Forbes watched him go. He was surprised to find that his mind was astonishingly clear. He immediately accepted the loss of Nell and realized with deep anguish that more than a little of himself had died with her. It was a permanent loss, and he did not expect to get used to it soon. He had loved her and never failed to show it; she had loved him and he had never failed to return it. He wept for a while, without shame or guilt. When someone you love dies, you weep because you miss them. He conceded with dull anger that Nell's death had not been a horrible, fortuitous accident and that he would probably never know the sinister events that led to it.

Presently his evident grief subsided. He knew in his heart that it would return again and again, but for the moment there was another matter to consider: Hamilton. He felt no shame about the stricken president, either, although he was shaken to the point where his hands trembled. It was as if he had been driving drunk and a collision that had nothing to do with him had occurred in the road ahead. For the moment he was gripped by a disconsolate sense of impending disaster, but he knew it wouldn't last. What would last, he knew in his bones, was the knowledge that he had been tricked into nearly murdering a man.

Gradually he began to feel a sense of relief, like taking off a heavy coat on a hot day. The feeling grew as he recognized that he had made a decision. He had been given the opportunity to murder again—and turned it down flat.

He was aware suddenly of someone next to him.

It was the rumpled man; the man who had rudely introduced himself four days ago as Mr. Walker; it was Coombes. He had on a new suit, but it was already wrinkled badly. He had shaved his mustache and goatee.

"That office across the hall. It's empty," he said. "Let's go in and talk."

To Coombes's amazement Forbes rose instantly from the

bench, as if he had been expecting him, and led the way. They stepped into the office. Forbes switched on the light and sat down in a chair by the door.

"Nice work," said Coombes after a few moments. He leaned against what obviously was a doctor's desk. He was smiling crookedly, but his tone was wary; the man across the room was definitely not the piece of putty he had encountered four days ago. He wondered if Forbes might somehow have learned his true identity. "I thought you might need some help. I was wrong."

Forbes lit a cigarette. His eyes were riveted on the seedy man who had thrown his life into wretched disorder. He felt a hot blob rising in his body. He knew it would burst soon.

"Were you on that plane, Walker?" he asked sharply.

Coombes looked bewildered. "No," he answered, puzzled by the question. He was not wearing his Colt Cobra; he wondered if he hadn't made a mistake in leaving it in his valise. He was relieved a fraction to know that his cover was intact. "I said I thought you did a good job," he repeated; he wanted to get back to the main topic of business.

"I didn't do anything," said Forbes; he sounded as if he wanted to dismiss the subject.

Coombes's hooded eyes widened with perplexity. "What the hell do you mean, you didn't do anything? Hamilton's dead."

"How do you know?"

"They just announced it out front," he said matter-of-factly. "Who's the doctor?"

"Brabham."

"He said it was a clot on the brain. A big one. He said Hamilton would have been paralyzed and blind if he had made it. He said the guy had a history of circulatory trouble. Somebody asked him whether that gamma globulin shot might have had anything to do with it. He said he didn't think so, but he wouldn't know for sure until he saw the autopsy report. He sounded pissed off."

Forbes took the news calmly; he had half anticipated it anyway. "Let me tell you something," he said. "I tried to give him that stuff. What were they called?"

"Pathogenic accelerators."

"I tried. But I didn't do it. Did you hear me? *I didn't do it.* Whatever killed him, I didn't have anything to do with it." He dropped his cigarette on the floor and crushed it with his shoe. "What I don't understand—" his voice gurgled with pain—"is why you had to kill Nell."

"Who?"

"Nell Leatherbee, goddamn it!" Forbes shouted.

Coombes shrugged. "Oh. The cunt from Treasury with the spinal meningitis."

The hot blob popped.

Forbes sprang from his chair and charged at Coombes. He flailed at him wildly. "You killed her, you slimy bastard," he screamed, swinging with his palms open as tears of anger flooded down his cheeks. His head was against Coombes's chest, and he shoved and slapped without landing a telling blow. He had never learned to fight properly.

Coombes back-pedaled until he was able to grab Forbes by the throat of his shirt and deliver a series of jackhammer punches to his solar plexus. When he felt that Forbes's resistance had dissolved, he released his grip and Forbes sank to the floor.

Forbes gasped and coughed. His esophagus seemed to be clogged with scratchy wool. Slowly he regained his breath. He snuffled and dried his eyes on his sleeve.

"You stupid son of a bitch," snarled Coombes. "I didn't kill her. I don't even know why she was killed. *If* she was killed. But here's one for you. They found a needle in her purse with enough of that bacteria in it to put half the country in the hospital. That means one thing to me. She was in on this. I don't know how—I don't want to know—but she was in on it."

Forbes leaned against the wall. "I loved her," he said softly, experiencing the sadness of betrayal as he heard himself say the words.

Coombes helped him to his feet. "I'm sorry the woman died. But an operation like this is loaded with risks. That guy Hibbitt. I don't know how he was hooked into it. But I can all but guarantee that he was. The only thing that counts is that Hamilton was stopped."

Forbes seemed not to hear. He shambled back to his chair by the door and sat down heavily. "I'll give you one now," he said; his strength was returning. "I don't think it was ever in Hamilton's head to defect. I know everything looked that way, but I swear to God I don't think it was something he ever meant to do."

Coombes snorted. "That's a lot of crap and you know it. You saw that letter. There were other things, too."

"That letter." Forbes tried to laugh. "That letter was the biggest joke since . . . since I don't know what."

"Maybe," Coombes said sullenly, "but it got you moving."

Forbes felt his anger rising again. "What got me moving was getting the shit kicked out of me and the threat of getting killed myself. In the end it didn't have a damned thing to do with whether I thought—or cared—if Joe Hamilton was going to defect. What I want to make clear to you is that I wasn't going to kill him—whether he was going to defect or not."

"Of course Hamilton was going to defect," Coombes said shortly, as if suddenly trying to convince himself of it. "I've *got* the letter to Roundtree. Or I did until somebody cracked my safe."

Forbes leaned forward in his chair. His heart began to beat faster. Images of the past four days flickered across his mind. Vest. The walk in Melville's garden. The death of Parisi. He shook his head vehemently. "You couldn't have the letter!" he cried. "It's impossible! I saw it shredded in Melville's office!"

A tangential thought struck Coombes at the same instant. "That's it," he said as a look of astonishment spread across his face. "That was what was wrong with it. That's why it didn't look right. *The letter wasn't folded.* Vest said it came in the mail, but it wasn't *folded.*"

"*Vest?*" asked Forbes. He, too, was astonished.

Coombes looked at him apprehensively. "What about Vest?"

"Doesn't he work for Melville?"

The two men stared at each other in silence. They recognized at the same moment the great ancient flame that follows the tiny spark. They no longer had cause to complain of the deception of the world. They had both been perpetrators and stupid victims of it. All that was left for them was to get a firm hold on the here and now and salvage something from it.

Coombes walked to the door. "I know what you've got in mind." His voice was hard. "Forget it. Don't ever think about it again."

Forbes looked up at him from his chair. The distance between them was not more than two feet. "What's in store for me?" he asked. "I know an awful lot."

"Nothing, I would guess," Coombes replied. "If you keep your mouth shut. You aren't thinking about going to the newspapers or anything like that, are you?"

"Hell, no. I'm a politician, not a reformer. Or a martyr."

"Remember this." Coombes glared viciously at Forbes. "You can't touch him. You understand that, don't you?"

Forbes started to laugh. Wonderful, he thought. He threw back his head and laughed some more.

"What's so goddamned funny?" Coombes was worried that Forbes might not have understood his warning.

"Don't you see it?" said Forbes; he struggled against bursting out again. "We were pulled into a sucker play. But *Melville* loses. He wanted to be president so badly he ruined himself. He got so involved in plots and conspiracies that he forgot to win the nomination. So what does he get? The chance to be president for five and a half months!" He laughed some more.

Abruptly Coombes thrust his nose within an inch of Forbes's face. "You can't touch him. Hasn't that gotten through to you yet? I'd like to kill him, too. I got set up just like you did. But you can't touch him. Melville is one of those guys you can't touch."

Then he left. Forbes could hear his heavy, serviceable shoes clomping down the corridor.

A FEW DAYS LATER...

12 The Policy Decision

Coombes was reading a newspaper in the fast-food restaurant at Eighteenth Street and Columbia Road when Headlight arrived. There were several empty coffee containers on the table. Coombes had expected him an hour ago. Outside, it was pouring.

It had been an unpromising week.

"Hell of a day for a funeral," said Headlight. He shook his umbrella and took off his fashionable raincoat. "We're still debating, by the way, whether we ought to deliver the body or let the Chinese come get it."

"I'm still suspended," said Coombes. He was not interested in the international uproar over the discovery in President Hamilton's will of his wish to be buried in China next to his parents and of President Melville's decision to honor it.

The restaurant was nearly deserted. It was late afternoon. Most businesses in Washington were closed for the day. It is customary during a president's funeral. The government had taken the day off completely. Flags at all government buildings were ordered to half-staff for a ten-day mourning period. The order had come from President Melville.

"Another problem," Headlight continued—he did not want to discuss Coombes's personal difficulties at the moment—"is that the Chinese want the burial in Peking. Somewhere near Mao's shrine. For the propaganda value, naturally. Of course, Hamilton's parents are buried in Chungking, so State is pressing for burial there. Hamilton's wife has no objections, by the way."

"I'm suspended without pay," Coombes persisted. "You knew that, didn't you? Counter Intelligence did everything but take me up to the mountains before they turned me loose. What the hell am I supposed to do until I'm reinstated?"

Headlight's thoughts were still on the diplomatic complexities of Hamilton's burial in the land of his youth. "As you can imagine, we want to be in charge of the delivery. It would give us a chance to see things firsthand, confirm some reports, all sorts of things that Peking station can't do. State, on the other hand, favors letting the Chinese make the pickup. They contend it would be a gesture that would at least counterbalance the propaganda problem. We're still battling over it."

"Look," said Coombes desperately, "I'm damned near broke. This funny money I'm getting from you is all I've got until I get my job back. You know it's no use talking to me about where to bury Hamilton. What has it got to do with me?"

"I thought you might be interested, that's all," Headlight said coolly.

"I am, but, Christ . . ."

Headlight took out his gold case and lit a cigarette. "The entire Basement will be looking for work before long. Counter Intelligence is drawing up a disbandment request right now. It's a good bet the director will approve it."

Coombes stared out the window. Rain streaked down the

glass. He hadn't heard about the fate of the Basement. "I've been in offensive operations for nearly twenty years," he said dejectedly. "Nearly thirty if you count Burma. I don't know any of this other stuff."

"We're thinking of opening a new cover in Mexico, a proprietary, a camera business," said Headlight; he held his cigarette delicately. "We'll get it off the ground after the first of the year. It wouldn't be smart for me to launch any new projects before Melville's gone. I could outbrass him with the stuff you gave me, but there doesn't seem to be a point to it."

There was a silence and then Coombes said bitterly, "You played me like some goddamn Portuguese politician. I could have got killed in California."

"It was a risk. You weren't supposed to be involved," said Headlight. "That man Vest. I had no idea he would pick you. He was given a list. Apparently he ignored it." He put out his cigarette. "What do you think about the Mexico thing?"

"A foreign posting at my age?" Coombes sounded skeptical. "You'll have a hell of a time selling that to Personnel. We both know Mexico isn't much—but me? Not with this Counter Intelligence thing hanging over me."

"I think I can swing it," said Headlight. "There's not much else I can offer you, anyway. I can't keep you on conditional status indefinitely. Finance will spot it if it goes on much longer."

"I need a steady paycheck, for Christ's sake," Coombes said forlornly.

After another silence Coombes held up his newspaper. He pointed to a small item.

"Did you see this?" he asked.

Headlight glanced at the item. It was from New York. The headline read: POLITICAL CONSULTANT AND SECRETARY KILLED IN ELEVATOR CRASH. The story went on to say that Forbes had once been a key aide to the late President Hamilton and that the accident had occurred in the secretary's apartment building at eight in the morning.

"I hadn't seen it," he said. "I haven't had a chance to look at the papers. This funeral and the China business." He put the paper aside. "This was a messy operation from the start," he added dispassionately. "It fell to pieces and the broken glass had to be swept up. That included a one-shot agent who might be tempted to confess to his secretary—or who might start nosing around to find out why his father committed suicide."

"But I told you Forbes was all right," said Coombes; his voice wavered; he bit at a fingernail. "He would have laid off. I know he would have. He was a politician. He wasn't the type to do anything."

Because Coombes didn't have an umbrella, they ignored their ritual of his always leaving first. Headlight shared his; it was expensive and had a teak handle. Cabs were scarce. It was the rain. Headlight dropped him at a bus stop.

Coombes looked at a schedule. He hadn't bothered to learn the suburban bus routes.